"DON'T HURT ME," SHE SAID AS HIS MOUTH CLOSED ON HERS.

The moment was filled with a new kind of tension. Natalie felt her heart hammering and a faint dizziness. She gripped his broad shoulders while thoughts tumbled over each other in her spinning brain.

Surely she must be going insane! She was sitting on a bed in the darkness at a remote outpost with the arms of a dangerous outlaw around her.

And she wanted him.

"I want you," he repeated, and Natalie could not find the strength to say no. She felt her stomach flutter violently as her heart drummed an erratic beat. Right or wrong, foolish or wise, she wanted to know this stranger's arms, to surrender to the dark desire his words had stirred.

Other *Love Spell* books by Nan Ryan:
WAYWARD LADY

Cloudcastle

Nan Ryan

LOVE SPELL BOOKS   NEW YORK CITY

For my charming, affectionate, witty, supportive, volatile,
entertaining, sometimes childish, always lovable husband.
"Seems like happiness is just a thing called Joe."

LOVE SPELL®

May 1999

Published by

Dorchester Publishing Co., Inc.
276 Fifth Avenue
New York, NY 10001

ISBN 0-505-52310-8

The name "Love Spell" and its logo are trademarks of Dorchester
Publishing Co., Inc.

Printed in the United States of America.

Chapter One

The high desert shimmered in a haze of late August heat. A Wells Fargo Overland stagecoach, half a day behind schedule, rattled across the parched ground toward Spanish Widow station in the New Mexico Territory. Sunburned and sweaty, the weary stage driver's rugged face broke into a wide grin when he spotted the small, bleached adobe building through the thermals rising from the desert floor.

He licked his cracked lips in anticipation of the cool water and hot meal he knew awaited him. He could almost taste Maria's light, brown-crusted biscuits. It was her cooking that made Spanish Widow one of his favorite stops on this bone-jarring route up north to the Colorado Territory. That and the friendliness of her husband, Carlos.

The Mexican couple had been at the remote way station for a little over a year and in that year they'd handled their duties with a cheerful efficiency that impressed the old stagecoach driver. He knew that at this minute, late though he was, the grinning, good-natured Carlos would be standing before the tiny adobe building, spyglass lifted to his dark eye, watching tirelessly for the rumbling Concord coach to appear on the horizon.

And he knew that as soon as Carlos sighted the stage, he'd

bob his head happily and shout to his plump, pretty wife, "Put the biscuits in, Maria, they're here!"

In the close, stuffy confines of the Overland coach, Natalie Vallance tucked a lock of golden-red hair behind her left ear, blinked her green eyes, rolled her tired, slender shoulders in a circular motion, and wondered how much longer it would be before she would be able to step down and stretch her stiff legs.

Across from her, the Overland's other passenger, a short, heavyset man, snored loudly. The fatigued woman envied the sleeping man. She'd managed to doze only briefly since leaving Santa Fe and knew she'd get little rest until she reached her mountain ranch at Cloudcastle.

And she was days away from Cloudcastle.

Natalie drew a deep breath and smiled. Hard as the journey was, it had been worth it. The weeks in Santa Fe with Metaka had been enjoyable. The long, lazy summer had slipped past in a pleasant, dreamlike way and Natalie treasured every hour spent with the pretty Indian woman who was to her a sister.

Metaka's family was just as dear. Jake Thompson, good-humored and hardworking, was a devoted husband and loving father to the couple's two brown-skinned, boisterous boys. Natalie had liked Jake Thompson from the first day she and Metaka had seen the big, light-haired rider dismount before Gallen's General Store in Cloudcastle, Colorado Territory, that chilly October day in 1867.

And she'd known, from the way his hazel eyes twinkled when he looked at Metaka, that the young cowboy would be staying in Cloudcastle longer than he'd intended.

And he had.

Jake Thompson had stayed until he could persuade Metaka to marry him and go back to Santa Fe. And Natalie, heavy coat turned up against the biting winds, had stood beside the solemn old shaman, Tahomah, and waved goodbye to the elderly Ute chief's granddaughter and the beaming bridegroom.

It had been a happy day and friends of the newlyweds had thrown rice and shouted good tidings and shot off their revolvers in the cold, crisp Colorado air. She could hear the shots even now.

Natalie stiffened.

She *did* hear shots!

When she snatched back the dusty side-curtains and looked out, her heart froze. The whine of a bullet stirred the still air inside the coach and pierced the white shirtfront of the man seated across from her. A tiny circle of blood appeared just beneath his heart and the passenger slumped over dead, never having roused from his slumber.

The blood-curdling war chants of approaching Indians grew deafening, and, terrified, Natalie slipped from the worn leather seat to the dusty floorboard of the coach, while atop the cab the determined driver raised his long whip to the backs of the weary, lathered horses and the creaking coach lurched violently forward.

Maria Sanchez flashed a brilliant smile at the burly marshal and refilled his coffee cup. Her smile fled when she shifted her gaze to the dark, dangerous man handcuffed to the big lawman. The bearded desperado made her nervous and she was grateful Marshal Cochran had refused to unlock the iron bracelet subduing the criminal.

Maria reluctantly poured steaming black coffee into the cup beside the prisoner's empty plate, her dark eyes flashing with apprehension. The silent, bearded man seemed not to notice. Politely he thanked her and lifted the scalding coffee to his lips with his free left hand.

Maria bustled back to the stove. She was cutting a freshly baked apple pie when she heard the first shots. Fearing the bearded man had somehow broken his bonds, she whirled toward the table, heart hammering, sharp knife in hand.

"Jesus God!" the lawman swore, and leapt to his feet, bringing his captive up with him.

And the quiet summer afternoon exploded into earsplitting, spine-tingling mayhem.

Reports of rifles mixed with the unmistakable whoops of marauding Indians, snorting horses, and the terrified screams of Maria Sanchez.

Marshal Cochran's gunbelt hung on a peg beside the front door, but his Winchester rifle lay upon the wooden bench beside him. He managed to get the weapon unscabbarded. But he never lifted it. A speeding bullet ripped through the open window and tore away his Adam's apple. The heavy gun clanked to the planked floor as the lawman's stunned eyes opened wide with disbelief and his big fingers wrapped themselves about his bleeding larynx, the swift movement jerking upward the bearded man's cuffed hand.

The prisoner's alert eyes went to the woman, Maria. She was running toward the open door and he shouted her name even as he felt the weight of the big marshal slump against him. Wrapping his free arm about the dying man's waist, he lunged toward the screaming woman, purposely tripping her before she could reach the front door.

Maria crashed to the floor, bellowing her outrage, her dark eyes desperately searching the barren yard for her Carlos. The bearded man held her immobile with a long leg clamped over her body while he coolly searched the dead marshal's pockets for a key. He didn't see the frightened little Mexican frantically seeking the shelter of the adobe. But Maria did.

Through tear-filled eyes Maria saw her husband running for his life. Carlos never made it. His feet touched the flat stone porch at the very instant a bullet ripped into the middle of his back. Maria wailed and threw off the long leg trapping her. Before the bearded man could stop her, the hysterical woman dashed out the door and drew a barrage of bullets that turned her bright yellow blouse to crimson. She slumped atop her supine husband, dead.

Now free of his bonds, the bearded man jerked up the dead lawman's Winchester and took up his lookout at a front window. Calmly he began firing, picking off the painted braves with practiced precision and deadly aim.

* * *

Inside the clattering, bumping stagecoach, Natalie swiftly stripped the revolver from the dead passenger's waistband. Bracing herself against the worn leather seat, she cautiously peered out, lifted the Navy Colt .44, and fired, striking a determined warrior whose intent it was to board the fast-moving stage.

Fierce face contorted with pain, the young warrior fell from his war pony and disappeared. As Natalie again took aim, she heard the loud groan of the stage driver and knew he'd been hit.

Ned Cass felt the bullet shatter his third rib and slam upward. He gasped in pain, but his big, callused hands never went to the wound. The old stagecoach driver was a professional. His duty was to his passengers. His responsibility: their safety.

Ned was determined to get the Overland coach and its passengers to Spanish Widow station if it was the last thing he ever did. Teeth clamped firmly together, eyes narrowed with resolve, Ned Cass did just that.

The rattling, besieged coach rolled to a stop before the small station, the heavy reins held firmly in Ned's sure grip. Three bullets hit him at once; the brave driver died there atop his halted stage.

Inside, Natalie, terror rising to choke her, frantically searched the dead passenger for more ammunition. There were no bullets left in the Colt. The man wore no gunbelt. The stage driver was dead. The station's occupants were surely dead. She was alone without so much as a bullet to use on herself.

The door of the coach was jerked open.

Natalie screamed.

A strong arm encircled her narrow waist and she was roughly pulled up against a hard male body. The useless gun slipped from her hand and she jerked her head around to look into the face of her captor, expecting to see the grinning, painted face of a redskin.

She saw a face burned dark as any Indian's, and hair black

as a savage's, but a pair of cold, steady eyes, blue as the summer skies, looked into hers. A little sigh of relief escaped her open lips, and shakily she wrapped trembling arms around the man's strong neck and buried her face in his bushy black beard.

The bearded stranger said not a word but swiftly plucked her from the coach and carried her into the thick-walled adobe building. Inside, he promptly deposited her on the floor, jerked the Colt from the dead lawman's holster, crouched down beside her, and handed her the gun, butt first.

The man's alert blue eyes turned at once to the moving, shouting targets. He lifted the Winchester rifle, took aim with calm authority, and in a drawl soft yet audible above the melee, cautioned, "If you wish to keep it, you'd best keep your head down, miss."

He fired, and it was then she noticed the silver handcuff dangling from his right wrist. Natalie swallowed hard. Dear God, she thought despairingly, I'm pitted against a bunch of murdering savages with a southern desperado as my only ally.

She lifted the heavy black Colt, wondering whom she feared most. The revolver wavered in her shaking hand and she briefly considered aiming it at the dark, bearded man kneeling beside her. Surely he was every bit as dangerous as the redskins circling the adobe. The Indians were uneducated and untamed; they knew no better, while the dark, deadly man beside her, who spoke in those drawling tones she found so offensive, had no such excuse.

Natalie peered out.

The circling, whooping warriors were pincushioning the lifeless bodies with arrows. Appalled, she leaned forward a little, eyes wide with horror. A bullet whizzed through the air a fraction of an inch from her face. Heart pounding, she whirled away from the window, pressing her shaking shoulders against the smooth stone wall, and stared in horror at a heavy lock of red-gold hair lying upon the planked floor in a shaft of bright sunlight. The lock of hair had been cut by the bullet as though a pair of sharp scissors had purposely snipped it from her head.

The dark stranger, squeezing off another shot that found its mark in the skull of a daring young brave, said coolly, "I warned you. Unless you want me pinning you to the floor with my knee, you'll keep out of the line of fire except to fire yourself." He again pulled the trigger, then added, "That is if you know how to use that gun."

Natalie took one last stunned look at the lock of red hair on the floor, narrowed her green eyes at the outlaw beside her, and cautiously moved into position to take aim and fire.

Straightening her slender right arm, she chose a close, painted target, and pulled the trigger. The Indian clutched his naked chest and slithered from his paint pony, his life-blood streaming down his shining, sun-reddened skin into a bright crimson pool on the hard alkali earth.

The bearded man's lips tightened and he said almost grudgingly, "Not bad for a woman."

Ignoring him, Natalie took aim and fired yet again. And again, with one well-placed bullet, she brought to an end another life. "Not bad for a man," she responded coldly, emerald eyes remaining on the swarming, shouting warriors.

The bearded man's gaze shifted briefly to the remarkable female beside him. A ripping bullet blazed through the window and stung his high, dark cheekbone. A thin furrow of bright red blood rose in tiny droplets, as though he'd cut himself shaving.

"If you wish to keep it," Natalie said, glancing at him, rapidly assessing the severity of the wound, "you'd best keep your head down. And your mind on your work."

He gave no reply.

His blue eyes flickered slightly beneath thick, coal-black lashes and Natalie couldn't believe her ears when she heard him chuckling; the low, rumbling sound came from deep down inside his broad chest even as he fired his weapon.

"Who are they?" she shouted above the whine of bullets.

"Victorio and his band of Apaches," he responded immediately.

"It can't be," she protested, "this is too far north."

"Tell Victorio that," the bearded southerner drawled as he reloaded the Winchester repeating rifle and turned again to the window.

Had anyone told Natalie that she and the dark desperado would have lived through that long, hot afternoon, outnumbered fifty to two against rampaging, bloodthirsty Apaches, she'd not have believed him. But when the blazing August sun finally slipped below the western horizon, the weary, thwarted warriors thundered away toward the south while inside the walls of the small, stifling-hot adobe, the strange pair watched their retreat, exhausted but alive.

Natalie knew, at least until sunrise, they wouldn't return. More than once old Tahomah had told her an Indian killed at night would remain in perpetual darkness throughout eternity. She was safe for the night. At least from the Apaches.

Her eyes went to the bearded outlaw.

Wordlessly he laid aside the Winchester, rose to his feet, slung the dead marshal's leather gunbelt around his slim frame, buckled it over his hips, and reached for the Colt she was holding. Reluctant to release it to the stranger, Natalie shook her red head negatively and her eyes went again to the silver bracelet dangling from his dark right wrist.

He caught her worried glance, took a key from his pocket, unlatched the handcuffs, and threw the worrisome restraints out the window. As he massaged his wrist with lean brown fingers, his keen blue eyes were on her face, awaiting her question.

It never came.

Dying to know just what foul crime this tall, bearded man had committed, Natalie quelled her natural curiosity. He looked dangerous. She'd keep the gun.

Surprised that she did not question him, he lifted wide shoulders in a shrug and put out a hand to help her up from the hard floor. Again she shook her head and rose unaided.

He stood directly before her, tall and menacing. Those blue

eyes were on her, appraising, even as she studied him, and she felt the wispy hair at her nape rise.

Abruptly, he stepped around her, lithe and pantherine. He lifted the lifeless marshal up over his right shoulder and went out into the sunset. She turned to watch when he returned and knelt beside the dead Mexican pair lying just outside the front door. The outlaw gingerly smoothed down the bright-flowered calico skirt, modestly covering an exposed brown thigh of the Mexican woman. Gently, as though she could still feel pain, he plucked the arrows from her bloody body, lifted her up into his long arms, and disappeared around the corner of the adobe.

In minutes he returned and carried away the Mexican stage agent, Carlos. Natalie quit watching when the dark, lean man put a booted foot on the step of the stagecoach and reached for the dead driver.

She took a seat at the plank table, feeling faint and weak. Hand firmly gripping the heavy Colt beside her on the long bench, she remained there until her criminal companion came back inside, having completed his gruesome chores.

She looked up. His unsettling blue gaze was on her.

"You've buried them?" she asked, fingers nervously twisting a silver teaspoon she'd lifted from beside a cold cup of coffee.

He shook his dark head. "I'll do it tomorrow."

"There's still a little light," she said indignantly, "surely the poor souls deserve—"

"Miss," he coolly cut in, "we need them."

She stared at him incredulously and felt hysterical laughter threatening to overcome her. "Need them? Dear God, what manner of animal are you?"

"The bodies will man guns at the windows come morning," he calmly explained. "It's a long shot; it may not fool Victorio but it's worth trying." He stepped away from the table and took off his black leather vest.

Natalie drew a labored breath. He'd just confirmed her unspoken fears. The Apaches would return. They'd be back come dawn; rested, angered, and ready to finish what they'd begun. She felt her flesh turn cold beneath the sheen of perspiration covering her tired, slender body.

Natalie took out her frustration on him. "Quit calling me 'miss.' I'm not a maiden!"

The tall, spare man stripped the blousey-sleeved black shirt from his sweat-dampened torso and tossed it over a bench.

"I beg your pardon, ma'am," he said calmly as he went to the cluttered cupboard at the back of the one-room building and poured water from a big earthen crock into a flat tin pan. Dipping his hands into the tepid water, he brought them up to cover his dirty, bloodstained face.

As if she were not present, he grabbed up a huge bar of soap, rubbed his hands over it until they were covered with thick foamy lather, and then scrubbed his face vigorously. His back was to her. Natalie immediately noted the three long, ribbon-like scars slicing across his dark, muscled back. Satiny white, they gleamed starkly against his swarthy, sweat-slick skin.

She bit back a gasp.

Who was this man? Where did he get such deep, maiming scars? Why had he been handcuffed to the marshal? How many people had he murdered? Would he stop at murdering a woman?

Natalie's fingers tightened on the heavy Colt revolver.

The tall southern bandit had finished washing. He turned to face her while he slid long arms into his soiled black shirt. Not bothering to button it, he shoved the long tails down into his tight black trousers and shrugged on the worn leather vest. Natalie's eyes were drawn to the dark curly hair covering his hard chest, beaded with water, glistening in the soft gloaming of light from the dying sun.

"Now that I'm a little cleaner, allow me to present myself, ma'am, I'm—"

"I don't care who you are," she cut him off, gaze lifting to his dark, bearded face. "They will be back, won't they?" she questioned, then swiftly lowered her green eyes from the disturbing, dangerous sight of him. "The Apaches; they'll come back and . . ." She fell silent, waiting for him to speak. He did not, so she slowly lifted her eyes to his. "Won't they?"

He ran a lean, sunburned hand through his thick, long hair. "They will, ma'am." He swung a long leg over the wooden bench and took a seat facing her. Softly, in that drawling southern accent, he said, "They took all the horses, but if you leave now, you might make it to the foothills by midnight." The clear blue eyes looked at her intently. "Come daylight, you could head for Fort Garland. With any luck a scout might spot you, take you in, and—"

"I'm not a fool. It's a good twenty miles to the fort. The Apaches would spot me before the soldiers. I'll stay."

"It's up to you."

"I know that."

"Very well," he said, "there's food aplenty; why don't you eat something."

"I'm not hungry," she replied as she rose from the table, the gun still clutched in her hand.

Through thick, lowered lashes, Natalie distrustfully studied her strange companion while he went about lighting a lamp and dishing up food as though he had not a care in the world. She noted his compelling deep blue eyes as they flicked intermittently to her; the straight, prominent nose, the full male lips almost hidden by the thick black beard and mustache. His black hair was far too long, curling over the collarless black shirt that stretched across his wide shoulders. The worn vest of black leather reached almost to his trim waist, while tight black trousers of some thick serge fabric clung to his long legs and covered all but the toes of worn black boots. The dead lawman's black gunbelt rode low on his slim hips, the empty holster resting atop a hard right thigh.

He took a seat and leisurely ate with impeccable table manners, while Natalie stood, stiff and silent, watching. Presently he pushed his plate away, rose, and stood looking down at her. The flickering light from the oil lamp cast shadows on the hard planes of his face, giving him an evil, frightening appearance. Natalie felt her unease rise as they stood staring at each other, neither speaking.

It was he who broke the strained silence.

"In case one of the young Apache braves feels heroic, we'd better put out the lamp."

Natalie stiffened.

Ignoring her reaction, he walked across the floor and picked up the Winchester. "I'll stand watch; you get some rest." He inclined his dark head and Natalie's gaze shifted to the area he indicated. A double bed rested along the western wall, its brightly colored quilt and soft white pillows looking very inviting to the tired young woman.

Natalie ventured closer to the bed, her eyes seeking a partitioning curtain or screen. There was none. Nothing to close off the bedchamber from the rest of the room. No means of privacy so that she might wash up without being watched by those gleaming blue eyes that followed her.

Sighing wearily, Natalie sat on the bed. She was tired, so tired, and longed to strip her soiled dress away, wash the dirt from her face, and lie back on the soft mattress. She wouldn't have dared.

Her companion had carried the lamp with him and taken up his post beside the open front door. Back resting against the hard clay wall, he sat, knees bent and wide apart, the heavy Winchester resting between his legs, barrel pointed toward the ceiling. He fished in his shirt pocket, brought out a cheroot and stuck it between his teeth. With a thumbnail he scratched a lucifer until it flamed up, and he drew upon the cigar. He tossed the match out the door and said softly, " 'Night, ma'am."

Natalie didn't answer.

He blew out the lamp.

It was a dark, moonless night. The station was cast into total blackness. Natalie's straining eyes could see nothing but the red, glowing tip of a cigar moving slowly back and forth to the mouth of a dangerous badman.

Chapter Two

Natalie sat stiffly on the bed in the darkness. She strained to see the bearded face, the wide shoulders of the man who was as much an enemy to her as the Apaches were. She could see nothing.

There was no moonglow, no starlight to illuminate the hot room. It was pitch-black, the darkness seeming almost tangible. And she was helpless and alone with a hardened criminal who spoke with a despised southern accent.

Natalie smiled in the darkness. The irony of it all was comical. Her only protection against violent savages was a wanted outlaw who could commit murder with a cold ruthlessness that would scare even the Apaches.

His polite, menacing calm was frightening. She had no doubt the tall, bearded stranger had gunned down more than one man without so much as batting a black eyelash.

The red tip of the outlaw's cigar sailed out the open door and Natalie tensed. Would he decide to take the bed? Would he decide to take her as well?

The silence was deafening. So still and quiet was the small, hot way station, she could hear her rapid breaths. And his slow, even breathing. Hand tightening on the heavy revolver, she sat, eyes blinking in the darkness, trying vainly to make out his form, listening for any sudden movement from him.

Minutes ticked away. Nothing happened. Natalie's back
ached relentlessly, her head throbbed, her mouth was dry.
Perspiration dotted her upper lip and her long, wilted hair
clung damply to her stiff neck.

An hour went by. She reasoned that if he was going to
make a move, he would surely have done so. She relaxed a
bit, slumping tiredly, fingers loosening on the Colt's steel
handle. She squirmed and shifted and finally scooted across
the bed so that she might use the wall to support her weary
back.

When she leaned her head against the wall and closed her
eyes for a moment, her thoughts drifted from this remote
stage station that would likely be her tomb.

The smiling, handsome face of her late husband rose before
her in the darkness, and Natalie bit her lip. By nightfall tomorrow, she'd be with him once again.

She felt her chest tighten. How young and happy and full
of hope they'd been that glorious spring day a dozen years
ago when she'd exchanged vows with Devlin Vallance in the
flower-filled drawing room of Devlin's stately ancestral mansion in Ohio. She was but a girl of eighteen, Devlin a manly
twenty-five on that lovely April day in 1860.

How brief and precious their time together had been before
he had ridden away to that bloody war against the hated
Confederates. How sweet the laughter-filled days, the love-
filled nights . . .

The hoot of an owl nearby brought Natalie rudely back to
the present. She winced audibly and felt her heart speed with
fear.

"When the hoot owl calls in the darkness of the night, a
potent ghost from the Spirit World has come to claim your
soul." Those were the words she'd heard old Tahomah repeat
many times over the years. He believed it. She did too.

"It's a foolish Indian superstition, nothing more," came a
deep, drawling voice from out of the darkness, as though the
bearded man had read her mind.

"I know," she said weakly, wondering how the outlaw

knew of the legend. But she did believe and she was frightened. Very frightened. She was thirty years old, in good health, of sound mind, and she didn't want to die. Although her life was not nearly as joyful as once it had been, she wanted to cling to it, to see old age, to watch her unborn grandchildren play happily in the mountain-shadowed valleys of her ranch home, Cloud West.

Natalie hardly knew when the tears she'd been fighting back for the past hour started slipping down her cheeks. She was weeping quietly and she felt she might never stop.

A sound across that dark, hot room made her blink at the tears filling her green eyes. Her strange companion had set the rifle down and was rising to his feet. The leather gunbelt was unbuckled and dropped to the wooden floor.

Natalie clutched her throat and listened to the man's sure, even steps as he crossed the room. Nearer and nearer the footfalls came until she knew he was standing by the bed.

She couldn't see a thing but she could feel him. His presence was strong and potent in the dark, hot room. He said nothing, but Natalie knew he was standing directly before her, so close she could reach out and touch him.

His scent was in the warm, heavy air. He smelled of sweat and leather and maleness. She gulped for a breath when the bed groaned as he sat down beside her.

For an interminable time he was silent beside her; his body heat assaulted her perspiring flesh, his breathing was slow and heavy near her ear. Terrified, Natalie sat stone still, not daring to move a muscle, tears still streaming down her frightened face.

And then she jumped when she felt them.

Warm fingers brushed her left cheek and the strange, dangerous man beside her said, "I cannot bear to hear a woman cry. Please don't. Don't."

Insane though it was, Natalie now found his low, calm voice and his warm, gentle touch strangely comforting.

She turned more fully toward the sound of that deep, drawling voice and lifted her face so that he could more easily reach her. Then both of his strong hands were on her

cheeks and she closed her eyes while his thumbs carefully
wiped the tears away.

". . . and a good chance help will arrive," he was saying
in low, conversational tones. Natalie believed not a word he
said but liked to hear him speak all the same. And she wished
. . . she desperately wished there was a glimmer of light
coming through the darkened windows so that she could look
into those compelling blue eyes.

Natalie felt the tension leaving her shoulders and a strange,
pleasing lassitude spreading throughout her body. She
yawned, feeling drowsy, and her eyelids grew heavy. "Will
you do something for me tomorrow?" she asked softly.

"What?"

"Will you promise to shoot me so the Apaches won't get
me?" She asked it as though she were requesting some small
favor, her voice soft and true, and without fear. Lazily she
rubbed her cheek against his right palm. "I'm too much of a
coward to do it myself." Again she yawned.

A muscle jumped in his bearded jaw. He knew Apaches
well. They buried men up to their necks, then jerked off their
heads with ropes. They hung men upside down over low-
burning campfires, and watched while the victim took days to
roast slowly to death. They cut off men's eyelids, put honey
on their faces and genitals, and then staked them to ant hills.

And when they got their hands on a pretty white
woman . . .

"Yes," he said evenly, "I'll kill you."

She nodded her thanks.

She could see nothing, but she leaned toward him and let
him continue to brush away her tears. All at once she felt his
beard brush her face; she drew a shallow breath and very
nearly sighed when his warm lips touched her fluttering eyelids. And still he spoke softly, gently, willing her to believe
they would be safe.

"The stage from Yuma is due at Spanish Widow in the
morning." His mouth was amazingly soft and tender on her
cheeks. "By nine A.M. it will arrive." Those lips kissed a path
along her cheekbone.

For the first time since he'd handed it to her, Natalie released her grip on the heavy Colt revolver. She let it slip to the soft bed and her fingers moved tentatively up to a hard, muscular forearm. Her intent was to gently push this man away, to assure him that she was now all right, that she'd not cry any more.

"Yes, we'll be rescued, I'm sure," she said, believing her words no more than he did.

Lightly she laid her hand upon his arm and felt the muscles jump beneath her touch even as his soft, persuasive lips continued to kiss her face. Her heart lurched crazily and her fingers tightened their grip upon his shirtsleeve.

He was breathing more rapidly now as his long arms slowly went around her, pulling her to him. Soon she was pressed close against his hard, muscular frame and his heartbeat drummed against her breasts.

The lips that had been moving upon her flushed face were taken from her and he said into her hair, "I want you."

Nothing more. Simply that.

He was silent then, silent and completely still. His arms encircled her, his lips hovered just above her own, his beard brushing her mouth and nose, but he moved not a muscle. He was waiting. Waiting for her to pull free of his embrace, to jump up from the bed, to flee.

The moment was filled with a new kind of tension between them. Natalie felt her heart hammering and a faint dizziness. She gripped his broad shoulders while thoughts tumbled over each other in her spinning brain.

Surely she must be going insane! She was sitting on a bed in the darkness at a remote outpost with the arms of a dangerous outlaw around her.

And she wanted him.

God help her; she wanted this bearded criminal whom she should hate and fear to the depths of her very soul. He was deadly, dangerous, a hunted animal whose misdeeds would surely curl her hair if she knew of them. He was unmistakably southern. Most probably one of the legion of Confederate devils who'd killed her beloved husband.

"I want you," he repeated, and Natalie could not find the strength to say no. Come morning, they were going to die. This hot, dark night would be their last upon this earth. Never again would she hear the wind in the pines outside her bedroom window. Or warm herself before a blazing fire on a cold snowy night. Or eat a sumptuous meal. Or taste imported wine.

Or make love.

Natalie felt her stomach flutter violently as her heart pounded. Right or wrong, foolish or wise, she wanted to know this bearded stranger's arms, to surrender to the dark desire his words had stirred.

If die she must tomorrow, then live she would tonight.

"Don't hurt me," she said as his mouth closed over hers.

As they'd been upon her cheeks, his lips were tender, soft, gentle. He kissed her lightly, as though he were the consummate gentleman, and she a treasured love he'd come to court. Natalie began to relax in his arms and her hand stole up around his strong neck, her fingers touching the long raven locks that curled down over the collar of his shirt. She sighed when he continued expertly to mold her soft lips to fit his. And she felt like laughing giddily from the teasing, tickling beard and mustache that she found so tantalizing against her sensitive face.

The stirringly sweet kisses continued and it seemed to Natalie that the small stuffy room became even hotter. Eyes open or shut, it was the same. She could see nothing. She could only feel. And smell. And taste. And hear.

She could hear the rustling of her skirts as she strained in his arms, the distant call of a nighthawk, the creak of the bed beneath them. She could taste tobacco on his mouth and salt from the perspiration covering his dark face. And the strange, unfamiliar flavor of him, the man, like no one else, unique, frightening, arousing.

She could feel his hard, powerful body pressing her own, the masterful arms holding her tightly, and the practiced mouth moving upon hers, sending all her senses reeling.

His lips had hardened with passion, and his mouth had

opened wide to deepen his kiss. His tongue plunged rhythmically into Natalie's receptive mouth in a bold, sexual way that made her stomach contract with the beginnings of full-fledged passion.

While she was lost in the depths of a heated, intimate kiss, he gently lifted her up into his arms. She sat there on his lap in the darkness, his mouth devouring hers, her loosened hair spilling down over his supporting arm. And then he rose with her in his arms.

He turned and gently placed her upon the bed and lay down with her, his burning lips never freeing hers. They strained together there on that small bed, their clothed, perspiring bodies locked together, their passion flaring white-hot.

They rolled over and he lay atop her, kissing her, embracing her, his long legs tangling with hers through her full skirts. They rolled yet again and she was atop him. His hands slid down her body sensuously, caressing, stroking, seeking the gentle curves beneath her dress. He moved her legs outside of his and drew her knees up on each side of his slim hips.

She leaned to him and kissed him, and kissed him, her long red-gold hair falling into his face. And when, in the thick darkness, she felt his fingers upon the tiny buttons on her bodice, she sighed and raised up a little to make his task easier.

And then she felt those strong hands encircling her rib cage, urging her down to him. His mouth was a searing flame upon her bare, aching breasts and Natalie sighed and happily positioned herself over him so that his lips might remain upon her burning flesh without his having to lift his dark head from the mattress.

The soft sound of his sucking was somehow powerfully erotic and Natalie thrilled to this intimate language of loving and pressed her swelling breasts ever closer to the heat and hunger of his mustached mouth.

When he'd caressed her breasts until they were tender and swollen, and tingling from his kisses, the bearded stranger sat her up, gently pushing her down onto his hard thighs. Then he sat up also and managed . . . she'd always wonder how . . . to undress her, and himself, sitting there in the middle of the bed.

When her bare knee came down upon the discarded Colt, Natalie winced aloud. He lowered the gun to the floor and raised her knee to his mouth.

"Baby," he said soothingly, his lips and tongue vigorously kissing her injured knee.

Within minutes, still sitting astride him, Natalie was unashamedly naked and so was he. For a time they simply luxuriated in that newfound freedom, gently touching, exploring, appreciating the vast differences between their unclothed bodies.

While his hands swept gently over her slim, satiny shoulders, down the delicate curve of her back and to her flaring hips, his lips sprinkled kisses upon her temple, her hair, her nose.

She smiled dreamily in the darkness and let her searching fingers contour his strong male shoulders and scarred, muscular back. With her fingertips she traced the satiny ribbons that marred his smooth brown flesh.

"You're beautiful," he murmured, his tongue worrying her left earlobe.

She purred deep in her throat. "How would you know?" she questioned softly, letting her head fall back. "You can't see me."

His mouth slid down the side of her throat. "Ah, but I can," he drawled. And as his hands caressed her bare, slender curves, he clearly envisioned her flawless, alabaster skin, her huge emerald eyes and long, lustrous golden-red hair, and her upturned nose and soft pink lips. Oh, yes, he could see her as surely as if bright sunlight were flooding the adobe.

With his tongue he touched the rapidly beating pulse in her throat and repeated, "I can see you."

Natalie's hands tightened on his muscular shoulders as he began to slowly lift her up, his mouth never leaving her flesh.

She felt his hot lips once again upon her breasts and bit her lip with pleasure.

His mouth lingered but a short time and moved on down her rib cage even as his strong hands pushed her upward. She was kneeling then astride him, her breath growing short, her head spinning.

And still he kissed and lifted her, hands firmly gripping her narrow, naked waist.

"No . . . no . . ." she weakly protested as his mouth played provocatively upon her quivering stomach, moving lower and lower. She felt her knees leave the mattress as he lifted her higher. "No . . . ," she murmured breathlessly, "no . . . please . . . you must stop . . . please stop . . . oh . . . oh . . . oh, God, don't ever stop."

She was standing now, his sure hands clutching her hips. And he was caressing her knees and thighs and belly, his lips tasting and his tongue stroking, silky beard tickling her flesh. Her whole body ignited with incredible, consuming heat and she felt she could wait not one second longer for him to give her what her body cried out for. A sob of pain and pleasure was building deep within her and every muscle in her tense body was straining.

And finally, in answer to her craving, undulating body, his lips moved to that throbbing, most feminine part of her, and the grateful sob tore from her throat.

His mouth dazzled her as he pressed his bearded face between her parted legs, closer, deeper, sweeter, until he was buried in her, licking, lapping, loving her with endless caresses of fire.

Her body aflame, and the pressure inside it building, Natalie clung to his thick dark hair and pressed her burning pelvis to his experienced mouth. Never in all of her life had she felt as she did at this moment. Never in the years she'd been married had her husband loved her in the way this dark outlaw was now pleasuring her. Never before had she surrendered so completely, so brazenly, to the fleshly delights of raw, uninhibited sex.

She did this night.

She clung to his dark hair and tossed her head wildly, rocking forward against him. She moaned and sighed and urged him on, begging for more in a low voice that sent the blood pounding in his ears so that he felt he might completely devour her, so aroused was his passion.

And then it began.

That wrenching, tearing, exquisite release that caused the breath to catch in Natalie's chest. She looked down upon the naked man she could not see and her shoulders slumped forward, her knees buckling under her.

But for him, she would have fallen. While his knowing mouth stayed fused to her source of joy, his strong hands held her fast, until her out-of-this-world climax was completed and she was drained and limp against him.

Only then did he lift his head and gently fold her body down next to his. She looked at his face. And she could see him. Through the thick darkness she was able to make out his gleaming blue eyes and gleaming wet lips before he kissed her with a tenderness as devastating as the wild loving had been.

She was his then.

Whatever he wanted to do. Whatever he wanted her to do. She was willing, eager, and as passionate and bold as he. When he laid her upon the bed and stretched out beside her, he took her small hand and placed it upon his throbbing erection. She sighed and brazenly caressed him, thrilling to the sounds of his deep groans.

In the darkness she leaned over him, and let her long, loose hair tickle his furred chest and flat belly. He groaned aloud when she bent to him and kissed his hard, male flesh with soft lips and teasing tongue. He could stand the sweet joy for only a short time before he grabbed her up, kissed her deeply, and pressed her down upon her back.

Shifting quickly over her, he drove into her with sure, deep thrusts and felt her soft, moist flesh close tightly around him. As though they were made for each other, they moved in slow, graceful splendor, their damp bodies slipping and sliding sensuously together until the supreme sexual pleasure they found in each other pushed them at last into the fast, frenzied movements that led to total blinding ecstasy.

And so it was all that long, dark, steamy night.

The imminent danger they faced added a distinct urgency and total abandon to their couplings. Again and again they surrendered to raw, unrestrained passion, each pushing the other to new heights of rapture, each greedy for gratification, reaching out to take all the bliss the other could offer, and delighting in the giving of joy in return.

Deep in the dead of that strange, hot night, Natalie, naked and sated, lay in the arms of the bearded outlaw, her cheek pressed against his muscular, bare shoulder.

Drifting toward peaceful, much needed slumber, she pressed a kiss to his broad chest, and giggled when the crisp hair that covered it tickled her sensitive nose. She hugged him tighter and slid a long, slender leg over his hard abdomen. And she wondered.

Who was her dark, bearded lover?

Then his strong brown hands were lifting her and his mouth was back on hers and she didn't care who he was. She sighed and climbed astride him.

Once again they made love, unseeing, under the pitch-black cloak of darkness.

Chapter Three

High in the Colorado Rockies a full harvest moon shone brightly, bathing the shimmering summits and lush valleys in silvery light. Towering peaks of the 14,000-foot mountains glowed with a preternatural radiance, and the thick, fragrant flora clinging to their sides sparkled dazzlingly in the moonlight.

At Cloud West, the high meadow ranch located at the 9,000-foot level of Promontory Point's soaring western face, the sprawling white ranch house took on a luminous incandescence. Inside the comfortable, well-maintained house the moon's brilliant beams streamed through every tall window, and every skylight, leaving hardly an inch of hardwood floor unlighted, few corners untouched.

Upstairs, in a large white-walled and white-carpeted bedroom, Natalie Vallance lay naked on her white, silk-hung bed, her slender ivory body brightly illuminated. And Natalie felt as though the lustrous, vivid light exposing her body lay bare her guilty soul as well.

She folded a slender arm beneath her head and let her eyes slip from the gathered white canopy overhead to her undraped alabaster body. Her face flamed crimson in the white light. She longed for the darkness; the thick, oppressive blackness that had so completely covered her shame on that hot, hot night she could not erase from her memory.

She let a trembling hand trail down over her narrow waist and flat belly as thoughts of a dark, bearded stranger intruded once again into her well-disciplined, carefully planned life. Fingertips gliding over her flesh, she relived—as she'd done so many times—her shameful, and uncharacteristically wanton, behavior on that dark, strange night she'd spent with the outlaw.

Natalie told herself none of it would have happened if the moon had been shining brightly on that fateful night. It was that damnable caressing darkness that had made her cast away all inhibition and logic, and drown in a dark sea of desire.

Natalie rolled into a fetal position on the silky white sheets as the recollection of the wild mating and timely rescue caused a tightness in her naked chest.

She'd fallen asleep there in the outlaw's arms in the darkness. He'd shaken her awake sometime later, saying, "Get dressed, I hear horses' hooves."

Disoriented and fearful, she'd struggled with the tiny buttons on her bodice as the first faint gray of dawn seeped in through the windows. Twisting her long red hair on top of her head, she watched the tall stranger finish buttoning his black shirt, pick up the Winchester, and go out into the dim morning light.

She'd opened her mouth to call to him, but said nothing.

A detail of soldiers from Fort Garland galloped up to the station and dismounted. When Natalie came out onto the stone porch, she saw two sergeants tying the dark, bearded man's wrists behind him. Then they escorted him to a horse.

She heard little of what the solicitous lieutenant beside her said. Intently she watched the tall, lean bandit, flanked by two soldiers, walk away from her. He'd not so much as turned his dark head to give her one last glance. Mounted on a big gray gelding led by the junior officer, he rode into the rapidly rising sun.

". . . and you're most fortunate, ma'am, to be alive. He's

killed before." Natalie felt heartsick and remorseful, and strangely lonely.

It had meant so little to him, he'd not even looked back . . . not even looked back . . . not even looked back. That hurtful thought kept crowding out all the others. It seemed impossible to Natalie that a man—even a hardened criminal —could make love to her the way the tall bearded bandit had and walk away without looking back.

Natalie shook her head to clear him from her thoughts. She had to forget about their night of loving, pretend it never happened. If only she could convince herself it was just as she'd told everyone: The wanted man had fought off the Apaches until night fell and they rode away. Then he'd stood watch while she slept. Dawn came, the soldiers rescued them and took the man away. There was nothing more to it.

Natalie sat up and slid her long, bare legs over the edge of the bed. She rose and walked across the deep white carpet to the tall glass-doored armoire. Drawing out a white satin chemise, she jerked it down over her head, feeling an overwhelming desire to hide her nakedness. She knew it was illogical, but she was sure her body looked different now, as if the dark man had left his mark on it.

Natalie trembled and she wished for the darkness—that sweet, cloaking, secretive blackness that hid shameful indiscretions so well.

And the guilt that inevitably followed.

A thousand feet below Natalie's beloved Cloud West ranch, Cloudcastle's lights twinkled like a fine jeweled necklace on a bed of dark green velvet. Tucked between the mammoth Promontory Point to the east and the majestic Lone Cave Peak to the west, the sparkling alpine village was nestled in the wide natural valley, from foothill to foothill.

Ten miles northeast of the town, Mount Sneffels rose to an imposing height, while ten miles due south, Mount Wilson, at 14,246 feet, surpassed all the others, making it one of the tallest in the San Juan range, topped only by Uncompahgre.

At the grandest mansion in all of Cloudcastle, a slim, aristocratic-looking man slipped his long arms into a fine, well-cut evening coat. He stepped closer to the free-standing gold-framed mirror and meticulously tied his striped silk cravat.

Lord Ashlin Blackmore, Cloudcastle's most illustrious citizen, a British earl, had migrated to the small mountain city by way of Denver. Leaving his native England with the last of his inheritance, the handsome blond man sought adventure and opportunity in a brash new land.

He had arrived in Cloudcastle on the hot July 4 of 1870, telling one and all he'd come as an agent for the proposed Denver–Pacific Railroad. He wished to purchase right-of-way acreage. He'd bought no land, but he had immediately won the hearts, and the trust, of the citizenry of the bustling gold-mining town. Quick to claim residence, Lord Blackmore promptly purchased the city's most imposing house.

Located at the very end of South Main Street on a natural rise overlooking the well-planned, attractive hamlet, the Blackmore residence had been built a decade before by a silver baron who'd since gone bankrupt and departed. Times had been flush when the imposing Victorian mansion was constructed, and no expense had been spared.

The spacious living room on the upper floor boasted a large bay window that provided a spectacular view of the lofty mountain peaks as well as the storybook village below. It was to this room that Lord Blackmore went to await the arrival of his guest.

Glorious moonlight washed over the European statuary, the mahogany spinet, and the tapestry-covered French sofas and armchairs, as well as the brocatelle draperies and lace curtains gracing tall floor-to-ceiling windows and double doors thrown open to the warm, dry mountain air.

He was standing there at the doors, blond hair looking silver in the moon's glow, his lips curving into a smile beneath his straight, patrician nose, when the carriage turned into the drive. Lord Blackmore saw the gleaming black coach come to a stop in the circular pebbled driveway below. He took a drink of burgundy and his smile broadened.

She stepped down from the carriage and into the moonlight. Her golden-red hair shone with highlights while the turquoise satin gown she wore lightened to a soft aqua in the pale, penetrating light. She lifted her skirts and turned to look up, and the earl's breath caught in his chest. Her flawless white skin was pearlized; her emerald eyes flashed and her dewy mouth was red and gleaming.

In seconds she was ushered into the room and into his arms. Lord Blackmore embraced the beautiful woman and said into her ear, "My dear, you grow more beautiful each day. Each night. Come, I shall pour you a glass of wine and we'll enjoy the view for a time before dinner."

Natalie smiled and fought down the puzzling desire she felt to pull away from his arms, to rush out of the room, back to the seclusion and privacy of Cloud West. She stood with her cheek pressed to the immaculate white shirt covering Lord Blackmore's chest, and felt his lips upon her hair, his soft hands gently pressing the bare flesh atop the low-cut back of her turquoise satin gown. It was all she could do to keep from shouting, "Don't touch me; take your hands off me."

She did not.

She remained passively still in his embrace until he at last released her, set her back, and looked down at her, his hands lightly gripping her shoulders. Brown eyes troubled, he said softly, "My love, you're not yourself. I can't help but wonder . . ." His voice dropped lower. "Are you sure that outlaw didn't harm . . ."

Natalie shrugged from his grasp and turned away, afraid the answer was written all too clearly in her eyes. "Ashlin, you've asked me that several times." She strolled toward the front bay window. "For the last time, the man never touched"—she hesitated, then hurried on—"never harmed me. Please don't speak of it again."

"I'm sorry, love." He came to her, gliding his fingertips over her satiny white shoulder, and assured, "We shan't speak of it ever again, I promise." He leaned down to kiss the shoulder he was touching and Natalie instinctively flinched. Lord Blackmore straightened, cleared his throat, and said, "May I offer you burgundy, my dear."

"Yes, Ashlin, thank you." She sauntered closer to the gleaming bay window. Her emerald eyes swept over the village below. Shimmering in the moonlight, Cloudcastle was a fairyland with twinkling lights, wide tree-lined avenues, and attractive Victorian buildings. Against the breathtaking backdrop of the towering San Juans, she could pick out the opulent, marble-fronted Eureka Hotel and adjoining Gaiety's Gaming Hall, where lights blazed from every portal. And across the street was the ornate Cloudcastle Opera House with its turrets and gables and balconies. The tall spire of the First Presbyterian Church with its gold-capped bell tower glittered in the moonlight.

The newspaper office, the Federal Land Office, Gallen's Dry Goods, the firehouse, numerous shops, the apothecary and Dr. Ellroy's office.

Her eyes settled on the newly built white Castleton County Courthouse. Almost immediately her gaze shifted to the sturdy, two-celled jailhouse across from the courthouse. There was activity there; several men, some mounted, others on foot, were congregated in front of the small building. It was too far away for her to make out any faces.

"Darling." Lord Blackmore was at her side, a glass of burgundy in his outstretched hand. "What intrigues you so?" He smiled and put a gentle hand on her nape.

"Nothing really," Natalie responded. "Just some sort of action down at the jail and I wondered . . ."

"Please, Natalie." He set the wine aside and drew her into his arms. "Forget the activity. Forget the jail." He slowly lowered his golden head and covered her lips with his own, pulling her closer. "Know only the jail of my encircling arms, my beautiful Natalie, my precious fiancée."

Joe South, Castleton County's most frequently jailed citizen, blinked and sat up on his bunk when the door of his cell swung open to admit a new prisoner. Roused from a drunken slumber, the frail, sleepy Joe rubbed his eyes, scratched at an itchy underarm, and studied the tall, silent man through bleary, unfocused eyes.

The door clanged shut, and the deputy who'd brought in the new prisoner laughed and said loudly, "That ought to hold you. You go entertaining any thoughts of breaking out" —he lifted a heavy Colt .44, stuck it through the bars—"I'll make you a worse cripple than Joe." Loud laughter came from the excited townsfolk who'd crowded around the jail to get a glimpse of the criminal. Night deputy Clyde Percell reholstered his Colt, hitched up his drooping breeches with a yank of his beefy hands, and strode outside to accept more congratulations and praise.

Joe South, the town drunk, was rapidly growing sober. He didn't like the cold blue eyes of the fierce-looking stranger now sharing his cell. Warily he watched the tall, dark outlaw move toward the empty bunk across from his own. His walk, the set of his shoulders, gave the impression of dangerous power, recognizable even to the whiskey-soaked Joe.

Through nervous, bloodshot eyes, Joe watched his strange cellmate meticulously smooth out the thin mattress, spread the blanket, and sit down on the bed. In one quick, fluid movement the dark bandit sprawled out on his back, resting his dark head on his folded arms.

Moonlight streamed in through the high, barred window to illuminate the narrow bed and the man upon it. Crossing his long legs at the ankles, the outlaw looked directly at Joe South and Joe gulped in stunned confusion as the quiet, deadly man flashed him a sudden, brilliant smile, his pearly teeth gleaming amid a dense growth of beard.

"Covington's the name," he said in a gentle voice as his smile widened. "Kane Covington."

That smile changed his appearance entirely. His hard-planed face no longer looked so evil and Joe South recognized the name. His fear changed to shock. Then to awe. And finally back to fear. Not of the man, Kane Covington, but for him. He'd heard of Kane Covington, sure enough. He knew exactly what was in store for the smiling, dark fellow southerner.

"Lordy, sir, we gotta get you out of here." Joe rose unsteadily to his feet. Limping over to his new cellmate, he warned excitedly, "You're gonna wind up wishin' you had never been born." He was looking down on the lounging, bearded man, appalled that Covington appeared so calm.

"Am I?"

"Yes, sir." Joe South shook his head knowingly. "You'll stand trial now." He was trembling; from both the liquor and the excitement. "Know what they call the Castleton County judge?"

"Suppose you tell me."

" 'Hanging' Nat Vallance, that's what! Sends 'em right to the gallows!"

Chapter Four

Already there was the hint of approaching autumn in the air.

Judge Natalie Vallance, perched sidesaddle atop her big bay stallion, Blaze, cantered down Ranch Road toward Cloudcastle. The sun was high and brilliant in the blue September skies. Natalie knew the curious townsfolk who would crowd into the courtroom today would be shedding jackets and rolling up shirtsleeves before the afternoon was over. But at this early hour there was a definite chill in the air.

Natalie drew a long, deep breath. How she loved this time of year in the Shining Mountains. Nature was at its best from now until first snowfall. It was in early fall four years ago that she had proudly become the first female judge in the sovereign Territory of Colorado.

Some people were still outraged that the only magistrate in Castleton County was a woman.

Natalie laughed aloud, recalling how she'd quietly set out to obtain the lofty position. Night after night she'd studied her father's worn law books, telling only Judge Masters and swearing him to secrecy. Wisely keeping her hopes and her dreams secret from all others, she'd spent her days visiting the court trials, listening, learning, and planning.

She became friendly with the circuit attorneys, accepting

their dinner invitations, skillfully rebuffing their amorous advances while gleaning worlds of valuable legal information.

She hosted an important party just before the Territory's September election, inviting a good number of Cloudcastle's upstanding citizens: husbands and socially prominent wives, as well as the two candidates to the territorial legislature, Democrat Charles Dixon and Republican Benjamin Nunn.

While guests ate dainty cakes and sipped punch, Natalie Vallance made an important announcement. "We're all happy to have Mr. Dixon and Mr. Nunn with us this evening." She looked from one to the other, smiling warmly. "One of you gentleman will be elected. We desire, here and now, a public pledge from both of you, that whoever of you is elected will work for the passage of an act conferring upon the women of the Territory the right of suffrage."

Both men looked at Natalie, at each other, and agreed. They were heavily applauded, the applause led by an approving Natalie.

Benjamin Nunn was elected and he kept his word. With an impatient, excited Natalie at his elbow, he drafted the document handing political equality to women, and two days later introduced the bill on the senate floor to an amused, all-male gathering.

Nonetheless, the bill passed. Meanwhile, Natalie read for the bar and passed it with flying colors. Not a week later the Honorable Clement T. Masters, a good friend of Natalie's deceased father, and her mentor, sent a message to the board of commissioners expressing his intent to retire as soon as some lady elector could be duly appointed to fill the vacancy.

Natalie Vallance, at age twenty-six, became the Colorado Territory's first female judge.

Joe South was free and sober on this perfect September morning. He'd lifted but one strong whiskey when word came from the jail that the prisoner, Kane Covington, wished to see him. The skinny young man didn't hesitate. He left the nearly empty saloon and hurriedly limped toward the jail.

Out of breath, he rushed right in and excitedly informed

the jailor he'd been summoned by Mr. Covington. The jailer motioned him on back and Joe South was soon standing before the bars of Kane Covington's cell.

Kane lay in that lounging sprawl of his, his long body totally relaxed. Joe South shook his head. Somehow he'd expected to see the bearded criminal clinging to the bars in desperation.

Joe grinned.

He should have known better.

"Joe, my boy." Kane agilely came to his feet. "Thanks for coming."

"Happy to, sir." Joe plucked his battered Stetson off his sandy head as though he stood in the presence of true greatness. "Anything I can do?"

"You can, Joe, you sure can." Kane scratched at his bushy black beard and winked at the shorter man. He walked back and forth before the bars. "I've decided—since you tell me the judge is a lady—I'll see if I can't look like a gentleman. Go to the best tailor in town, express my wishes to have a fine suit of clothes ready and delivered by noon today. I'd prefer dove gray, I believe, and let's see, Joe . . . one of those white shirts with a stiff, uncomfortable collar, a subdued cravat, studs, and—" He stopped his restless prowling, and raised his lean brown hand to his hair-covered face. "And, Joe, send the barber around to the jail. I need a shave and a haircut."

It was nearing noon and Natalie threw open the windows of her small chambers. The chill had long since left the air and now it was hot.

Natalie flipped open two or three buttons of the tight-bodiced white blouse she wore, patted at her upswept red-gold hair, and softly sighed. It would be a long, uncomfortable afternoon. The entire community would try and crowd into the courtroom. It would be close and stuffy. And hot. Too hot. Almost as hot as . . .

Natalie bit the inside of her cheek and clenched her fists. She had to forget about that night! She had to quit torturing herself over it. All right, so she'd behaved outrageously with an animal on the wrong side of the law. That's unfair of me, she mentally scolded herself. Here I am a magistrate of the courts and I'm judging the man without even knowing the crime he's accused of commiting. She shook her head. Whatever he's done, whoever he is, there's no going back, no changing the past.

She drew a shallow breath. No one knew and no one would ever know, and although she'd betrayed Ashlin, she'd make it up to him. It wasn't as though she'd committed adultery. They were not yet man and wife. Had they been, that indiscretion would never have happened. She was not completely without morals. Never in her married life had she betrayed her husband, Devlin Vallance. And she'd never betray Ashlin once they were married.

"Forgive me, Ashlin," she said to the silent chamber, as she had a dozen times in the past month.

Determined anew to put the whole horrible episode behind her, Judge Natalie Vallance slipped her arms into her long black judicial robe, hooked it securely beneath her chin, glanced one last time at the clock, and proceeded into the already packed courtroom.

"All rise for the Honorable Judge Natalie Vallance," said the bailiff as Natalie entered the crowded courtroom and took her place upon the bench.

She promptly lifted her gavel and brought the proceedings to order. In a clear, firm voice, she announced, "The Third District Court of Castleton County in the sovereign Territory of Colorado is now in session." Hardly bothering to look up from her sheaf of papers, Judge Vallance read the charge.

"The accused, Kane W. Covington, is charged with the murder of one Jimmy Ray Leatherwood on July 8, 1872. Is the prosecution ready?" She lifted eyes to the county attorney.

"We are, Your Honor," said Doug Matthews loudly.

"Is defense ready?" she queried, returning her attention to the sheaf of papers before her.

"It is, Your Honor," came a gentle southern voice that made Natalie look up in alarm. She saw the slim, immaculately groomed man standing alone behind the defendant's bar. His tall, lean frame was draped in a light gray suit. Underneath it he wore a spanking white shirt with a tight collar. His handsome, hawklike face was smoothly shaven, and his coal-black hair was carefully trimmed and brushed. His cruel-looking mouth was fixed in a tight expression, and the eyes . . .

Natalie felt her heart stop. Then start again at a racing beat that left her light-headed and dizzy.

She was looking into the unforgettable blue eyes of her dark outlaw lover.

Chapter Five

And he was looking at her.

Those deep blue eyes gave no flicker of recognition, no hint of surprise or confusion. Not at first. But their gazes locked and held. And in his eyes, a contradiction, a touch of melancholy. Swiftly it passed and in its place, an icy, predatory glare that chilled her very bones.

Struggling to break the hold his eyes had upon her, Natalie closed her trembling fingers around the smooth, hard handle of the gavel and said as forcefully as she could manage, "This court is recessed until nine tomorrow morning." She didn't explain why and chose to ignore the mumbling that erupted from disappointed citizens who'd been lining up outside the courthouse since breakfast time. "Bailiff, take the prisoner to his cell," she directed, and brought down the gavel with such force, it sounded like a pistol shot.

Not daring to glance again at the defendant, Natalie, ashen-faced and feeling ill, hurried out of the courtroom with such haste that the townsfolk fell to gossiping. What on earth was the matter with the calm, self-assured Judge Vallance? Her behavior was decidedly strange and puzzling. Never in the four years she'd been on the bench had the coolly composed judge dismissed court proceedings before they'd begun.

Lord Ashlin Blackmore rose from his seat in the rear of

the courtroom. Alarmed and eager to make his way through the disappointed departing crowd, he smiled and good-naturedly dismissed the questioning looks and shouted appeals for an explanation of his fiancée's strange behavior.

Ashlin stood before the closed door of Natalie's private chambers. He knocked softly, and entered before she invited him inside. Still wearing her billowing black robes, Natalie whirled from the window to face him. Her green eyes held a look of sheer terror.

"Darling," he said, hurrying over to her, "what is it?"

Longing to tell him the truth, anxious to pour out the whole horrible story, Natalie violently shook her head, afraid if she spoke, this man who trusted and admired her would never forgive her for betraying him. She felt his chest beneath her hot cheek and his comforting arms about her.

She squeezed her eyes tightly shut.

And she lied.

"Nothing, Ashlin, really. I'm not feeling well physically and I just thought—"

"I knew it," he interrupted, pushing her back a little and taking her chin in his hand, "you're ill, you're as white as linen." His soft brown eyes were filled with concern. It made her feel even more dreadful. "Natalie, I shall summon Dr. Ellroy, at once."

"No, Ashlin. I've no need of a doctor." She dropped her eyes from his searching gaze. "A slight stomach upset, nothing more. I'll lie down here in chambers. Within an hour I'll be fine . . . good as new."

"I don't like it, darling. I do wish you'd let me bring the doctor—"

"Absolutely not. I feel a little better already." She eased herself from his grasp and turned her back to him. Taking off her black robe, she repeated, "All I need is some rest."

"I'll drive you up to Cloud West so Jane can look after you," he offered.

"I've work to do, Ashlin," Natalie replied, fighting to keep the rising irritation from her voice.

"Very well, dear, but at lunchtime I'm taking you up to the

ranch. Have you forgotten I'm due to leave on the Overland stage for Denver this afternoon?"

"No . . . no . . . I've not forgotten," she murmured, although she'd forgotten completely that he would be gone for a couple of days. Reminded of it, she felt a measure of relief instead of the disappointment she knew she should be experiencing. She turned to face him, and smiled. "Ashlin, please don't worry about me. You go on to Denver. I'll rest a bit, then ride home before sundown."

"You're certain you don't wish me to cancel my trip and stay. . . ."

"I won't hear of it." She was shaking her head and he smiled resignedly.

Natalie sighed heavily when Ashlin finally departed. Massaging the back of her tense neck, she crossed the room to draw heavy drapes against the glare of the September sunlight. She kicked off her slippers and lay down upon the worn, uncomfortable sofa along the room's west wall.

There she remained for the rest of the autumn afternoon. She kept telling herself she'd get up and go home. But still she stayed where she was, a strange, mounting sense of urgency claiming her. She was exhausted, yet exhilarated. Tired, yet restless.

When the hot September sun was sliding beneath the jagged peaks of the westernmost range, Natalie was still alone in her chambers. The long, tormenting hours had been divided between lying trancelike on the sofa and pacing, stocking-footed, back and forth across the waxed hardwood floors, her long, hot skirts swirling with her quick steps.

There was barely a glow of fading pink to the clear Colorado sky when finally she stepped out of her chambers, red-gold hair carefully redressed into a neat, tight bun at the back of her head, white blouse rebuttoned to her chin, back straight. Everything about her conveyed placidity and self-possession.

Natalie nodded briskly to a couple of miners as she made her way toward the livery stables. Both men tipped their hats deferentially and stepped aside to let her pass. The hard-

packed dirt street stretched empty before her as most of the
town's inhabitants were in their homes enjoying the evening
meal.

She neared the new Castleton County jail.

Her pulse began to speed. She told herself she'd walk right
by without so much as a passing glance. She drew up even
with the open door and her gaze automatically drifted into
the gaslit interior.

Feet atop his desk, mouth gaping open, the night jailer,
burly, barrel-chested Dwayne Ward slept peacefully. Natalie
paused. And she looked up and down the empty sidewalks.

It was easy to tell herself she should proceed at once into
the jail. She was, after all, the highest-ranking law enforce-
ment officer in Castleton County. Within the walls of the
county jail was a dangerous criminal and the man paid to
guard him was sound asleep. The situation called for immediate intervention. She had no choice, it was up to her to see if
the prisoner was securely restrained in his cell.

Natalie ventured inside, past the snoring jailer. He slept
on, undisturbed. She went at once to the door behind his
desk, which led into a narrow corridor between two small
cells. She paused there, debating. Should she go inside?

She had to.

Had to find out if the prisoner planned to put her life in
jeopardy along with his own. Would he tell—had he told—of
their heated night of passion at Spanish Widow? Would word
of her lustful behavior soon reach Ashlin's ears? Would the
entire community of Cloudcastle soon realize that the judge
they respected, the woman they thought a lady, was in truth
no better than an alley cat?

Her heart pounding, Natalie neared Kane's cell. He was
lying on his back in the moonlight, his hard-planed, hawkish
face half-silvered by the light, half darkened in the shadow.
His long, lean body reclined with a kind of lazy grace and
ease. The white shirt he'd worn in the courtroom was now
opened down to his waist, exposing the crisp black hair of his
chest. His gray suit trousers clung snuggly to a flat belly, slim
hips and long, stretched-out legs.

Natalie felt her cheeks grow warm. She could remember all too well how that hard masculine body felt pressed to her own.

Before she'd spoken a word, Kane turned his dark head and saw her. His blue eyes gleamed with interest. Backlit from the outer room, her golden-red hair made a halo about her small, well-shaped head. The slender, gently curved body, covered from chin to wrist to toes, still managed to look seductive and inviting.

The flaming hair, the sparkling eyes, the pouting mouth, silently announced the identity of his unexpected night visitor.

Agilely, Kane rolled from the bunk and was on his feet, crossing to stand before the iron bars that separated them.

As though a wild, dangerous animal had come near the confining bars of its cage, Natalie clasped a hand to her throat and took a step backward.

Kane's mobile lips twisted into a sardonic, accusing grin. "I'm well restrained, Your Honor." He wrapped long, tanned fingers around the narrow, metal bars. "I couldn't get to you if I wanted . . . or vice versa."

Natalie glared at him but moved closer, casting a quick glance over her shoulder at the dozing jailer. In a soft voice she said, "Mr. Covington, I've come to . . . to see if your cell is secure. To check on your accommodations. To be assured you've been properly fed."

"Beefsteak, mashed potatoes, snap beans, biscuits, cherry pie, and plenty of hot coffee. I appreciate your concern," said Kane, shoving his hands into the pockets of his tight trousers as he moved away. His deep, drawling voice held a scornful inflection.

"A little respect for my office, if you please, Mr. Covington!" Natalie's green eyes flashed in the dimness and she stepped closer, gripping one of the bars with her right hand.

He was back facing her before the words were out of her mouth. "Say what's really on your mind, Your Honor." His lean fingers swiftly snaked through the bars and wrapped themselves around her wrist.

Irritation turning to alarm, Natalie hissed, "Let go of me or I'll—"

"You'll what?" he taunted coldly, refusing to release her. "Wake the jailer and tell him you couldn't resist a visit with the prisoner?" He smiled then, his quick blue eyes scanning her face. The smile fled as swiftly as it appeared. "Do you often visit the men incarcerated in the county jail?" His fingers continued to hold her, not tightly but securely. She refused to struggle and relinquish more of her dignity than she'd already lost.

"No." She looked him in the eye. "I do not."

"I thought not." His thumb absently rubbed the soft inside of her wrist. "We both know the reason for your visit."

"Do we?" She lifted her chin defiantly.

He was nodding his dark head. "Your Honor, if you were the first young lady who had come to me in secret to ask that I remain silent about an indiscretion, I might be—"

"I don't have to listen to your insults."

"Who's insulting you?" He was smiling again, a wide, infuriating grin that was somehow intensely cruel. "I'm saying you can relax. I'm not going to tell the good townsfolk that the honorable Judge Natalie Vallance, respected magistrate of Castleton County and revered fiancée of the noble Lord Blackmore, spent a sultry night in—"

"Damn you, Kane Covington." She snatched her wrist free. "Tell anything you please!"

"No, Your Honor," he said softly, in that cultivated southern voice she so loathed and which was so at odds with the chisel-featured face that had gone cold and expressionless, the blue eyes bleak and somber. "I should expose you to the man who foolishly loves you, but I won't." He fell silent then, looking at her. Natalie felt she would never forget the icy contempt she saw in his cold eyes.

"I shall—"

"Tell him yourself?" Kane cut in on her. "No, you won't."

Natalie glared at him, but had no reply. Tension hung heavy in the air; the two of them looked at each other with a mixture of extreme distaste and undeniable attraction.

Natalie felt the magnetic pull of this dark, strange man who spoke to her with such scorn. Revolted by her own weakness, she took out her disgust on him.

Stepping closer, she said through gritted teeth, "Covington, you, are a southern killer who will be brought to justice at my hands! Think about that tonight when you're trying to sleep!"

Kane smiled lazily and every line, every bone and muscle of his lean body bespoke repose. "As I recall, Justice Vallance, those judicial hands brought this southern killer to ecstasy. Think about that tonight when you're trying to sleep."

"I'll see you in court!" Natalie snapped heatedly, and left the man laughing confidently behind her.

Seething, she swept into the outer room, past the jailer's desk. Then she stopped, turned around, and shoved his big, booted feet to the floor, rudely waking him. "You're supposed to be guarding a man accused of murder. Wake up and do it!"

The big jailer blinked and nodded and watched the violent swish of the angry judge's skirts as she stormed out into the night.

In his cell, Kane, still chuckling, stretched out once again upon his narrow bunk. The haughty judge had had a shock when she looked up and saw him this morning; she had an even bigger one coming in tomorrow's hearing.

Kane's smile fled and his eyes grew hard.

Seeing her had been a shock for him too. Joe South had told him that the Castleton County judge was a beautiful, genteel lady who was engaged to the community's most illustrious citizen, the respected, wealthy Lord Ashlin Blackmore. Joe had told him that Lord Blackmore was the only gentleman who'd managed successfully to court the pristine judge.

Joe said that many a miner, cowboy, circuit attorney, and even one preacher had tried and failed to find favor with the lovely Natalie Vallance. But the judge was ever the lady. She'd loved her dead husband very much and had remained true to his memory for years. Lord Blackmore had come to

Cloudcastle a couple of years ago and it had taken him half that time to persuade Mrs. Vallance to accept his invitations. Now the pair were inseparable and were planning a wedding within the year.

Kane grimaced in the moonlight.

Was there an honest female to be found? Were they all like his angelic-faced Susannah? He sighed and patted his breast pocket, searching for a cigar. Apparently, the lovely judge was no different from the cold, conniving little belle who'd betrayed him.

Teeth grinding, Kane was up off the cot, swift as a cat. And like a caged tiger, he paced restlessly about the small cell, his face hard in the moonlight, his mind filled with thoughts of a beautiful, lying enchantress.

Kane drew on the cigar, squinting at the smoke swirling up into his eyes. All at once he ceased pacing and shook his dark head, bewildered. The lovely face in his thoughts, he realized with surprise, was not Susannah's sweet, heart-shaped countenance with the big dark eyes and dark, bouncing curls.

It was a fragile, high-cheekboned face with enormous emerald eyes, a proud small nose, and softly curved lips. And the hair was not dark at all, it was a glorious red-gold hue that, when unloosed, fell softly about ivory shoulders almost to a narrow waist.

Kane cursed softly and tossed his cigar out the one high, barred window. He flung himself onto his bunk and dismissed both fair feminine faces from his thoughts. Within minutes, Kane Covington was asleep.

Sleep was more elusive for Natalie Vallance. It had been that way for a month. Since the dark, hot night at Spanish Widow. In all of her life, Natalie had never knowingly done anything to hurt another human being. She'd made mistakes, as all mortals must, but never had she carried within herself a guilt for deeds committed, then hidden.

She did now, and she would always. It had been bad enough before today, now it was near to unbearable. To look

up and see the face of the outlaw she'd . . . she'd . . . and
then to have him accuse her of being fraudulent and . . .

Natalie groaned in the moonlight. His accusations had hit
home. She was every bit as bad as he said. She, an engaged
woman, had behaved disgracefully with a total stranger, a
hardened criminal. And now he had turned up in her life, his
burning blue eyes denouncing her, shaming her.

Natalie flung her slender arms up over her head and bit her
lip. Was the man a murderer? According to the prosecuting
attorney, he'd shot and killed Jimmy Ray Leatherwood on a
July day on Promontory Point above Cloud West; her own
property. She'd been in Santa Fe for the summer; a circuit
judge had filled in for her while she enjoyed her stay with
Metaka and her family. She'd heard nothing of the shooting.

After she'd been rescued and had returned to Cloudcastle,
she'd been told of the murder. But she had no idea that the
man she had made love to at Spanish Widow was responsible
for Leatherwood's death. Vaguely she recalled Ashlin men-
tioning Kane Covington, but the name meant nothing to her.

Natalie's tortured mind continued to spin until, much,
much later, she drifted toward the welcome release of slumber. Half asleep, Natalie jumped violently.

A graphic vision had flickered past her closed eyelids. She
was looking into the deep blue eyes of Kane Covington as she
handed down the sentence of death by hanging.

Natalie bolted upright in bed. Would she be the one responsible for closing those beautiful blue eyes for eternity?

"Dear God," she murmured in the moonlight, "how much
guilt can I bear?"

Chapter Six

The following morning, the Seth Thomas walnut-cased clock on top of Natalie's desk chimed softly. The judge looked up; it was 9:00 A.M. Dressed in her black robe with her flaming hair secured severely at the back of her head, Natalie drew a deep breath, rose, and opened the door of her chambers. She entered the noisy courtroom and gracefully climbed the three steps to the tall bench. There was only standing room available in the large courtroom. Tall windows, spaced two feet apart, were thrown open. Curious faces peered through each one as men jostled and jockeyed for a better look at the dark outlaw responsible for the death of the wild and rowdy Jimmy Ray Leatherwood.

Purposely keeping her eyes from the black-haired man standing behind the defense table, Natalie looked out at the crowd and noticed several well-dressed ladies seated among the men. She swiftly noted the expressions on their faces were not ones of disgust and condemnation. More than one feminine face was flushed with color. The women preened and patted their curls and waved fancy fans before their blushing cheeks, engaging in the age-old ritual of flirtation. Sensible, prim ladies were behaving like foolish females in the presence of the virile defendant.

Natalie was disgusted.

She rapped the heavy gavel loudly, and brought the room to order.

"Be seated," said Natalie in a clear, sure voice. The shuffling, coughing, and whispering tapered off as the curious took their seats, eager for the trial to commence. Natalie sat down, touched the sheaf of papers before her, and announced, "The first and only case on this morning's docket is the Territory of Colorado versus Kane Covington." Her green eyes lifted.

Looking down from the bench, she said, "Charges have been brought by one Damon Lee Leatherwood, Cloudcastle, Colorado Territory, against the defendant, Kane W. Covington, state of Mississippi." Pointedly, she looked at the territorial prosecutor's table, where the smugly confident county attorney, Douglas Matthews, was leaning eagerly forward in his chair.

Then her eyes went to the defendant's table. Kane Covington, slouched in an almost disrespectful pose, was there alone, the chair beside him once again empty. Natalie bit the inside of her bottom lip and cleared her throat.

"Does the defendant wish to have a county attorney appointed by the bench?"

"No, Your Honor," Kane said smoothly. He rose agilely, and added, "May it please the court, defendant asks permission to approach the bench."

"The defendant may approach the bench along with the prosecutor." Big Doug Matthews bounded noisily from his chair and lumbered forward, arriving at the tall podium before Kane stepped up beside him.

"Mr. Covington?" Natalie questioned quietly.

"Your Honor," Kane responded, "I wish to act in my own defense and as such I request a trial by jury."

Natalie's mouth gaped open while Doug Matthews boomed, "Don't be absurd, Covington. You aren't qualified to act as counsel in your own defense."

Ignoring the big man at his elbow, Kane said softly to Natalie, "Your Honor, I'm duly qualified. I passed the bar examination in my home state of Mississippi and practiced there until the onset of the War Between the States."

He may as well have waved a red flag before a raging bull. Green eyes snapping angrily, Natalie said under her breath, "You mean the War of the Rebellion, Mr. Covington?" The image of his tall, lean frame wearing Confederate gray flashed before her eyes; vividly she could see him, musket in hand, blue eyes cold, killing Union troops.

"As you will, Your Honor, nonetheless, I am, in fact, an attorney. I mean to act in my own defense and I am asking for a trial by jury."

"Can he do that?" Doug Matthews scratched his head.

"May it please the court," Kane spoke up, giving her no opportunity to answer, "and my esteemed colleague, the prosecutor." He glanced briefly at Matthews. "The fact is that every person accused of a capital crime must be granted trial by jury, under the United States Constitution and the statutes of the sovereign Territory of Colorado."

"But we ain't sure you're a citizen, Covington." Matthews looked from Kane to Natalie. "Did you sign your allegiance to the United States of America after the war? If you didn't, then you can't—"

"I signed nothing, Mr. Matthews, nor do I intend to do so at this late date. I'm instructed that regardless of my loyalties, I am entitled to a trial by jury." He looked at Natalie. "Am I in error, Your Honor? Will I be punished for an alleged act committed on the soil of the Territory of Colorado without so much as a fair jury trial?"

"Counsel for the defense is well informed," Natalie said grudgingly. "You are entitled to a trial by jury." She picked up the gavel and promptly brought it down, announcing, "Court will be recessed for an hour. The defendant, Kane W. Covington, is herewith bound over for trial by jury under the purview of this court."

At Natalie's bidding, the bailiff hurried outside to round up veniremen from the crowds of miners and ranchers on the courthouse square. Exactly one hour later, a jury was empaneled and Big Doug Matthews, the county attorney, strutted before the jury box, thumbs hooked into the armholes of his vest, proclaiming boldly that the great Territory of Colorado would swiftly prove the charges brought against the defendant, Kane W. Covington.

At the conclusion of his opening speech, Douglas Matthews felt self-satisfied. He took his seat and cast a smiling glance at Kane Covington.

"Will the defense come forward and make his opening remarks," Natalie said to Kane.

He shook his dark head. "Defense waives that right, Your Honor."

The first prosecution witness was called to the box. Damon Lee Leatherwood, brother of the deceased, swaggered up the aisle. His broad, ugly face wore a smirk as he stood by the box and took the oath.

Doug Matthews walked to the box, smiled at the witness, and said, "Did you and your younger brother, Jimmy, encounter a stranger in the high country above Cloudcastle— the Vallance property—on July 8, 1872?"

"We did."

"What did this trespassing intruder do when he saw you and Jimmy?"

"He shot and killed Jimmy."

"I see." Doug Matthews shook his big head. "And how old was Jimmy?"

"Just a baby; hadn't celebrated his twenty-third birthday." Damon Leatherwood's eyes narrowed.

"A shame, a cryin' shame," said Matthews, and Natalie looked at Kane, wondering why he didn't object. "Do you see that heartless killer in this courtroom, Damon?"

"Yes, I do."

"Will you point him out to the jury."

Damon pointed a blunt finger at Kane. "That's him. That's the southern bastard that shot and killed little Jimmy!"

The questioning progressed.

The prosecutor continued to lead the witness into testimony undeniably damning to the defendant. Still, Kane made no objection to stop him. Natalie began to doubt the southerner was an attorney. Could she, in all good conscience, sit by and allow him to be rushed to the gallows for want of a decent defense?

Her gaze drifted once again to the defense table. She blinked, unbelieving. Kane Covington's dark hand was lifted to his mouth, stifling a yawn, and his lids drooped low over drowsy blue eyes. His long, lean body suggested total languor and Natalie fleetingly wondered if the man was quite right in the head. Didn't he know that this was a murder trial—*his* murder trial—and that unless he shook off his lassitude and defended himself he would be swinging from the hanging tree before sundown?

Kane hardly listened to Damon Leatherwood's testimony. His mind had long ago wandered and he found the beautiful judge of far greater interest than the witness. From hooded eyes he casually observed her, thinking amusedly that he'd better take a good, long look. Likely it would be his last chance, considering what he was carrying in his breast pocket. He had a feeling that once it was introduced as evidence, the beautiful judge would hate him with a passion far greater than the one now claiming her.

Kane sighed.

Even now, wearing those long judicial robes with that flaming hair restrained, she was desirable. Too vividly he recalled the sweet, clean fragrance of that lustrous wild hair, the velvet smoothness of her ivory skin, the lusty timbre of her voice speaking words of passion. Too clearly he remembered the way her long, slender arms and legs had wound around him, the taste of her lips beneath his, the tight, glorious fit of his hard flesh in the moist softness of hers.

Kane shifted in his chair.

". . . and we asked him to leave peaceably, me and Jimmy," Damon Leatherwood was saying.

Shaking his head in sympathy, the prosecutor patted Damon Leatherwood's forearm, and said to the judge, "No further questions, Your Honor." He glanced at Kane, "Your witness."

Kane nodded, rose, and approached the man seated in the witness box. "Ever see me before, Mr. Leatherwood?" Kane's cold blue eyes were riveted to Damon Leatherwood's face.

Leatherwood glared at Kane. "You know I have, you murdering—"

"Where have you seen me before, Mr. Leatherwood?"

"You know where!" Damon Leatherwood's eyes shifted nervously between Kane and the twelve rapt men seated behind the jury rail.

"Yes, I do, but I want you to tell the jury where you saw me," Kane prodded, turning his back on Damon Leatherwood. He shrugged out of his tailored gray jacket and Natalie's gaze was drawn at once to his wide shoulders and muscular back, which was clearly outlined beneath his sweat-dampened white shirt. He turned around and she hastily lowered her eyes, wondering dismally if she was blushing like some foolish schoolgirl. "Where did you and 'little Jimmy' encounter me?" He walked slowly back to the box, rolling up his shirtsleeves over dark forearms as he came.

"You was up there on the Vallance property where you had no business being!"

"Can you give a more exact location. I understand that Cloud West—the Vallance property—is extensive. Where on Cloud West did you run into me?" Kane gracefully pulled at the crease in the right leg of his fine trousers, lifted his foot to the brass rung attached to the witness box, and crossed his long arms over his chest.

"I don't see what difference it—"

"The exact location, Leatherwood."

"Objection, Your Honor." Doug Matthews bolted up out of his chair. "I can't see what the—"

"Your Honor," Kane said as his arms came unfolded and his right foot went back to the floor, "I assure you this line of questioning is consequential and if you'll allow me to continue, I shall prove it."

"Objection overruled," said Judge Natalie Vallance. "Defense may continue if location is needed to prove a point."

"Thank you, Your Honor." Kane smiled and turned back to Leatherwood.

"Where?"

Leatherwood squirmed in the witness chair and said heatedly, "You was up there on Promontory Point about a hundred yards below timberline, watering your horse in Primrose Lake."

"Absolutely correct, Mr. Leatherwood. That is precisely where I was that day." Kane smiled at the scowling man. "And what did you and 'little Jimmy' do when you saw me there?"

"We told you you was trespassing."

"That's all. Just like that. You merely informed me I was trespassing. Nothing more?"

"Just told you to leave." Leatherwood narrowed his eyes.

"Do you know the penalty for perjury, Mr. Leatherwood?"

"The penalty for what?"

Kane leaned close to Leatherwood's face. "Lying under oath?"

"I ain't lying, I'm—"

"You're lying, all right, Leatherwood. You did more than ask me to leave. You shot at me, isn't that right?"

"No, it ain't!"

"You started shooting and I had no choice but to defend myself."

"No, no, it wasn't like that . . ." Leatherwood looked at the jury, then at the county attorney.

"It was exactly like that. You shot at me and I defended myself. For, in fact, it was you and your brother who were trespassing that day."

"Objection!" The county attorney was again on his feet and a loud buzz swept through the crowd. Members of the jury were looking at one another in bafflement. Natalie was rapping for order, feeling as confused as everyone else.

Of those occupying the Castleton County Courthouse on that hot September day, only Kane Covington seemed coolly in control. He went to the defense table, where he'd laid his folded jacket. From the inside breast pocket he drew out a document. Every eye was on him.

Kane walked directly to the bench, spread the legal-looking paper before Natalie, and said, "Your Honor, may I introduce as evidence, this legal deed to said property upon which I did shoot and kill one Jimmy Ray Leatherwood on July 8, 1872, while he and his brother, Damon Leatherwood, were trespassing on my property."

The county attorney had joined Kane at the bench. He was reaching for the document while Natalie, stunned and uncomprehending, stared down at Kane Covington, her questioning green eyes demanding an explanation.

"Your Honor," Kane said softly, looking directly at her, "you'll find, when you examine it, this deed to be legal and binding. I am rightful owner to the entire top forty-five hundred feet of Promontory Point, that mostly vertical property located at the eastern boundary of Cloud West; said property fully defined by metes and bounds and containing exactly—"

Natalie heard no more than the words *Promontory Point . . . Cloud West.* After that she could see Kane Covington's lips moving, but heard nothing of what he said.

Promontory Point. Treasure Mountain. The Manitou gold.

The vows I made to Tahomah to protect the gold! she thought. Dear Lord, this can't be happening . . . it's not possible . . . The hidden Cliff Palace with its rooms of gold. The Anasazi's sacred burial ground.

"No!" she shouted, banging the gavel and jumping to her feet. "No! It can't be! It's mine, all of Cloud West is mine! Tahomah gave it to me a decade ago!"

Chapter Seven

The crowded courtroom erupted.

Joe South, almost sober, stood at the back of the room nervously twisting his soiled Stetson, staring wide-eyed at Kane Covington. Thin, pallid Burl Leatherwood, the older of the two brothers, shifted in his seat, lips tightening with displeasure. Sourdoughs scratched their heads and questioned one another. Ladies gasped, their eyes sparkling, inwardly pleased that the tall, dark stranger in their midst might be saved from the hangman's noose.

"Your Honor," Kane softly broke in on Natalie's declarations, "if you continue with this outburst, I'll ask that a disinterested third party be—"

Natalie was well versed in the law. She knew she was dangerously close to making prejudicial statements that would most certainly disqualify her in her own court.

Face red with anger, she fought to calm herself. While the excited spectators continued their commotion, Natalie looked directly into Kane's blue eyes and said softly, so that only he could hear, "You won't get away with this, Counselor. I don't know what sleight of hand you're trying to pull, but it won't work. Cloud West is mine—all of it—and if you ever again set foot on it, I'll finish what the Leatherwoods started."

Kane's full lips curved into a cruel smile, but he made no reply.

"Order!" Natalie rapped the gavel. "This court will come to order!" Voices lowered to a hum and finally fell silent. "New evidence has been offered for introduction by the defense. Said evidence will be examined at this time by prosecution and the bench." Her frigid green gaze fell on Kane. "Defense will hand over the alleged deed."

"Ah, I believe you're holding it, Your Honor," Kane said levelly.

Clutched so tightly in her right hand that the paper was crinkling, the damning deed lay before her. Natalie loosened her hold upon the document and said calmly, "So it is. Will prosecution approach the bench."

The county attorney hurried forward while Natalie read the words deeding sections of Cloud West to one Kane W. Covington. Natalie scanned the document dated 1865. There, in bold, telling strokes, was the signature of her deceased husband, Major Devlin Vallance. There was no doubt in her mind that Devlin had signed away the property. She recognized his distinctive hand; she'd seen it so many times at the closing of his letters.

"Your Honor." Kane directed her attention to the signatures of the two witnesses to the document. "If proof of your husband's signature is needed, may I suggest the court call one of the undersigned for testimony. I'm told said witness, Colonel James Dunn, now resides in Denver. He could be in Cloudcastle by—"

"Colonel Dunn's presence is unnecessary." Natalie resignedly lifted her green eyes from the document. "This is my husband's signature. The deed is valid."

Suppressing a weary sigh, she passed the deed to Doug Matthews. He studied it thoughtfully, scratched his head, and reluctantly gave it over to the foreman of the jury. He returned to the bench and said, "Your Honor, I'm not certain this man can own land in the United States or its territories. He's already admitted that he never signed the—"

"Your Honor, may I quote from Lancaster versus the Territory of Montana, wherein the—"

"Please, no, Mr. Covington." Natalie gave him a negative shake of her head. Then, to the county attorney, "Defendant can legally own land, Counselor. Please continue."

"Yes, Your Honor. Prosecution calls Kane Covington to the witness stand."

Matthews strode up and down before the witness box, purposely silent, intentionally dramatic. The room grew quieter and quieter. Just as Doug Matthews had hoped. At last he came to stand before the witness. He spoke softly so that those in the back of the packed room and the ones peering through the windows leaned forward in an effort to hear.

"Are you aware, Mr. Covington, that something a man coerces another to give up does not rightfully belong to the man who takes it."

"I'd agree with that."

"You would?" Matthews smiled and glanced smugly at the jury. "Then may I suggest, Covington, that no part of the Vallance property is rightfully yours." He leaned close and added, "May I further suggest that the deed you have in your possession is completely worthless." His voice was steadily growing louder. "Is it not a fact that the land in question did change hands in a military prison?"

"Yes."

"I thought so!" Matthews's eyes danced with delight. "May I suggest, sir, that the land is not yours! The facts speak for themselves. A prisoner relieved of his property by his captor! I contend that Major Vallance's land was taken from him under extreme duress!"

The county attorney's voice had boomed to a deafening crescendo. He was pleased with his stirring performance, feeling certain he'd moved the enrapt jury, sure every person in the room was mentally applauding. So convinced was he of his swaying oratory, he swiftly pivoted about and faced his large audience.

"Only," drawled a deep voice from behind, "the duress of three ladies."

Matthews's satisfied smile slipped a little and his ebullience was dampened by the sure, calm tone of the accused. He turned to face Kane.

"Three ladies?" he repeated foolishly.

Kane laced long, tanned fingers atop his hard abdomen. "Yes. A poker game in prison. But a Federal prison, not a Confederate one. And it was I who was the prisoner, not Major Vallance." Kane paused, glanced at the jury, then continued, never lifting his voice, speaking in level, conversational tones.

"I was temporarily a guest of the Yankees. Major Devlin Vallance visited the prison with a group of fellow officers to inspect the accommodations. He expressed his penchant for poker; I assured the major that we had at least one thing in common. I was released from my cell for an evening of cards in the officers' quarters. I was quite lucky . . . at cards, that is. The major ran out of money. He insisted the game continue."

Kane lifted his wide shoulders in a shrug. "I was his prisoner; could I refuse his request? When reveille sounded, Major Vallance owed me a small fortune. The land he owned was his only means of payment. An honorable man, he deeded sections of this land over to me, and as you have seen it has been duly witnessed by two field grade officers." Kane paused. "Officers of the Union army." He stopped speaking.

Matthews was completely deflated. The big man looked much like a five-year-old boy about to burst into frustrated tears after failing to get his way. Knowing he was beaten on the question of the deed's validity, he dropped the issue and altered his line of questioning.

"Why, I wonder, Mr. Covington," Matthews said hurriedly, "have you waited all this time to claim what is rightfully yours?" He lifted his eyebrows in puzzlement. "You tell the court you won the property during the war. Why did you wait seven long years to come claim it? What were you doing all that time?"

Kane smiled at the big man. "Counselor," he said flatly, "I can't see that where I've been and what I've been doing since

the war should be of particular concern to you or this court."
He refused to elaborate.

The ladies in attendance tittered and nodded, and wondered just what the appealingly mysterious dark man had been up to for the past seven years.

So did Judge Natalie Vallance.

"Mr. Covington," Matthews said, walking over to stand before the jury, "if it was your property you stood upon the day you encountered the Leatherwoods, why in heaven's name didn't you tell them what you were doing there?"

"I didn't feel it was my duty to explain my presence on my own land."

"Oh, you didn't," Matthews said hatefully, leaning over the wooden rail of the jury box. "I see. And you didn't feel it was your place to have the decency to inform Mrs. Natalie Vallance that a portion of her ranch now belonged to you. You didn't bother with telling anyone at all and then after you killed Jimmy Leatherwood and wounded his brother Damon, you fled like a thief in the night! Why? If it was your land, why run?"

"Had I stayed, I'd have been a dead man by sundown," Kane stated calmly. "Only a fool would have remained. The facts are this, Counselor. I rode through Cloudcastle on July eighth, not stopping in town. I proceeded on up to Promontory Point and there did encounter the Leatherwood brothers. They fired on me and I returned that fire, hitting both men. I left immediately. I rode for Bernalillo in the New Mexico Territory that very night."

"Why?" Matthews spun about and rushed back to the witness box. Lifting his arms in a questioning gesture, he said, "It was your land. You were defending yourself. Why was it necessary to leave the Territory? Why didn't you come into town and tell Sheriff Gifford what had happened?"

"That deed." Kane nodded his dark head to the document a jury member was studying. "The deed was in the New Mexico Territory. I knew I didn't have a chance without it to prove ownership. No sooner had I collected the deed than I was arrested by federal marshal Jake Cochran." Kane hesitated and Natalie, holding her breath, wondered if he now intended to tell everything. Kane's blue eyes flicked to her, touched her briefly, and dismissed her. He said nothing more.

Natalie sat stiffly on the bench and fought the waves of nausea engulfing her. She had had no choice but to sit quietly by while this coldhearted southerner calmly explained how her beloved husband had gambled away Treasure Mountain, the sacred burial ground she had vowed never to disturb.

She had not told Devlin of the gold. Had she done so, this terrible thing would not have happened. He had never known; he'd thought he was relinquishing untillable acreage, far less valuable than the lower spread. He had let go only of land that was for the most part vertical, therefore useless, worthless. Dear God, she should have broken her vow of silence and told him.

The trial continued, but Natalie knew she was beaten. And she knew as well, as she watched Kane Covington present his closing arguments to the jury, that he was going to beat the murder charge against him.

His speech was eloquent and convincing. The jurors listened, transfixed, and Natalie could tell by the expressions on their weathered faces that they intended to set him free.

They didn't like the man, that was evident, but they were honest, law-abiding men who meant to see justice done. It was almost a relief when, after only thirty minutes of deliberation, the verdict was brought in.

"Have you reached a decision?" Natalie questioned the foreman.

"We have, Your Honor. We find the defendant, Kane W. Covington, not guilty."

Damon Leatherwood jumped up from his seat. "Why they can't let that—" A hand on his sleeve silenced him as his older brother, Burl, shook his head.

"This court is adjourned," said Judge Natalie Vallance, and brought down her gavel with a resounding ring.

Burl Leatherwood guided his enraged younger brother toward the door. Joe South laughed happily and headed for the nearest saloon. The room swiftly emptied.

Natalie stepped down from the bench and made her way toward her chambers. Kane beat her. He stood, arms crossed over his chest, waiting.

Not caring if anyone heard her, Natalie said hotly, "Get out of my way, you dirty, thieving Rebel!"

"Why, Your Honor," Kane said with mock despair, "is that any way to talk to a neighbor?"

Horrified, Natalie gasped, "Surely you don't—"

"Ah, but I do. I begin work on my cabin within the week. Need to get it built before the first snowfall, don't you agree?"

Chapter Eight

Furious, Natalie tightened her jaw and her green eyes blazed. Brushing past him with no further comment, she rushed into her private chambers and tore off the long black robe, angrily flinging it down on her desk. Snatching her sensible gray bonnet from the coat tree, she shoved it onto her head, grabbed up her reticule, and stormed out the side door.

Moments later Natalie sat regally in the uncomfortable sidesaddle atop her bay stallion, Blaze. Her composed face belying her shock and anger, she guided the big mount out of the livery stables.

Men stood about on the wooden sidewalks, talking excitedly of the unexpected turn of events that had taken place in the Castleton County Courthouse. They turned to stare when Natalie rode the big beast into the street and rounded the corner. Determined she'd not let anyone know the depth of her despair, Natalie nodded and smiled, as though she were out for a Sunday ride.

The serene smile remained in place, but the green eyes were stormy when they fell on the tall, lean man lounging against the colored barber pole on the east side of Main. All alone, away from the crowd, Kane Covington, gray jacket hooked over a thumb and slung over a wide shoulder, stood indolently surveying her.

Natalie looked straight ahead, riding slowly past him, and let out a breath of relief when she reached the north edge of town. Turning onto Paradise Road, Natalie slapped the reins on Blaze's sleek flanks and urged him into a canter. By the time she reached Ranch Road and started the ascent up to Cloud West, she was muttering to herself.

Ashlin would be far away when I so desperately need him! Why did he choose to go to Denver at a time like this? What on earth am I going to do about that thieving, low-down . . .

Natalie quickly decided. She would visit Tahomah. She had to tell him what had happened. He'd know what to do.

Dressed in tight-fitting doeskin pants that were as soft as velvet, a comfortable poncho, leather boots and gloves, her red-gold hair freed of restraints and falling about her shoulders, Natalie buckled a leather gunbelt around her hips. Assuring her housekeeper, Jane, that she would be back come morning, she hurried to the stables to resaddle Blaze.

She rode astride, enjoying the feel of powerful, responsive horseflesh between her long, trousered legs. Barely touching the heels of her boots to the stallion, she spoke his name and he bolted away toward the southeast, as if he knew where they were going.

Natalie let him have his head and leaned low over his neck, feeling her body become an extension of the stallion's. A rush of exhilaration spread through her.

It was a warm, glorious autumn day in the high country; color-change season. Rose-colored mountain laurel carpeted the broad open meadow. And high above, mountain sumac colored the rising slopes with scarlet foliage and clusters of dark red fruit. There were even a few lingering alpine gold flowers dotting the meadows with vivid yellows . . . long past their blooming season.

In minutes horse and rider had crossed the wide upland valley and were rapidly leaving the plateau behind, ascending the soaring Promontory Point. The thin air cooled instantly as the pair plunged into the dark forest of towering trees.

White-trunked aspen had begun their seasonal change, blazing brilliantly in breathtaking yellows while the maples shone vivid red. The scrub oaks were already dark brown, but the towering evergreen and fir trees remained a lush dark green.

Natalie smiled, breathed deeply of the cool, thin air, and laughed happily when a big-eyed doe flashed through the woods above her. These forests were teeming with antelope, prairie wolves, and coyotes. Occasionally she'd spotted a majestic mountain lion moving with lazy grace through the underbrush, and once she had come face-to-face with a grizzly bear. She'd been fortunate that the big brute had looked her over, turned, and lumbered away.

Natalie was happy to share her isolated mountain paradise with these creatures. They belonged here in this wilderness, just as she belonged, she and the old shaman who had given it to her.

Natalie's mount carried her steadily higher past a cold mountain stream where tall, splendid blue spruce trees shaded the crystal-clear waters. Blaze stepped into the stream, carefully picking his way across the boulder-strewn bottom. Pulling up on his reins, Natalie said softly, "Stop a minute, boy, and let's drink."

The mount's ears pricked up and he halted at once. While Natalie, laughing like a little girl, jerked off her gloves, leaned low to the side of the horse, and scooped up a palmful of the icy water, Blaze drank noisily, lapping and blowing contentedly.

Thirst quenched, the pair were back in motion. On the far bank, the horse once again climbed higher and Natalie let the reins go slack, trusting him to pick his way over the jagged bluffs.

And then they reached the timberline where pines, gnarled and bent from frigid mountain winds, seemed to writhe in agony from their constant punishment. Soon the terrain became too harsh for even the hardy pines, and the big bay stallion labored, as he climbed cautiously up the barren rocky ledges.

Natalie reined up sharply and raised a hand to shield her

eyes. Above stark rocky outcroppings, wide slashing ridges and deep trenches, caves hidden by embrasures of half-sunken rock had been twisted and gouged and formed by prehistoric heat into a labyrinth that was supremely beautiful and totally confusing.

Her gaze moved upward until she could pick out the high, jutting edge of rimrock that concealed the opening of the sacred Cliff Palace. The low-riding sun turned the ancient walls a golden color. And within those walls even where the sun couldn't reach, Natalie knew, the walls still shone yellow because they were made of gold.

Natalie sighed, shook her head thoughtfully, and once more reined Blaze into motion, quitting the rocky ramparts. Continuing eastward around the mountain, she rode several miles before she reached the high pass between Promontory Point and El Diente Peak. Again she halted and looked up at the majestic peak, which soared even higher than Treasure Mountain.

Thick, wet mist enshrouded the spires, piercing the bright, clear turquoise skies. Already the towering summits were dusted with snow. Natalie's eyes lingered on the jutting snow-capped ridges and she reflected on how this vast, remote fairyland had once come to be hers.

It was hers because of snow. Bright, beautiful snow. Dangerous, killing snow. The "white death."

It was in the early spring, 1862. The Civil War raged. Natalie's husband of two years, Captain Devlin Vallance, was fighting for the Union in far-off Tennessee. Natalie had completed her studies at Oberlin College in Devlin's home state of Ohio. Until the powerful Union forces could claim their victory and Devlin could return to her, Natalie had agreed to live with her parents in the wild Colorado Territory where her father, Will Carpenter, was the Castleton County judge. Natalie headed west with her parents.

There was snow, lots of deep, wet snow beneath the wheels of the crowded Concord stagecoach. The stage had crossed the great Continental Divide and was no more than a day's journey from its final destination when it happened. There was little warning. No time to avert the tragedy. A small, strange vibration shook the lumbering stage just seconds before a deafening, roaring curtain of snow came sweeping down the mountain.

"Merciful God!" Judge Carpenter exclaimed, reaching for his wife, and those words were to be his last.

Natalie screamed as the stage and its occupants tumbled over. In an instant that seemed like a lifetime, she felt herself being sucked from the coach's window and tossed high into the air. Eyes wide open with horror, she saw the coach, with her parents inside, being hurled down the steep white mountainside. Her screams were choked off by snow filling her mouth and before her eyes there was now only snow. Blinding white snow. Brilliant, impenetrable snow. Suffocating, smothering snow.

The next thing she saw was a shiny, polished panther's claw swinging close to her face.

Natalie blinked in confusion and let her gaze move upward from the powerful, sun-darkened throat where the strange neckpiece hung on a thin leather strip. A pair of black, glittery eyes peered down at her from a broad ugly face, and a wide mouth was grinning.

Terrified, she tried to rise, only to be pushed gently back to the floor by a strong hand. "Do not fear," said the old Indian, whose long, coarse gray hair swung about his blunt features. "You are safe, Fire-in-the-Snow."

Thinking it must surely be a nightmare, Natalie closed her eyes and drifted back into unconsciousness. But when she awakened, again the same furrowed face was peering at her. And there was another face beside his ugly countenance. A lovely young girl with coal-black hair, tawny skin, and flashing black eyes was holding her hand.

"My parents?" Natalie pleaded, and girl's dark eyes flickered.

"Dead," stated the old Indian without preamble, and Natalie found herself plucked from her bed of animal furs and

pressed almost roughly against his massive chest when she
cried out in despair. A broad hand patted her back while the
old Indian rocked her as though she were an infant.

The young Indian girl spoke quietly.

"My name is Metaka. My grandfather, Tahomah, is the
respected shaman of the Capote Ute tribe." Her dark eyes
went to Natalie's tousled red-gold hair. "You are Fire-in-the-
Snow." The girl's eyes came back to Natalie's tear-stained
face. "Grandfather was told of your coming in a vision."

A deep voice rumbled then from deep inside the old Indian's immense chest, its resonance vibrating against Natalie's
breasts as he continued to trap her in his gargantuan arms.

He said, "The great spirit, Manitou, spoke to me. He said I
must go to the summit of Red Mountain pass and wait inside
the safety of Bear Creek Cave. When I hear great thunder of
snow pass over me, I will know the time has come for Fire-in-
the-Snow."

Natalie managed to free a hand and rub at her red-rimmed
eyes while the old man, his flat black eyes fixed and staring,
continued. "I obey. I wait in cave for two suns. While I
waited, snow grew deeper and heavier. Then the giant spirit
hand pushed the snow down the mountain. The White
Death." Old Tahomah shook his great head, eyes dazed. "I
see fire in the snow just as the Manitou foretold. I go to the
fire and examine it." The glittery eyes rested on Natalie's
head. "Your flaming hair," he said somberly. "A lock of fiery
red hair sprouting from the snow."

Natalie waited, but the old shaman said no more.

"He will tell more tomorrow." Metaka's sweet, girlish
voice broke the silence. "Rest now."

Confused, grief-stricken, but strangely no longer afraid,
Natalie nodded her tired head and felt herself being lifted by
those huge, strong arms back among the soft, warm furs.
Square, callused hands tenderly pulled the covers up about
her shoulders and the old Indian smiled down at her, "Sleep
now, my chosen-daughter. I will watch over you till all my
days here are run out."

Natalie fell asleep.

She remained in the lodge of old Tahomah and his grand-daughter, Metaka, through the winter. While strong icy winds roared outside and new snows blanketed the silvery mountains, the old shaman, firelight flickering on his coarse features, sat cross-legged staring into the flames, his deep voice reverberating off the shadowed walls, telling Natalie of the legend:

"When time began there was nothing but the sky. The Manitou lived alone in the middle of the sky, ruler of all. He told the wind to blow, the suns to shine. Beneath the Turquoise Sky were white, thick clouds. Manitou punched a great hole in the clouds and poured stones from the floor of the heavens to make the 'Shining Mountains.' He touched these mountains with his hand and made the forests grow, the rivers run, the beast to roam."

Tahomah studied Natalie's face. She met his gaze and said softly, "Please, Tahomah, continue."

"All was good and my people lived here; built their cliff homes and prospered." His broad, ugly face suddenly furrowed into a deep frown. "Then the white-eyes come in search of the yellow and white metals." He shook his great gray head and his eyes grew fierce. His hand shot out and he took Natalie's arm. "Manitou has sent you to protect the sacred burial ground of my people, the Anasazi. It is a trust you must never betray."

Abruptly he released her arm and continued, idly fingering the polished panther's claw at his throat as he spoke. "Deep inside a hidden Cliff Palace where the ancient ones sleep in death, a vast fortune in gold was left by the Spanish. The walls of this secret room shine yellow with rich veins of gold ore." Tahomah paused, his eyes cold, hard. "Only one white man has ever found the secret palace. I killed him and fed his bones to the wolves."

Ignoring Natalie's openmouthed shock, he continued to speak commandingly in a deep, sure voice. "You, Fire-in-the-Snow, are the one who must protect the gold. The Manitou has ordained it. To you I give all of these lands." His hands made a sweeping gesture.

Natalie protested. "You cannot, Tahomah. This land should go to your blood-kin granddaughter, Metaka, when you—"

He raised his hand to silence her. "Metaka will not be here. I have seen in a vision that she will go to another land."

Natalie looked at the girl, who was not yet fifteen. Metaka smiled and nodded her dark head. "Grandfather knows. The Manitou knows. The land must be yours."

It was settled.

Summer came.

Natalie said a tearful good-bye to Metaka, climbed atop a big paint pony, and followed Tahomah away from the lodge. He led her through stone corridors and craggy, cloud-high peaks thrusting to the clear sky. At last they reached the concealed Cliff Palace high on the southern face of a rugged, rocky mountain. Solemnly, Tahomah announced, "Treasure Mountain, my chosen-daughter. No white man shall ever remove the gold and live to spend it." His ugly face was hard, his eyes fierce. She nodded. Mounted, they sat in silence, listening to the winds, echoes of the past surrounding them.

"Come, chosen-daughter," Tahomah said, at last breaking the spell, "I will lead you down to the white man's village where you will make your home." He inclined his gray head to the northwest.

Natalie nodded and followed the old man down through the hovering clouds, in and out of canyons, over rugged terrain, until finally the old man halted his mount and Natalie drew the paint up alongside.

"Cloudcastle," he said, pointing to the small hamlet below. "I will leave you now. If you cannot find your way back to me, I will find you."

"Beware when you come down to Cloudcastle," Natalie said softly.

He grinned, black eyes gleaming. "No one will know I'm there. I will wear my invisible shirt."

"Tahomah, if the land is to be mine, won't I need something . . . a paper of some kind with your mark on it?"

Tahomah's grin broadened and his eyes twinkled mischievously. "Yes, it is called a deed and the mark is called my signature." He reached inside his calico shirt, brought out a folded document, and held it out to her.

Natalie's face reddened. "Tahomah, I'm sorry I—"

"Supposed all redmen are illiterate? It is all right; I am not offended." He thrust the deed into her hands. "This was drawn up by smart young Indian lawyer practicing in Denver." He grinned once more and his blunt fingers toyed with the panther's claw at his throat. "Harvard graduate. Speaks three languages . . . four, including his native tongue. Take deed to Tom Fairhope at the federal land office in Cloudcastle. He remember me from his bluecoat days."

Without another word, Tahomah whirled his big pony around and thundered back up the mountain, his coarse gray hair gleaming in the brilliant summer sunshine.

The sun had slipped below the horizon, its afterglow burnishing the rocky mountains with blood-red light. Natalie was smiling to herself recalling that long-ago day.

She'd kept her word. When Devlin had been furloughed and came to the Colorado Territory to spend his leave with her, she'd told him only that she'd been deeded the land; she didn't tell him of Treasure Mountain and its gold. She'd shown Devlin the deed, and he'd happily kissed her and said they'd build their ranch house at once. The shell was already going up when he'd ridden back to war, promising to return to her soon.

But Devlin never came back. He was killed in the war's last days, and Natalie was left a widow at age twenty-three.

Devlin never knew, he couldn't have known, about the sacred burial ground. If he had, he'd never have gambled away the land. He didn't know. It wasn't his fault.

Natalie felt eyes upon her. She raised her head.

On a rocky ledge twenty feet above her, old Tahomah stood peering down at her, his arthritic fingers toying with the shiny panther's claw. His broad, flat face, reddened by the dying sunlight, looked as though it had been chiseled from the rugged stone surrounding him. His long gray hair

lifted in the winds and his black eyes shone with a mischievous twinkle.

"Fire-in-the-Snow," he said happily, and Natalie knew the
old shaman had known she was coming.

"Tahomah," she said affectionately, and gently spurred
Blaze. The old Indian took the horse's bridle in his huge
hand and quietly led him into one of the thousands of narrow
corridors slicing through the towering Shining Mountains.

Chapter Nine

Lids low over icy blue eyes, Kane Covington had calmly watched Natalie ride past and out of sight. Casually brushing the dark, unruly hair back off his forehead, Kane stepped from the sidewalk and crossed the street. With unhurried steps he strolled down Main, his intimidating gaze, aimed like a deadly weapon, slowly sweeping over the milling crowd of gossiping, staring townspeople.

There was about him a quiet, lethal deadliness that lowered loud voices, stilled wagging tongues, and caused even the surliest of men to move out of the way so he could pass. A buzz of excited chatter followed him, but Kane Covington didn't care what was being said.

In moments Kane stood on the shaded front porch of a large three-story boardinghouse on Silver Street. He knocked softly and nodded at the short, chestnut-haired woman who answered.

Kane didn't hesitate. He said, "Ma'am, I need a room. So there will be no surprises, I'm Kane Covington. I've just come from the courthouse, where I was tried and acquitted of the murder of Jimmy Leatherwood." He studied her round, plump face, his penetrating eyes on her doubtful countenance.

Marge Baker had heard of Kane Covington, though she

had not been present at his trial. She wished she could tell this dark man with the intense blue eyes that he would have to find lodgings elsewhere. But Marge had two rooms vacant and she badly needed money.

"Come in, Mr. Covington," said Marge Baker, forcing a smile to her lips. "I'll show you the room."

At six thirty that evening, Kane joined the other boarders in the downstairs dining room. Loud talking dropped to low mumbles when he took his seat. Ignoring the disdainful looks directed at him, Kane spread his napkin on his knees and began to eat.

Marge Baker brought in a huge platter of pan-fried steak.

A young woman followed Marge, a gleaming silver pitcher in her hands. Kane's eyes swiftly settled on her. Glossy dark hair was held back off the girl's pretty face with a ribbon as red as her succulent mouth. A simple gingham dress failed to hide the voluptuous curves of her ripe, seductive body. Breasts, high and rounded, bounced temptingly with her steps, and full, womanly hips swayed beneath the folds of her gathered skirt. The smallness of her waist further accentuated the soft female curves and a natural grace added to her alluring sensuality.

Kane's appreciative gaze climbed back to her face. She was smiling, her wide, generous lips curved beautifully over even white teeth, her large and dark eyes fixed on him.

"Belinda, honey, this is our newest boarder, Mr. Kane Covington." Marge Baker set the platter of meat on the table and put an arm around the tall, dark-haired girl. "Mr. Covington, this is my only daughter, Belinda."

"Kane," he corrected. "Nice to meet you, Belinda."

"Hello, Kane," Belinda said cheerfully, and came at once to his chair. She leaned over, tipped the silver pitcher, and poured fresh milk into his glass. A soft, full breast pressed against his shoulder and Kane's eyes met hers. She was smiling warmly at him and her dark, luminous eyes gleamed. But in their velvety depths Kane noticed an oddly blank, unreadable expression.

Kane's gaze shifted to the girl's mother. He caught the

unmistakable flicker of alarm crossing Marge Baker's plump face. The lovely young woman moved away from him, filled other glasses, and exchanged easy banter with the hungry boarders, though her beautiful yet strangely vacant eyes kept returning to Kane.

Hungry miners wolfed down their food as though they'd never before eaten, then excused themselves and left the table. Only Kane remained.

"Start the dishes, Belinda," Marge Baker said, and gave the girl a gentle shove toward the swinging kitchen door.

"Okay, Momma," Belinda agreed. "See you at breakfast, Kane." She again favored him with a smile.

" 'Night, Belinda," he said, smiling, and saw Marge Baker's hazel eyes cloud with worry.

The girl had no sooner disappeared than Marge Baker took a seat beside Kane. Nervously she dusted crumbs from the white tablecloth and cleared her throat. "Mr. Covington, my beautiful daughter, Belinda, is eighteen in years, but only eight mentally." She drew a deep breath. "She was kicked by a horse when she was a little girl, and . . . and . . . she . . ." her voice trailed away, her head bowing.

Kane's voice was low, soft. "Mrs. Baker, I would never touch your daughter."

Marge lifted her head. Her eyes sought Kane's. She trusted this hard man. He was telling the truth. Her lovely, retarded Belinda would be safe with this dark, handsome stranger. She was sure of it.

Natalie felt better after telling Tahomah of Kane Covington and his deed to Treasure Mountain. And she felt a measure of relief when the old shaman shook his gray head and said in that gruff, fatherly voice, "Do not worry, Fire-in-the-Snow. This Kane does not know of the gold." His glittery eyes shone in the firelight. "And if he finds it . . . remember that no white eyes takes the gold and lives."

For the remainder of the evening the two of them enjoyed each other's company. They shared a tasty meal of roasted elk, and when Natalie drowsily snuggled down into her bed of furs across the dying fire from Tahomah, she felt safe and unworried, just as she always had with the wise medicine man.

It was late morning when she awakened. She stretched lazily, glad there was no rush to get home. Her day was free; she had no cases on the docket. She could enjoy a leisurely ride back to Cloud West and be well rested and at her best for Ashlin's return from Denver come midafternoon.

Shortly after lunch, Natalie embraced old Tahomah, buckled the gunbelt around her hips, mounted her stallion, and rode away. Blaze picked his way carefully among boulders and steep, narrow passageways, weaving in and out of the shadowy, rugged cliffs and scarps above timberline.

It was cool and dim inside the fissures of the great peaks, but once Natalie and Blaze emerged into the harsh grandeur of flat, barren rock below the veiling clouds of the summits, a fierce sun beat down. The intense sunlight was so severe, Natalie could feel its stinging heat on her bare head and perspiration beginning under the heavy poncho. Wrapping the mount's reins around the saddle horn, Natalie drew off the woolen garment, turned, and tied it behind the cantle.

Shedding the poncho helped little. Natalie was still warm. She was wearing the top half of men's heavy underwear, and she couldn't take it off because there was nothing beneath it. Plucking at the itchy, clinging cotton, Natalie adjusted the hot leather gunbelt and ran a hand across her warm face. She sighed, knowing she'd be perspiring heavily by the time she reached the welcome canopy of the dense mountain forest below.

An idea took hold. Natalie smiled. She could alter her course slightly and ride up to Turquoise Lake. She kicked Blaze into a trot, her mind made up. Eager to reach the cold glacial waters of the ice-carved basin, Natalie was already debating with herself whether, once there, she'd merely sip some of the cold waters and dash some on her steaming face, or if she would pull off her tight boots, roll her up leather trousers, and wade for a while. It was a pleasant dilemma.

Natalie was disagreeably hot by the time she reached the

clear, jewel-like tarn. Her face was flushed; a sheen covered her throat and the scratchy undershirt clung to her. Dismounting well below the lake, Natalie tied Blaze to the one lonely pine struggling to survive high on this rocky point. She unsaddled the big stallion, patted his sleek, hot neck, and hurried away.

Busily flipping open the top buttons of her undershirt, Natalie climbed agilely up a barren, windswept conelike ridge, stopped, and gasped in horrified shock. Mind and muscle paralyzed, Natalie stood openmouthed, staring.

Below her, on the opposite side of the Turquoise tarn, ankle-deep in the shallow water, stood Kane Covington. As naked as the day he was born.

His dark, lean body glistened in the strong sunlight. He stood unmoving, a living bronzed statue poised in a pool of vivid turquoise. Natalie's shocked eyes clung to the bare length of his body and she grew breathless, unable to move or to look away.

Terrified he would glance up unexpectedly and see her, Natalie was in agony; she could neither safely leave nor stay.

Damn you, Covington, dive in, she said to him mentally. Are you afraid of water? Dive in and let me escape. Please!

Kane moved, but he did not dive into the water. He slowly twisted his torso first one way, then the other and turned so that he was more fully facing her. Natalie's misery increased.

Heart now thundering in her chest, Natalie, amazed that he'd not raised his dark head and caught her, stared unblinkingly at the naked male body whose every plane and hollow her hands had once explored in the warm darkness.

God he was magnificent!

Muscular arms and shoulders had a sculpted, marble appearance. Chest, deep and wide, was covered with a dense growth of coal-black hair where crystals of water, clinging to the thick curls, glistened in the glaring sunlight. That dark, dark hair narrowed to a thick, straight line going down his hard abdomen and flat belly to widen again at his groin.

Natalie commanded her eyes to leave that most private part of his splendid anatomy: that virile maleness that caused her throat to go dry, her stomach to contract, her knees to grow watery.

She tore her gaze from that which he was so innocently displaying and noted the white scars across his smooth, deeply tanned back. Vividly she remembered how those three satiny ribbons dissecting his flesh had felt beneath her fingertips. Beneath her lips.

Water was dripping in rivulets down his shimmering hard buttocks; the dusting of dark hair on his long, well-shaped legs clung to his hard thighs and muscular calves. He'd obviously been in the water before. Why, oh, why, didn't he go back in.

Dive in! Dear God, dive in and let me escape. It won't take me a second to hurry back over the ridge. I'll be gone by the time you clear the surface and you'll never know I've been here . . . never know I've seen you like this. Dive in, Covington, I beg you!

Kane didn't dive.

He lifted long arms up, folded them behind his head, and drew in a slow, deep breath. And Natalie watched, fascinated, as his wet, wide chest swelled with indrawn air and his stomach became concave beneath his rib cage. He stood there like that, his long legs apart and his eyes closed and Natalie's attention was once again drawn to that masculine flesh that could give such wild, wild pleasure.

She could feel the heat of the sun beating down on her head; the temperature of her body rising feverishly, an ache starting deep inside that she recognized as a threatening physical hunger. A hunger for Kane Covington.

Dive, you sensuous son of a bitch!

Kane's long arms slowly unfolded. He stretched them high above his head, and clasped his hands together. He raised himself on tiptoe. He remained motionless for an instant, then dived gracefully into the turquoise waters, piercing the cold depths with poised precision, disappearing immediately, sending tiny ripples spreading in an outward circle on the placid surface of the lake.

Stifling a cry of relief, Natalie whirled and ran up the conelike rocky embankment. She topped the granite ridge and scampered over its side, sliding, slipping, hurrying to get out of sight. She had escaped.

Natalie halted, caught her breath, and waited. And while she waited, her indignation steadily grew. Kane Covington was swimming naked in her favorite tarn on her private property, and she deeply resented it!

When her breathing had slowed to normal and she no longer heard the splashing of water, Natalie waited a few more minutes. Then, instinctively touching the revolver, she turned and started back toward the tarn.

She made as much noise as possible, purposely kicking at boulders while she hummed loudly. She would give him plenty of time to know that someone was coming . . . ample time to get fully dressed.

Natalie topped the rise and encountered him standing on the near bank, wearing only a pair of close-fitting denim pants that were not yet buttoned up over his belly. Her humming ceased and, feigning great surprise, Natalie stopped, glared at him, and said in a cold, cutting voice, "Mr. Covington, you'll have to go at once. You are trespassing!"

"Really?" Kane fixed her with those bold blue eyes and his wet, sensual lips turned up into a mocking smile. "Why didn't you serve your warrant when you were here a moment ago, Your Honor?"

Natalie's jaw dropped. Shock was quickly replaced with fury, and she snapped, "Why didn't you acknowledge my presence?"

Kane chuckled and started toward her, long fingers raking the thick wet hair back off his face. "Why didn't you acknowledge mine?" Before she could reply, he added devilishly, "You examined me thoroughly. Do I please you?"

Natalie smirked hatefully. "You flatter yourself, Covington. I was merely—"

"Seeing if it looked as good as it felt in the darkness?" he taunted.

Natalie's face reddened, but her delicate jaw hardened. "Let me repeat, Mr. Covington, you are trespassing on my property and I want you to leave. I'll give you exactly five minutes to finish dressing and get out of here!"

Unruffled, Kane, moving catlike on bare, brown feet across the sunbaked rock, neared her, his naked, wet shoulders shimmering in the sunlight. Natalie felt a sudden weakness.

"Your Honor," he said in that gentle drawl of his, "it's you who are trespassing, not I."

"I?" she said indignantly. "This is Turquoise Lake, Covington. Within the boundaries of Cloud West and . . . and . . ." It was dawning anew. She was above the timberline of Promontory Point. This portion of Cloud West no longer belonged to her.

Kane was shaking his wet head. "That's correct, Your Honor. You're standing on my land." He lifted a bare shoulder. "My lake."

Natalie felt a trickle of perspiration coursing down the valley between her breasts. A headache was beginning behind her eyes. And her hatred for this dark southern man was steadily growing. She glared at him when he said, "Not to worry, though. I'll be more than happy to share the lake with you." His blue eyes widened a trifle as they swept over her slender body. "Why don't you shed those hot clothes. I'll give you a nice cold bath and then make love to you." He moved steadily nearer.

Furious, Natalie warned, "Don't take another step."

"Or you'll what?" Kane tortured.

As swiftly as any dangerous gunslinger, Natalie whipped the .38 revolver from its holster and leveled it on him. "Or I'll blow your arrogant southern head off."

Kane never hesitated. He continued to come, his eyes flickering for an instant, more with excitement than with fear. He felt the slight hardening of his body inside his pants as he approached this angry, flame-haired female whose glacial, green-eyed beauty was somehow strangely enhanced by the threat of danger she posed.

He recalled with vivid clarity the way she had coolly fired and killed Apaches at Spanish Widow. She was now training her gun on his bare belly. Would she pull the trigger?

"I mean it, Covington," Natalie said contemptuously. "Take one more step and I'll fire."

Kane took another step.

Natalie's finger tightened on the trigger of the .38. Her breasts heaved beneath her undershirt and she bit the fleshy underside of her bottom lip until she tasted blood. A cornered lioness, Natalie Vallance was dangerous.

Kane stood directly before her, so close, the steel barrel of her gun was only inches from his bare stomach. His eyes held hers for a moment, then lowered to settle on her mouth. Natalie felt her gun hand tremble.

Kane smiled triumphantly. And he slowly bent over and kissed the shaking hand that held the revolver. His warm lips sprinkled soft kisses over her white, fragile knuckles, the smooth back of her hand, the inside of her wrist, while Natalie, stunned and speechless, stared at the back of his dark, wet head.

Of its own volition, her hand, with the revolver still clutched tightly in it, began slowly to lower. Kane raised his head to look at her. His blue eyes flamed and a shiver skipped up Natalie's spine.

"Kiss me, Your Honor," Kane murmured huskily, and leaned close.

Natalie's free hand shot out and shoved his dampened chest. "Kiss you?" she shrieked, "you're lucky I didn't kill you!"

"You desired me when I was a bearded outlaw," he reminded her, "I'm the same man who—"

"Don't speak to me of that night! It's past and forgotten and—"

"Justice Vallance," he drawled lazily, "you haven't forgotten, nor have I. We're out here alone . . . on my land . . . you needn't pretend with me."

"Pretend?" She was almost shouting as she looked up at that smooth, sunburned face with its sharp, chiseled features and burning blue eyes. "I am not pretending! Get this through your thick Rebel skull, I do not want you!"

His dark eyebrows lifted skeptically. "Don't add perjury to trespassing. You want me."

"No, I don't!" she assured him haughtily, insanely noting the way his long, wet eyelashes clung together.

Kane grinned knowingly down at her. And with a movement so swift, it rendered her powerless, his deft hands jerked the tail of her thick cotton undershirt from out of her tight trousers, shoving it up under her arms. Her full, creamy breasts spilled out to him, but Kane's eyes remained locked with hers. His long arm encircled her and he pressed her against his lean frame.

"Feel my heart beat against yours and then tell me you don't want me," he commanded, and Natalie winced as her bare breasts were flattened against damp, crisp hair and hard muscle. She swallowed, too surprised to speak, to think, to move. His heart thundered with her own, thrilling her, exciting her.

His eyes, those deep, mysterious cobalt eyes, seemed to look right into her soul, and he said huskily, "You want me, Your Honor. Just as I want you."

"No . . . no, I don't," she murmured weakly, and squirmed with mingled emotions when his mouth sank down to hers.

Kane kissed her, but her mouth stayed closed and trembling beneath his searching lips. Desperately fighting the white-hot passions flaring within her, Natalie turned her face away to escape his plundering, passionate mouth. It did little good. His hand came up to cradle her head against his warm, slick throat, and above her ear he ordered enticingly, "Let yourself go. Let's do the things we did at Spanish Widow in the darkness. No one will ever know."

"You . . . you're making me wet," she whispered insanely.

"I'll make you wet in more places than one," he growled, and Natalie felt the tightness rapidly building in her lower belly, her breasts swelling painfully against his hair-roughened chest, nipples taut with desire.

Why did she continue to stand here, half naked, against

this man who obviously had not a shred of respect for her, a man who was her enemy, a reckless southerner who'd taken her beloved land.

"You are disgusting and dirty," she said feebly, feeling the same wild rush of sexual excitement she'd experienced at Spanish Widow.

"Be disgusting and dirty with me, Justice," he said, seeming to read her thoughts. Gently he pulled her head away from his shoulder, tipped her chin up, and said throatily, "Kiss me, baby. Kiss me."

His mouth slowly settled on hers and it was just as it had been at Spanish Widow. Kane caressed, molded, tasted her lips with heart-stopping tenderness, gently persuading, expertly enticing, silently seducing. Natalie was powerless—just as before—against such exquisite lovemaking. His lips were smooth and surprisingly soft, the kiss like a slow, sure fire burning its way through her.

"Ah, baby," he groaned just as his kiss deepened. His mouth was on hers again and Natalie could no longer fight it. With a soft sigh of resignation, her lips parted to accept his hot, thrusting tongue and Kane trembled as his long arms went around her to mold her slim body to his.

Here under the burning Colorado sun, Kane's thrilling, ardent kisses set Natalie aflame, just as they had on that dark, hot night. She anxiously returned his caress, her tongue seeking his, her fingers trailing over the harsh planes of his handsome face, her body pressing eagerly to the hard, inviting length of his.

"Baby," he said when at last their lips parted, "say you want me. Tell me." His lips played on her temple.

"No," she gasped, awed by the powerful passions claiming her, "I don't . . . I can't . . ." His lips stifled her protests.

And he murmured into her mouth, "It's all right, baby, all right," before he kissed her again.

Kane stood, legs apart, mouth devouring the sweetness of hers, hands cupping her soft, rounded bottom, anxiously drawing her hips and thighs to his own. One hand slid up her bare back to press her naked breasts closer to his chest and he heard her catch her breath in a gasp of startled ecstasy. A hard, ungiving object was between them. Kane lifted his head and smiled druggedly down at a flushed Natalie.

His hand found hers. Hers still held the .38 revolver. The gun was trapped between their bodies, its steel barrel resting dangerously close to his rigid masculinity. Gently he pulled her hand and the gun away and said teasingly, "I'd hate to lose the part of me that gives us both so much pleasure."

He may as well have tossed cold water from the tarn into Natalie's hot face. With that one careless sentence, he'd dashed her desire.

"You smug bastard!" Natalie recoiled in outrage, wriggling frantically from his arms, her emerald eyes flashing. Gun raised once again, she angrily jerked her rumpled undershirt down over her naked breasts. "I ought to shoot you! You're vulgar and insulting and I despise you."

"Hey, I'm sorry, baby," Kane offered, the blood still rushing through his veins, his groin aching.

"No, you're not," she hissed. "You're only sorry that you failed to seduce me again. You show no respect whatsoever, Mr. Covington! Well, I'll tell you something, you'd best remember who I am. I happen to be the highest-ranking law officer in the county of Castleton!"

"So?" Kane felt his own anger rising as his passion dissipated. This fiery beauty dressing him down had stood in his embrace seconds earlier, molding herself to him. This haughty redhead had once done things to him in the darkness no shy, retiring lady would know about, much less do. Now, like a typical female, she was pretending to be shocked and distressed at his behavior. It rankled Kane.

Stepping closer, a muscle jumping in his lean jaw, Kane grabbed her gunbelt and pulled her roughly to him. "Your Honor, you wear no awe-insiring judicial robes of virtue with me. As you recall, I've been under those robes." A light gleamed in his hot blue eyes as she struggled impotently against him. "And I will be there again."

Chapter Ten

Natalie was still very much upset come sundown. Dispirit-edly playing croquet on the well-manicured lawn of Ashlin's mountainside mansion, she struck the bright red-wooden ball with her heavy mallet, lifting her eyes as it shot across the grass.

"You don't understand, Ashlin," she insisted heatedly, "the man holds a legal deed to Cloud West. He fully intends to live on it and—"

"Darling girl," Lord Blackmore placated soothingly, "is it so terribly tragic?" He took careful aim, tapped his purple ball easily, and smiled when it went directly through the wire hoop set up on the turf.

"I don't feel like croquet this evening," Natalie told him. "Haven't you heard a word I've said, Ashlin? A southern stranger has taken my land!"

"Come, darling, we'll go inside." He dropped his mallet and motioned for her to do the same. Placing a hand to her back, Ashlin guided her across the vast yard, reasoning calmly, "Natalie, you know very well that the land this Mr. Covington has laid claim to is of little use." He smiled down into her face and shook his golden head dismissively. "Please don't let it concern you, my love." His lips brushed her temple and his arm went around her.

Natalie shrugged out of Ashlin's embrace as they climbed the front steps of the house. "Ashlin, the man owns the peak that—"

"That what, Natalie?" His soft brown eyes were calm, reassuring. "That is unsuitable for even the heartiest of wildlife? That has absolutely no value? That is only rock; vertical and so barren nothing can live there but moss and lichen?" He opened the front door, led her inside, and again pulled her to him. "How long can the man last up there, pray tell?" Softly he laughed, wrapping his arms around her and pressing his lips to her lustrous red-gold hair. "My guess is that by the time the first snowstorm wreaks havoc on the high slopes, this Mississippi drifter will be anxious to hasten back to a warmer clime."

Natalie wanted to believe it. After all, Kane Covington knew nothing of the gold. The land he'd won did appear to be useless. Maybe he would soon become discouraged and move on. Or sell Treasure Mountain back to her. Perhaps she should mention that the next time she confronted the tall southerner. Natalie shivered. She had no intention of ever again being alone with the exasperating man.

"Darling." Ashlin Blackmore felt the shiver. "What is it? Are you so worried then that—"

"Kiss me, Ashlin." Natalie lifted her face to his, willing him to drive out the memory of Kane's blazing caresses at the tarn earlier in the day.

"My love." Ashlin was delighted. They stood embracing in the gathering dusk, the chandelier over their heads not yet blazing with light. Ashlin's lips swiftly covered Natalie's, and he kissed her passionately. Natalie ran her slender fingers through his hair and drew his golden head down, responding eagerly, hopefully. Closing her eyes, she kissed her fiancé with an unfamiliar abandon that both startled and pleased him. Ashlin's blood rapidly heated and he held her slim body close, caressing the bare milky shoulders so exquisitely framed in the tall, puffy sleeves of her dress. His heart pounding in his chest, he was certain this beautiful woman he held was as inflamed as he.

But at the edge of Natalie's mind, thoughts of another man's kisses taunted her, shamed her, and made her pull free at last and say, "Ashlin, I . . . isn't it time we had our dinner?" And she was out of his arms, leaving her bewildered, aroused fiancé blinking in bafflement and disappointment, his breath short and labored, his ardor fully stirred.

Facing away from him, Natalie closed her eyes tight and brought her arms up to hug her ribs. Feeling ghastly for treating this kind, loving man so unfairly, Natalie apologized. "Ashlin, I'm sorry." She opened her eyes, dropped her arms to her sides, and slowly pivoted to face him. "I'm upset— needlessly, perhaps—over this whole Covington affair." She forced a smile to her tight lips. "Think you can forgive me for behaving like a foolish female?"

Ashlin Blackmore unloosened his uncomfortable, perfectly tied cravat, and managed a smile. Brown eyes warm and understanding, he came to Natalie. Cupping her bare shoulders in his soft hands, he promised gently, "My dear, I could forgive you anything. Put all cares away for the evening. Cook has outdone himself for you."

Natalie smiled, took the arm he offered, and lifted the skirts of her elegant green gown. As they climbed the imposing staircase to the second floor, she silently promised herself and this handsome man who loved her that she would put the disturbing Kane Covington completely out of her mind.

In the high-ceilinged dining room, tall white candles in heavy silver candelabra cast soft shadows on the snowy white linen, the gold-rimmed china, the heavy sterling cutlery, and on the classically handsome face of the golden-haired man smiling at Natalie over his stemmed wineglass. Natalie's wide-set green eyes lingered on the familiar features and she told herself, as she had so often in the past year, that Ashlin Blackmore was an extremely attractive man, as well as charming, intelligent, and kind. She was the luckiest of women.

Natalie returned Ashlin's loving smile and ladled a spoonful of claret consommé to her lips. Ashlin kept the dinner conversation light and amusing but did not fail to notice

Natalie's lack of appetite. She picked listlessly at the citrus salad, barely touched the lamb cassoulet, and left the lemon-raspberry ice melting in its sparkling crystal dish.

Ashlin didn't say a word about his fiancée's unusual behavior. Instead, he patted at his mouth, placed the linen napkin beside his empty plate, and rose. "Let's take our champagne into the drawing room, where we'll be more comfortable."

"Ashlin, no . . . I . . ." She looked up at him over her shoulder when he pulled her tall, velvet-covered chair from the table. "Would you be terribly unhappy with me if we called it an evening?"

"Not in the least," he said graciously. "After all"—he smiled knowingly—"we'll soon be man and wife and we'll need only to walk down the hall to our bedchamber when we wish to retire early." His brown eyes gleamed and Natalie forced herself to smile.

On Thursday morning, Kane Covington sat in the dining room of the boardinghouse on Silver Street, enjoying his third cup of coffee after the other tenants had eaten and left. As he lighted a pencil-thin cigar, he grinned good-naturedly at the plump, industrious woman who was clearing away the breakfast dishes.

Marge Baker smiled indulgently at Kane. "I can't believe, Mr. Covington, that you actually intend to build a house way up on Promontory Point." She shoved dirty plates into a tall stack and deposited a mound of silverware atop them. "There's no way you . . ." She was distracted by her daughter stepping forward to help. "No, Belinda, honey, that's all right. It's time for you to put on your bonnet and get on up the hill."

Pretty as a spring flower in her simple cotton dress of pink and white checks, dark curls bouncing prettily, big brown eyes shining, Belinda said, "I can't wear my bonnet, Momma. The ribbon's gone."

Marge Baker frowned.

"It so happens," drawled Kane, "that I was in Gallen's Dry Goods yesterday afternoon." He drew from his shirt pocket a bright pink satin ribbon. The long, pretty ribbon was entwined in his lean, dark fingers. Belinda's huge eyes settled on it and she began to laugh happily.

Starting toward him, Belinda asked excitedly, "Can I have it?"

Kane's eyes cut quickly to Marge Baker. Silently she nodded, smiling. "You sure can, Belinda. I bought it for you."

Childlike, Belinda snatched the pink ribbon from him and asked, "Why?"

"Because you are my friend," said Kane, and smiled with pleasure when the beautiful young girl, forgetting about her bonnet, swept the wide ribbon under her long, heavy hair and tried, unsuccessfully, to tie it into a bow atop her head.

Kane snuffed out his cigar and rose. "Let me," he offered, and deftly tied the shiny ribbon into a perfect bow amid a mass of dark, glossy curls.

"Thanks." Belinda beamed, kissed his smooth cheek, and ran to her mother. "Pretty?"

"Very pretty," Marge assured, hugging her daughter. "You'd better be on your way." She urged her to the door, issuing rapid-fire instructions. "Look both ways before you cross the street. Don't get into a carriage with a stranger. Don't dawdle and arrive late. And be back here by noon." As an afterthought, Marge added, frowning, "Mind the ice wagon, Belinda; it's due to pass here any minute."

"I will," the young girl promised, and jerked open the front door, calling over her shoulder, "Thank you, Kane."

Kane smiled and nodded his head yes to another cup of coffee. Marge Baker poured and explained. "Every week Belinda cleans Lord Blackmore's mansion."

"I see," Kane mused. "I would have thought Lord Blackmore employed a full-time housekeeper." He drank his coffee.

"Oh, he does," Marge assured, "but the housekeeper gets Thursdays off."

Kane leaned back in his chair. "Does a mansion get dirty so quickly?"

Marge pinkened. "No, I'm sure it doesn't. Lord Blackmore

is such a good man and he knows our financial situation. He
pays Belinda handsomely for a morning's work, Mr. Covington. I'm very grateful to him. He makes Belinda feel needed
and the money is a godsend."

"How kind of Lord Blackmore." Kane finished his coffee
and left. He stepped down off the sidewalk, looked up, and
swiftly retreated. The ice wagon, loaded down with huge ice
blocks, sped recklessly past, dust from the hooves of four
galloping horses rising up to choke Kane and bring a curse to
his lips.

It was ten minutes past noon when Kane, walking down
Main on his way to the Eureka Hotel, spotted Belinda Baker
skipping toward him, her cheeks rosy with color, and her
dark hair spilling around her shoulders and back.

The new pink hair ribbon was missing.

"Hello, Belinda," he greeted her warmly.

"Hello, Kane." She stopped abruptly and smiled up at
him, a tiny dollop of chocolate candy clinging to her full
upper lip. "I can't stop and talk; Momma expects me home."

"Yes, she does," agreed Kane. "Better hurry on, I'll see
you at supper."

"At supper," she repeated, and darted away, calling greet-
ings to others as she passed. She knew most all of them, and
they, her. It was an unspoken rule in Cloudcastle that these
life-hardened men keep an eye on the pretty girl in case a
stranger rode into town with notions of taking advantage of
her. She was as safe on the streets as in her own bedroom on
Silver Street.

Kane was still smiling after Belinda when Natalie stepped
out of a doorway onto the sidewalk.

"Hello, Judge Vallance," greeted Belinda cheerily. Natalie
looked up from her letter and smiled warmly at the younger
woman.

"You've just come from Ashlin's, dear?" Natalie was pleasant.

"Yes, ma'am," Belinda said, and hurried on down the

street. Natalie's eyes went back to the letter as she walked slowly in Kane's direction.

Kane stood, unmoving, watching her approach.

She wore one of those prim, stuffy suits he so disliked. A drab gray color, its sleeves long and fitted, waist tight; long, heavy skirts flounced up in back over a small bustle. Her titian hair was parted in the middle, pulled tight over small ears, and knotted into a shiny bun at the nape of her long, delicate neck.

Kane smiled and shoved his hands into the pockets of his snug-fitting buff-colored trousers. He much preferred the judge as she'd been dressed a week ago at Turquoise tarn. What a vision she'd been in those tight trousers that outlined her womanly hips and long, slender legs. Her high, full breasts had pushed provocatively against the cotton undershirt and her hair, that glorious red hair, cascading down about her shoulders, had combusted in the sunlight, blinding him, bewitching him.

Natalie was so engrossed in the correspondence she'd just received from her beloved uncle Shelby Sutton, she was oblivious to her surroundings. Wide emerald eyes eagerly reading every word of the missive, she had no idea that Kane Covington stood on the sidewalk directly in her path.

"Oh! I beg your pardon," Natalie hastily apologized when she slammed into a hard male chest. "I'm sorry. I . . ." Her eyes flew to the dark face above hers and embarrassment changed to anger. The letter dropped from her fingers.

Strong hands gripping her slim waist to keep her from falling, Kane smiled down at her. "I'm not, Your Honor." His piercing gaze traveled boldly down her slender form. "I had almost forgotten how your body feels against mine." His burning blue eyes were mocking her.

Threatened, furious, Natalie glanced around to see if people were looking. "I have forgotten," she said angrily.

"I've warned you about perjuring yourself, Your Honor," taunted Kane. "You've not forgotten and to pretend that you have is—"

"Get out of my way, you thief!"

Unruffled, Kane stepped aside to let her pass. Purposely waiting until she had walked half a block, he called, "Justice Vallance, you're forgetting something." He agilely bent from the waist and picked up the note she'd dropped. "Your letter."

Natalie whirled about. "Give it to me."

Kane grinned wickedly and brought the crumpled missive up to his chest. Eyes squinted, he said, "Come and get it."

Fuming, Natalie again looked quickly about. A pair of widows were stepping out of Gallen's Dry Goods. The Reverend John Bellingrath was exiting the Eureka lobby. Several cowboys were crossing the street. She had no choice but to retain her dignity, though she longed to shout insults at him.

Daintily she lifted her long gray skirts and went to him. " 'Morning, Mrs. Taylor, Mrs. Dunston," she said, nodding to the widows. They greeted her warmly and moved on. Natalie spoke to the reverend, politely introduced Kane, and heard Kane say, "Why, yes, Reverend, I shall be at services on Sunday."

Natalie rolled her eyes skyward.

The Reverend Bellingrath left and Natalie, the sweet smile never leaving her face, looked up at Kane and said, "I want my letter this instant!"

"What letter, dear?" It was Lord Blackmore and he was standing at Kane's right elbow.

Natalie was momentarily flustered. Kane, however, was not. He lifted the crinkled paper, smiled easily at Ashlin Blackmore, and said, "Judge Vallance dropped this as she passed." He gave the letter to Natalie and put out his hand to Ashlin. "Covington," he said, still smiling. "Kane Covington."

"Ashlin Blackmore." Ashlin shook the outstretched hand. "Natalie has mentioned you, sir."

"Has she?" Kane drawled, his eyes never leaving Lord Blackmore.

Ashlin wrapped a protective arm around Natalie's waist. "She tells me you are soon to be her neighbor. That being the case, I feel we should all become better acquainted." Natalie stiffened.

"I wholeheartedly agree," said Kane.

"Good, good." Lord Blackmore's smile was warm and friendly. "Natalie and I were planning to have lunch at the Eureka. Perhaps you'll agree to join us, Mr. Covington."

"No, Ashlin." Natalie was quick to answer for Kane. "I'm sure Mr. Covington already has plans." She held her breath.

Kane's eyes left Lord Blackmore for the first time since the blond man had joined them. A mischievous light dancing in their blue depths, he looked pointedly at Natalie and said in that gentle southern voice, "You're in luck, ma'am. I'm free all afternoon." He turned back to Ashlin. "I'd be delighted to join you two for lunch."

Natalie wasn't certain which man she was more angry with.

Chapter Eleven

If Natalie had been irritated with Ashlin for inviting Kane Covington to join them for lunch, she was downright angry with him when, not a week later, he arrived at Cloud West for an afternoon outing on horseback. With Kane Covington in tow.

"Look who I ran into on the ride up, Natalie, dear." Lord Blackmore, golden hair gleaming in the September sunlight, strode rapidly up the front walk ahead of Kane. As was his custom when riding horseback, Ashlin wore a fine, ruffled shirt of softest silk. A pair of brown whipcord jodhpurs bloomed voluminously around his thighs and tapered tightly at the knees, where they were tucked into tall, brown riding boots of imported calfskin. A colorful scarf was knotted at his throat and under his arm he carried a British swagger stick.

Natalie looked from the earl to Kane Covington. Rugged in a pair of tight, faded denim pants, a white shirt unbuttoned down his dark chest, and a battered black Stetson pulled low over his sultry eyes, his expression, as always, was inscrutable.

Nonetheless, Natalie instantly wished that her fiancé had worn something a bit less dandified. Then she immediately berated herself for such traitorous notions. Never before had she thought Ashlin looked foolish in his riding costume. Why should she now?

She didn't, she insisted to herself. And she was glad that she had dressed in a fashionable riding habit of dark navy gabardine. The long, split skirt hugged her hips and fell elegantly about her booted feet. The short loose bolero jacket accentuated her tiny waist, and the colorful red cummerbund was the perfect splash of color against the ruffled white blouse. A flat-crowned black hat resting on her shoulders, drawstrings secured at her throat, completed the ensemble. Yes, she was glad Ashlin insisted on maintaining Old World customs here in the wilds of the Colorado Territory. He was, after all, a nobleman, and she was delighted that such was the case.

Natalie took Ashlin's arm and smiled up at him. "You shouldn't have taken Mr. Covington away from his work, Ashlin." Her green gaze turned icy when it shifted to Kane. "Whatever that might be."

"Kind of you to be concerned, Your Honor." Kane touched the brim of his hat but did not remove it. "As a matter of fact, I was all finished. You see, I was up on the point, choosing the location for my cabin." He watched her beautiful eyes blaze with anger. "After a morning of riding over my property, I believe I've found the ideal spot."

Natalie felt her insides twist. She silently cautioned herself to remain calm. As casually as possible she asked, "Oh?" and managed a smile. "I presume it's to be above my home here on the western slope."

"Nope."

"Where will you build, Kane?" said Ashlin Blackmore, and Natalie held her breath. "If not here on the west side, I'd choose the north. You'd be able to see Cloudcastle and the valley below from the north slope."

"Actually, there's a small, flat clearing just below timberline on the south face of the——"

Natalie heard no more. She felt the blood drain from her face and was afraid she was going to be sick. The south side! He was building his cabin directly below the Cliff Palace!

"—and start felling lodgepole pines as early as next week," Kane continued.

Natalie felt her shock give way to anger. "Bear in mind, Mr. Covington that Trea—that Promontory Point is exactly 14,156 feet tall and you own only the top 4,500 feet!"

"Natalie, dear!" exclaimed Ashlin Blackmore.

"Why, ma'am, I'm well aware that your boundary reaches to . . . hmmm . . . 9,656 feet. That correct?" He shoved his hands into his back pockets and grinned.

Natalie's hands went to her hips and she took a menacing step toward him. "Good for you, Covington. You can add and subtract." She lifted her chin challengingly. "Cut down one tree below your property line and I'll haul you into my court!"

Ashlin Blackmore, shaking his head, reached out and put a calming hand on Natalie's arm. "Darling, Kane wouldn't dream of disturbing your trees." He gave her a gentle silencing squeeze that thoroughly annoyed an already irritated Natalie. Instinctively, she flinched. Ashlin withdrew his hand, but said commandingly, "Why don't you offer Kane some refreshment while I go out and saddle Blaze?" Ignoring her look of dismay, he said to Kane, "Have her show you around." Ashlin was off the porch then, slapping the swagger stick against his whipcord breeches, crossing the yard to circle the house.

"Why don't you show me around," said Kane as soon as he and Natalie were alone.

"I'll show you nothing," she retorted coldly. "What are you doing here?"

Kane lifted wide shoulders. "Your fiancé has already told you. I was on my way into town. Lord Blackmore kindly invited me to go horseback riding with the two of you. Here I am." Kane swept the Stetson from his head, releasing an unruly forelock of raven hair. He tossed his hat onto the green-and-white-cushioned wicker settee, took off his black leather gloves and stuffed them into a hip pocket, all the while looking appraisingly at Natalie. "I liked your tight pants and undershirt much better than—"

"Will you keep your voice down!"

Kane grinned. "Have it your way."

"I intend to, Covington."

"A woman after my own heart."

Natalie ignored the remark. "Ashlin mentioned refreshments. What do you want?"

"You."

"I beg your pardon?" Her pulse speeded up, despite her anger and dislike for the man.

"You heard me."

"Mr. Covington, my fiancé was kind enough to invite you here this afternoon. How could you undermine him?"

"How could you?"

"I couldn't . . . I . . ." Her voice faltered, then trailed away.

Kane swiftly moved in for the kill. "You could. You did. And you will again." He was suddenly standing so close to her, Natalie could see the sheen of perspiration covering his dark throat and chest. She breathed shallowly and felt a premonitory twinge of fear.

"Never again," she said, defiantly lifting her chin.

A lean male hand quickly captured that chin and Kane's electric blue eyes went to her trembling mouth. "You will, Judge. And we both know it."

"You're no good, Kane Covington," she accused.

"Ah, that's so true, but then neither, Your Honor, are you." He smiled and added, "The only difference between us is that I don't pretend to be something I'm not."

"Are you saying that I do?"

Kane softly chuckled and skimmed his tanned thumb back and forth over her chin. "No more so than most women."

"You have no use for women, do you, Covington?" She brushed his hand from her face.

"I've a very good use for you. Shall I come visit you tonight and show—"

Violently she shoved on his chest, recoiling when her hands touched damp, male hair. "Get off my porch, Mr.

Covington, and don't ever come here again! Go back to your—"

"Natalie!" Ashlin Blackmore called, leading Natalie's saddled stallion. "How could you be so rude? I invited Kane to ride with us." He looped the big steed's reins over the hitching post close to the other horses and came up the walk. "Just what is going on here? Natalie? Kane?"

"Mrs. Vallance was just commenting that perhaps I shouldn't be losing time away from my house-building." Kane smiled easily. "She suggested I get to cutting lumber immediately."

"Nonsense," said Ashlin Blackmore. "You can start bright and early tomorrow."

"So I can," drawled Kane, retrieving his Stetson from the settee. Then swung down the front steps into the sunlight.

To Natalie's dismay, she found herself being lifted into her sidesaddle by Kane Covington, and she wondered how, when only the man's hands touched her waist, he could manage to make the gesture somehow sexual, intimate, unseemly. And she also wondered why on earth Ashlin couldn't see it. Was he so blind and insensitive that he noticed nothing?

"Shall I show you where I'm to live?" asked Kane, addressing Ashlin.

"By all means," the blond man responded pleasantly while Natalie ground her teeth.

Kane nodded, swung loosely up into the saddle, reined his mount next to Natalie's bay stallion, and said, "Shall we?"

"By all means," Natalie sweetly parroted Ashlin's words.

The riders cantered across the rolling valley to the southeast, Natalie flanked by the two men. They talked little as they rode and Natalie, still smarting from Kane's cruel words and threatening presence, wore a sullen expression that worried Ashlin and amused Kane.

Half an hour into their ride, Lord Blackmore's fair face was flushing bright pink and Natalie, irritated to begin with, found that, too, somehow exasperating. Why was he foolishly riding bareheaded under the fierce Colorado sun? He'd blister for sure.

"Ashlin, you're turning red," she said, leaning in his direction.

"We're not far from the south fork of the San Miguel." He pressed a hand to his jaw. "We'll stop there and rest in the shade."

She nodded in agreement.

In minutes Ashlin was helping Natalie dismount beneath a stand of blue spruce at river's edge. Kane remained in the saddle.

"Kane, don't you want to join us? The water's cold and pure," Ashlin said.

"You two go ahead. I'll enjoy a smoke." Kane caught Natalie's look of relief.

No sooner had Ashlin taken Natalie's arm and guided her down the grassy banks, than she was questioning him, "Why, Ashlin, would you bring that man to my home? Invite him to ride with us?" She was scowling, high brow puckered, lips tight with annoyance.

"Darling, it's not like you to act this way. What do you have against this man?"

"Are you deaf and blind, Ashlin! The man is a thieving southerner who has taken my land!"

Ashlin shook his golden head. "Natalie, your husband is responsible for Kane's owning Promontory Point." Natalie opened her mouth, but Ashlin hurried on. "Now, darling, I'm not speaking ill of the deceased, I'm saying that Mr. Covington came by the land in an honest game of cards and it's not fair—"

"Fair?" Natalie snapped, and jerked her arm free. "Do you think it's fair that a worthless southerner—one of the Rebels who killed Devlin—should live not a stone's throw from my home? Should own my land!"

"Natalie." Ashlin again took her arm and urged her toward the river. "The war has been over for years, it's time you forgot."

"I shall never forget!"

Ashlin sighed. "Dear, your uncle you speak of so often . . . is a southerner, a—"

"Uncle Shelby is a Texan; there's a difference, he—"

"He fought for the Confederacy, Natalie, just as Kane did." Ashlin suddenly halted, pulling her back to him. "I think there's more to it. More than Kane's being a southerner. More than his owning a worthless tip of Cloud West. Is there something I don't know?"

Natalie felt heat rising to her cheeks. She had never told Ashlin of the secret Cliff Palace with its gold treasure; a treasure that now lay upon land owned by Covington. Nor had she revealed that Kane Covington was the man with whom she had spent the night at Spanish Widow. She'd not told anyone. Obviously, neither had Kane Covington. It was too late now. If she confessed, Ashlin might suspect why she hadn't told him before.

Anxiously she changed the subject. "I just received a long letter from Uncle Shelby the other day. He'll be coming to Cloudcastle this winter."

"Dear, that's wonderful. I'll finally meet the man I've heard so much about. I hope he can stay for a nice long visit."

"I do too," Natalie said, wondering just how well her brash, outspoken uncle would get along with the refined Lord Blackmore. "I'm thirsty," she said, hurrying away and calling over her shoulder, "Look, Ashlin, how high the river is from all the summer rains."

Tons of fast-moving icy water surged rapidly downstream, splashing and spilling over the river's stony banks. The rushing current sped along the river's rock bottom with a velocity that caused white, lacy foam to spray off the jutting boulders in midstream and lap at the sloping banks. The loud roar of the tumbling waters made it necessary to shout in order to be heard above the roaring din.

"Careful, darling," Ashlin called to Natalie, "don't slip on the rocks."

"I won't," Natalie yelled, and sank to her knees beside the crashing, pounding river.

Kane, blue eyes squinted, looked out over the wide, rushing river, glinting silver in the distance. His gaze drifted to the couple on its rocky banks. Natalie had taken off her flat-crowned hat. Her russet hair was blazing in the sunlight. Kane found himself wishing Ashlin Blackmore were nowhere in sight.

Kane shifted in the saddle and gritted his teeth.

After the couple drank of the cold, clear water, Ashlin gallantly bathed Natalie's warm face with his clean white handkerchief, then lifted it to his own. At last he smiled at Natalie and said, "Darling, go on back, I'll follow in a few minutes." And his handsome face grew redder still.

Irritated anew, Natalie said nothing. She whirled away and stormed back up the trail while Ashlin Blackmore disappeared into the trees.

Natalie neared Kane.

He sat relaxing in the saddle, turned in the seat, a long leg around the horn, resting on the horse's shiny neck.

From underneath the brim of his black hat, he watched through cold blue eyes as Natalie came toward him, her delicate jaw set in obvious displeasure.

From his breast pocket Kane pulled a small canvas sack of Lone Jack smoking tobacco, found a packet of thin cigarette papers, took one, and held it delicately with thumb and forefinger. He tapped some tobacco into the paper, pulled the drawstring tight with his teeth, and dropped it back into his pocket. With both hands he rolled the paper around the tobacco.

Natalie was nearly to him.

Bold blue eyes on her unhappy face, Kane slowly put out his tongue and moistened the edge of the paper, purposely taking his time, so that the haughty beauty on the ground below him could closely observe his actions. When he saw her lips part and her tongue dart out to wet them, Kane stuck the handmade smoke between his teeth and lit it.

Drawing on the cigarette, he sat there with the dark hat pushed low over his handsome face. Gazing down at Natalie from narrowed blue eyes, the cigarette jutting from his mouth, long leg swung over the horn, he had an unconsciously arrogant, disdainful look that was both immensely annoying and undeniably appealing.

She was staring. She couldn't help herself. While he unemotionally observed her, she was drawn by the compelling animal magnetism he effortlessly exuded. There was about this man an air of bored superiority that made her long to smack his smug face. At the same time there was a brooding sadness that made her yearn to kiss away the hardness from his cruel mouth. But above all, there was about him a barely leashed sexual power that tempted her to know again the ecstasy of his arms. So potent was that power, she caught herself imagining him climbing down from his horse and taking her right there on the ground with her fiancé only yards away.

"I feel the very same way," drawled Kane knowingly, and Natalie knew that the dark devil had read her dirty daydreams in her eyes. He watched through a curtain of smoke from his smoldering cigarette as Natalie's cheeks caught fire and she whirled away in angered frustration.

Natalie was silent on the ride back to Cloud West, paying little attention to what either man said. All she wanted was to get home and for both of them to leave so she could be alone.

"That's a fine-looking stallion you're riding, Judge Vallance." Natalie was drawn back into the conversation by Kane.

"Yes, he is," she responded without turning her head.

"One of the finest," offered Lord Blackmore. "Natalie paid a handsome price for him, but he's worth every penny."

"Where did you buy the stallion, Judge?"

"A neighboring rancher," she was noncommittal.

"Jude Monroe's place is down the mountain from Natalie, just off Paradise Road. He breeds and sells cow ponies. Has a brother to Natalie's stallion for sale, or so I've heard. Looks just like Blaze, same color, same deep chest and—"

"I'll go buy him today," said Kane.

"Good, good," Lord Blackmore said, smiling sunnily, not noticing how Natalie had stiffened in the saddle. "Nothing like fine horseflesh and lots of open space to make a man feel alive."

Kane inhaled deeply and nodded. "I'm sure pleased I'll be living here in the Territory." He knew Natalie was about to explode. "This is beautiful country, Blackmore. Breathtaking."

"That it is. You'll have to join Natalie and me again some time. It's most pleasurable to ride at night this time of year. Air cold on your face and a big harvest moon bathing these mountains and valleys in silvery light. I do enjoy the cool moonlit evenings!"

"Oh, I don't know," drawled Kane musingly. "I'm rather partial to sweltering summer nights that are moonless. The kind that are so dark, you can't see a hand before your face or the sweat covering your body." His narrow-eyed gaze swung to the silent Natalie. "How about you, Justice Vallance?"

Longing to slap his dark, arrogant face, Natalie smiled and replied with calm composure, "No, Mr. Covington, I do not like hot, moonless nights. One never knows what kind of distasteful animal might be lurking in the darkness."

"Hmmm." Kane's full lips stretched into a devilish smile. "That's true. Or," he added pointedly, "what kind of animal one might turn into in the darkness."

He chuckled softly when Natalie, hat bouncing off her head, dug her silver-trimmed spurs into her big mount's flanks and angrily thundered ahead.

"I say, dreadfully sorry about Natalie's rudeness. Women are damned difficult to understand at times," Ashlin said in embarrassment.

Kane Covington simply smiled.

Three days later, Natalie and Ashlin were seated in the Blackmore carriage outside the Castleton County Courthouse. Kane, astride a gleaming bay stallion, rode around the corner from the blacksmith shop. Ashlin immediately waved and called to him. Kane reined in his freshly shod, newly purchased mount and approached them.

Determined to hold her temper, Natalie managed a polite
smile. For Ashlin's benefit. Not for Kane's. She knew it was
vitally important that she learn to treat Kane with a degree of
civility whenever Ashlin, or anyone else, was around.

"You purchased the horse," Ashlin noted.

Kane swung down from the stallion's back and came to the
open buggy. Reins held loosely in his hand, his eyes flicked
over Natalie, dismissed her, and went to Lord Blackmore. He
lifted a booted foot to the carriage step on her side, put a
gloved hand on the back of the seat behind her, and addressed Blackmore.

"I'm very much obliged that you told me about Satan."

Natalie's eyebrows shot up at once and she opened her
mouth to make a snide remark, caught herself, drew a breath,
and smiled sweetly at Kane. "A novel name."

"Is it?" He looked over his shoulder at the shimmering
bay. Satan shook his great head and whickered. "He answers
to it," Kane assured Natalie.

Natalie had no choice but to smile and listen patiently
while the two men conversed about Kane's stallion. She paid
little attention, but when Ashlin changed the subject, Natalie
could hardly hold her tongue.

"Kane, you ready for El Dorado Day?" Ashlin questioned.

"Beg pardon?"

"Haven't you noticed the decorations going up all over
Cloudcastle?" Ashlin indicated the red, white, and blue bunt-
ing that graced many of the storefronts and hitchrails. "Each
year the miners celebrate El Dorado Day. A gold prize goes
to the sourdough who brings in the largest nugget." Ashlin
took Natalie's hand. "Tell him about it, my dear."

Reluctantly, Natalie explained to Kane that the celebration
had grown each year; that it was an all-day affair with the
gold-weighing as well as the strong-man competition, various
games and entertainment, plus a meal at both noon and
night.

"You coming?" asked Kane, looking directly at her.

"She'll be there," Ashlin answered enthusiastically. "Natalie judges some of the contests. And by the way, the whole

thing is topped off by the big El Dorado Dance that night. I'm sure I'll be called on to share Natalie at the dance." He laughed and added, "There's hardly enough females to go around."

"When is the big day, Your Honor?" Kane's lean fingers played idly upon the smooth leather of the carriage seat, almost, but not quite, touching Natalie's shoulder.

"A week from Saturday, although I'm afraid, Mr. Covington, you might find the festivities a bit quaint."

"I'll be the judge of that, Judge," drawled Kane, taking his foot down from the buggy step. He nodded good day to Lord Blackmore, and grinned at the blaze of fire he saw flickering in the emerald eyes of the woman who was so desperately trying to maintain her composure.

Chapter Twelve

The nip of the crisp autumn days sharpened with winter's approach. The clear, thin air was invigorating and exhilarating. But the chill of the high-country nights was extreme; the mercury plummeted with the abrupt setting of the sun. Extra logs were tossed into fireplaces and heavy blankets were taken out of trunks and chests to be spread upon beds. Lightweight clothing gave way to woolens, and shivering miners and cowboys imbibed large quantities of bracing whiskey in the local saloons as bets were taken at the bar on the date of Cloudcastle's first snowfall.

And it was still only September.

Kane Covington was racing against the calendar. He was anxious to get his cabin built before the onset of deep snows. Knowing the job was too much for a man alone, he looked in town for hired help.

On a morning so frigid, his breath was a white vapor on the air, Kane descended the front steps of the Baker house, dodged the oncoming ice wagon, and went directly to the Gilded Cage Saloon. He stepped through the slatted, hinged doors and looked about, his eyes dilating in the dim room. A couple of weary miners stood at the long, polished bar. It was obvious by their state of drunkenness that they had been there all night. A poker game was in progress at a green baize table beneath the west stairs.

Kane squinted, looked about. He didn't notice the slumped, frail figure in the darkened corner shakily lifting his glass.

Kane ordered whiskey and before the barkeep brought down the bottle, loud voices filled the quiet room. Kane never turned around. He watched the bewhiskered bartender pour the amber liquid into a heavy shot glass, glanced into the mirror above the back bar, and saw the three ruffians approaching. All were huge. All were disheveled. All were mean-looking. One was Damon Leatherwood.

"Well, what have we here?" Leatherwood's voice boomed, startling the two drunken miners. Leatherwood's two companions swiftly flanked Kane at the bar, while Leatherwood, grinning broadly, tapped Kane's right shoulder.

Kane turned to face him.

Damon Leatherwood's gaze flicked over Kane's lean body and came back up to his face. "Where's your gun, Covington?"

"At Mrs. Baker's boardinghouse," replied Kane levelly.

"Afraid if you wear it to town somebody'll spank you with it?" Damon Leatherwood grinned, pleased with himself, and his companions burst into laughter. One added, "Maybe he's got the wrong building. Sunday school meets down the block."

Kane remained silent.

All at once the saloon was filled. The curious rushed in, eyes wide, hearts pumping, eager for a showdown. All jockeyed to get a ringside seat.

Damon Leatherwood knew he had an audience and his boldness grew. "Covington," he said, narrowing his eyes evilly, "I believe that's my whiskey you're fixin' to drink." The crowd held their collective breath, their transfixed gaze on the tall, dark southerner.

Kane said nothing.

Damon Leatherwood reached around Kane, took the freshly poured glass of whiskey, smiled, and downed the fiery liquor. He slammed the empty glass back on the bar, wiped his mouth, and stepped closer. "And that's my spot you're standing in."

Again the crowd muttered and waited and assured one another that now the quiet southerner would make his move. He did not. Roughly, Leatherwood shoved Kane aside, moved up to the bar, and turned around.

"This is my waterin' hole, Covington. Find yourself another, I don't like looking at your ugly murderer's face." The room fell silent. More than one excited, staring male hoped that this dark, icy-eyed stranger would pick up the gauntlet the loud-mouthed Leatherwood had thrown down.

Surely the man who had shot and killed Jimmy Leatherwood and had wounded the brute now baiting him, would not act the coward. Surely this deadly quiet southerner would step forward and defend his manhood. Surely there breathed one soul among them who was not afraid of the dangerous Leatherwood brothers.

One, avidly watching the drama, hoped it above all the others. From his table in the darkened corner, a sobered Joe South was expectant, certain the man with whom he had shared a jail cell would wordlessly step up and take a well-aimed swing at the bullying Damon Leatherwood.

As if a knife stabbed deeply into his heart, Joe South felt a pang of misery and defeat when he watched Kane Covington nod his dark head in acquiescence, turn, and quietly leave the saloon. Wearily dropping back into his chair, Joe poured himself another drink, swallowed it down, and felt a childish desire to weep.

The bottle before him empty, Joe sighed, rose unsteadily, and went out into the cold. Limping wearily down the sidewalk, head bowed, spirits low, he was startled by a greeting called to him from across the street.

Joe South looked up. Kane Covington was crossing toward him, his dark hair blowing in the wind, his bearing as self-assured as ever.

"Joe, my friend." Kane clasped his shoulder. "How would you like to go to work?"

"Work? Me?" Joe was so taken aback, he forgot his disappointment.

"You, Joe. I need help. You interested?"

"Doing what?"

"Building my cabin on the mountain."

Joe South stared at Kane. "I'm crippled. My leg is . . ."

"You don't saw or hammer with your legs, Joe." Kane's compelling blue eyes were on his face.

"Some say I'm a drunk too."

Kane smiled. "Folks say a lot of things about me."

"I know."

"So what'll it be? You coming to work for me?" Kane smiled.

Joe South forced the incident in the saloon from his mind. What difference did it make that Kane Covington was afraid of Leatherwood and his gang? He, himself, was terrified of them. Everybody in Cloudcastle was afraid of the Leatherwoods. Why should Kane be any different. It wasn't Kane's fault; it was his own for holding Kane up to being something he wasn't. Kane was like him. Just a man. A man who was afraid.

"Sure, Kane, I'll work for you. But, if I take a drink now and again, that's my lookout."

Kane laughed suddenly, and there was a magic in his laugh. Joe South decided he would never let the laughing man know he'd witnessed his cowardice.

When she heard of the confrontation in the saloon, strange as it seemed, Natalie felt a mild twinge of surprised disappointment.

No sooner had she shed her heavy woolen cape and untied her bonnet on that cold Thursday morning, than Ashlin Blackmore came striding into the courthouse chambers, his fair face flushing from the cold.

"Ashlin." She looked up and came to greet him. "I wasn't expecting you."

Looking dapper in a fine cloak of beige cashmere, Ashlin drew her to him. "I know, dear. I just have a moment, then I must run." He kissed the top of her head. "I was at the bank and heard some news about our new friend, Kane Covington."

Natalie pulled back to look up at him, fighting down the curiosity she was feeling. "Your friend, you mean." She toyed with the supple collar of his cloak.

Lord Blackmore repeated the story of Kane's encounter with Damon Leatherwood and his companions. He expressed chagrin that Kane would behave in such an unmanly way.

"I'm disappointed, truly I am. However, that's unfair I suppose. Those brutish Leatherwoods are frightening and dangerous. I steer clear of them and Kane will learn to do the same." He waited for a reply. Natalie said nothing. "Well . . . I must be off, darling. I'll see you at lunch. I'll send the carriage for you."

"Now, Ashlin, that's not necessary. I can walk up the hill to your—"

"I won't hear of it, dear, it's so cold." He gave her a brief hug. "Must dash, I've a million things to do."

"Yes, Ashlin," said Natalie, and her thoughts returned to Kane Covington.

Hugging herself, she went to stand before the crackling fire, reluctant to start reviewing the stacks of pretrial briefs piled high atop her desk. Kane Covington a coward? Hardly. She'd seen the man up against the Apaches. Still . . . would Ashlin would have allowed such insults to go unanswered?

No. He would not.

The thought gave her a warm feeling. Ashlin was the better man in every way.

Belinda Baker flicked the feather duster over the gleaming cherrywood sideboard. She hummed happily as she cleaned the spacious dining room of Lord Blackmore's hilltop mansion. Thoughts of the upcoming El Dorado celebration filling her head, she didn't hear the man climbing the stairs to the wide marbled corridor.

"There she is," said a beaming Lord Blackmore, standing

in the wide, arched doorway, his handsome face flushed with color, his brown eyes gleaming.

"Yes," giggled Belinda. "Here I am."

Ashlin Blackmore, smiling warmly at the pretty young girl on the far side of the long dining table, shrugged out of his cashmere cloak, tossed it over a chair, and approached her.

"What color today, Belinda?" he asked.

Belinda took a deep breath, tilted her dark head, and thought for a few seconds. "I know," she proudly announced. "Gold! I want gold!"

Ashlin reached her, took the feather duster from her hands and let it slip to the deep piled Aubusson carpet. "Very well. You know where it is." He touched a beribboned pigtail lying over her left shoulder. "And you know what you must do, don't you?"

Belinda eagerly nodded, stepped away, and disappeared through the arched doors. Ashlin Blackmore smiled, went into the drawing room across the corridor, and drew an imported, ready-made cigarette from a silver box atop a handsome pier table.

Meticulously fitting the cigarette into an ivory holder, he placed the holder in his mouth, lit the cigarette, and drew smoke deep into his lungs.

And he slowly walked down the long marble-floored hall to his bedroom.

Cigarette holder between long, pale fingers, he swung open the heavy carved door. A drawer was pulled open in the circular drum table near the bed. Atop its inlaid surface sat an open satin-covered box of expensive chocolates, their colorful, shiny wrappers catching the rays of the bright morning sun. There were blue ones and red ones and green ones. Purple and pink ones. Silver ones.

And gold.

Ashlin sighed with satisfaction and his brown eyes shifted to the bed. There on his huge four-poster, amid shiny satin sheets of palest gold, Belinda Baker, as naked as Eve in the garden, sat cross-legged, hungrily eating a piece of creamy chocolate from a shiny gold wrapper.

Ashlin leaned back against the door frame, drawing on his scented cigarette and savoring the sight of the girl in his bed. Unashamedly displaying her many charms, Belinda paid no mind to the tall blond voyeur hungrily eyeing her.

Ashlin's heated gaze took in her huge, melon-shaped breasts tipped with discs of pink satin. Belly slightly rounded with baby fat, flaring, voluptuous hips, strong young thighs that held him tightly. Long, well-shaped legs, soft, fleshy arms, and beautiful shoulders.

A dark plait, with its gold ribbon bow, fell over her right shoulder, partially concealing one white breast. She changed her position, uncrossing her legs, reaching to the open box of chocolates, and Ashlin's hot eyes went to that dense, curly growth of dark hair between her silky thighs.

Ashlin nervously stabbed out his cigarette in a crystal ashtray and undressed with trembling hands. While Belinda unpeeled the shiny gold paper from another piece of soft candy, he stripped and came, naked, to the bed.

She continued to lick the candy when he pushed her over onto her back. His sex already swollen with urgent need, he roughly shoved her legs wide apart, thrust immediately into her, and lowered his head to greedily suckle a ripe, tempting breast.

Belinda only giggled, popped the last of the chocolate into her mouth, licked her fingers and then twined them into Lord Blackmore's luxuriant golden locks.

Ashlin lifted his head. Eyes glazed with lust, he huskily commanded, "Belinda, put your legs around me and lift your hips."

Immediately she obeyed, bucking up against him, her hands clutching his shoulders, her big, trusting eyes wide open. A great groan issued from his open mouth as it came down upon the chocolate-smeared, wide lips of his young, willing playmate. In seconds he climaxed deep within her and fell away, knowing, but uncaring, that he had left her yearning, burning, needing release.

It didn't matter.

Lord Blackmore knew that the delectable child, body afire,

breath hot upon him, would now do all the things he had taught her that aroused him. Smiling, he lay back, relaxed, content, pleased, feeling no guilt.

After all, he was an engaged gentleman whose pristine, prim fiancée refused to sleep with him. Save an occasional trip to Denver, he had no outlet for his sexual desires. He didn't dare visit the prostitutes in Cloudcastle; the news would have spread up and down Main before he was back into his trousers.

No, this was the answer. This lovely naked child who liked to eat candy in his bed. She was perfect for his needs. After that first time when he'd had to cajole and coax her to undress and then she'd cried and carried on because he'd had difficulty getting it in, Belinda had been nothing but supreme pleasure for him.

She obeyed his every command, performed any act he desired, was as insatiable as he, and kept their trysts to herself. He was confident of her silence. Had she so much as hinted to her mother what went on, Marge Baker would never have let the child darken his door again.

Their secret was safe. No one knew. No one would ever know. Blackmore never really worried about it. Who would take the word of this half-wit over his? So once again he had three glorious hours to lie here and enjoy the delights of her nubile body.

He sighed and smiled as he watched her, dark plaits dangling over her shoulders, bare, bouncy bottom pointed skyward while she leaned over him, hugging him, pressing her bare curves to his naked length, frantically trying to arouse him anew. He stretched contentedly, raising long arms up to cradle his own head, refusing to embrace her.

He closed his eyes, feigning sleep, savoring, enjoying to the fullest one of his favorite rituals of their weekly sexual encounters. It was a delicious game to lie stretched out beneath her, putting forth an immense effort not to become aroused too quickly.

Sometimes it was easy. Sometimes impossible. On occasion he'd managed to draw out the love-play for an hour, maybe more. Other times he could stand it for only minutes before driving into her hot, moist flesh.

He could tell this was going to be one of the delightful mornings when he could hold out for a long, enjoyable time. He yawned lazily, turned his head, and peered into the tall beveled mirror near the bed. He watched his hand go to the dark head of the beauty leaning over him.

"Belinda," he murmured drowsily. "Remember how I told you we can't put it in until you make it hard?"

"Yes." She lifted her face to look at him.

Ashlin touched a forefinger to her succulent mouth and said, "I want you to kiss me all over. Start at my eyelids and go down to my toes. Then it will be hard and you can have it."

Belinda never questioned the command. Her hot, wet mouth went immediately to his closed eyes as she eagerly began kissing his face, his throat, his chest. She never made it to his toes. By the time her lips were scattering fiery caresses down his belly, she felt him stirring against her.

"Look," she said happily to Ashlin, "you're hard. See." She wrapped long fingers around his pulsing flesh.

"Yes," he groaned, "I see. You've done good work, Belinda."

"Can we put it in now?"

"You put it in," he huskily commanded, and sighed when she climbed astride him and guided him into her. Again he turned his golden head to the mirror and watched her wildly ride him until her climax came and she tossed her dark head and screamed and brought him to the same, blinding ecstasy claiming her.

At noon, Ashlin stood in the downstairs corridor helping Belinda on with her wrap. "Now remember, dear," he said, winding the long, striped muffler about her young throat, "we don't tell anybody what we do."

"We don't tell." She nodded.

"And why is that, Belinda?"

She didn't hesitate. "We do the things we do because we are 'very special friends.' "

"Correct. 'Very special friends.' That makes it right. But we don't want anyone to know." He gave her full left breast an intimate squeeze. "It's our secret." He bent and kissed her parted lips, thrusting his tongue deep into her mouth. He lifted his golden head and murmured, "The secret of 'very special friends.' "

Gravel crunched beneath the wheels of a carriage. Natalie, red hair gleaming in the cold sunlight, stepped down and dashed up to the porch. Ashlin opened the door, a relaxed smile on his face.

"Darling," he greeted warmly, "say hello to Belinda. She was on her way out." He put an arm about his fiancée's narrow waist. Over Natalie's head he winked at the young girl. "Belinda does good work."

Chapter Thirteen

Cold northeasterly winds whispered softly against the windows. Natalie paced restlessly before the roaring fireplace in her parlor. Try as she might, she could never fully dismiss from her mind the dark, defiant southerner who was cutting timber just around the mountain from her.

Little seemed to bother—or interest—Kane Covington. She had heard the gossip following the Leatherwood taunting at the Gilded Cage. Covington had been mistrusted before that, now he was laughed at as well. Men on the streets said he was yellow, a lily-livered southerner who needed a gun in his hands to be any part of a man.

They, however, said it out of earshot of Kane Covington.

Covington went about town just as before, unruffled by his reputation, insensitive to the disgust now showing clearly in the eyes of Cloudcastle's citizens.

Kane drank alone in Cloudcastle's saloons. He played cards, coolly winning from drifters and gamblers who respected only money. He worked tirelessly on his cabin in the mountains, Joe South at his side on Joe's sober days, alone when Joe was drunk.

There was one faction of Cloudcastle's population who harbored no ill feelings toward Kane.

The ladies.

With them he had no trouble and many a female heart fluttered pleasantly when the dark, handsome man touched the brim of his hat and smiled. Pretty girls flirted with him and daydreamed about him. Young matrons blushed and smiled and dropped their gaze from his bold blue eyes and wondered why their husbands had nothing to do with the man. Older ladies openly admired his exquisite lean physique, his dark good looks, his cool, courtly manners, and silently said to themselves, If I were thirty, even twenty years younger . . .

Natalie grimaced and picked up the heavy black poker.

She prodded and jabbed at the smoldering logs with a vengeance. It was downright disgusting the way the women of Cloudcastle whispered about Kane Covington. Only yesterday she'd had lunch at the Eureka Hotel with Esther Sanders, young mother of two, and Carol Thompson, widowed by last year's accident down in the Paradox mine.

Plump and good-natured Esther, who was deeply in love with her miner husband and devoted to their adorable little boys, had mentioned that she thought the handsome Mr. Covington was a fine gentlemen despite what others might say and she had invited him to come to Sunday services to worship. Carol Thompson, a small, fair blonde with sparkling hazel eyes, a teasing smile, and an irreverent sense of humor, confided laughingly, "I wish the good-looking southerner would quit being such a gentleman. I'd like him to come over to my house and worship me."

"Carol!" Natalie was appalled at her friend. "You can't mean that, why—"

"Oh, but I do, Nat." Carol leaned over the table and confided, "I loved Benny Thompson, but he's been dead for more than a year." She smiled and added, "Kane Covington makes me feel very much alive."

"The man is a southern renegade, Carol," Natalie reminded her.

"Who cares? He was cleared of all charges and I love his drawling voice and polished manners."

"And don't forget those brooding blue eyes," put in Esther

Sanders. "Carol is right, Natalie. He's terribly attractive and mannerly and I hope he comes to the El Dorado Day celebration. I'd trade both my babies for one dance in his arms." Carol laughed and Natalie forced herself to smile.

"I want to spend more than a dance in his arms," admitted Carol, and Natalie felt her insides twist. She longed to warn Carol that Kane Covington was no gentleman at all, that he was hard and dangerous, an uncaring thief with no heart.

Instead she said, "Ashlin told me he's not what he appears to be." She plucked absently at the white linen napkin on her lap. "His demeanor suggests defiance and strength. In fact he's turned out to be quite weak and fearful . . . he was—"

"For heaven's sake, Nat," Carol Thompson cut her off. "The man's enlightened, that's all. Only a fool would tangle with that horrid Leatherwood clan again. I, for one, am delighted those bullies didn't get under his skin."

"Amen," agreed Esther Sanders.

Staring into the leaping flames, Natalie realized she'd been standing there too long. Her face was flushed and her long, full skirts were near scorching. Withdrawing the glowing red poker, she replaced it by the andirons and left the overwarm room.

A walk, that's what she needed. She'd take a short walk in the cold, brisk air and enjoy her free Saturday morning. All too soon the ground would freeze and heavy snows would make walking impossible. Lifting her long skirts, Natalie rushed up the stairs to her bedroom and swept a warm, green wool shawl about her shoulders. Tying the fringed ends into a firm, tight knot below her breasts, she rushed downstairs, went to the back of the house, and stepped outdoors, smiling and gasping at the rush of frigid mountain air that enveloped her.

She took a deep, cold breath, crossed the rear gallery, and went down the steps. The hot, bubbling springs hidden between the tall walls of Escalante Canyon would be about the right distance to walk on this blustery autumn morning.

She climbed at a brisk pace, her red-gold hair and long

green skirts whipping in the rising winds. She didn't care. The wind in her face felt good and seemed to sweep all unpleasant thoughts and worries from her mind. Natalie hurried up the rocky incline to the canyon's mouth, smiling when she reached it.

She lost the bright sun when she entered the narrow, steep-walled canyon, and soon she lost her smile. Eyes squinting, she nimbly picked her way around an upthrust of ragged rock rimming the nature-concealed springs. Stopping abruptly, she stared, unbelieving, at the newly built stone enclosure rising above the near end of the gurgling, steamy brook.

"That damned Covington!" she said aloud, and felt her fury rising. Did he leave no stone unturned? Was he everywhere at once?

Fuming, she skirted the enclosure, seeking its open end. Bending to peer inside, she halfway expected to see Kane lounging about naked, just as he'd been that day at Turquoise Tarn. Heavy, vaporous white steam rose thickly within the stone building and Natalie could see nothing.

She called out and, getting no answer, rose, her green eyes snapping with displeasure. She would confront the presumptuous interloper immediately! Was he sure the springs were on his property? Would it have been asking too much that he check with her before he altered a favorite landmark that was practically in her backyard? Was he intent on taking everything she valued?

Natalie was back out of the canyon in no time and rushing down the mountain. Without thinking of the distance, she stormed off in search of Kane Covington. And as she walked at a brisk, unwavering pace, she rehearsed all the things she would say to the swarthy Rebel!

Her legs were growing weak and shaky and Natalie realized she had come a long way. Her throat was dry, her lungs were laboring, and she had a catch in her right side. Swallowing with difficulty, she continued, pressing her hand against her waist. She stopped, turned her head, and listened. And new resolve spurred her on.

She heard the rhythmic thudding of an ax against a tree trunk. So he was there, even though it was Saturday. Good! She'd waste no time in giving him a piece of her mind. She didn't give a damn; she had something to say to Covington and nothing and no one would stop her!

Natalie halted a hundred yards above the cabin site. And her breath quickened. Kane, shirtless, his dark, scarred back gleaming in the October sunshine, swung the heavy ax in sure, fluid movements. And he was alone.

Natalie ventured forward, transfixed by the powerful play of sleek muscles moving in Kane's shoulders and chest with each swing of the heavy ax against a tall lodgepole pine tree. Coal-black hair disheveled and falling over his forehead, sweat glistening on his long arms and in the thick mat of dark hair covering his chest, he moved with a graceful freedom that was spellbinding.

Natalie gave no warning of her approach, did not call out to announce her coming. But Kane slowly lowered the ax and looked up, as though he could feel her presence.

Expecting his hard, handsome face to break into that knowing, mocking grin she so hated, Natalie was confused when he let the smooth handle of the heavy work tool slip from his fingers and stood watching her approach him, his beautiful blue eyes fathomless and haunting, his wide, mobile mouth compressed.

Each time she had been near this man, she'd felt a mysterious excitement. Approaching him now, alone in the wilderness, with those hypnotic indigo eyes holding her, Natalie wondered at the wisdom of confronting him. He looked almost vulnerable, and she found the effect totally devastating.

As if the strong mountain winds blew it away, the almost sad expression in his eyes vanished and was replaced by a cynical, familiar gleam. "Your Honor," he said, folding long arms over his bare chest, "welcome to my mountain home. Sorry it's not yet completed, I would offer you coffee."

Natalie's wrath returned.

"And I'd refuse." She fell easily into the jabbing banter that was their custom. "I'm here to—"

"—to admire a dark-skinned god working in the wilds?" He lowered his long arms to his sides and drew in his breath, the posture causing his low-riding trousers to fall away from his flat, hard belly.

"You conceited fool; the last thing in this world I want to look at is your sweaty body."

"Ah, that's right." Kane shook his dark head. "You don't like to look at it, you like to feel it—"

Boiling by now, she cut him off. "I came to here to voice a complaint, Mr. Kane Covington!"

"You? Complain about something! I can hardly believe it."

"Why did you build that stone enclosure over the Escalante Canyon hot springs?"

"You saw it?"

"I did and I don't like it."

"Well, I'm heartbroken. I built it for you."

"You're a liar, Covington. You never do anything for anyone other than yourself."

"Well, it's for us both, actually. Now we can enjoy the springs both winter and summer. Won't that be delightful?"

"I want it torn down immediately!" she informed him indignantly.

"No. Judge, it's like an Indian sweat-house." He took a step closer, looming tall and menacing against the clear blue sky. He casually lifted a hand to finger the green fringe of Natalie's shawl while he spoke. "Even in winter, you can be inside steaming the aches and pains from your body." He grinned boyishly, his long, tanned fingers idly toying with the wool fringe.

"I will never use it, Kane." She hurriedly brushed his hand away.

His fingers returned to the fringe, plucking and twisting. "Have you ever enjoyed the springs?"

"Yes, but now you've ruined it. You had no right . . . you . . ."

His fingers released the green fringe and moved with slow determination beneath the woolen shawl. Her breath stopped when that hand gently touched her waist and he said in a

low, persuasive tone, "I haven't, Your Honor. You'll see."
His fingers caressed her. "We'll make love in the stonehouse."

"We'll make love nowhere, Kane Covington, nowhere!"
Violently, she shoved away his hand. "I made a mistake at
Spanish Widow and I'm sick of you holding it over my
head!" Her eyes were hard and she unintentionally swayed
toward him as she tilted her head back and looked up angrily.

"You're imagining things, Judge." Kane's fingers were
back on the fringe, twirling, twisting, and teasing.

"No, I'm not. You feel you have the upper hand, but I've
got news for you, Kane Covington. Nobody intimidates me,
nobody! I do as I please, when I please, and you'll not sit in
judgment on me, no matter what has passed between us."

"Your Honor." Kane feigned surprise. "I'd not dream of
judging you." He shook his dark head. "That's the farthest
thing from my mind. Shall I tell you what is on my mind?"

"Spare me," she snapped, but he grinned and told her.

"I want to make love to you."

"No."

His smile remained in place and he moved closer. "Lots of
pretty girls say no when they mean yes." His free hand came
up to her wind-tossed red hair.

Natalie jammed a forefinger into his chest and informed
him, "It's been more than a decade since I was a girl and
when I say no I mean no!"

Kane caught her wrist and held her hand against his bare
stomach. Ignoring her struggles, he raked long fingers
through the fiery tresses falling about her shoulders and said,
distractedly, "God, your hair is pretty. You should always
wear it loose like this." His azure eyes met hers.

"Let go of me," she ordered.

"I can't," he answered huskily, "I can't."

And Kane saw the fire ignite in her eyes, despite her anger.
He fully realized that a war was raging within her and knew
it was much like the battle he fought. He reminded himself,
each time he thought of her, that what he felt for this lovely

red-haired woman was nothing but desire. Pure, basic lust. It
was normal, natural, and nothing to concern him.

And here she stood before him, that beautiful face tilted up
to his, red, silky hair glinting gold, sultry emerald eyes half
hidden by full-lashed lowered lids. His gaze locked with hers
for a time, then focused on her mouth. Dewy, parted lips
tempted him to kiss her. He wanted her; it was that simple.
She had been a responsive and satisfying lover that night at
Spanish Widow and he wanted more.

He had a hunger for what she could give him. He cared
nothing for her. Nothing. She was the epitome of all he disliked in a woman. She had everyone fooled. Everyone.

But not him. And as much as he wanted her, he also
wanted her to know that she meant nothing to him. So, instead of using the persuasive charm that might have made
her melt in his arms, powerless to fight the raging fire that
blazed between them, instead of behaving gallantly, as a man
would with his adored sweetheart, instead of even remaining
mute and bending to take her lips in a heated kiss of passion,
Kane promptly set her straight.

"We're two of a kind, Judge Vallance. You want it, so do I.
Why hold out? Let me. Let me, baby." His fingers tightened
their hold on the long, flowing mane of red hair even as he
urged her slender body to his with a hand moving around her
back to press her to him. Natalie winced and squirmed
against him, feeling, even through the heavy folds of her
skirt, what was happening to him. "Feel that," he said huskily, his breath hot upon her face, "it's for you, baby." He
moved his slim hips in a slow, rotating motion that made her
pulses race, made her aching breasts seek closer contact with
his naked chest.

Natalie's senses stirred alarmingly from the contact with
his tall, hard body. The heated masculine scent of him assaulted her with such frightening force, her knees buckled.
His hand still held her own against his flat stomach and she
could feel his pulse beating there. Throbbing there.

Her heart was at odds with her head, but it was broad
daylight and there were no Apaches threatening to end her

life tomorrow. And this sexual animal pressed against her was just that. A sexual animal who cared nothing for her and was so convinced of his power, he thought he could coldly, cruelly insult her and still seduce her.

Well, she could be just as cold, just as cruel, and she would enjoy every minute of it. Natalie lifted her free hand to his face, fingers gently urging his mouth toward hers. Her lips found his and she kissed him teasingly, teeth playfully nipping at his full bottom lip.

She pulled back a little when his open mouth tried to claim hers in a deep, anxious kiss. She lifted her gaze to see his lids lowering over passion-glazed blue eyes and she waited no longer. She said softly, "I feel it, Kane." She purposely wet her lips and smiled seductively up at him. "Remember what I did that night at Spanish Widow?" She held his smoldering gaze, pulled her hand free of his fingers and moved it provocatively, boldly down over his belly.

His breath quickened. "Yes, honey, yes," he said, his mouth coming down to hers.

"Wait." She turned her head just as his hard, hot lips touched hers. "Move back just a little, Kane."

He obeyed instantly. Her eyes lowered to his groin. She teasingly licked her bottom lip as her hand moved steadily toward the rigid maleness straining against his tight trousers. "Know what I'm going to do to you, Kane?"

"Do it, honey, do it!"

"All right," she purred, "you asked for it." With that, Natalie pressed her middle finger against her thumb and gave his hard male flesh a swift, resounding thump, laughing in his startled face as desire vanished and he was instantly limp.

Shocked, speechless, he stood there unmoving, his dark, stricken face suffused with crimson. Natalie walked away, laughing gaily.

She had not felt so lighthearted in weeks.

Chapter Fourteen

El Dorado Day!

A bright, warming sun filled the cloudless blue Colorado skies on that Saturday, October 19, 1872, and the citizens of Cloudcastle awoke and rejoiced at their good fortune. Mother Nature, that fickle female of the elements, had bestowed on the jewel-like high country hamlet a day of brisk, golden excellence. Had they put in an order for a perfect day, it could have been no better than the one delivered.

Throughout the mountain community and all the surrounding ranches and farms, from the smallest toddler to the most hardened of old sourdoughs, everyone arose with a measure of excitement causing the blood to zing through their veins as the fun-filled day they had looked forward to for weeks finally arrived.

Households bustled to life as last-minute preparations were carried out and families rushed through their morning meals to get on with the more important business at hand.

Kitchens all over the valley were filled with the pleasing scents of cinnamon and nuts from sweet breads baking in overworked ovens, while on cupboards covered with clean white dishtowels, baked hams, fried chickens, and rare roasts of beef lay ready to be transported to banquet tables downtown.

In bedrooms throughout Cloudcastle, young girls pressed their best dresses while boys polished their scuffed boots, fathers shaved extra close, and mothers hurriedly dressed, calling instructions and orders to their children and husbands. "No, Janie, I've told you repeatedly, you are not to wear that raspberry frock, no daughter of mine is going to be seen on El Dorado Day in a neckline so daring" or "James, I'd give my hair an extra turn with the brush, your cowlick is still sticking up," or "Now, dear, promise me you'll not drink too much whiskey; it's a long time until night and I want to dance every dance."

At the Blackmore mansion in the cul-de-sac end of Main Street, Lord Ashlin Blackmore, wearing a dressing gown of claret satin tied loosely about his trim waist, lounged on top of his tall four-poster bed, sipping coffee while he studied, as he had so often in the past two years, the crude parchment map his late brother had once sent him.

Ashlin set the fragile cup on the drum table and placed his forefinger on the map where young Titus Blackmore had drawn a heavy black *X*.

"Damn it to hell!" spat a frowning Lord Blackmore. "The very land that now belongs to Kane Covington!"

From the folds of the map he drew a yellowed document. It was a letter from his younger brother. A letter written over a dozen years before.

Dearest Brother Ashlin,

I'm enclosing a map of great value. Each day brings me closer to the gold treasure my young Indian maiden spoke of. Do not despair, after I killed her, I hid her body well. And had I not, it would have made no difference. These Americans think nothing of killing the savages.

I pretend I am American . . . it has been not been difficult as I spent so many years in one of their universities. I thought it wise to conceal my true identity as I plan to return to England once my fortune is secure and I certainly would not wish to bring any whisper of scandal on the Blackmore name.

Only one obstacle now stands in my way. An old Ute shaman; but I'm confident I can surprise and kill him as I did the girl who told the secret of Treasure Mountain. Millions of dollars in gold will then be mine!

> Your loving younger brother,
> Titus

Ashlin refolded the old letter.

He had paid little attention to it when he had first received it. Actually, he hadn't been all that interested in his brother's message. As the eldest son, he had inherited his father's sizable fortune and at the time Titus's letter had arrived, life had been a splendid one of country estates, fox hunts, gleaming coaches, sleek Thoroughbreds, fine French wines, and beautiful women.

When word came of young Titus's death, Ashlin had merely shrugged his shoulders, waved away the message-bearing servant, and turned back to the little tailor meticulously measuring him for a new wardrobe. The map and letter had been tossed into a drawer and forgotten. Until the Blackmore fortune had dwindled away over the next decade.

Ashlin sighed wearily and rose. Replacing the worn documents in a drawer of the tall mahogany chest, he shook his fair head.

All had gone well following his arrival in America. He had promptly discovered that the land with its hidden gold was owned by a beautiful widowed judge. He'd pretended he was purchasing railroad right-of-way and had made an offer to Natalie. She refused, so he had begun to court her, reasoning that once she was his wife, he would merely take what was rightfully his and once again live in graceful ease.

Then Kane Covington had arrived.

"God damn that thieving southern bastard," Lord Blackmore said furiously, tearing off his luxurious robe. "He is not going to take my gold! I'll see him in hell first!"

A knock on his bedroom door caused him to whirl about and shout sharply, "What is it?"

"Your coach, sir," called William politely. "It is ready."

Lord Blackmore rapidly composed himself. "Thank you, William. I'll be ready in fifteen minutes."

He rolled his eyes disgustedly. If there was anything he detested, it was primitive celebrations like El Dorado Day.

At Cloud West, Natalie brushed her long red-gold hair before the mirror and realized she was not looking forward to El Dorado Day as she had in years past.

The reason?

Kane Covington.

His mere presence at the celebration would spoil the day for her just as his presence around the mountain shattered the peace of Cloud West. When the wind was out of the south, she could hear the ringing of his ax and the loud thumping sound of tall lodgepole pines crashing to the ground. On one occasion she had heard his low, clear voice belting out a bawdy drinking song and her blood had boiled.

The man was going to be her neighbor!

And he would be in town today, lolling insolently about, spoiling her pleasure. How would he behave? She had not seen him since she'd behaved so impulsively—and crudely—that morning at his cabin site. It was almost impossible now to believe she had actually reached out and . . . and . . .

Natalie smiled at her reflection. It was amusing, albeit unforgivable. The shocked expression in those blue, blue eyes, the immediately wilting of his—

Natalie's smile broadened to a pleased grin. Then she began to giggle foolishly. Her slender shoulders shook with her merriment, and dizzily she threw herself on top of her bed. She rolled from side to side, laughing, holding her sides, reliving with glee the moment on the mountain. What a joy it had been to so completely get the best of him!

Finally she calmed down a little and her smile faded as she wiped her eyes.

The man brought out the very worst in her, no doubt about

it. With him she had done things she had never before considered, to him she had whispered words she had never before uttered, for him she had been the willing wanton.

And because of him she was having sleepless nights. The bastard had taken the three things that meant the most to her: her husband, her land, and her . . . her . . .

Natalie bounded off the bed. To hell with Kane Covington. She was going to put on her prettiest winter frock, her finest slippers, her most expensive bonnet, and she was going to ride down to Cloudcastle in a gleaming black carriage with the Blackmore coat-of-arms crest emblazoned on its door. And seated beside her, on the supple ebony leather, would be the handsome blond nobleman who loved her. Together they would enjoy the daylong festivities and she would pay no attention to how Kane Covington spent his time. Perhaps, if she was very lucky, he would be angry enough over their last meeting to leave her completely alone.

"Lord Blackmore's carriage is pulling in the drive," called Jane, the housekeeper.

"Thank you, Jane." Natalie flew to the armoire and took down the new sky-blue dress of merino wool. She stepped into the lovely frock and nimbly buttoned the tiny covered buttons that ran up the middle of the bodice to the low, square neckline. Tight, long sleeves hugged her slender arms, and softly gathered skirts fell about her feet. Well aware that the summer-blue color enhanced her red-haired, ivory-skinned fairness, Natalie gave the low bodice of her dress an upward tug, reached for the velvet-trimmed bonnet and matching cape, and descended the sweeping staircase.

Marge Baker's Silver Street boardinghouse was bustling with activity. Miners and cowboys were taking their baths, shaving, drinking, milling in and out of one another's rooms, and speculating on who would win the prize for the year's biggest golden nugget.

As was his custom, Kane remained alone at the dining room table, while Marge and Belinda cleared the breakfast dishes and checked on blueberry pies bubbling in the big oven.

"Kane," squealed Belinda, "I'm so excited, aren't you?" Kane smiled at her. "But then you don't know, you've never been to El Dorado Day before. Oh, it's just the most fun of anything."

"Belinda, I'm not going."

"Not go?" Marge Baker, hearing that, rushed out of the kitchen. "You can't mean that, Kane. Everyone celebrates El Dorado Day!"

"It's such a warm, clear day," reasoned Kane, "I'm going to work on my cabin."

". . . and I'll wear my dress with the green stripes and the green velvet hair ribbon you bought me," Belinda continued, describing her outfit for the big day. "And I'll eat potato salad and ham and . . . oh, Kane, you just have to come, please."

Kane pushed back his chair and rose. "Belinda, I honestly have too much to do."

She was at his side in an instant. "Work all day and come to the dance tonight."

"Maybe." He smiled and touched her shiny hair. "You have a wonderful time. 'Bye, Marge," he called.

She appeared in the doorway. "You won't have anything to eat if you don't come to the celebration. You know I'm not serving any meals here today."

"I'll manage," Kane said as he departed.

At the livery stables where his stallion, Satan, was boarded, there were already dozens of horses filling the stalls and tied up at the hitchrail outside. Kane saddled the bay and led him out of the building even as buggies, carts, wagons, and saddle ponies clogged the streets. His alert eyes did not fail to notice the finest of all coaches among the throng, a gleaming black carriage adorned by a gold crest.

Kane swung lithely up into the saddle. He urged his mount into a canter, leaving the town behind, and thought about the woman he knew was riding inside the impressive black carriage. The fierce anger he had felt following her outrageous humiliation of him had long since departed. And though he would never in a million years have let her know, he rather admired her earthy defiance. Never had a woman so thoroughly—and literally—deflated him.

While he was sure no real lady would behave as she had, and that the bold temptress would certainly benefit from a good, sound spanking to her beautiful, bare backside, he had to admit he was more intrigued by her than ever. And more determined to get even.

At the outskirts of Cloudcastle, Kane abruptly pulled up on Satan. The big horse halted at once, turning smoothly when his master reined him about in a half circle. Kane crossed his hands atop the horn and sat looking back at town, an evil grin playing at his lips.

Perhaps he should forgo work on his cabin for one day. Go back and join in the festivities. Return and make his presence known first thing so that Judge Vallance would realize there could be no avoiding him. Kane pondered the delightful possibility, idly patting Satan's sleek neck.

No.

He'd not go back to town. It would be far more unsettling for Her Honor to search for him throughout the day, afraid each time she looked up she might see him in the crowd. When finally she dropped her guard, certain he was not coming . . .

Kane's sky-blue eyes danced with mischief. He stood in the saddle, threw back his dark head, and laughed. Just when the deceitful beauty least expected it, there he'd be. Smiling at her. Threatening her.

Laughing still, Kane lowered himself back into the saddle, wheeled his mount, and galloped away. He found himself looking forward to the celebration with as much enthusiasm as any resident of Cloudcastle.

Lightly gripping Ashlin's right arm, Natalie smiled and nodded and told herself she most certainly was not looking about for a dark, hard face with eyes as blue as the new dress she wore.

The wooden sidewalks were spilling over with people and everywhere laughter and goodwill abounded as Main Street was roped off and contests and games commenced. Natalie hardly expected Kane Covington to join in the planned activities. He was far too cynical to be a good sport.

Ashlin, however, was not. Shrugging out of his fine gray jacket, he laughingly rolled up his shirtsleeves and picked up the heavy ball peen hammer. He raised it high over his blond head and brought it down with all his strength, trying unsuccessfully to break apart, with one crushing blow, a huge, solid boulder.

Laughing harder than anyone when he failed, he shook his head and urged another contestant forward for a turn at the rock, stepping back to watch with the others. Natalie's attention drifted from the man straining to put great power behind his blow. Nonchalantly she studied the sea of male faces before her.

Kane Covington's hard, handsome face was not among them.

By noon all the participants had worked up hearty appetites and plates were piled high with smoked ham, golden-fried rainbow trout, roast beef, and so many different vegetables they all ran together. Women stood behind long, linen-draped tables dishing up the beets, string beans, cauliflower, stewed celery, and potato salad.

Standing behind the long food table next to Natalie, Carol Thompson confided in a whisper, "I'm so disappointed."

Natalie smiled up at a bearded miner as she handed him a heaping plate, and accepted his thanks. Then she turned to her friend and questioned, "Why? The weather is perfect, we've more food this year than ever before, and a bigger crowd."

"Kane Covington is not here," stated Carol emphatically.

"Oh?" Natalie acted surprised. "I hadn't noticed."

"Well, then you're the only female present who hasn't."

Cakes and pies were paraded out and placed at the table's end. There were chocolate and white layer cakes, puddings and pies, and fresh fruits.

Belinda Baker leaned across the table to hand Ashlin Blackmore a slice of rich pumpkin pie. He smiled warmly at her.

"Belinda, how pretty you look." His tone was pleasant and friendly. Through his mind flashed the vivid recollection of the past Thursday at his mansion. As soon as Belinda had entered the upstairs corridor, he had guided her into the drawing room and had taken her there on the floor, jerking off only her drawers and unbuttoning his trousers. His blood raced as he recalled that his old carriage driver had almost caught them in the act. While they'd grunted and bucked upon the Aubusson carpet, fully clothed, William, after leaving the mansion, had returned unexpectedly. Fortunately the old servant had the good breeding to knock softly on the closed drawing room doors to announce that he had returned for a broken vase in need of repair. The vase was in the drawing room.

While the beautiful Belinda panted beneath him, Ashlin had called out hurriedly, "Never mind, William, I'll take care of it," and resumed at once the lusty coupling.

Now looking at Belinda, Ashlin fleetingly entertained the notion of finding an excuse to spirit her away to the confines of his parked carriage. He could think of nothing more titillating than to have a go at the beautiful girl while the child's mother and his own fiancée, as well as the rest of Cloudcastle, stood not a stone's throw away.

Rapidly remembering all that he had to lose, Ashlin dismissed the fanciful notion. He would just have to wait until Thursday.

Marge Baker, standing beside her daughter, looked up at the blond nobleman with awe. What a kind, thoughtful man Lord Blackmore was. What a lucky young woman Judge Vallance was. Marge's attention left Lord Blackmore. Joe South stood before her, a shy, embarrassed grin on his scrubbed face. Marge flashed him a warm smile, filled his plate, and told him he should have Kane bring him along for supper at the boardinghouse some night soon.

After the midday feast, activities lulled for a time as the

ladies cleared away the uneaten foods and the men smoked
their cigars and home-rolled cigarettes and visited. Natalie
quietly worked while her eyes wandered restlessly over the
crowd.

Kane Covington was nowhere to be found.

Soon the emptied street was filled once again as the afternoon activities began. Contests and games were enjoyed not
only by the men but by the women and children as well. No
one was left out; everyone eagerly joined in the fun.

Belinda Baker won the prettiest girl contest. Zeke Brad-
shaw, a weathered, bewhiskered prospector, the ugliest man.
Nathan Park, six foot four, three hundred pounds, and a
father of seven, took the title of the strongest man after much
shouting and flexing and lifting. Natalie smilingly placed a
painted-gold crown atop the curly brown head Nathan lowered for her.

And finally, the most important event of all—the prize for
the largest single gold nugget brought down from the hills—
went to Bobby Clayborne, a skinny fourteen-year-old boy.
Bobby's prize was a shiny golden double eagle.

And then it was time for supper. The noontime crowd had
swelled as new faces appeared at the bountiful tables. Natalie
scanned the long queues of men; the tall, dark southerner was
not in line. Natalie's smile became more sure, her manner
more relaxed. Finally she could enjoy herself. At last she
could stop looking about for Kane Covington.

After another heavy, filling meal, Natalie expressed the
need to "walk off her food." Ashlin demurred, saying he was
far too full to move.

"Come on." Carol Thompson heard the exchange and
stepped forward. "I'll walk with you."

"Good," responded Natalie. "Where's Esther? I haven't
seen her since the sack races. Does she want to go with us?"
She nodded to Ashlin and sauntered away.

"Esther took the boys to the buggy for a nap before the
dance. Let's go."

Away from busy, crowd-filled Main, the streets of Cloudcastle were deserted. The two young women ambled lazily

along the wooden sidewalks in the waning autumn sunshine. Neither spoke. Full, a little tired, and pensive, they enjoyed the brief respite from the boisterous celebration.

Turning off Main, they strolled down Denver, passing shut-down businesses, the assay office, the creamery, and the dentist's office. Only saloons remained open and they appeared empty. Everyone in the city of Cloudcastle was down on Main.

A block ahead of the two young women stood the Mother Lode Saloon. All was quiet within. Outside, one lone man hunkered against the front wall. He was tilted back in his chair, black hat pulled low over his eyes. The upper part of his lean body was in the shade and his long legs were stretched out in the sunlight.

Natalie's heart began to pound. It was him. She knew it was. The lounging sprawl. The hat pulled low. The wide shoulders. The long legs. The loner was Kane Covington.

"Carol." She put out her hand to stop the other woman. "We've walked far enough. Let's turn back now and—"

"Will you stop it. We haven't been gone five minutes." Carol continued walking.

"But . . . but . . ."

"What is wrong with you?" Carol wanted to know.

"Shhh," cautioned Natalie. "He'll hear you."

"Who'll hear me?" Carol looked again at the man in front of the Mother Lode. "Who do you think . . ." Her eyes grew wide. She grabbed Natalie's hand. "My Lord, that's him. That's Kane Covington."

"I know, let's turn around."

"Not on your life," stated an eager Carol Thompson. "Come on."

Natalie was trapped. If she made too much of a fuss, Carol would wonder about her anxiety. She fell back into step beside her friend.

Just when the two young women drew up even with Kane, he shifted his weight, slowly forcing the front chair legs down to the porch. With catlike grace he rose before them, pushed back his hat, and said in that flat, drawling Mississippi accent, " 'Evening, ladies. Enjoying the celebration?"

His blue eyes were on Carol's smiling face. He was purposely ignoring Natalie. She knew he was. He'd not so much as glanced at her. That was just fine with her.

"We'll enjoy it a great deal more if you promise to come to the dance tonight," Carol said saucily, and brazenly laid a hand upon Kane's white shirtfront.

"That's flattering, Mrs. Thompson." Kane's hand covered Carol's. "I hadn't planned to attend." He moved her hand away and his eyes came at last to Natalie. Her breath caught in her throat as she felt an electricity so intense, so sudden, she was fearful Carol would sense it.

"Call me Carol and please change your mind," Carol replied as Natalie drew a labored breath that directed Kane's steady blue gaze to the low, square bodice of her merino wool dress. She saw a brief flicker of fire leap into his eyes and her breasts swelled against the soft fabric even as gooseflesh prickled her ivory shoulders and bosom. Kane's attention swung back to Carol.

"Carol," he drawled lazily, "perhaps I will change my mind." He smiled down at Carol, but Natalie knew the message was meant for her. He would be at the dance, and that knowledge filled her with dread.

"Promise us," cajoled Carol as Kane pulled the brim of his black hat back down over his eyes and stepped down off the wooden sidewalk, blue eyes squinting in the dying sun.

"There goes a man," Carol sighed as both women watched Kane make his unhurried way to the opposite side of the street and disappear around the corner.

Chapter Fifteen

Savoring a moment alone, Natalie stood on the upper landing of the crowded two-story Hotel Eureka ballroom. Below her, flushed, joyful dancers swayed and turned beneath blazing brass-and-crystal chandeliers. The dance had been in progress for well over an hour.

He wasn't coming.

If he were, he would have arrived. And if he had arrived, she would surely have seen him. Natalie expelled a grateful sigh of relief and let her sweeping glance once more encompass the cavernous ballroom.

At the room's east end, on a raised marble dais, a small, loud orchestra played a rousing rendition of "Buffalo Gal, Won't You Come Out Tonight," while dozens of pairs of nimble feet lifted from, then touched once more, the shining marble dancefloor. Carol Thompson's blond curls shook as she spun about in the arms of a flashy faro dealer from Gaiety's Gaming Hall.

Esther Jones and her husband were on the floor, smiling at each other as newlyweds might. Belinda Baker danced with a clumsy twelve-year-old boy, the pair laughing as they stepped on each other's toes. Next to them, Ashlin guided the plump Marge Baker about, towering over her, bending to listen attentively when she spoke.

Natalie continued to scrutinize the crowd, missing no one, double-checking, making sure. Satisfied she could finally relax and enjoy herself, that he was nowhere in the ballroom, Natalie headed for the stairs. She reached the wide center staircase and looked down.

And her heart stopped beating, then raced madly.

Kane, stunningly handsome, stood below her, an arm resting on the gleaming bannister, a booted foot propped on the first stair step. He wore a frock coat as black as his raven hair and a shirt as white as the mountain snow. His blue eyes were fastened upon her, in them a puzzling yearning and sadness.

Instantly it was gone, replaced by that cool, cynically impertinent gleam she'd come to expect. Refusing to look away, he held her gaze and stood silently challenging her to descend the stairs and confront him.

Telling herself she had no fear of him or of anything he might choose to do or say, Natalie tossed her head, lifted her blue merino skirts, and swept down the marble steps to him. Kane lowered his foot to the floor, awaiting her, white teeth flashing in the dark face, the exasperating glint lighting his azure eyes.

Fighting the uneasy feelings this man always aroused in her, Natalie would have been greatly surprised at the thoughts filling his dark head as he appraised her.

Kane watched the flame-haired beauty descending to him and his heart hammered heavily beneath his ribs. She was looking straight into his eyes, daring him to misbehave, assuring him she was not afraid, warning him she could hold her own against him.

Never would he have given her the satisfaction of knowing just how appealing she was. It was not her fair, feminine beauty alone that made him want her with a passion that burned hot and constant. He'd had dozens of women as beautiful, although it was true that her glorious hair was of a bright copper color that seemed afire under the chandeliers and her skin was so flawlessly white, it looked like fine ivory porcelain.

It was more, much more. It was the flash of stubborn defi-

ance in her beautiful emerald eyes, the slightly arrogant lifting of her proud, straight nose, the determined set of her
firm, small chin. And the rebellious, puffy pout of her lovely
lips made him want to mash them in for her.

Natalie reached Kane.

"Mr. Covington, I'm glad you could come." She extended
her hand.

Kane took it and reached for the other. She withheld it,
drawing it behind her. "What do you want?"

"Only to protect my manhood, Your Honor." He grinned
tauntingly, "I'm afraid you'll be tempted to give my—"

"Will you keep your voice down!" Natalie hissed, her face
turning crimson. Temper flaring, she snatched her hand free.

"Yes, if you'll keep your thumb and forefinger to yourself."

"Do you never tire of being crude, Mr. Covington?" She
looked around to be sure no one heard him.

"I? Crude?" Kane pretended surprise. Then he grinned
and added, "Your Honor, of all your many talents I do believe acting is your greatest."

Natalie ground her teeth. "I have no idea what you mean."
She gave him a bored, impatient look.

"You know exactly what I mean." He leaned closer, his
breath ruffling the wispy curls on her temple. "Only with me
are you yourself. Real. Alive. Crude." He added softly, "And
then only when we're alone. Let's slip outdoors and be our-
selves." He chuckled softly.

Natalie rolled her eyes skyward. "You should never try to
be amusing, Mr. Covington. It doesn't suit you."

"Perhaps you are right, Judge. I'm much better suited to
lovemaking, don't you agree?" His long fingers cupped her
elbow, giving it a gentle squeeze. "I'll make you a bargain,
you stop being an actress, and I'll stop being a comedian.
We'll be lovers."

Her jaw tightened and her green eyes flashed with anger
and outrage. "Listen to me, Covington, and try your best to
comprehend. I want—"

"Your Honor," he broke in, smiling easily, "your fiancé is
coming this way. Either prove me wrong and go right on

chewing me out"—he nodded to the approaching blond man
—"or prove me right and put on your charming, actress
smile.

Seething, Natalie was bested.

She turned and smiled at Ashlin even as she inconspicu-
ously ground the heel of her slippered foot into the instep of
Kane's right foot. He didn't flinch or make a sound.

"Kane," greeted Ashlin warmly, "there you are. We've
missed you all day, haven't we, dear?"

"Oh, all day," said Natalie, not daring to look again into
Kane's accusing eyes.

"Kind of you, Lord Blackmore." Kane shook hands and
exchanged pleasantries with the only man in the ballroom
likely to acknowledge his presence.

Kane wondered what this man wanted. He didn't trust
Lord Blackmore. No more than he trusted the beautiful
woman who was to become Blackmore's wife. The man went
out of his way to be friendly. Why? It did not add up to
Kane.

"If you two will excuse me," Kane said, his hand acciden-
tally brushing Natalie's as she stood close. Both automatically glanced at each other, then away. "I see Marge Baker
waving to me." He left them as the music started once again.

Ashlin took Natalie in his arms and questioned, "What
was all that about?"

"All what?"

"I watched the two of you from across the room," Ashlin
told her. "I'm not sure I like what I saw. Should I be jealous?"

"Certainly not," answered Natalie, inwardly cringing. She
was doing exactly what Kane had accused her of doing. She
was acting. Pretending. Lying. "Yes!" she wanted to shout
loudly and ease her conscience, "you've every reason to be
jealous. I've gone to his bed when I've never been to yours!
And the callous devil is trying to get me there again. Yes, yes,
yes, you should be jealous!"

"I'm glad," he said, squeezing her hand and pressing her
closer. "I can see in his eyes that he desires you and—"

"Now, Ashlin—"

"Hear me through, darling," Ashlin chided. "I know Kane desires you . . . he doesn't bother to hide it when he looks at you." He lowered his lips to her ear and whispered, "I don't mind. I'm flattered, actually, for although I'd not trust Covington with my pocket watch, much less my fiancée, I know I can always, unfailingly, trust you, my dear."

The rest of the evening was sheer agony for Natalie. She dutifully danced with miners and cowboys, laughing and spinning and pretending she was having the best of times. From thick, veiling lashes she cast nervous glances at the unscrupulous man responsible for her misery.

Carol Thompson had managed to drag Kane onto the floor, and the glow on the pretty blonde's face could have lighted the big ballroom. Carol was a short, curvaceous woman, and her shiny golden head barely reached Kane's wide shoulders. She was leaning back in his long arms, her face lifted almost worshipfully to his, her fingers toying with the thick, dark hair at the back of his head, her full breasts resting against his white shirtfront. Her lips were parted, her eyes were shining, her demeanor was one of complete surrender.

Natalie guiltily looked away. Then back. Her eyes went to Kane's dark face. He was smiling down at Carol, but the expression in his blue eyes was enigmatic. Carol suddenly giggled and pressed her cheek against his chest and Natalie felt her stomach lurch unpleasantly. Kane's gaze lifted from the golden head beneath his chin and fell on Natalie. Their glances collided and held. His eyes flickered, his smile fled, his handsome face stiffened.

Natalie made a misstep, apologized to her partner, and bit the inside of her cheek.

What did it mean? What did Kane want of her? One minute he was teasing and goading, making her squirm and bristle with anger, the next he was looking at her as though she had somehow hurt or upset him. But how could that be? He cared nothing for her and had made that clear from the beginning. He delighted in torturing her, never missed an opportunity to remind her she was no lady, so why—

"—is that the reason?"

"I . . . I'm sorry." Natalie looked up into the harshly lined face of her dancing partner. "Could you repeat the—"

"I was just askin' why you ain't married the earl yet," said the old sourdough, "was you waitin' till the Christmas season?"

"I . . . yes, for Christmas," she said, wondering if she meant it. "We're waiting for the holidays."

The dance continued and Natalie made a point to steer clear of Kane Covington. Ever conscious of his whereabouts, she managed to stay on the other side of the room from him. After his dance with Carol, Kane left the floor. Alone, he lounged against the wall near the orchestra, arms folded over his chest, seemingly impervious to the whispers about him. Lazily his eyes followed the dancers, and if he was aware that dozens of females were hopefully awaiting his invitation for a dance, he didn't let on.

The liquor flowed. The music grew louder. The room fairly rocked with gaiety. And finally the inevitable happened. A fistfight erupted . . . two drunken cowboys wanted to dance with the same young lady. At the same time.

The orchestra fell silent. Dancers scattered. Ashlin promptly released Natalie and made his way toward the troublemakers, even as others hastily moved out of harm's way. Natalie could not hear what was being said, but she saw Ashlin step in between the angry pair. In seconds the trouble had been quelled and peace restored. Ashlin lifted his hand and signaled the orchestra to resume playing.

Ashlin was quickly surrounded by admiring, approving friends. His hand grew tired from all the congratulatory shakes. Impressed with his cool show of heroism and forceful exertion of authority, everyone in the room pressed forward to express their thanks.

Everyone but Kane Covington.

"Can't you get close enough to tell your handsome knight

how proud you are?" Kane's deep, derisive voice caused Natalie to jerk her head around.

"You may poke fun if you wish, Covington, but I am quite proud of Ashlin." She pushed at a rebellious red curl falling onto her forehead, and needled, "I'm told you let the Leatherwoods run you out of the Gilded Cage." She paused, expecting to see the scoffing grin leave his face. It never happened. Faintly flustered, she pressed on, intent on embarrassing him. "You did not stand up to them as Ashlin would have done."

"Would you have been proud of me if I had?"

"Certainly not!"

"Ah, well, there you are. Why do it?"

"Are you suggesting that Ashlin—"

"I'm suggesting nothing beyond your hand for the next dance."

Natalie gave him a smug look. "I will be enjoying the next dance in the arms of my fiancé."

"Nope," drawled Kane, "it seems his virile display of manliness has had quite an effect on the ladies." He inclined his dark head across the room.

A usually shy young matron, her face pink with excitement, was clinging to Ashlin's arm, drawing him toward the dance floor. He was smiling down at her, politely obliging.

"I suppose you think I'm jealous." Natalie hated herself the moment the words were out of her mouth. The orchestra struck up a Virginia reel.

"No," Kane said, shocking her, "I don't think you give a damn."

She opened her mouth to protest, but was not allowed to respond. Kane's warm fingers took hold of her elbow, slid down her arm to her hand, and entwined her fingers through his. He led her to the floor.

Couples queued up facing each other in parallel lines. Ashlin, four couples away from Kane, looked at Natalie, smiled warmly, then bowed to his beaming partner as Kane bowed to Natalie.

The dance began.

It was fast and strenuous and dizzying. Natalie, warm and out of breath, had no choice but to cling to her tall, graceful partner as he whirled her swiftly about the floor, swept her beneath the canopy of the other dancers' upstretched arms, and released her so he could prance grandly behind her before pulling her back into his arms.

Despite the vigorous, fast pace of the reel, Natalie was ever aware of the hard male chest and lean thighs pressing against her. Each movement of his tall, agile body seemed to singe right through her dress as though she were unclothed. She offered silent thanks that the furious timing of the dance and the frequent swings and spins made uninterrupted closeness impossible. She could never have made it through a waltz.

The music stopped at last and, breathless, Natalie immediately stepped from Kane's arms. Hand at her throat, she swallowed, trying to speak, as all about them the winded dancers headed for the refreshment tables to quench their thirst.

The music started once more. A waltz. Natalie was backing away. Kane was advancing. She shook her head wildly from side to side. He nodded his slowly up and down. She tried to speak. He said not a word. She held her hands up in an unconsciously defensive gesture. He aggressively took them both in his own.

"No," she finally managed.

"Yes," he calmly countered.

Natalie winced softly as Kane masterfully pulled her slender body into his sure embrace and the sweet, soft strains of the music filled the room. His touch was firm upon her waist. His long, lean fingers clasped her hand warmly while his eyes, half hidden beneath thick, coal-black lashes, fastened on her parted lips.

Feeling as though she would surely suffocate, Natalie drew a labored breath and focused on his dark throat above the stiff white collar.

When she could speak, she said coldly, "Please do not hold me so tight, people are staring."

"Are they?"

"Yes, they'll talk."

"Let them."

"Ashlin might be displeased."

"Let him."

Her eyes lifted to his. "Mr. Covington, I realize you don't care what anyone thinks, but I do."

"Why?"

"My life is here in Cloudcastle. While you will stay but a short time, I will live here for—"

"I plan to stay."

"You're so wealthy, then, that it is unnecessary for you to work?" She knew better.

"No. Perhaps I shall find my fortune here." He smiled down at her.

Natalie started. "Doing what?"

"Prospecting."

"I see. And just where do you plan to pan for gold? Turquoise tarn? San Miguel River? Escalante hot springs?"

"Oh, not pan, Your Honor. I'm not interested in a few ounces of gold dust washed from the streams." He folded their linked hands against his chest. "Thought I'd explore my mountain; see if I can't uncover a rich vein above the clouds."

Natalie fought the panic rising in her throat. "You're out of your mind, Covington. There's no gold on Cloud West."

"Hmmm, maybe you're right. Still, I'll take a look."

"It's winter," she frantically reminded him, "the snows will—"

"Slow me down, no doubt." He grinned. "I'm in no hurry."

"Mr. Covington, I really don't think—"

"Kane," he corrected her. "Can't you be a bit less formal, our relationship being what it is."

"We have no relationship," she quickly snapped.

Deep blue eyes looked at her accusingly. "Don't we?" drawled Kane, coldly. "Tell me, Judge, do you really suppose this self-denial is going to restore your virtue? To me it's a bit like closing the barn door after the horse is loose." He felt her struggle against him, but his arm tightened, pressing her closer to his hard, ungiving length. Against her ear he murmured, "Self-indulgence may be a sin but a pleasurable one, if I recall." He blew teasingly on a wispy red curl and added, "And I recall the sound of your sighs, the taste of—"

"My God, I hate you!" she cut him off, her fury rising, slender body trembling.

Kane stared at the beautiful, angry face turned up to his. Her passions erupted, the green eyes were turbulent, willful, blazing. "I know you do," said Kane, feeling much the same way about her, "I know."

Chapter Sixteen

On Sunday morning following the El Dorado Day dance, no sun appeared. Dark, ominous clouds filled a bleak, leaden sky. Outside it was freezing cold, and getting colder. Strong, frigid winds howled at windows. At 9,000 feet, Cloud West was eye-level with the dark base of the rising storm.

By noontime rain was falling in the high, windswept valley. Black clouds enclosed the mountain peaks as bolts of lightning lit up the darkened drawing room and claps of thunder rattled the windows of the big ranch house.

Natalie's mercurial mood was as tumultuous as the tempest. Her mind kept returning to Kane Covington. And the mere thought of him was enough to stir her ire.

She despised his brooding cynicism and cool, condescending manner. His fondest desire was to humiliate her and he was quite adept at it. Recalled insults filled her with a violent anger and around the drawing room Natalie paced, cursing the day he was born.

Then her wrath would be swept aside as a feverish sensation of white-hot lust came rushing in to overwhelm her and she could think of nothing save the waltz they had shared. Of how his tall, lean body felt against her own when he had held her much too closely. The warmth of his breath and lips when he spoke into her ear, drawling coaxingly, over and

over, in that soft Mississippi accent, "I want you, baby. Say
you want me." All the while managing small accidental
touches of those warm lips against her ear; touches that
caused unbearable excitement.

Fear suddenly claimed her. Kane had said he intended to
do some prospecting. The Cliff Palace was not safe. The gold
was not safe. And Natalie, pacing nervously back and forth,
felt certain that neither she nor the gold would ever be safe
again.

Her fear lasted but a brief time. Swiftly it changed back to
all-consuming anger. Anger at Kane Covington. Of all her
changing emotions, it was strongest. Dominating and engulfing her, it remained with her.

Natalie was still pacing moodily when Tahomah appeared
at Cloud West on that cold, dark afternoon. The Ute shaman
came riding down out of the thick black clouds, unfazed by
the wild wind and weather. His mahogany face wet with rain,
he burst into the warm house, saying without preamble, "Tell
me what is troubling you, Fire-in-the-Snow."

Natalie was not surprised to see him. The old Indian had
the uncanny ability of knowing when she was upset or unhappy. Absently running his gnarled, arthritic hand over the
shiny panther's claw, he mutely awaited her answer.

She could not reveal, even to Tahomah, all that burdened
her on that bleak Sunday. Assuring the glum-faced chief it
was nothing to concern him, she smiled warmly and attempted to wave the worry from his eyes with a dismissive
gesture of her hand. Promptly she turned the subject to the
worsening weather.

Tahomah shook his gray head solemnly and warned that
the "demons of winter" were loose upon the land and before
they again crawled back into the earth, great changes would
take place in the Shining Mountains. Some good, some bad.

When night fell, Tahomah took his leave, disappearing
into the thick clouds and pelting sleet. And Natalie was again
alone, and troubled.

Tahomah's visit had not worked its usual magic. She had

told him of the daylong El Dorado celebration and all that had happened and he had listened attentively, nodding and smiling. But when she mentioned that Ashlin would soon arrive for dinner and that she would like Tahomah to stay and share the evening meal, his broad, ugly face became expressionless and he said simply, "No."

Tahomah did not like Ashlin, had never liked him, and made little effort to hide it. From the first time the two men had met, Natalie had sensed a deep coolness between them, though both denied such was the case. Tahomah had asked today, as he had a half-dozen times before, if Ashlin had a brother. It baffled her why the shaman would pose such a strange question. The first time it happened, she had asked Ashlin. His answer was to pull her into his arms, kiss her, and laugh, saying calmly, "My dear, I'm an only child. One of a kind."

Natalie stood pensively at the window long after Tahomah had disappeared into the thick darkness. The shaman's barely concealed disapproval of Ashlin troubled her. Tahomah was generally such a good judge of character. What did he see in Ashlin that made him withhold his friendship? Why did his black eyes cloud each time he gazed on the handsome blond nobleman?

Out of the blue the idea struck her: Tahomah would like Kane Covington. Natalie felt a chill skip up her spine. Perhaps Tahomah wasn't such a good judge of character after all. Surely the dark devil was Satan's own spawn, hatched in hell!

Less than a mile from where Natalie stood peering into the darkness, the man from Hades rode his bay stallion through the punishing sleet. Hat brim pulled low, coat collar turned up over his cold ears, Kane spoke to the surefooted stallion and the beast lunged forward.

Riding back into Cloudcastle after a long, miserable day of cutting timber, Kane squeezed the big bay with his thighs and knees and felt the horse's powerful heart thundering between his legs, the sleek wet muscles pounding and driving.

And he wondered why, when riding this beautiful red-hued animal through blinding sleet in the cold, rugged mountains, his thoughts turned to the beautiful red-haired tigress whose firm, satiny body had once, on a sultry hot night, moved so responsively under his.

Kane ground his teeth as his groin swelled and he silently cursed the overwhelming desire that overtook him at the most inopportune times. Kane touched Satan with his spurs.

All he needed was a cold night in the warm arms of one of madam Mollie Madison's girls. Mollie's house reputedly had the most beautiful prostitutes in Cloudcastle. High-toned, refined, and exotic. Best of all, the girls were clean and accommodating. He would go there as soon as he reached town.

The temperature was dropping when Kane cantered into Cloudcastle. Needles of icy sleet stung his cold face and his fingers felt stiff inside the tight leather gloves. He went directly to the imposing three-story structure where lights blazed from every portal. An obliging servant appeared from nowhere and Kane, dismounting, tossed him the reins and hurried up the frozen front walk.

The madam herself answered the door, her round, powdered face lighting up with a warm, welcoming smile when she looked up at the dark-skinned, wide-shouldered man standing on the cold verandah.

"Mr. Covington," she greeted, "come in, come in at once."

She motioned a red-jacketed servant forward to take Kane's wet coat and hat. Tapping Kane's chest with her feathered fan, Mollie Madison said coyly, "My girls have been wondering when the handsome southerner would come to see us. They'll be delighted." She steered him into a softly lit parlor where a man was playing "The Man on the Flying Trapeze" on a gold-trimmed piano. A musical backdrop for the seductive sounds of tinkling female laughter, the clink of champagne glasses, and whispered promises of what pleasures could be expected upstairs.

Kane was in no mood to wait. His blue eyes quickly swept the rose-colored room and settled on a tall, voluptuous beauty with hair as black as his own and eyes the color of warm sherry.

"Ah, your taste is excellent, Mr. Covington." Mollie beamed. "Katrina is my most exotic, prized courtesan. She is also very expensive." Mollie cautiously studied Kane's hard face. It was impassive. She pressed on. "Katrina sees only one gentleman an evening, so if she is your choice . . . you can stay until morning."

"I'll do that," said Kane, and without another word made his way across the room. Katrina smiled at him when he put his hand on her small, corseted waist. Together they climbed the wide, carpeted stairs.

Eager to please the quiet, handsome man in whose strong arms she would be spending the night, Katrina was waiting expectantly in the oversize bed when a clean, naked Kane came out of the ornate bathroom, towel-drying his thick, dark hair. Her sherry eyes greedily traveling down the dark, lean length of him, Katrina could hardly believe her good fortune.

Kane's gaze moved slowly about the softly lit room and he felt a measure of pleasurable anticipation overtaking his tired, tense body. Outside it was sleeting and cold, but in here . . . A warm fire blazed brightly in the black marble fireplace. Champagne was chilling in a silver bucket beside the bed; two long-stemmed crystal glasses were ready to be filled. Black satin sheets and huge fluffy pillows made a sensuous playground of the big canopied bed.

Katrina's sherry eyes were brazenly promising unspoken delights, while her white, voluptuous body was provocatively concealed beneath slick black satin. Long, silky hair had been brushed out and now lay in shiny waves upon the pillow. Bare ivory shoulders were visible as the slithery sheet rode just above the crests of her full, rounded breasts. One long, shapely leg, purposely left outside the covers, was bent at the knee, foot flat upon the mattress.

Could any man want more?

Kane let the wet towel slip from his grasp to the scarlet-carpeted floor. With slow, determined strides he went to the bed, put a knee on the mattress, and ran his fingers playfully along the edge of the top sheet, all the while looking down at his beautiful companion.

"Katrina, are you going to pleasure me all through the night?" he drawled, still standing above her, dark thumb and forefinger sliding back and forth along the sheet's border, his knuckles brushing the rise of her bare, soft bosom.

"Yes, darling, I am," purred Katrina, and inhaled deeply, causing the sheet to lift with her full, jutting breasts.

"Good," said Kane, slowly peeling the black satin sheet away, not stopping until it lay at her feet. He stood for only a moment admiring her naked charms before the girl laughed deep in her throat, lifted a slender hand and pulled him into bed with her.

Half an hour later Kane stood buttoning his trousers while Katrina, full red lips pouting, sherry eyes flashing with anger, sat naked in the rumpled satin bed and chided, "We've only begun. I will show you a wonderful time, Kane."

Kane smiled at her. "You already have, Katrina."

Katrina petulantly swatted a fat, shiny pillow. "You paid for the whole night. Stay and let me fulfill you."

"I'm fulfilled," said Kane gallantly, exiting the room.

In no time he was undressing again and crawling between the cold white cotton sheets of his third-floor room at Marge Baker's boardinghouse.

Kane lay on his bare belly, long arms folded beneath his cheek. He sighed wearily. Sexually, he had performed with zest and hunger and the beautiful Katrina, an expert at her craft, had brought him to a draining climax. The act itself had been pleasurable enough.

Why, then, did he feel as unfulfilled as ever?

Unbidden, Natalie's beautiful face appeared in the gloom, so real and so near, yet so unreachable. Kane's fingers ached to touch her flawless skin. His arms trembled with longing to hold her. His abdomen tightened painfully and his hands clutched his lonely pillow as intense, blinding desire overtook him. He cursed aloud in the darkness, swearing at the rigid rod of passion pressing against his bare belly as though he were not responsible, as though it had a mind all its own.

"Damn you," he swore raggedly, and flipped over onto his back, cursing his weakness, his lack of control, and his longing. Forcing himself to envision the beautiful Judge Natalie Vallance lying naked in the arms of Ashlin Blackmore, Kane's hot, coursing blood cooled at last and the physical evidence of desire disappeared.

The empty longing remained.

Chapter Seventeen

During the night the drizzling sleet changed to softly falling snow. By the time Natalie arrived at the Castleton County Courthouse on that wintry Monday morning, the craggy, cloud-high peaks of the rugged mountains were mantled in white and the tiny hamlet of Cloudcastle was lightly dusted with its first snow of the season.

Natalie unlocked her private chambers behind the courtroom and stepped inside, shivering. Shrugging out of her heavy cashmere cloak, she hurriedly hung it on the coat tree and went about laying a fire in the grate.

Deciding to leave on the warm, fur-lined boots she was wearing, Natalie stepped behind her desk, idly wondering who had won this year's lottery by correctly predicting the date of Cloudcastle's first snowfall. Most likely it was a flatlander, someone unfamiliar with the region, since October 21 was unusually late for the season's first snow.

Natalie pondered for a moment. The first snow last year had fallen on September 29th . . . no, the 28th. She smiled and lifted her eyes to the north window. Huge, wet flakes, driven by a rising west wind, swirled from out of the skies. The sight of them filled her with good cheer.

Turning to the legal work arrayed before her, Natalie breezily went about the business at hand. She had a civil case to conduct after lunch, but could spend the morning clearing titles, processing deeds, and legalizing partnerships and enterprises.

Natalie flipped open the top folder on a neat stack and began. She hummed softly as she skimmed the long legal document. She felt lighthearted because in the back of her mind was the pleasing notion that, due to the onset of the snows, Mr. Kane Covington could not continue the construction of his mountain cabin. Nor would he be apt to roam the high, treacherous peaks of Treasure Mountain, hunting for gold.

Natalie lifted a black pen from its inkwell and thoughtfully tapped her bottom lip with its sharp tip while her green eyes gleamed mischievously. "Covington," she said aloud, "you'll find working out-of-doors up here a bit different than it is way down on the Mississippi Gulf Coast." She laughed then, satisfied that the southerner, who was unaccustomed to the harsh weather in the Rockies, was still, at this late hour, sound asleep in his warm boardinghouse bed. And would most probably remain there. "Welcome to the Colorado Territory, Mr. Covington!"

Kane added his signature to the brief letter that lay before him on the little writing desk. Then he put down the pen, and reread the words he had written to Colonel James Dunn, the Federal officer who had witnessed Devlin Vallance's signature on the deed Kane held to Promontory Point.

Kane's path had crossed with Dunn's more than once over the past few years, and despite their different loyalties during the war, the two men had become, if not good friends, reasonably friendly. There was a mutual respect and understanding between the two and Kane was confident the man, who made his home in Denver, would promptly answer his letter.

Colonel Dunn,
    I am in need of a favor and trust you will give me a

hand. As an elected territorial official, you are surely privy to the information I solicit.

A distinguished Cloudcastle citizen, Lord Ashlin Blackmore, claims he is an agent for a group of influential Denver businessmen seeking to purchase right-of-way land for the proposed Denver–Pacific railway. To my knowledge he has bought nothing although he apparently makes frequent trips to Denver to meet with the board. Do you know anything of him or about him? My reasons for asking are strictly personal; I know you will keep my inquiry confidential, as I will most certainly keep your reply.

My best to your Mary and the children.

Kane Covington

Natalie found the morning's tasks tedious and tiresome. While she loved the challenge and excitement of the courtroom, she disliked the routine paperwork, which piled up as quickly as she could process it. Within an hour she was squirming about in her swivel chair, feeling restless and distracted.

Natalie rubbed her eyes and glanced at the walnut-cased clock. It was only 9:30 A.M. Sighing, she rose and stretched her arms high over her head, reluctant to continue with her work. The thought struck her that the morning mail had most likely arrived.

With a heavy cloak around her shoulders and a hood covering her hair, she stepped out into the gently falling snow and carefully picked her way across the nearly deserted street. She reached the wooden sidewalk, placed her hand on a skinny porch pilaster before the barbershop, and stood stamping the loose snow from her boots.

When Natalie looked up, she saw Kane Covington coming up the sidewalk toward her. Her fingers tightened reflexively on the wooden pilaster and her lips compressed firmly.

He was bareheaded. A fine dusting of snow adorned his broad shoulders and thick, dark hair. He was smiling warmly, as though it were a balmy summer's day and she were an old, dear friend he was coming to meet.

It infuriated Natalie.

"Why aren't you in bed?" she snapped thoughtlessly when he reached her.

Kane immediately seized the opportunity. "Your Honor," he said with mockery in his blue eyes, "I'm delighted bed comes to mind when you look at me."

"That is not what I—"

"When I see you I'm reminded of big, soft four-poster beds," he interrupted smoothly. "It must be something about your—"

"You," she cut in, "are disgustingly vulgar."

"But fun, don't you agree? Speaking of fun, I had a bit this morning. I won the lottery; picked the date of Cloudcastle's first snowfall." He patted his breast pocket. "Let me buy you breakfast with part of my winnings." He gave her a maddeningly serene smile, lifted a white envelope he carried in his right hand, and teasingly tapped her high cloak collar.

"Certainly not." Natalie swatted his hand away and the white envelope slipped from his fingers, fluttering to the snow-covered sidewalk. Kane bent to retrieve it and Natalie's eyes fell on the addressee. Without thinking she blurted out, "James Dunn. That's the man who witnessed your deed to Promontory Point."

Kane replied calmly, "Yes, it is. Since you're obviously dying of curiosity, shall I tell you what it says?" He knew full well his statement would make her quick to assure him she did not care.

"Mr. Covington, let me assure you I do not care what you have to say to Mr. Dunn."

Kane chuckled and took her arm. "Then walk with me to post it, Judge."

"Never." Natalie snatched her arm free, stepped around him, and started down the sidewalk. Kane watched the sway of her long, billowing cloak. In two strides he caught up to her, fell into step, and taunted, "Afraid to join me for breakfast? Afraid I'll try to—"

"I am afraid of nothing. If you'll kindly excuse me." She quickened her steps.

Kane grinned and pursued her, saying pointedly, "I must get this in the mail and ride up to Promontory Point."

Natalie stopped walking. "Whatever for? Surely you don't plan to work in this weather?" She gave him a smug smile. "You can't be serious about planning to stay on in Cloudcastle."

"But I am. This place has seduced me." He grinned evilly and added, "It's rather like you, Judge. Cold, austere, but ah, what priceless treasures lie hidden."

Natalie ground her teeth. "Covington, you won't last! You're used to muggy heat and mosquitoes, but you will find—"

"I find this climate invigorating, Judge." Kane purposely took a long, deep breath. "I'm filled with energy that has to be worked off." His gaze shifted to her mouth. "Sexual energy. Any suggestions?"

"Just one."

"Tell me."

Natalie glanced about. "Stick it in the snow!"

His deep, rumbling laughter followed her as she flounced away, disappearing inside the Wells Fargo office. The tall clerk looked out from under his green visor, smiled, and handed Natalie a letter.

Natalie saw the familiar handwriting and eagerly tore open the envelope, a happy light warming her eyes. Anxiously she read the letter, far too engrossed in it to pay any mind to the man so engrossed with her.

The letter contained the message she had been looking forward to receiving. Uncle Shelby Sutton, her only living blood relative, was coming to Cloudcastle in three weeks.

Kane stood studying her as she read the letter. Her beautiful eyes shone happily and her full, pouting lips were lifted in a disarming smile. Kane's lean fingers tightened on the missive he was holding when she absently raised a small white hand and impatiently pushed the hood off her mass of reddish hair.

Always beautiful, she looked incredibly luscious on this cold, snowy morning with her green eyes glittering and her flawless skin glowing with healthy color. Kane felt an unfamiliar attraction to her that was more complex than basic passion.

Swiftly he reminded himself that although she looked so fresh and young and innocent standing there reading her letter, her appearance was deceiving. She was, in fact, a deceitful, conniving thirty-year-old woman who had been around, and plenty. That slender, tempting body had known the arms of more than one man, including his own.

Like the beautiful, viperous Susannah, Natalie Vallance was about as vulnerable as a serpent.

Nonetheless hot desire rose in him and Kane silently vowed he would have this experienced russet-haired woman again. Once had not been enough. If he could get her into his bed for a couple of nights—or a couple of days—he would no doubt get his fill of her and promptly forget her.

He would have a better chance to do so when he lived near her. As soon as he had his cabin completed, he might persuade her that no one need know if they chose to share a few hours of carnal pleasure. Cloud West was remote. No close neighbors. Just the two of them, miles from town, sharing a fierce environment. Paired against the elements, battling blizzards on crackling cold nights. He and the redheaded judge, cut off from civilization, turning to each other in their need.

Kane pushed away from the wall. He stepped past Natalie, but she didn't notice him. Quickly posting his letter, he hurried out of the Wells Fargo office.

He had work to do.

Lord Blackmore's gleaming coach wound slowly up the icy escarpment toward Cloud West. It was night and the snow was so thick, the city of Cloudcastle, a thousand feet below, was almost hidden from view in the icy haze. A few bright lights twinkled through the snow ghosts of tall pine trees and naked aspens.

A cold, rising wind buffeted the enclosed carriage and Natalie, safe and warm inside the confines of the luxurious coach with her attentive fiancé beside her, felt more secure than she had in weeks. The evening had been a pleasant one. They'd enjoyed a tempting buffet at Dr. and Mrs. Ellroy's, which had been followed by games of cribbage. Four couples had been at the Ellroy home, all old friends, all good company, and Ashlin had been in an especially entertaining mood, charming her and the others with amusing stories of his youth in England.

Natalie was almost content on this cold, starry night, and mentally counted her blessings. In a matter of days her beloved uncle would arrive, and Ashlin seemed eager to meet him. She had not seen the worrisome Kane Covington since the day at the Wells Fargo office, but she felt confident the construction of his cabin was at a standstill. It had snowed every day for the past week.

Rumors abounded that the southerner had run desperately short of money before winning the lottery. Before that bit of luck, one of the miners who lived at the Baker boarding-house, swore he had overheard Marge Baker telling Kane Covington that she would be glad to carry him for a time, that he could pay when he had the money.

Natalie frowned.

If only he hadn't won the snow lottery. Carol Thompson had told her there was more than a thousand dollars in the pot. Damn! He might last for months on that kind of money.

No, no he wouldn't. He was far too self-indulgent and undisciplined. He spent his nights—and his money—on gambling and women, so the gossips proclaimed. A thousand dollars would not last long; not with his appetites. And he would have a difficult time finding employment in Cloudcastle. A great majority of the mines had closed over the past five years and of the ones operating, she could think of no foreman who would offer him a job.

Natalie sighed and snuggled deeper beneath the soft, furry lap robe. Ashlin smiled in the darkness and drew her close. "You sound like a satisfied woman, my dear."

"I am," she said, and smiled up at him.

Ashlin bent down and found her mouth. He kissed her softly, gently, as a gentleman would. Natalie put her arms around his neck and kissed him back. And told herself it did not matter if his kisses did not stir her to raging passion, as the despicable Kane Covington's had. Ashlin loved her, respected her, was going to marry her.

He was not the kind of man to use a woman for his own selfish pleasure.

Natalie's serenity was shaken the next day.

The snow had stopped for a time, but great drifts had piled up against the sides of buildings and Cloudcastle's unpaved streets were covered with heavily rutted ice. The sun was out and Natalie, standing in the upstairs salon of the talented French couturiere Madame Du Bois, was not cold even though she was clad in only a soft satin chemise, silk stockings, and high-heeled shoes.

Through gleaming skylights above her head, brilliant sunshine streamed in to bathe her nearly nude body with lustrous light and welcome warmth.

Natalie smiled at the short, dark-haired woman and dutifully stepped into the half-finished shimmering yellow taffeta frock. With an off-the-shoulder neckline and a long, tight basque, the gown, fashioned from a pattern Natalie had admired in *Godey's Lady's Book,* looked stunning even in this incomplete stage.

"Magnifique!" trilled Madame Du Bois as her nimble fingers tugged at the hidden hooks that ran down the gown's snug back. Before Natalie could agree, the bell downstairs tinkled and the tiny dressmaker shouted shrilly, *"Ne quittez pas!"* and scurried down the stairs, leaving Natalie alone to admire the lovely yellow creation.

She was still staring, transfixed, into the tall beveled mirror when Madame returned with Carol Thompson.

"Nat!" exclaimed her friend. "You are beautiful!"

"Oui, oui," Madame Du Bois agreed, "she have the slender body, the regal bearing to do justice to Madame Du Bois's designs!"

Carol nodded, untying the streamers of her blue felt bon-

net. "You look like a delicious bowl of lemon ice, Nat, and
I'm pea green with jealousy."

Natalie's slender hands smoothed the stiff, shiny fabric
hugging her midriff. "Thanks, Carol, but doesn't it seem a bit
daring to you?" Her eyes lowered to the expanse of bare
white flesh showing atop the gown's rounded décolletage.

"Heavens, no!" assured Carol, then added teasingly,
"Looks like the lady judge has decided to offer new evidence
that she is decidedly all woman." Her gaze rested on Natalie's nearly bare bosom.

Madame Du Bois, nodding her dark head vigorously, proclaimed happily, "Ah, this yellow taffeta is sedate!" Her eyebrows lifted impishly. "Wait until she put on the sumptuous
turquoise velvet! Is cut to here!" With short fingers she drew
imaginary lines from Natalie's bare shoulders to a point at
her narrow waist. "You will be as tempting as that shameless
beauty, the exotic Katrina." The little dressmaker laughed
and darted behind Natalie to fuss with the scalloped taffeta
overskirt hitched up into a small bustle.

"Katrina?" questioned Natalie, "I don't—"

"I do." Carol sat on the tufted-velvet love seat. "Katrina is
the long-legged beauty at Mollie Madison's." She frowned
suddenly. "Rumor has it she is simply wild for Kane Covington."

"Ah, this is true, this is true," offered Madame Du Bois in
low, confidential tones. "That Katrina, she and some of the
other girls come to me for new gowns. Katrina speaks of the
handsome Mississippian in glowing terms."

"What does she say?" Carol leaned forward eagerly.

"Carol, I'm sure Madame Du Bois does not wish to—"

"Ah, but I love to gossip; I am French, no?" said the dressmaker. Her voice lowered almost to a whisper. "Katrina tell
her friends Mr. Covington is the expert at *amour* and that she
'trembles with passion' when he—"

"Madame, isn't it a bit too warm in here?" Natalie felt her
face flushing hotly.

The little couturiere sighed, but crossed the sunny room to
open a window.

Carol said dreamily, "Isn't it a shame that—"

"I think perhaps pearls would go well with this gown, don't you?" Natalie interrupted, desperate to change the subject.

"I mean, I made it clear to Kane," Carol continued, "that I find him very attractive. Yet he refuses to give me a tumble and I have to believe it is because he stays away from decent females."

"But why?" asked Madame Du Bois. "He is well-bred gentleman, no?"

Carol shrugged. "I thought so, but Jake—ah, an acquaintance who deals faro at Gaiety's—says that Kane comes there often and never brings a respectable lady with him, but almost never leaves alone." She lowered her eyelashes suggestively. "Jake says it's downright lewd the way those loose, fancy women drape themselves all over Kane while he's gambling."

Natalie felt the breath inside her body growing short.

"Ah, *oui,*" beamed the openmouthed couturiere, "and then he go home with them, no?"

"Of course he does," nodded Carol. "Let's face it, the man likes bold, beautiful whores."

"He never courts fine, eligible ladies of Cloudcastle?" wondered Madame Du Bois.

"Never," stated Carol emphatically. "The man is obviously decadent and base. He prefers his affairs to be cheap and vulgar and meaningless." She sighed sadly. "The southern gentleman is actually no gentleman."

"Ah, is *tragique,*" lamented Madame Du Bois. "He is so handsome!"

"He sure is," agreed Carol, wistfully, "but he's . . . he's always so quiet and distant. I've tried to draw him out, but he . . . he—" Abruptly Carol looked questioningly at Natalie. "Come to think of it, the only time I have ever seen Kane animated is when he was talking to you, Nat. What is the explanation?"

Natalie, dying a little inside, smiled and calmly replied, "Perhaps he does not consider me a lady."

Both Carol and Madame Du Bois laughed merrily, and when the dressmaker helped Natalie step out of the rustling yellow taffeta, she was puzzled to see Natalie hastily donning her street clothes. "But, *mon amie,*" she reminded, "we are to fit the turquoise velvet, no?"

"Tomorrow," said Natalie, "we'll do it tomorrow."

The cold air felt good on her hot face when Natalie exited the downstairs door of Madame Du Bois's little shop. She drew a deep breath and hurried away, giving silent thanks that Carol had remained behind for a fitting. She had heard more than she ever wanted to know of Kane Covington. Shaking her head to clear the unpleasant pictures painted by Carol's enlightening gossip, Natalie turned the corner onto Denver Street.

If she had been mildly upset in the upstairs fitting room of Madame Du Bois's, she was now almost overwhelmed.

There stood Kane Covington with a gorgeous, stately beauty clinging possessively to his arm. The door the handsome pair had just exited? The town's assay office!

Her heart pounding, Natalie sailed back around the corner to avoid a confrontation. Fear gripped her. What was he doing in the assay office? Dear Lord, had he already discovered the gold?

Feeling shocked and alarmed, Natalie walked dazedly in the opposite direction, hardly realizing where she was headed until, short of breath, she climbed the steep steps of the Blackmore mansion.

Upstairs, bright sunlight streamed through the big bay windows of the spacious drawing room. Across the marbled corridor, however, in the vast dining hall, the cut-velvet drapes were tightly pulled; double doors securely closed.

On the heavy sideboard, a single white candle burned in a tall crystal candlestick. The matching candlestick was empty. The long dining table, draped with snowy-white damask, was elaborately laid for lunch. Fine china, sparkling crystal, and heavy sterling had been meticulously placed for two.

But it was not yet noontime.

And atop that massive, regal table, at its far edge, away

from the dazzling place settings, a beautiful young dark-haired girl sat upon the table.

Naked.

Before her stood a handsome blond man, also naked, a long white candle held loosely in his right hand. The blond man was kissing the dark-haired girl, his hot mouth devouring her hungrily.

He raised his golden head at last and smiled down at her, lifting the candle to her chin. Stroking teasingly, he trailed the tallow taper over the curve of her white throat, around each full, jutting breasts, down her bare white belly and lower.

Belinda Baker's pale thighs fell apart. Ashlin Blackmore filled them.

Natalie Vallance lifted the downstairs door knocker.

Chapter Eighteen

Dear Captain Covington,

In reply to your inquiry regarding the titled Blackmore: the gentleman, although he is acquainted with Moffat, Tabor, Evans, and Bedford, and frequently dines with the entrepreneurs when in the city, is in no way connected with their railroad interests. I am told that Lord Blackmore's visits are purely pleasurable ones and that when he is not being entertained at the homes of Denver's socially elite, he spends his hours in drunken debauchery at Mattie Silk's establishment.

From all I can gather, the pleasure-seeking nobleman is quite wealthy and has no profession, other than that of being the charming, sought-after European gracing Denver's drawing rooms.

Next time you are over the Divide, stop in and spend a few nights with us.

Regards,
James Dunn

Kane folded the letter and put it inside his breast pocket, his dark face devoid of expression. Exiting the Wells Fargo office, he unlooped Satan's reins from the hitchrail, swung up into

the saddle, and cantered down the street, his thoughts on the
contents of Dunn's letter.

Pondering Blackmore's reason for dissembling, Kane
kicked his steed into a trot on the outskirts of town, blue eyes
squinting against the glaring reflection of the bright winter
sun on the snow-covered ground.

Past the old shut-down Shining Mountain mine rode Kane,
climbing rapidly now, Satan laboring through the deep drifts
of snow. Kane did not put Blackmore from his mind until he
saw, at last, the sturdy shell of his mountain cabin nestled
amid the ice-glazed pines.

Kane smiled.

Amazingly enough, the structure was near completion,
though hardly a day had gone by without snow falling. Kane
unsaddled the big stallion, anxious to begin work. With any
luck he could occupy the cabin in a couple of weeks.

Satan whinnied and tossed his great head. Kane turned to
see a grinning Joe South, mounted atop a skinny dun mare,
loping toward him. Joe lifted a hand and waved. He looked
sober. Together they might get the roof on.

Shortly before ten o'clock on that same morning, the Overland stage rolled to a stop on Cloudcastle's Main Street.

Colonel Shelby Sutton pushed the coach door open and
stepped down to the icy street. He reached for the passenger
within. The petite, well-dressed lady placed her gloved hands
on top of his broad shoulders and laughed prettily when his
hands went to her tiny waist.

Effortlessly, the tall, slim man swept the enchanting
woman out of the coach and into his arms. While people
stared and whispered, Colonel Sutton, gray-haired and gray-
eyed, posture still that of erect military bearing, gallantly
carried the small, curvaceous female to the sidewalk.

There he gently lowered her, pulled her small hand around
his arm, and escorted her to the Eureka Hotel while every eye
followed them.

Inside the ornate hotel, the colonel saw the lovely lady
settled in a comfortable second-floor suite, and paid to have
her many trunks and valises transported from the coach.

Squeezing her gloved hand, he said charmingly, "My dear, until this evening."

The pale blond woman lowered her lashes demurely and smiled up at the tall, attractive man. "Colonel, I shall count the hours."

Back outside, Shelby Sutton's gaze went immediately to the Castleton County Courthouse and he smiled broadly. Stopping a youth, he clamped a hand down on the boy's bony shoulder and said, "Want to make a dollar, son?"

"You bet, mister."

"Run down to the courthouse and see that Judge Natalie Vallance gets the message her uncle has arrived." He handed the boy the coin, and added. "I'll be at the Gilded Cage Saloon. Fetch me when she's free and there's another dollar in it for you."

Ashlin Blackmore sneezed.

A cold was coming on; he was certain. Of all the days to catch a cold! Natalie's uncle was due in town and she'd made big plans for the evening. He sneezed again. Ashlin dreaded the whole miserable affair. The old man would most likely question him, pry, probe, be the typical protective relative. That's all he needed.

"Are you catching a cold?" Belinda questioned, and Ashlin realized he had been so preoccupied, he had forgotten her presence.

They were in his opulent drawing room on this cold Thursday morning. He stood with his back to the fireplace; Belinda sat, cross-legged, on the floor at his feet.

The sight of her there below him brought an involuntary tremor of remembered terror. How close they'd come to being caught the last time the young girl had been at the mansion. Never would he forget the panic that had gripped his chest when he realized Natalie was at the front door! The frantically issued orders to Belinda, the frenzied dressing, the racing about, the pounding of his heart when at last he'd flown down the stairs. The anxious moments when Natalie swept into the dining room where Belinda stood lighting a tall white candle in its crystal holder.

"Ashlin?" Belinda's voice interrupted his thoughts. He smiled down at her and reached for her hand.

"Stand up, child." Belinda rose before him. "Undress."

Ashlin watched while she discarded her clothes. When she stood naked before him, he commanded, "Turn around, Belinda." Belinda turned. "Now get down on all fours," he said huskily.

He looked at the bare bottom turned up for his pleasure as his hand went to the buttons of his trousers. Slowly he sank to his knees behind her.

Ashlin sneezed.

In the Castleton County courtroom, Natalie read the look in the darting eyes of the bailiff, Theodore Burford. He was signaling that he had a message, something to tell her. Almost imperceptibly, she nodded to him, then immediately redirected her attention to the nervous young defense attorney who was bent on clearing his client of claim-jumping charges.

The bailiff silently stole to the front of the room, sidled over to the tall podium and laid his hand upon it. He quickly retreated, leaving behind a folded piece of paper. Natalie's fingers closed over the note and she slid it across the polished wood.

Waiting for the opportune moment, she unfolded it in her lap.

Uncle Shelby Sutton is in the Gilded Cage Saloon. Send young Frank Dallas to get him when you are free.

Natalie's heart filled with joy. He was early. The stage was supposed to arrive at eleven that morning and it was not yet ten.

Time dragged and Natalie fidgeted. Court dismissal came at last.

Feeling happy and carefree, Natalie eschewed young Frank Dallas's offer to fetch her uncle. Smiling down into the youth's narrow face, she gave him a coin and told him she

wouldn't need his help. Judge Natalie Vallance hurried down
the sidewalk, paused but a brief moment outside the swinging
doors of the Gilded Cage, drew a deep breath, and strode
inside.

Immediately she spied him, his back to her, at the brass-
trimmed mahogany bar. The tall, lanky frame, the wide, erect
shoulders, the gleaming silver hair: it could only be Shelby
Robard Sutton.

Natalie went directly to where he stood drinking his whiskey. Lifting a foot to the brass rail, she forcefully slammed a
small fist down upon the bar and said loudly, "Can't a girl get
a drink around here?"

The entire room fell silent as miners, gamblers, and cowboys gaped, openmouthed. Shelby Sutton turned, looked
down into the pretty, smiling face of his niece and his gray
eyes widened. He threw back his silver head, laughed loudly,
and reached for her.

Sweeping her from the floor, he spun her around and said
over his shoulder, "Barkeep, a whiskey for the lady!"

Never had Natalie been more happy to see him. When at
last he released her, she stood at his side, sipping her bourbon, oblivious to the disdainful glances being sent their way.
Uncle Shelby, it seemed to her, never aged. At fifty-seven he
was as trim as a man of half his years. The bronzed skin of
his face was tight and unwrinkled, save the squint lines
around the gray, mischievous eyes. Nose straight and prominent, mouth pink and constantly smiling beneath the neatly
trimmed silver mustache, he was a dashing figure of a man
even in middle age.

On the ride to the ranch Natalie considered telling her
uncle of her misfortune . . . of losing her land. She
promptly discarded the notion. Tomorrow would be soon
enough to burden him with her troubles. For now, she
wanted only to enjoy his company and to let nothing mar a
perfect day.

"I've a wonderful evening planned, Uncle Shelby," Natalie
announced while she sat on the bed watching him unpack his
fine leather valises.

"Shall I guess?" the tall man asked, smiling fondly at his niece as he placed neatly folded shirts in a bureau drawer. "Let's see . . . your young man is taking us to the opera."

"Uncle Shelby!" Natalie's face screwed up in a frown. "I wanted it to be a surprise. How did you—"

"Baby girl, I'm sorry. I didn't mean to spoil your fun." He took a seat on the bed beside her, putting a long arm around her slender shoulders. "It so happens that my fellow passenger on the stagecoach was the noted opera star Noel Salvato. Miss Salvato told me the Cloudcastle opera season opens tonight. She is its star and has invited us to attend the performance this evening."

Natalie's eyes widened like a child's. "You met Miss Salvato? What's she like? Is she pretty? She's very famous, you know."

"I know." He nodded and rose to continue with his unpacking. "Noel is a charming, lovely woman. Not young by your standards, but certainly young by my own." He grinned. "My guess is the singer is on the wrong side of forty, but remarkably well preserved. But enough about her, tell me about your young man."

"No. Soon you'll meet him and you can be the judge." She rose, smiling. "I'll leave you to rest now and knock on your door in a couple of hours. Ashlin is to come for us at seven o'clock. We'll go to the Eureka for a light dinner, then on to the opera house. Afterward, we'll return here for a midnight supper. Sound pleasant?"

"Sounds wonderful, honey. I'll put on my best bib and tucker."

"You'd better, because I intend to show you off."

Natalie added a splash of rosewater to her bath. Heavy hair pinned up off her neck, she luxuriated in the sudsy warmth of the tub, lazily studying the crystal snowflakes glistening on the windowsill above her.

Only a small sliver of gray light remained on the western horizon and Natalie's big bath, the gas jets not yet lit in the brass wall sconces, was semidark, the only illumination being the snow-glow of the mountains beyond her uncurtained windows.

Natalie liked it this way. She could recline, naked and relaxed, in this warm, cozy atmosphere, looking out at a world that could not look in on her. Natalie smiled dreamily and lifted a fluffy washcloth to her throat. Languidly she washed her shoulders, her arms, thinking of the hours ahead.

Then she moved the soft, soapy washcloth down to her breast. Natalie suddenly shook her head thoughtfully. Her exquisite new turquoise gown revealed a great expanse of bosom. Did she dare wear it tonight?

When she'd finished bathing, Natalie slipped on a satin wrapper, and Madame Du Bois's scoldings came flooding back into her mind: *No, no, no! You may not wear these bulky underthings with my fabulous creation! Chérie, the gown is fully lined; do not be a silly girl! You will wear only corset under the turquoise velvet, nothing else, I demand it.*

Natalie held the beautiful new gown up before her. It was magnificent! She longed to wear it to the opera; to be stunning on this gala evening.

It was settled. She was going to wear this lush, gorgeous gown. Natalie carefully laid the soft velvet frock across her bed. Humming happily, she sat down and drew on a pair of sheer black silk stockings, carefully pulling the turquoise satin garters up above her knees. She stepped into the scandalously high-heeled silver slippers and stood up.

Natalie untied her robe, tossed it aside, and drew the hated corset around her slender body. Bottom lip sucked behind her teeth, she tugged, she pulled, she struggled until finally her already small waist was nipped in so a man's hands could easily span it.

While the stiff, ungiving corset minimized her waist, it maximized her curves. Reaching from underneath her breasts down to just below her hipbones, the rigidly boned garment pushed her full breasts up and out.

Suddenly embarrassed, Natalie snatched some satiny underwear from a drawer and stepped into it. Then she drew on the dress. And she sighed with exasperation. There was absolutely no way she could wear lingerie under the velvet gown. The delicate lace ruffles on her underdrawers made ugly ridges through the soft, luxuriant velvet. The narrow straps and at least an inch of her chemise showed above the low neckline of the dress.

Frowning, Natalie peeled off the new dress. In seconds she was putting it on once again. The underwear lay discarded on the white carpet. She stood before the tall mirror staring at herself as though she were a stranger.

The glamorous gown was of the very latest Parisian style. As it was sleeveless, her slim, bare arms looked creamy white against the deep turquoise hue. The rich, soft velvet that barely covered her full breasts was caught up at small fabric-covered buckles on top of her shoulders. And the bodice of the gown, in both back and front, plunged sensuously low.

From waist to knee the gown was skintight, pulling snugly across Natalie's flat belly, over her hips, and thighs. It flared like a petal from the knees down and swirled grandly upward to a small bustle, then fell once again into a small, trailing train.

Natalie looked at the woman in the mirror and admitted she was indeed beautiful. And the feeling was so heady, she would not have changed gowns for anything in the world. She smiled, and naughtily thought that it was strangely fun to wear a lovely dress with nothing beneath it.

Wearing white silk gloves on her small hands and carrying a tiny reticule of crystal beads and a fur-lined cape over her arm, Natalie descended the stairs to join her uncle.

Shelby Sutton stood in the parlor, a glass of port in his hand. Nattily attired as usual, he looked grand in a dark dinner coat and matching trousers, white shirt, striped four-in-hand tie, silver hair gleaming and neatly brushed.

He turned and saw his beautiful niece across the room. Lifting his glass to her, he said honestly, "My dear child, you shall surely turn all heads this night. I wager no gentleman is safe from—"

A knock at the door interrupted.

"It's Ashlin," Natalie said, glowing. "Will you let him in, Uncle Shelby?"

Shelby sat his glass aside. He threw open the door, and saw not a tall, blond young man, but a short, old one.

Ashlin's old servant, William, said apologetically, "Lord Blackmore sends his regrets, he has caught cold and cannot join you this evening."

Chapter Nineteen

There was a full, white moon. A billion stars twinkled brightly in the clear sky. The snow-glazed peaks glistened as though sprinkled with diamond-dust. Trees wreathed with frost loomed ghostly white against the star-studded firmament. Waterfalls, frozen in mid plunge, hung suspended above frigid mountain streams. Gelid gleaming granite, shrouded in snow, formed seductive statues of milky monolithic magnificence. Icicles fringed the eaves of brightly-lit residences.

It was a glorious winter night in the Shining Mountains, but Natalie, stepping into the warmth of Lord Blackmore's opulent covered carriage, wore a small frown of annoyance. For weeks she had been planning this perfect evening for her uncle. Now Ashlin was home with a bad cold and would not be joining them. Natalie leaned back against the high leather seat and drew her fur-lined cape more tightly about herself, feeling a chill skip up her spine.

She had the strangest feeling that Ashlin's absence was not to be the only unexpected occurrence on this beautiful, bitter cold night.

Shelby Sutton, the velvet collar of his chesterfield coat pulled up close to his throat, silk top hat covering his shiny silver hair, stepped into the roomy interior of the Blackmore

coach, took a seat beside his lovely niece, and said cheerfully,
"Don't fret, child. I'll meet your young man soon enough."
Shelby smiled at her and added, "The evening's not spoiled.
And remember . . . badly begun, well ended."

Natalie returned his smile, determined to shake off her
mild disappointment and odd apprehension. Looping an arm
through his, she pressed her cheek to his shoulder, and said
softly, "It's been a long time since we went out for the evening, just the two of us."

Shelby's kid-gloved hand patted the silk-covered fingers
clutching his forearm. "Too long, honey. We'll have a fine
time tonight, I promise."

The pair chattered spiritedly on the long ride down into
Cloudcastle, and Natalie recaptured the jovial, lively frame of
mind she'd enjoyed earlier that afternoon.

The coach rolled up to the crimson-canopied door of the
Eureka Hotel, and William, Ashlin's faithful servant, was
quick to open the carriage door and assist his master's fiancée
down to the sidewalk.

"A good night to you, William," said Shelby Sutton, smiling at the stooped little man.

William shook his head and, grinning broadly, said, "No,
Colonel Sutton, sir. I'll be driving you and Mrs. Vallance
back to Cloud West later this evening."

Shelby Sutton looked from the smiling servant to his nodding niece. She laughed at his puzzled expression and took
his arm. "William," she told the waiting driver, "the opera
should be over around eleven. We'll meet you in front of the
theater."

By the time Natalie and Shelby had shed their wraps and
she preceded her uncle into the fourth-floor Roof Garden of
the Hotel Eureka, she was aglow with happiness, color high
in her ivory cheeks, emerald eyes sparkling with delight.
Head held regally aloft, shoulders back, she strolled proudly
into the impressive room of glass and stone, sensing—and
enjoying—the quick turning of heads, the immediate animated whispers, the approval, and disapproval, that her dar-

ing, gorgeous turquoise velvet gown was eliciting from the well-heeled diners.

Following a carpeted path among royal palms, hanging baskets, and gold-gilt tubs of lush greenery and hothouse orchids, Natalie and Shelby were led to a choice table "on the glass," its strategic location insuring a degree of privacy as well as a breathtaking view of the streets of Cloudcastle stretching in twinkling splendor to the tinseled, towering San Juans bathed in magic moonlight.

"*Mon colonel,* welcome to the Eureka," the maître d'hotel, Philippe D'Ortega said, beaming, shaking Shelby's hand, complimenting Natalie on her turquoise gown, and expressing his regret that Lord Blackmore was ill.

"A pleasure to be back, Philippe," assured Shelby Sutton as the small Frenchman motioned the sommelier forward, bowing as he backed away.

Shelby glanced at the silk-tasseled wine list while Natalie smiled up at the slim, sophisticated wine steward and fought the urge to laugh aloud when she saw him swallow nervously. His dark gaze jerked guiltily up from her exposed bosom.

Shelby made his wine choice. The sommelier nodded approvingly and hurried away. Shelby's encompassing gaze swept around the lavish room, coming back to rest on the flame-haired young woman seated across the table, which was graced with Irish linen, Haviland china, a cut-glass candelabrum, and fragrant white orchids.

When the wine was poured, Shelby lifted his stemmed glass to Natalie, toasting her with chilled vintage Moselle. "May the most beautiful woman in Cloudcastle have an evening she will not soon forget." He touched his glass to hers and they drank. As Natalie sipped the smooth wine, she felt her heart skip a beat. The premonition she'd had earlier returned; the excitement of this glorious hour was going to be overshadowed before the night ended. She was sure of it.

Fresh French bread arrived, and square pats of golden butter afloat in small silver bowls of ice water. At just the right moment, huge, crisp salads were set before the pair.

While Shelby Sutton ate heartily of Rocky Mountain trout,

French peas, and mashed potatoes, Natalie was far too excited to eat. Scarcely touching her tender filet of beef, aspara-
gus on toast, and string beans, she hung on to her uncle's
every word, completely absorbed, enjoying the sound of his
deep, familiar voice, enthralled with his tales of adventure
and travel.

Ignoring her food, Natalie interrupted and questioned her
uncle, and reached again and again for her wineglass, sipping
from it happily. Ever the loving, indulgent uncle, Shelby
made sure the glass stayed filled for the beautiful young niece
whose sparkling emerald eyes never failed to warm his weary
heart.

Regarding her as he always had, as he always would, a
beautiful child to be pampered and spoiled, Shelby ordered
Neapolitan ice cream to tempt her. But he did not scold when
Natalie took only a few bites and let the rest melt in its
crystal bowl. She didn't touch her cup of steaming Vienna
coffee. She ignored the silver plate bearing bonbons, Malaga
grapes, and new figs.

Shelby sipped his coffee and grinned contentedly. The
child was too excited to eat; it was obvious. And Shelby was
pleased and flattered that his presence was the cause of her
excitement. She could eat a big supper later at Cloud West.

Uncle and niece laughed happily as they dashed across the
street to the Cloudcastle Opera House, dodging carriages and
slipping and sliding on the ice. Up the steps they hurried, to
be swallowed up in the eager throng of culture-hungry first-
nighters. Into the grand vestibule they were swept, a part of
Cloudcastle's elite, all decked out in their finery, laughing,
waving, and calling to one another, while from above an orchestra was tuning.

Natalie was breathless and happy after they'd checked
their wraps and she took her uncle's arm and crossed the
gleaming marbled floor of the semicircular foyer to one of the
main staircases that swirled grandly from the first floor to the
second. A blinding richness of shimmering marble, glittering
gilt, hammered bronze, swagged drappery, and plush carpet-
ing was everywhere in the ornate opera house.

Shelby handed Natalie into their private box on the theater's third tier, its location close to the stage. The couple sat on plush velvet chairs and looked out at the magnificent theater.

Eight giant Corinthian coupled columns supported the dome. Cherubs and flying angels of pure white stucco carried the arches, and from the very center of the high round ceiling, a spectacular gasolier hung suspended on a heavy gold chain, hissing softly, pouring honeyed light down upon the glittering crowd below.

A white-gloved waiter held out a silver tray and Shelby took the two champagne cocktails. The huge gasolier dimmed and the heavy crimson stage curtains lifted. Handing a glass to his niece, Shelby rose from his chair, lifted his own glass in salute, and smiled down upon the small, curvaceous woman costumed in a white peasant blouse, a colorful skirt, and a long, dark wig.

Noel Salvato looked up, smiled seductively at the tall, silver-haired man who was bowing at her while the orchestra waited. Sure of herself and of her hold on the expectant audience, she took a moment to throw a kiss to her tall admirer. Then she abruptly lowered her hand and snapped her fingers, and the long awaited *Carmen* began.

The performance was excellent, the entire cast extremely talented and professional, their superb voices ringing true and clear in the cavernous auditorium. And of them all, Noel Salvato, the diva, was most gifted. Her strong soprano voice tinkled the crystal prisms of the gasolier and sent shivers down Natalie's spine.

Or was something else making her shiver? Some event yet to happen, some crowning glory to an already remarkable day? No matter. Natalie sipped her champagne cocktail and let the performance enchant her.

After the last rousing curtain call, Natalie and Shelby remained in their box, finishing their champagne, waiting for the star of *Carmen* to change from her stage costume into evening dress. After a time, Shelby lifted his gold hunter-cased watch from his vest pocket, flipped it open, and said, "Noel should be ready, Natalie. Shall we go?"

In a backstage dressing room filled with garlands of cut flowers, Noel Salvato stood, dressed in shimmering white satin. She lifted her hand to Shelby's bronzed face and beamed up at him.

"Come in, come in, Colonel." She dropped her hand to his lapel when he stooped to kiss her cheek. "Need I be jealous?" said the pale blond, her soft brown eyes shifting to Natalie.

Shelby chuckled and pulled her close. "No, my dear, you needn't. May I present my only niece, Judge Natalie Vallance."

"Miss Salvato," said Natalie. "A thrill to meet you. Your performance was outstanding."

"A female judge?" The singer's light eyebrows lifted quizzically.

"Indeed. The only female judge west of the Mississippi," Shelby bragged proudly.

"Good for you, Natalie," complimented Noel. "But does this mean I shall have to watch my step this evening?" Her smile was directed at Shelby.

"I'll be doing good to watch my own, Miss Salvato," admitted a slightly tipsy Natalie.

"I'll be honored to watch you both," offered Shelby. "Now, where shall it be, ladies?" He looked at Natalie. "To Cloud West and our midnight supper?"

"I'm in your hands, my handsome colonel," Noel replied, laughing, as she impatiently jerked down her luxurious white ermine wrap and held it out for Shelby to drape about her shoulders.

"William is waiting out front, but . . ." Natalie tilted her head.

"But what, dear?" Shelby's attention came back to her.

"I don't know. I'm not . . . let's not go home yet." Her emerald eyes gleamed brilliantly and her words were just a little slurred from all the champagne she'd drunk during the performance.

"Then we'll not go," assured Shelby Sutton. "Let's have a magnum of champagne at the—"

"Let's go to Gaiety's Gaming Hall," Natalie interrupted, then turned and walked purposefully out of the dressing room, a sly smile curving her soft lips.

"What are we waiting for?" said a delighted Shelby Sutton.

"I love the roulette game," Noel Salvato added excitedly.

Into Gaiety's plush gaming hall strode the laughing trio. Wraps hastily discarded, they stood on the threshold, leisurely surveying the big room.

The after-theater crowd was out en masse. The big room overflowed with handsomely dressed customers and liveried servants. The whir of the roulette wheel, the clatter of the dice upon green felt, deep laughter and shouts of lucky winners, filled the air. Grinning happily, Shelby's gray eyes cast about, searching for a roulette table with room for them all.

He saw it far in the back of the casino. On a raised, partially curtained landing, one lone man sat at the roulette table, his back to the room. A hushed crowd stood at a respectable distance, watching his play.

"Come along," said Shelby, guiding the two women through the crowd of smiling patrons. Unattached males looked up from their games to stare admiringly at the russet-haired judge whose slender, sensual body was so temptingly displayed in a daring gown of turquoise velvet.

Whispers followed in her wake, and more than one man who was supposedly a good friend of Lord Blackmore's secretly daydreamed, wishing that the beautiful judge might, on this evening, behave as befitted a woman dressed in the breathtakingly revealing gown. Each inwardly sighed and turned back to his game. There was no chance of such an occurrence.

These men knew that Her Honor, Judge Vallance, although seductively clad and exuding sensuality, was ever the lady. Any hopes they harbored that she might misbehave were ludicrous. She never had. She wouldn't this night.

Shelby, Noel, and Natalie reached the far side of the big, loud room. Directly before them, up three carpeted steps, sat the roulette table with its lone player. Natalie blinked, recognizing the seated man with golden jetons stacked before him.

The wide shoulders in the ebony velvet coat. The wavy raven hair. The lean brown hand holding a thin, dark cheroot.

"Uncle Shelby . . ." she began nervously.

"Shhh, honey," he silenced her, his gray gaze resting on the player. He waited with the others, watching, until the little white ball, madly whirring around the varnished roulette wheel, came to rest in the number eight slot. Whistles and cheers went up from the spectators, although the seated man made not a sound.

Languidly, the winner pulled tall stacks of gold jetons toward him. Only then did Shelby Sutton, grinning widely, shaking his silver head in joyous disbelief, urge both women up the carpeted steps. And Natalie felt her heart stop beating when her uncle said in a voice loud enough to be heard above the din, "Captain Covington, tenn-*hut!*"

The brown raking hands slowed and paused. The well-shaped dark head snapped up. The wide, velvet-draped shoulders straightened. With astounding grace and speed Kane was up out of his chair and pivoting. His unblinking blue gaze went at once to the beaming face of the silver-haired man standing below him.

"Colonel Shelby Sutton!" drawled Kane warmly, his lean hand snapping off a crisp military salute.

Chapter Twenty

Natalie could not believe it.

It could not be true! A case of mistaken identity, that's what it was. These two men couldn't possibly know each other.

Natalie blinked and shook her head incredulously. Hand clamped firmly on Kane's right shoulder, Shelby Sutton turned quickly, his gray eyes dancing, and proclaimed happily, "Noel Salvato, Natalie Vallance, I want you to meet a very dear friend!"

Kane nodded politely to the singer, spoke her name, then let his blue gaze settle on Natalie. Looking directly into her horrified green eyes, he said in a low, even voice, "Judge Vallance, how nice to see you this evening."

"You two know each other?" Shelby asked ecstatically.

"Know each other?" Natalie's tone was deceptively calm. "Why, we're neighbors, aren't we, Mr. Covington?" She smiled then, and only Kane read the icy contempt in that smile.

"Will wonders never cease!" exclaimed Shelby. "I had no idea. Let's get a private salon and visit, and—wait—wait, Kane, you finished playing?"

"Yes, Colonel Shelby."

Shelby glanced over his shoulder at the tall stacks of shiny golden jetons. His smiling mouth stretched wider. "Win much, Captain?"

Kane grinned at Shelby. "Ten thousand."

Shelby Sutton laughed merrily. "This is your lucky night, Captain Covington!"

"It seems to be," said Kane, nodding to the croupier to collect and hold his winnings, while Natalie silently ground her teeth.

Ten thousand, she thought desperately. Dear Lord, he can last for months on ten thousand.

". . . . and we'll order up some champagne," Shelby Sutton was saying, and the next thing Natalie knew, the foursome was ensconced inside an intimate, tastefully decorated second-floor salon. Shelby and Noel sat side by side on a peach brocade sofa, facing her across a marble-topped table on which a white-coated waiter deposited a silver bucket, a magnum of champagne chilling in its icy depths.

Natalie sat on an identical sofa. Beside her was Kane Covington, looking strikingly handsome in a finely cut dinner jacket of soft, ebony velvet, snug black trousers, white shirt, and black silk tie. He exuded the insufferable self-confidence that was, to him, second nature. The sprawling, relaxed posture of his long, lean body seemed to emphasize the insolent demeanor that most females found irresistible. Natalie found it irritating.

Was the man never ill at ease?

Gratefully, Natalie accepted the glass of champagne Kane handed her. She listened distractedly as her uncle spoke of the days the two men spent together in the war. It was clear that Shelby Sutton was genuinely fond of the younger man and that Kane looked up to her uncle more than she would have thought him capable of respecting any man. Or woman.

Shelby didn't so much as blink an eyelash when Kane coolly told him how he'd come to be living in Cloudcastle, Colorado Territory. And Kane was not at all hesitant in speaking of his deed to Promontory Point, remarking casually that he intended to live on his land. If Uncle Shelby was shocked or outraged, he didn't show it. He was grinning and nodding his gleaming silver head, while his long arm moved about the blond singer, drawing her close. Noel Salvato talked animatedly with both men, obviously charmed and having a grand time.

Natalie wanted to have a good time as well. She didn't want anything, or anyone, spoiling this beautiful wintry evening. Forcing her dislike of Kane into the background, she sipped her champagne and let the bubbly wine continue to warm and relax her. She caught herself laughing responsively at something amusing Kane said.

"I've an excellent idea," stated Shelby Sutton shortly. "The four of us will ride up to Cloud West and finish our celebration." He squeezed Noel's bare shoulders. "I'm famished, aren't you, Kane?"

Natalie's gaze happened to be on Kane's face. "Ah . . . you're very kind, Colonel, but I must decline."

"Nonsense, Captain." Shelby shot to his feet. "We won't let you decline. It's been how long—three, four years?—since last we met. You're coming to Cloud West, Captain Covington. That's an order!"

Natalie would have sworn she saw a flicker of unease in Kane's blue eyes before he graciously accepted. "By your leave, Colonel."

Outside, the tall, coatless Kane fell into step beside Natalie, gallantly taking her arm when they stepped down into the icy street. Shelby Sutton and his pretty companion followed closely, Shelby bending down to hear what the blond singer was whispering.

Parked before the now darkened opera house, the Blackmore carriage waited, old William dozing atop the box. Kane handed Natalie into the coach's warm interior and followed, stepping past to take a seat beside her.

The other couple reached the big carriage, stopped, and stood framed in the open door. Pretty, blond Noel Salvato was laughing gaily, as though she knew a delightful secret. Shelby grinned down at her, leaned inside and said with a sly smile, "We'll see you in an hour at Cloud West. Noel has a carriage and driver at her disposal, provided by the opera company. We'll ride up in it." He lifted a hand and tipped the brim of his silk topper, purposely ignoring Kane's and Natalie's protests. Shelby grinned wickedly, closed the carriage door, and stepped back, arm encircling Noel Salvato.

Old William clicked his tongue to the matched blacks and the polished carriage rolled away while two laughing people stood in the street, waving their good-byes. Neither noticed a tall, thin man standing in the shadows outside Gaiety's. But he noticed them.

His cold-eyed gaze rested on the pair for only a second, then went once again to the black carriage rapidly receding in the distance. He watched until it disappeared. He had been watching from the moment Kane Covington had followed Natalie Vallance across the big gambling hall, placed her long cape around her shoulders, and ushered her out into the cold, moonlit night. He had watched the dark man guide the slender beauty across the slippery street, his hand holding her possessively, as though he owned her. And he had watched when the pair stepped into the Blackmore coach.

Burl Leatherwood turned and walked away.

Dead certain that Kane would seize this opportunity to tease and torment her, Natalie pulled her fur-lined cape protectively around her. Alone with the disturbing man, she became, for the first time all evening, acutely aware of her nudity beneath the velvet gown.

Keeping her long, slender legs tightly crossed, she cast an indifferent glance at Kane, fully expecting to see him leaning threateningly close, a leering, lascivious smile on his hard, handsome face.

Ever the enigma, Kane stared moodily straight ahead, mute and unsmiling. Sitting with his lean fingers clutching his bent knees, he looked for all the world as though he were the nervous, endangered prey, rather than the brash, menacing predator.

Natalie frowned and pondered this strange turn of events. What was his game now? Why was he ignoring her when, for the next hour, he literally had her captive inside this darkened, moving coach.

Studying the quiet, dark man from beneath her lowered lashes, Natalie momentarily solved the puzzle. She knew why Kane was distant, unreachable, so little-boy-shy all of a sudden. Natalie surmised that this dark, sullen southerner had his own strange set of values. While he had no qualms about seducing the fiancée of an acquaintance, Lord Blackmore, he drew the line at making love to the niece of a fellow officer, Colonel Shelby Sutton.

Natalie began to smile. Her fun was not over after all.

Lifting her silk-gloved fingers to her throat, Natalie unfastened the braided clasp holding together her long, fur-lined cape. "Would you give me a hand, Kane?" she asked, softly.

His dark head turned toward her and he stared in bafflement. "It's freezing cold," he told her, "surely you don't mean to—"

"Yes. I do," she assured him, opening her wrap. "I'm warm. Much too warm."

She could hardly keep from laughing when he reluctantly eased the cape off her shoulders. A muscle jumped in his hard jaw when she turned a little in the seat, lifting her body up, motioning him to pull the voluminous wrap from under her.

Eyes quickly averting from the generous expanse of bare bosom before him, Kane swore under his breath and snatched the cape free, holding it awkwardly on his lap.

Natalie's laughter tinkled in his ears. "Kane, toss my wrap across to the other seat. You needn't hold it all the way to Cloud West."

Kane didn't look at her. He carefully folded the luxurious cape and placed it on the empty seat. His dark head swung around swiftly when Natalie placed a warm hand on his arm. "You're going to freeze to death," Kane bit out, brooding blue eyes holding hers.

"Not if you keep me warm." She smiled seductively and tightened her grip on his arm.

Kane moved her hand away, looking confused and annoyed. His eyes strayed back to her ivory shoulders, her full bosom, and he swallowed hard. "Don't flirt with me, Judge. It's not becoming. It's boring."

"Boring?" she said with a smile. "Why, Kane, I can't believe that." Ignoring the dark scowl on his harshly planed face, she moved closer to him and ran her forefinger up the black velvet sleeve covering his right arm. "I don't believe I bore you, Kane." Her fingers slid over to his satin lapel. "I think I frighten you."

Kane brushed her hand away. "Behave yourself, damn it."

Unperturbed, Natalie smiled naughtily and leaned close to his ear, whispering in an exaggerated southern drawl, "Why, Cap'n, honey. Hush my mouth! I can't believe you'd speak like that befo' a lady."

"You're not acting like a lady."

"No?" she said, smiling prettily, "Well, Cap'n, I didn't figure you wanted some simperin' southern belle who might come down with an attack of the vapors if a man so much as kissed her. No, sir, I know you like—"

"Stop it, Judge, or I'll—"

"You'll what, Cap'n?" Natalie laughingly interrupted. "Turn me over your knee? Tell my uncle on me?"

Kane was angry. His eyes were hard, flinty. Lean jaw set. He was madder still when Natalie teasingly accused, "You're afraid of me, Cap'n. You want me and that scares you."

Kane felt his muscles tighten. "No, Your Honor, I don't want you." His eyes, meeting hers, were wintry.

"You do," she whispered huskily, "you want me, Kane. I know you want me."

"No," he repeated harshly, "I don't."

Natalie ignored the statement. Lifting a gloved hand to the perfect knot of his black silk tie, she said, "You do, and I'll prove it."

Kane's long fingers swiftly closed over hers, stopping her, his grip so firm, she felt that the fragile bones in her hand might shatter. "What the hell do you want?" he asked coldly.

Natalie gazed into his angry eyes and said softly, "I want you to release my hand and relax for a moment. If you are not afraid, you'll do it."

Kane's fingers loosened and fell away. "I don't want you, Judge." His tone was flat and determined.

"I know," she responded, and turned more fully to him. Kane sat stiffly, allowing her to undo his tie. That accomplished, Natalie deftly unfastened the top button of his crisp white shirt and heard his quick intake of air. Still he did not move. Silk-clad hands amazingly dexterous, Natalie hastily drew four more buttons through their buttonholes and Kane's immaculate shirt fell open to his waist.

She pushed the shirt apart and let her emerald eyes drift down to the dark, muscular chest with its mat of black hair. She licked her bottom lip provocatively and slowly lifted her eyes to Kane's. His were unreadable. Coolly he said, "That about do it, Mrs. Vallance? You've half undressed me. Are you satisfied now?" A cruel, cold smile curled his full top lip.

"No, Cap'n," Natalie told him, "not quite."

With a bravado made possible by the champagne she'd consumed and the sure knowledge that the niece of Colonel Shelby Sutton was as safe as an infant with Captain Covington, Natalie lifted her hand to the soft velvet covering her full bosom. Purposely waiting until Kane's eyes had followed that hand, she let her fingers slowly, seductively move to her left breast. They touched, they slid, they moved over and directly beneath, while Kane's rapt gaze followed.

Transfixed, he watched as that small, silk-clad hand glided up over the straining velvet and went to the buckle on top of her shoulder. Hooking a thumb beneath the buckle, Natalie teasingly pushed it down over her shoulder and released it. The turquoise velvet bodice remained in place, but Natalie's left shoulder was totally bare. And when she drew a deep, long breath, the lush velvet slipped lower still.

Natalie loved the tortured expression that crossed Kane's dark face. Swiftly he lifted his eyes to hers. Natalie smiled and slowly leaned toward him.

"Let your heart beat against mine, then tell me you don't want me," she said triumphantly.

She pressed her torso to his bare chest and heard Kane's deep, shuddering groan. At once she felt the sexual danger of her foolish game. She trembled, reading the look in his beautiful blue eyes. Steaming anger had changed to steaming desire, and she was afraid.

Quickly using her hands to lever herself from his chest, Natalie said apologetically, fearfully, "Kane, I shouldn't have—"

But her sentence was never finished. Kane's hot, hungry mouth swallowed the words as his shaking arms crushed her to him. Natalie could feel his heavy heartbeat thundering with her own and knew in that instant that she was lost.

His lips and tongue were sweetly plundering her mouth and Natalie had neither the strength nor the inclination to stop him. No one had kissed her the way Kane kissed her and she gloried in the pleasure of it. His kiss was at once abandoned and ravenous, yet tender and lingering. Eager and demanding, yet languid and solicitous. Brutal and lustful, yet gentle and affectionate.

His full, smooth lips molded to her own, his tongue did wild, wonderful things to the sensitive inside of her mouth, his sharp white teeth nibbled and raked, biting her playfully, and by the time that first consuming kiss ended and Kane lifted his dark head, Natalie, murmured hopelessly, "We can't, Kane. Let me go, let me up."

At sometime during that long, deep kiss, Kane had completely turned her about and pulled her across his knees. Now she half sat, half reclined against him, her shoulders supported by his encircling arm. Lips nuzzling her ear, Kane murmured heavily, "No, I'll not let you go. Witch, beautiful, tempting witch. Yes, I want you. I must have you or die."

He pulled back a little to peer down at her. Natalie looked up into those passion-heated blue eyes and felt totally powerless against the intense sexuality of this man. She whimpered softly, but made no earnest effort to stop him when Kane unbuckled the velvet buckle on top of her left shoulder. She held her breath as the lined-velvet bodice fell away and her bare, trembling breast spilled out. Kane lowered his dark head, placed a closed-mouth kiss on the bloom of her nipple, then straightened. Urging her body next to his own, his

Thrill to the most sensual, adventure-filled Romances on the market today...

FROM 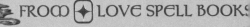 LOVE SPELL BOOKS

As a home subscriber to the Love Spell Romance Book Club, you'll enjoy the best in today's BRAND-NEW Time Travel, Futuristic, Legendary Lovers, Perfect Heroes and other genre romance fiction. For five years, Love Spell has brought you the award-winning, high-quality authors you know and love to read. Each Love Spell romance will sweep you away to a world of high adventure...and intimate romance. Discover for yourself all the passion and excitement millions of readers thrill to each and every month.

Save $5.00 Each Time You Buy!

Every other month, the Love Spell Romance Book Club brings you four brand-new titles from Love Spell Books. EACH PACKAGE WILL SAVE YOU AT LEAST $5.00 FROM THE BOOK-STORE PRICE! And you'll never miss a new title with our convenient home delivery service.

Here's how we do it: Each package will carry a FREE 10-DAY EXAMINATION privilege. At the end of that time, if you decide to keep your books, simply pay the low invoice price of $17.96, no shipping or handling charges added. HOME DELIVERY IS ALWAYS FREE. With today's top romance novels selling for $5.99 and higher, our price SAVES YOU AT LEAST $5.00 with each shipment.

AND YOUR FIRST TWO-BOOK SHIP-MENT IS TOTALLY FREE!

IT'S A BARGAIN YOU CAN'T BEAT! A SUPER $11.48 Value!

Love Spell ◆ A Division of Dorchester Publishing Co., Inc.

Get Two Books Totally
FREE —
An $11.48 Value!

▼ Tear Here and Mail Your FREE Book Card Today! ▼

PLEASE RUSH
MY TWO FREE
BOOKS TO ME
RIGHT AWAY!

Love Spell Romance Book Club
P.O. Box 6613
Edison, NJ 08818-6613

AFFIX
STAMP
HERE

mouth came back to hers. Pausing, lips hovering so close to her own that she could feel his breath, he told her hoarsely, "And I'll have you right here, right now."

His mouth took hers then and Natalie felt her bared nipple, and the one still draped in velvet, tighten into pebble-hard points of aching pleasure. The crisp, thick hair on Kane's warm, muscular chest rubbed against her bare nipple and Natalie instinctively pressed closer to him, her heart thrumming a wild out-of-control rhythm.

At last Kane's lips left hers and Natalie, a part of her wine-drugged brain still capable of logical thought, once more tried to collect herself and bring to an end this frivolous sport so rapidly escalating out of control. She clutched feebly at her loosened bodice and struggled to move from Kane's grasp.

Anger mixed with his passion and Kane jerked her back, depositing her on his lap. "No, Judge, I'll not let you go." His voice sounded deadly. "Come to me."

Strong fingers cupped the back of her head and he forced her mouth once more to his. Natalie tried to turn her head, but the effort was futile. His lips held hers prisoner and she could not move, even though her gloved hands pushed violently against his bare, warm chest.

While he kissed her, Kane's free hand moved beneath her twisted velvet skirts and Natalie made a little strangled pleading sound deep in her throat. Kane ignored it. He continued to drink from her lips while his exploring hand moved up a silk-stockinged leg. Natalie squirmed and struggled and remembered, almost hysterically, that she was naked beneath the gown. There was no protective barrier to keep him from her.

Soon Kane knew it too.

A warm, determined hand moved above the silky stocking and satin garter, and encountered bare skin. His mouth released Natalie's instantly and his eyes flew to the exposed flesh before him.

Ashamed and afraid, Natalie said brokenly, "Please . . . Kane . . ." And her damp forehead fell against his cheek.

Enthralled, Kane pulled the lush velvet skirt higher and

the heart inside his chest doubled its fierce beating. The long, luscious legs, the bare moonbathed thighs, and the blazing auburn curls between them caused Kane to groan, "Jesus. Baby, baby."

Feeling as though she might perish from shame and from passion, Natalie squeezed her eyes shut and murmured, "You must think—"

"Hush," rasped Kane, toying for an instant with a shiny satin garter before seeking that tempting red-gold triangle between her pale thighs.

Natalie's body spasmed slightly when his lean fingers raked through the tight curls and moved downward. And she knew she didn't want him to stop. She wanted him to touch her there; her body was begging for it, craving it, and she didn't care if it was right or wrong, foolish or wise.

"Yes, Kane," she breathed, and kissed his throat. "Oh, yes."

"Sit up and part your legs a little, baby," whispered Kane raggedly. Sighing softly, Natalie shivered and obeyed. Kane's fingers sought out and found that damp, throbbing nubbin of flesh protected by the dense curls. "Unbuckle the other shoulder of your dress," he commanded huskily. Willingly she did so, pushing the garment down to her waist. Her bare, swelling breasts were near his dark face, and Kane, his fingers caressing her between her legs, leaned his head back on the tall leather seat and urged her to him.

Natalie's green eyes closed in ecstasy when his warm lips enclosed her throbbing right nipple. He took only a brief second to tease at it with his tongue, licking, circling, painting, before he drew hungrily upon it, sucking eagerly, anxiously.

Purring deep in her throat, Natalie's silk-gloved fingers ran through the dark hair at the sides of his head to draw him closer, closer even as she arched her slender back, instinctively pushing her breast against his hot, loving mouth.

Kane drew on the taut, sweet nipples. He felt he would never get enough, so delicious was the taste of her, so drugging the texture of her bare, soft breasts against his hot face.

And between her legs . . . that slick, hot satin flesh responded so erotically to his eager hand. He wanted never to be free of it. He'd keep her naked and throbbing forever, his hand, and his alone, stroking, exciting, possessing her.

When both Natalie's breasts were pink and glowing from his kisses and Kane's brown fingers were wet from her surging passion, Kane picked her up and laid her upon the opposite seat. He came to her then, his clothed body moving swiftly over hers, his hand between them to release his aching, horizontal-thrusting masculinity.

Natalie felt it throb against her bare belly and almost sobbed from wanting. Kane kissed her deeply and said into her mouth, "Do you want me?"

"Yes."

"Then, take me. Take all of me, baby."

Natalie let out a strange little half sob and lowered her hand. Fingers closing around the naked rigid flesh, she guided him easily into her waiting warmth, emerald eyes sliding closed in rapture.

With the glorious melding of his flesh into hers, they murmured unintelligible words of passion while they moved eagerly and primitively, his thrusts deep and rapid, her response wild and abandoned. So aroused was she when he came into her, Natalie felt her climax beginning almost at once. Her eyes flew open in distressed apology. Kane's smoldering eyes were looking down at her and he whispered huskily, because he could feel what was happening to her, "Yes, baby, yes. It's okay. Let it come."

And she did.

Wave after wave of shuddering pleasure washed over her and she clung to his velvet-clad shoulders and tossed her head and bucked up against him and felt his silencing mouth come down on hers when her release became too vocal. And in that kiss, Kane's own release began and heightened Natalie's to near-hysterical splendor. He thrust deeply, rapidly with his hard, exploding body while his tongue thrust deeply, rapidly in cadence with the other.

And then they were over the top and into that brilliant

nirvana meant only for passionate, uninhibited lovers. They clung to each other desperately until rapture subsided, and, totally sated, they lay exhausted, their mingled breath vaporing in the cold, moon-splashed carriage.

But reality soon came rushing back to engulf them.

Passion slaked, hunger fed, each found it suddenly unbelievable—and unforgivable—that this had been allowed to happen. Broad, bare chest still heaving, Kane levered himself off Natalie, adjusting his clothes as he did so.

He moved at once to the seat across from her as Natalie sat up blushing and hurriedly lowered her gown to hide her naked belly and thighs. She struggled with the velvet shoulder buckles, pulling frantically at the bodice of her gown. And as she struggled, she felt an almost uncontrollable anger at Kane as he sat across from her, lolling lazily, quietly observing, not offering to help. The more she struggled, the angrier she became.

Kane's hooded eyes never left her, and while he sat coolly watching her labor to cover herself, a frown on her beautiful face, one breast still bare and shimmering in the moonlight, he felt his disgust and anger swiftly rising.

They were both angry. Thoroughly, unreasonably angry. Angry with themselves. But being human, they took it out on each other. Natalie was the first to speak. Finally managing to get her gown back together, she jerked her cape around her shoulders and said hatefully, "Thanks for all your help!"

Kane snorted. "A shame you're not as adept at dressing as you are at undressing."

"I beg your pardon," she said furiously. "It was you who—"

"Tell me, Judge, do you always go about naked? Is it so you'll be able to take on a man without bothering to—"

"Stop it! I don't go around naked. This gown makes it—"

"—damned easy for you to behave the harlot."

"Who are you calling a harlot, you bastard!"

"Would you prefer tart?" he said coldly. "Tell me, Judge, how many times have you brought your blond knight to ecstasy in this carriage? Does Lord Blackmore like to make love in here? How do you go about it? Seated? Lying down, or—"

"You name a position, Covington," Natalie cut in, stung by his cruel words, frantic to hurt him in return. "Ashlin is very innovative. We experiment every time we ride in the carriage." She laughed then, a low, throaty laugh, as though recalling something amusingly naughty. "I'll never forget the time we—"

"Shut up!" Kane roared. "God damn it, shut up!"

Natalie blinked her eyelashes and said innocently, "Why, Kane, I thought you wanted to hear about it. I'll be glad to relate all the delicious details of our amorous escapades."

Kane leaned forward menacingly and said in a voice tinged with cold steel, "I don't care where or when or with whom you spread your legs, Judge Vallance, as long as it's never again with me."

Natalie leaned forward to meet him and, looking straight into his stormy eyes, drawled cruelly, "Why, Cap'n Covington, you mean you didn't enjoy makin' love to Colonel Shelby's only niece in the back of her fiancé's carriage?"

Chapter Twenty-one

Natalie awoke with a start. Through her bedroom door came a deep, familiar voice with a hint of a Texas twang.

"Wake up, lazybones," called Shelby Sutton, knocking briskly. "Rise and shine. If you're not downstairs in five minutes, I'll be back for you." Deep, chuckling laughter followed, then the sound of his booted feet descending the stairs.

Natalie wished she never had to get out of bed. Never had to go down the stairs. She was tired, so tired. Her eyes were scratchy and her head ached ferociously. And her heart ached too.

Natalie had lain awake until the first gray smudge tinged the eastern horizon. It had been a long, agonizing night of self-reproach and soul-searching. She was confused and upset; little was clear save two things. She hated Kane Covington now more than ever. And she could not marry Ashlin Blackmore.

Natalie pushed the cascading auburn curls off her pale face and sat up. She would wait until Uncle Shelby left town, then, as gently as possible, she would tell Ashlin she could never be his wife.

Natalie had faced some hard facts during the long, sleepless night. She had admitted to herself that she was not and had never been in love with Ashlin Blackmore. A woman in love with one man did not make love to another.

Ashlin was a kind, charming man and she was fond of him. He had come into her life at precisely the appropriate moment. For years she had been forced to use her will alone to determine the course of her life. Weary of the constant loneliness, starved for the company of an intelligent, cultured man, longing to have children, she had easily convinced herself the relationship with Ashlin was one that would grow into a deep and abiding love. But it had not happened.

Her feelings for Kane Covington were just as clear. She hated him more than ever. He was a callous southern bastard with a heart of stone. A dangerous devil who possessed the power to bewitch her. One heated kiss and her bones had turned to jelly, her body had dissolved into his. And afterward, he'd called her a harlot!

After dressing in a colorless day-dress of drab gray wool, Natalie tiredly went downstairs. She would say nothing to Uncle Shelby of her decision not to marry Ashlin. He would be in Cloudcastle for only a short visit, and it had been so long since he had been here. She'd not spoil their time together. She would pretend all was right with her world. Then, after his departure, she would go at once to Ashlin and tell him of her decision.

As for Kane Covington, she'd never, of course, speak of the tawdry tryst they had shared, but she would not hesitate to tell her uncle just what she thought of the miserable Mississippian!

"There she is!" exclaimed her beaming uncle when Natalie stepped into the dining room. Swiftly he rose and planted a kiss on her cheek.

" 'Morning, Uncle Shelby." She tried to sound untroubled.

"My God, child." Her uncle's alert, gray eyes were on her pale face. "What is it? You look terrible."

Natalie smiled weakly and took the chair he pulled out. "A bit too much champagne, I believe."

Her uncle reclaimed his chair and quickly poured her a cup of steaming black coffee. "It's my fault. I should have insisted you eat your dinner at the Eureka last evening." He shook his head. "Then when we came back here, why . . . neither you nor Kane ate a bite."

Natalie took a sip of the dark brew, placed the thin porcelain cup back in its saucer, and said, "Uncle Shelby, I'm thirty years old. You're hardly to blame for my not eating properly. Or drinking too much champagne." Or, she added silently, for making love to your unprincipled friend in the back of Ashlin's carriage.

"Honey, you'll always be a child to me, don't you know that?" He gazed at her fondly and she could see the worry in his warm gray eyes. "You look so peaked, so drawn."

"Uncle Shelby, you actually approve of Kane Covington?" She hadn't meant to blurt out the question.

"Nat, I think a lot of the boy. I sure do."

"He stole my land!"

Shelby passed her a platter of crisply fried bacon. She shook her head no. He set it back on the table and said evenly, "Natalie, Kane stole nothing. He won that land, fair and square."

"You too?"

"Me too what, honey?"

"You're taking his side against me. How could you? Can't anyone see that the man is . . . is . . ." Natalie saw the puzzled expression in her uncle's gray eyes, and stopped speaking.

"Natalie, I would never take anyone's side against you on anything. Surely you believe that."

Contrite, Natalie reached out and patted her uncle's strong, bronzed hand. "I know. I'm sorry." She made an effort to smile.

"That's better," said Shelby. "Darlin', that land up on Promontory Point, the acreage Kane won, is worthless. Besides, I know Kane, he'll be gone by spring. He's a wanderer, a vagabond. He never stays in one place very long."

Natalie sighed wearily. "I hope you're right. Uncle Shelby, your fondness for the man truly puzzles me. You two are such opposites. You're kind and caring and brave, while Kane is hard and heartless and a coward."

"Coward?" Shelby's silver eyebrows shot up incredulously. "Kane Covington a coward?"

"Yes, he's cowardly. He let the town bully scare him out of the Gilded Cage Saloon. Everybody in Cloudcastle laughs about it."

Shelby Sutton laughed himself. "Do they, now?" He opened the gleaming silver biscuit box, took out a light, fluffy biscuit, and laid it on Natalie's plate, urging her to butter it. "I'll wager they do their laughing when Kane's not around, don't they?"

"I don't know . . . I . . . well, yes, but—"

"Natalie, if Kane Covington let a man run him out of a saloon, it was not because of fear. It was because he didn't care enough to fight. Kane doesn't care about much of anything anymore, but I assure you, he's no coward. I fought by his side in the war, remember?"

Seeing how passionate her uncle felt on the subject, Natalie shrugged slender shoulders and let it drop. But she found herself continuing to question him, as casually as possible, about Kane.

"So you two served together in the war? Were you stationed at the same place?"

Relieved to see her mood softening, Shelby bobbed his silver head up and down. "Bravest damned soldier ever under my command."

"Really?" she murmured, lifting her coffee cup.

With little prompting, Shelby Sutton spoke, with great affection and admiration, of Kane Covington. And Natalie caught herself leaning forward with interest, hanging on to every word, intensely absorbed in the revelations.

Shelby told her that Kane Covington was a wealthy southern aristocrat whose happy youth had been spent at his family's Mississippi coastal plantation on the Gulf of Mexico. Educated at Harvard, Kane had read for the bar before reaching his twenty-second birthday. Not a year later, the

War Between the States broke out and Kane, heir to vast land holdings and hundreds of slaves, valiantly volunteered.

"Kane was under my command in the early days of the war," mused Shelby, "and from the beginning I was impressed with the mannerly Mississippian. He was smart, industrious, and always cheerful, a truly remarkable young man. And when we went into battle . . . well, Kane was all a commanding officer could hope for in a soldier.

"He was sharp and daring, and closely escaped death more than once." Shelby suddenly stuck a long arm behind him and with a forefinger stabbed at his spine. "Kane has three deep scars that go all the way across his back. Got them from a mounted Yankee's saber slashing him down on a hot August day in Virginia. Kane's horse had been shot from under him and his musket was empty of ammunition."

Natalie hoped her face was not flushing. She knew, all too well, of the ribbon-white scars that marred Kane's back. "Was Kane discharged then? Did he return to Mississippi?" Natalie prodded.

"No, honey. He lay in the field hospital near death for several days, not making a sound though we had run out of supplies and the doctors had nothing to ease his pain. I'd go by and see him and give him an awkward pat and say, 'Don't let go, son. Hold on, hold on,' and Kane would smile bravely and say, 'Don't worry, sir, I'm going to live, I have to live for my sweet Susannah.' "

Shelby fell silent and Natalie realized she was practically holding her breath.

"Go on," she prompted, refusing to ask who Susannah was, but hoping he would reveal it.

"Kane did live, of course," said Shelby Sutton, "and went on to become a decorated officer. He was taken from my command the next year and sent to Tennessee; still, we kept in touch. He was wounded twice more and awarded medals for bravery. When the war finally ended, it had been more than two years since he'd last seen his Mississippi home." Shelby sadly shook his silver head. "He had nothing to go back to. Kane's daddy, also a Confederate officer, died at the bloody battle of Shiloh. His mother and baby sister, fleeing the Yankees, took refuge in a small Alabama town, caught the yellow fever, and died in the sweltering summer of sixty-three. The big plantation on the Mississippi coast was occupied by Federal troops and when they no longer had a use for it, they burned it to the ground."

"No!" Natalie was horrified.

"They did," said Shelby. "Destroyed a thirty-room mansion that had been standing for fifty years on the peaceful shores of the Gulf. A shame, a damned shame."

"It is," admitted Natalie.

"Kane didn't stay long in Mississippi. After the war he took to drifting . . . wandered all around the country, not caring much where he went or what he did. He punched cows on a big ranch in West Texas for a while; he went to Europe and lived for a time in a castle with a rich widowed duchess. Kane soon tired of her, came home and gambled on the riverboats one summer, then . . . hell, he even lived among the Comanches for a year."

"He lived with the Indians? Did he take a squaw?" The words were out of her mouth before she thought.

Shelby laughed at the wide-eyed expression on her pale face. "No, a squaw took him. I ran into Kane once back in those days in a Texas saloon. He insisted I ride with him up to the Comanche camp in Palo Duro Canyon. He assured me my scalp was safe long as I was with him, so I accepted the invitation." Shelby's face broke into a wide grin. "The prettiest little dark-eyed gal you ever saw was living with Kane, and I could see she fairly worshiped him."

Frowning, Natalie said, "But what about . . . ah . . . Susannah, was it?"

"I didn't tell you about her?"

"You mentioned her name, but you didn't say what became of her. I assume he tired of her and set her back on the shelf."

"Hardly." Shelby's smile fled. "Kane was deeply in love with Susannah. She was the daughter of a fellow Mississippi planter and Kane had known her since the day she was born.

Susannah Hamilton was tiny, dark-eyed, dark-haired, and beautiful, but several years younger than Kane. Kane promised her daddy they would wait to marry until Susannah turned eighteen. The war got in the way. Susannah was sixteen when Kane left; he had just turned twenty-three. He carried a small ambrotype of her beneath his uniform blouse, next to his heart. He used to take it out and study it fondly. He'd proudly show it to the other men and I couldn't blame him. She was just as pretty as an angel. Kane said she was as sweet as she was pretty."

"Then I don't understand. Why didn't he—"

"I'm coming to that. While Kane was away, the Yankees occupied the Hamilton mansion. The Hamiltons didn't move out; they remained in their quarters and . . . well, it seems Kane's little Susannah was not quite as sweet as he'd thought. Within weeks the pretty child Kane loved was . . . hmmm . . . sharing her girlish charms with a Federal officer."

Natalie was astonished. "But how did Kane find out? I mean . . ." Her words trailed away.

"The Federal officer was to be only the first in a long line. Eventually Susannah went north with a middle-aged naval captain whose family had vast real estate holdings and prosperous banking interests in Illinois. The bride dropped Kane a short letter saying she was dreadfully sorry, but she could not 'bear the thought of being poor.' "

"That's terrible," Natalie said, stunned. "Why, he must have . . . Kane surely—"

"Suffered. Kane suffered. He loved that little girl and thought she loved him. It changed him, I'll tell you that."

"Yes . . ." she mused. "I would imagine he doesn't much like women."

Shelby grinned suddenly and the sparkle crept back into his expressive gray eyes. "Kane? Why, he's crazy about women."

"I don't see how he could—"

"Honey, there's a big difference between liking women and respecting them. To Kane, women are merely a source of amusement . . . physical pleasure. One is pretty much like the next to Kane, long as she's good-looking and likes to—" Shelby cleared his throat. "He has no problem replacing one female with another and does so often."

"I'm sure he does," snapped Natalie.

"I'm afraid the boy will never again fall in love," offered Shelby thoughtfully. "The girl he believed to be every inch the lady turned out to be a mercenary little tramp. Since then, well, Kane's had lots of women . . . too many, and every last one of them fall right into bed with him the moment he snaps his fingers." Shelby scratched his chin and added, "Is it any wonder his opinion of the fair sex is less than it should be?" He brightened once more and stated, "I believe if Kane Covington could just once meet a female that behaved like a lady, he'd be smitten!"

Later on that same day, a tall, thin man quietly stole through the frozen, terraced backyard behind the hilltop Blackmore mansion shortly after dusk. Hurriedly climbing the steps to the rear verandah, the man knocked lightly upon the door and turned his back against the bitter, chilling winds swirling under the eaves of the house.

Old William opened the door, peering questioningly up at the chilled, light-haired man standing on the porch. Recognizing the caller, he stepped back, almost cowering, as the man swept past him and said, "Tell your master I'm here. I'll be in the study." He took off his worn coat and shoved it at the old man.

"Yes, sir, Mr. Leatherwood." William backed away, anxious to leave the presence of this cold, threatening man. In moments the servant was back, and Burl Leatherwood, pouring his second glass of bourbon from a heavy leaded decanter, heard the little man say, "Lord Blackmore has a bad cold, sir, but if you feel you must see him this evening, you may go up."

Burl Leatherwood downed the whiskey without a grimace, handed William the empty glass and headed for the stairway.

Not bothering to knock, he went into Ashlin Blackmore's large bedchamber.

"What in God's name do you mean coming here?" Ashlin asked. He was propped up in bed glaring at the tall, pallid man.

"Relax, boss," said Burl Leatherwood, "no one saw me. I came down through foothills in back. The moon's not yet up."

Ashlin blew his nose. "I don't give a damn. I've told you before, you are never to come here, it's far too risky."

"Keep your gown on, Blackmore, I said no one saw me." Leatherwood pulled up a ladder-back chair, turned it about, and straddled it. "I thought you'd want to hear what happened last night."

"I'm sure I'm going to, so if you'll kindly say it and leave."

"The Rebel horned in on the judge's little party last night, boss."

"God damn it, spit it out. What the hell are you saying?"

"I am saying that I was in Gaiety's Gaming Hall and saw Judge Vallance, the judge's old gray-haired uncle, and that blond opera singer arrive. Your fiancée was wearing a revealing gown that left very little to the imagination. Every man in the place was panting by the time she crossed the floor." An evil light flickered in his light eyes. "And who do you suppose they bumped into? Covington."

"Go on."

"The cozy little foursome went upstairs to one of those private salons. Later, when they came back down and got their coats, I followed them outside. The uncle took the singer to the hotel or somewhere and the judge . . . she and Covington left town together in your carriage."

Before the last words were out of Burl Leatherwood's mouth, Ashlin Blackmore was shouting at the top of his lungs. "William! William, get up here at once!"

Trembling, the old servant stood, head bowed, while his master questioned him. "Where did you drive Mrs. Vallance and her companion? How long did it take for you to reach Cloud West? How long did you remain there?"

William had seen the dark side of Ashlin Blackmore's nature before. He had been with his master since Blackmore had been a youth and would remain with him until one of them died. He loved the spoiled Blackmore, despite the nobleman's shortcomings. He would have laid down his life for the earl, but on this cold night, he lied to him. Not by commission; but by omission.

If William's eyesight was not what it once had been, his hearing was perfect. And he had heard the unmistakable sounds of lovemaking inside the Blackmore coach the evening past. Too old to be shocked, too compassionate to judge, William had sat atop the box and silently told himself—and the handsome pair inside the carriage—that their secret was safe with him.

William knew and admired Judge Natalie Vallance. And he surmised that unless he was mightily mistaken, the brave and beautiful lady would set things right on her own. He hoped it was so. For her sake, not for his master's. Because William also knew—and would take with him to his grave—the tormenting knowledge of Ashlin Blackmore's shocking sexual secrets.

"I drove Mrs. Vallance and her escort directly to Cloud West, Sir. Less than ten minutes after we got there, her uncle and his companion arrived in another carriage."

"Did you see anything that might suggest improper behavior on the part of Natalie's escort?"

"Nothing, sir. Mrs. Vallance invited me inside when we reached Cloud West. I drank hot coffee at the table with Mr. Covington while Mrs. Vallance changed her clothes. When she came back down the stairs, her uncle and the singer were there. Will that be all, sir?"

"Yes, yes. Get out of here!" thundered Ashlin Blackmore. "And William, next time you drive my fiancée anywhere in my carriage, you are come to me the moment you get back and tell me who was with her."

"I didn't wish to disturb you, sir. It was late and you—"

"You've had all day today to tell me!"

"I didn't think it important, milord."

"All my possessions are important, old man. I catch you holding things back from me, you'll wish you had stayed in England!"

The servant scurried away and Ashlin turned his attention back to Burl Leatherwood. "We can't do anything now, not with the uncle in town, but soon as he's out of the way . . ."

Burl Leatherwood grinned. "Yes?"

Ashlin's brown eyes narrowed. "I want that Covington bastard taken care of once and for all. I need to get at that gold soon; I've borrowed all I can in Denver." His perfectly arched brows came together as he frowned thoughtfully. "We take care of him; I marry Natalie immediately and . . ." He paused, and as an afterthought said, "That Indian must be done away with as well; the old savage tries to poison Natalie's mind against me."

Burl Leatherwood, shaking his light head negatively, rose slowly from his chair. He stepped close to the bed. "Boss, you pay us, we'll be happy to kill Covington. But not the Indian."

"Leatherwood, you work for me! I give the orders here. I want Tahomah dead."

"You want him dead, you kill him."

Ashlin snorted derisively. "Are you afraid of an ignorant Ute chief?"

"I am," Burl Leatherwood admitted. "That old Indian sees things, knows things. He has a power."

"My God, you sound like my foolish fiancée," Ashlin ground out scornfully. "I'll pay you double what I give you to get rid of Covington."

"Not for any amount, boss."

"I'll kill him myself," stated Ashlin Blackmore, and blew his red nose on a soft linen handkerchief.

Chapter Twenty-two

On Sunday evening a pale but Byronically beautiful Lord Ashlin Blackmore assured one and all he was fully recovered from his nasty cold as he hosted a sunset buffet in his palatial mansion. The honored guest was, of course, Colonel Shelby Sutton.

An assortment of Cloudcastle's citizens gleefully attended the sumptuous affair. Nabobs and dandies, decked out in their finest, mingled with merchants and miners, cowhands and farmers. Paris-gowned wives of silver barons and professional men mingled freely with excited, simply clad rancher's daughters and miner's shy, mannerly wives. Powerful, aging matrons and lonely, respected widows braved the bitter cold to attend the important event.

Most had been to previous parties at the Blackmore mansion, so they knew to expect a grand time with plenty of good food. They were not disappointed. Inside the candle-lit dining room, on the long, linen-draped table, a feast fit for kings was laid out.

A pineapple-glazed ham, a brown, crisp roasted turkey, a tender, pink-centered roast of beef were expertly sliced with rapier-sharp carving knives and placed upon fine china dinner plates. There were partridges, mutton chops, and rainbow trout as well. Oyster pie and cold chicken. Spinach and cauliflower and carrots and string beans. Chicken salad, ham salad, potato salad. Mashed potatoes, baked potatoes, scalloped potatoes.

Jellies, custards, cakes, blancmange, sweetmeats. Pyramids of grapes and oranges and apples. Sugared almonds and glazed pecans.

Champagne and port and sherry. Kentucky bourbon and aged cognac for the gentlemen. Cherry, peach, and raspberry brandy for the ladies. A typical Blackmore buffet!

The tempting foods and fine wines were not, on this occasion, the foremost reason Cloudcastle's mixed gentry filled the Blackmore mansion. They had come to welcome back Colonel Shelby Sutton, the tall, silver-haired Texan all agreed had stayed away from Cloudcastle far too long.

From the first time Colonel Shelby had ridden into the little mountain town years before to spend a summer with his pretty young niece, Natalie Vallance, he had been taken instantly to their hearts. A gentle, understanding man with a flair for the dramatic, a talent for putting people at their ease, and a warm, witty sense of humor, his very presence insured any gathering's success.

Loved by men and women alike, Shelby, possessor of a remarkable memory, called everyone by their given names when they stepped up to shake his firm hand. And, often as not, he brought up some amusing anecdote from a long-forgotten conversation out of the past. Flattered and astonished, the charmed, happy guests would sweep on into the drawing room, lighthearted and pleased, feeling very special.

Natalie, wearing a pretty ivory wool frock with long sleeves and a high collar, stood between her uncle and Ashlin, greeting the many callers. She was grateful that Kane Covington had declined Ashlin's invitation to join in the festivities.

Kane had told her uncle, as well as Ashlin, that this particular Sunday was to be his moving day. His alpine cabin was completed.

So Natalie stood, the personification of primness, smiling, nodding, and feeling like the worst kind of hypocrite. Her tormented thoughts were never far from the absent man who aroused dark, shameful passions in her.

From this night forward, he would be living on Promontory Point. Less than three miles around the mountain from her home. Less than three thousand feet below the hallowed Cliff Palace.

A fierce alpine sun came out at midweek and burned away the misty fog. Wet, deep snows melted and rushing mountain streams, filled with bobbing ice blocks, flowed swiftly downhill. On a bright, vision-blinding day of unfiltered sunlight, Kane walked among the snow-laden pines surrounding his cabin. His breathing was labored and his buckskin shirt was unbuttoned.

Trekking steadily up and eastward, he traversed the high, craggy peaks of Promontory Point. Savoring the solitude, the sunny day, and the clear, crisp mountain air, Kane had tramped several miles when he caught a glimpse of something glinting in the strong sunlight. Sucking in deep, long breaths, he continued to climb, his curiosity piqued. He drew closer, paused, squinted. Again the object winked at him, and intrigued, Kane made his way up to the massive monolith looming against the clear blue sky.

With his intent gaze never leaving the mysterious twinkling, Kane rapidly covered the distance and soon stood before the towering boulder. He reached out, wrapped his fingers around what appeared to be an arrow, and yanked. Loosened from a deep crevice in the rock by raging mountain winds, the arrow came unlodged with only the slightest pressure.

Pulling it free, Kane stared, unbelieving. The arrow in his hand was no ordinary one. The exquisitely carved tip gleamed brilliantly in the Colorado sunshine and Kane's lips curved upward into a grin as his fingers caressed the cold, shiny yellow.

The arrow was tipped in gold.

Kane felt his heart speed delightfully. The arrow was very, very old. Chances were it had been wedged in the boulder for

many years. It could well have been there long before gold
fever had caused eager prospectors to swarm up into the
Shining Mountains.

Kane's smile broadened. The wood of the arrow was unmistakably native to the region and had undoubtedly been
taken from this very mountain. Had the gold come from here
as well?

Experiencing an almost childlike rush of hope and excitement, Kane broke off the weathered wood and studied once
more the gleaming gold tip before shoving the arrowhead
into the pocket of his buckskin trousers. Whistling happily,
he continued exploring the rugged mountain he owned.

Shortly after noon, he discovered a dark, deep cave. It was
on the frozen east side of Promontory Point, and the thick,
hard ice that coated the fissure's walls never melted. And
Kane wondered, might there be gold beneath the covering
ice?

He spent an hour methodically chiseling at the ice just
beyond the cave's mouth. Perspiring from the strenuous exertion, Kane paused to remove his buckskin shirt. Tossing it
carelessly aside, he eagerly returned to his task.

Winded, arm and back muscles aching, he stopped an hour
later to smoke. Rolling the cigarette with deft fingers, Kane
made his way outside into the warm sunshine. Leaning lazily
against a tall, slanted boulder, he was cupping his hands to
light his smoke when he heard the snort of a horse. His eyes
slowly lifted to see three mounted Indians on a small, snow-
covered rise above. Their dark, flat eyes were studying him.

Kane puffed his cigarette to life and slowly shook out the
match. He drew smoke deep into his lungs and released it as
the trio rode down the winding incline. Two of the Indians,
who were young and spirited, spoke excitedly in their native
tongue. The third, an aging man with a broad, ugly face,
long, graying hair, and a squat, powerful body, held up his
hand for silence.

The young, muscular braves stopped talking, but they
lunged down from their ponies and ran straight toward
Kane. Kane felt the hair on the back of his neck rising.

The old Indian gingerly dismounted and called brusquely to the eager pair. The lean, fierce braves halted two steps from Kane. Their gray-haired leader ordered them back. Clearly unhappy, they obeyed.

Ignoring their displeasure, the aged one came to stand directly before Kane. Blue eyes holding the Indian's black ones, Kane continued to smoke his cigarette leisurely. The Indian said nothing; he stared at Kane's brown face, at his wide, bare shoulders, at his sweat-drenched chest. Scratching a broad jaw, the Indian walked slowly around Kane, pausing to examine three white slashes cutting across his bare back.

Kane could feel the man's intense eyes upon him; still the old Indian did not speak. Kane was silent too, his eyes calmly going from one belligerent young brave to the other. Sullen and poised, they clearly were eager to have a go at him. Kane coolly plotted which of the two young warriors he would take out first. Or should he go for the old chief?

The aged Indian circled and once again stood facing Kane. Kane tossed his smoked-down cigarette away. The Indian finally spoke.

"My strong young braves want to kill you." His black eyes were somber.

"And you?" Kane's voice was low and calm.

"Maybe I kill you myself."

"I'll take you with me, Chief," promised Kane.

"You have no weapon," the old Indian scoffed.

"My hands," said Kane, and pushed away from the boulder, coming into a relaxed, but ready, stance: feet apart, hands at his sides.

"You not afraid?"

"No," replied Kane. "I am not afraid."

The chief shook his gray head scornfully. "You afraid." The young braves behind him nodded and grinned, murmuring excitedly. "I know you afraid," stated the old Indian.

Kane's hands went to his hips. "No, Chief, I am not afraid."

The chief frowned. "I say you afraid. I will feel your heart to see if there is fear." Instantly, his rough, square hand reached out to Kane. He placed it firmly upon the left side, gripping the hard wall of Kane's chest. Under his blunt, broad fingers he felt a steady, rhythmic beating. After what seemed a lifetime to Kane, the old man moved his hand away.

"Your heart is not afraid," admitted the Indian. "You are brave warrior. I will let you live. I am Tahomah, medicine man of my people, the Capote Utes." With that his stern mouth lifted into a hint of a grin, and he put out his hand to Kane.

Kane took it and they shook.

"I'm Kane Covington, Chief Tahomah, and I am honored to meet and shake the hand of a brave Ute medicine man." Kane saw a brief flicker of recognition in the black eyes when he told the Indian his name.

Tahomah dropped Kane's hand abruptly and grabbed his right shoulder. "Where you get scars, Kane Covington?"

"From the bluecoats," said Kane.

Tahomah's black eyes suddenly sparkled. His massive hands went to the fringed bottom of his own buckskin tunic. He swiftly jerked it up under his chin and proudly displayed a badly scarred chest. "I fight bluebellies too," he said, grinning, his blunt, gnarled fingers trailing over the zigzagging scars, lifting a polished panther's claw out of the way.

Kane smiled and nodded, even as the two young braves angrily mounted their waiting ponies, disappointed that they were not to be allowed any sport on this fine, sunny day. Kane felt himself relaxing completely when the old Indian, smiling happily, lowered his shirt, then almost at once raised his hands to the rawhide band about his thick neck. He lifted it over his gray head.

The chief's black eyes grew somber once more. Raising his hands toward Kane's dark head, he draped the rawhide band with its shiny panther's claw around Kane's neck. And he told him, "You are in danger, Scarback. I give to you my lucky panther's claw. I killed the cat with my bare hands long time ago. Wear it at all times; it will keep you safe. Will ward off dangers."

Kane, his eyes on Tahomah's weathered face, lifted a lean hand to finger the animal claw resting at the base of his throat. "Tahomah, I cannot take your amulet. You need it to—"

Tahomah shook his gray head, interrupting. "I am an old man. My life is ending. You wear it." He turned abruptly and strode toward his horse. Then he came back. He looked up at the tall, bare-chested white man and said, "You know my Fire-in-the-Snow, Scarback." It was a statement.

Kane stared at him. "I'm sorry, Chief, I don't—"

"Fire-in-the-Snow. My chosen-daughter, Natalie Vallance. The white man's judge with the hair of fire and the eyes of emerald. Fire-in-the-Snow," said Tahomah.

Kane's mouth gaped open. "Yes," he managed. "Yes, I know Mrs. Vallance."

"She told me of you," admitted Tahomah.

"Did she?" replied Kane for want of something better to say. He could well imagine what Natalie had said.

Tahomah nodded thoughtfully and again walked away. When he'd almost reached his horse, he halted. "Scarback, you love Fire-in-the-Snow."

Ready for any remark but that one, Kane swallowed hard and said, "I . . . no. No, I don't." He shook his dark head forcefully. "I do not love Fire-in-the-Snow?"

Tahomah glowered fiercely at Kane. Then the smile crept back to his lips and the light danced once more in his obsidian eyes. "Your heart loves Fire-in-the-Snow."

Chapter Twenty-three

Later in the week Kane walked down the wooden sidewalks of Cloudcastle alongside his old commanding officer, Colonel Shelby Sutton. Around his neck, for all to see, swung the shiny panther's claw.

Censuring glances and whispered conversations followed the two men. The good townsfolk were troubled. Colonel Sutton, a man they so admired, was openly hobnobbing with a coward. And an Indian-loving coward at that. Why, Covington was wearing a savage's charm around his neck and odds were he didn't take it by force!

"Colonel," drawled Kane, his blue eyes steady, "you want to keep in the good graces of these people, it might be wise to stay away from me."

Shelby Sutton never slowed his pace. "You trying to get out of buying me a drink, Captain?"

Kane grinned and pushed open the swinging doors of the Gilded Cage Saloon. "After you, Colonel."

On Saturday, Tahomah rode into Cloud West at lunchtime. He grinned impishly, explaining he had a dream that Colonel Shelby Sutton was in the Territory. Shelby Sutton greeted the old chief warmly and immediately brought down the whiskey bottle. Natalie took it from him, smiling good-naturedly, and herded both men into the dining room.

After a big meal, the three spent the long, pleasant winter's afternoon in the fire-warmed drawing room, the two men enjoying their whiskey and cigars while Natalie sipped spiced hot tea. The three discussed everything from politics to peace treaties, and the hours sped past.

At four o'clock Shelby made his apologies to the old chief, explaining that he had a commitment to meet a lovely blond singer down in Cloudcastle for an early supper before her performance at the opera house. Tahomah's black eyes twinkled and he nodded his gray head knowingly. The two men shook hands and Shelby made the Ute promise to visit again and soon.

It was not until then that Shelby Sutton said casually, "Chief, I understand you met Kane Covington."

Natalie gaped, openmouthed, as the old shaman bobbed his head happily and quizzed, "He your friend?"

Shelby grinned. "Has been for years, Chief."

"Brave man, brave man," muttered the Ute.

"Indeed he is, and he says the same of you."

It was while the two men discussed Kane that Natalie noticed Tahomah's amulet was missing. No sooner had she closed the door behind her uncle than she whirled and questioned him. Calmly, Tahomah admitted he had given it to Kane.

"You gave it to Kane Covington!" Natalie blazed, and her hands went to her hips.

"I did," said Tahomah resolutely.

Natalie rolled her eyes heavenward while the old Indian stalked back into the parlor and took a seat on the sofa. Sighing heavily, Natalie crossed the room to sit beside her unrepentant friend. She placed a small hand atop his gnarled, arthritic one and smiled at him.

"Tahomah," she said gently, "how could you give your panther's claw to Covington? I've told you about the man; he stole Treasure Mountain. He will—"

"He is in danger," interrupted Tahomah.

"What if he is?" snapped Natalie. "He wouldn't be if he would get off this mountain and leave Colorado!" She folded her arms across her chest. "Why you would wish to save a . . . a . . ."

"He is brave man."

"How do you know he's brave?"

"I see his scars. Bluebellies give him bad scars." Tahomah frowned. "Try to kill him."

Natalie flushed. She rose and began pacing. "Very well, you saw the scars on his back, but—"

"I did not say I saw the scars on his back."

"You did, you just said you—"

"I said I see scars." His black eyes impaled her. "I did not say where they were."

"Well . . . ah"—Natalie nervously cleared her throat— "wherever his scars are . . . he . . . they . . ." She floundered, her face pink. Tahomah's accusing grin angered her. "Scars do not mean he is brave! I'm very displeased and disappointed that you would befriend him. First Uncle Shelby. Now you. I don't like it and I'll tell you—"

"Fire-in-the-Snow." Tahomah rose, again interrupting. "I am your father; you my chosen-daughter. You cannot speak to me like that. I am old and wise; you are young and foolish."

"Now, Tahomah, you—"

He silenced her with a lift of his hand. His twinkling eyes grew somber and his broad, copper face took on a deep, forbidding scowl. He came to stand before her. "I see things, Fire. Things that you do not see." Black eyes grew fixed and his voice dropped to a hoarse whisper. "Fire, for years you have had upon your slim shoulders the burden of protecting the Manitou gold. That burden will be lifted at noon of the twelfth full moon."

Eyes wide, Natalie asked anxiously, "What will happen, Tahomah? How will I know? . . .'

"I cannot reveal it, but it has been foretold. And one who is now in great danger will then be forever safe."

"If you're speaking of Kane Covington, I don't care what

happens to—" Tahomah's fierce expression silenced her. She drew a breath, lifted a hand to his weathered cheek, and murmured contritely, "Forgive me, Tahomah. I meant no disrespect, but you told me that you killed the panther with your bare hands; that you've worn the claw ever since. Now you've given it away. Won't you be in danger?" Her green eyes filled with concern.

"I am afraid of nothing; I am old, time to go."

"No," she protested sadly, "don't speak like that. What would I do without you?"

"You marry soon; have husband," said Tahomah, then quickly changed the subject. "I came today not only to see your uncle. I came for my Christmas present. Where is it?"

Natalie smiled brightly. "This will be the earliest we've ever exchanged our gifts."

Tahomah grinned sheepishly. "I could wait no longer. What day is it?"

Natalie laughed gaily as she hurried into the corridor. "November sixteenth. Not even Thanksgiving yet," she called over her shoulder.

"Hmmm. I thought it was nearly Christmas Day," mused the old chief, more to himself than to Natalie. He dropped back onto the sofa, shaking his gray head. His memory was not what it once was; yet another sign that his time on this earth was running out.

Natalie momentarily returned carrying a large, brightly wrapped box tied with ribbon. She laid it across the old chief's knees and sat down by him. As he did every year, Tahomah meticulously worked at removing the shiny paper, his heavy gray eyebrows knitting together, black eyes mischievous, a sly smile on his lips. And Natalie, as she did each year, grew impatient.

"Here, Tahomah," she said shortly, "let me help."

In seconds she'd ripped the paper off and tossed it to the floor. Jerking the lid from the box, she pushed aside tissue paper and lifted the turquoise velvet shirt up for him to admire.

His gnarled fingers swept over the supple velvet, and Natalie clapped her hands with delight when he peeled off his buckskin tunic and drew the colorful velvet shirt over his head.

"How I look?" he asked, rubbing his fingers over the rich softness covering his massive chest.

"Magnificent," praised Natalie.

Tahomah preened proudly, then leaned over and kissed the top of Natalie's fiery head. "Thank you, Daughter. I will wear to meet the Great Spirit in the Sky."

"Not for years yet," countered Natalie. "Now give me mine."

"Your what?" he teased. "I bring nothing. You saw no presents when I entered."

"Where have you hidden it? I know you brought me something."

He chuckled happily and went to the heavy blanket he had worn over his shoulders for the ride down to Cloud West. From out of its folds he drew a necklace. An exquisite lavaliere of smooth, shiny gold. Natalie gasped when he draped the gold chain with its round disc about her throat. Set in the center of the large golden pendant, a smooth turquoise stone was the color of a Colorado summer sky.

"Tahomah! It's splendid, but where did—"

He smiled. "Do not question your father," he gently scolded.

"Never," she promised, and hugged him tightly.

Shelby Sutton's visit lasted longer than he had intended. Enjoying himself thoroughly, he was in no hurry to leave. He liked the people of Cloudcastle, and they, him. Enchanted with the blond opera singer, Noel Salvato, Shelby spent many a gay, lively hour in her company. Ashlin Blackmore went out of his way to gain Shelby's approval, so the Texan spent pleasant, entertaining evenings with Natalie and her Englishman. And Shelby happily renewed his friendship with Kane Covington.

Untroubled by the fact that Natalie disliked Kane, Shelby frequently passed cold, snowy afternoons at the younger man's mountain cabin while Natalie presided over her courtroom.

It was on such an afternoon that Shelby, long legs stretched out to the roaring fire, gray eyes staring sleepily into the flames, took the last swallow from his tumbler of bourbon and said, "What is it between you and Natalie?"

Kane's lean fingers tightened on his whiskey glass. Plagued with guilt, feeling like the worst kind of heel, he said evenly, "Colonel, your niece resents me for owning this land." He took a long, thirsty pull from his whiskey.

Shelby Sutton shook his silver head. "It's more than that, Kane. I can sense it. It's like . . . if I didn't know better, I'd think . . . Ah, hell, who the devil can understand women?" He held out his empty glass to Kane.

Relieved, Kane reached for the half-filled bottle and tipped it to Shelby's glass. "As you know, sir, I quit trying a long time ago."

Shelby's gray gaze swung to Kane's face. He looked the younger man in the eye and said, unsmiling, "Kane, when I leave here, I want you to do me a favor."

"Name it, Colonel."

"Keep an eye on her for me."

It was two days before Thanksgiving. A cold, snowy Tuesday afternoon in Cloudcastle. Joe South, terrifically thirsty, stumbled into the Silverton Saloon. He knew the Silverton bartender. Old Bart, a spidery little man with beady black eyes and a sparse, drooping mustache, was good for at least one free whiskey. Joe, pupils dilating in the dimness of the room, glanced blindly about. Seeing no one he recognized, he limped up to the bar.

"How about it, Bart?" he questioned hopefully, taking off his dark felt hat and shaking the snowflakes from it. "Suppose an old friend could have one shot of whiskey?"

Bart was already pouring even as he nodded his head. Joe, hands trembling, mouth dry, reached for the glass, turned it up, and sighed with satisfaction as he felt the bourbon's fiery warmth burn his parched throat and go down into his cold chest and empty belly.

Old Bart smiled and poured another.

"Well, what have we here?" came an all too familiar voice, and Joe South immediately wished he had never come into the Silverton. "I do believe it's the puny southern gimp," said Damon Leatherwood, stepping up beside the uneasy Joe.

"Sure looks like the crippled little drunk," observed Leatherwood's bearded companion, beefy Nate Sweatt. He took the bar at Joe's other side.

"Where's your Indian-lovin' friend, Joe?" Leatherwood grinned and glanced about. "He afraid to come into town to drink?"

Joe South fought the panic threatening to choke him. He was alone. Old Bart was backing away, his beady eyes darting nervously between the two big men.

"I don't know what you're talking about." Joe wished his voice sounded surer.

Leatherwood, smiling broadly, picked up Joe's felt hat from the bar. "Joe, I believe this is my hat you've got here." And he dropped the hat to the floor and dramatically wiped his muddy boots on it. Joe said nothing. "And this"—Leatherwood nodded to the full glass of whiskey sitting before Joe —"this is my drink, isn't it, Joe?" Joe nodded reluctantly. "What Joe? I didn't hear you? Isn't this my drink?"

"Yes." Joe bowed his head. Damon Leatherwood grabbed a handful of Joe's light hair and pulled his head back.

"Tell you what, Joe. I'm going to drink my whiskey and while I'm drinkin', I want to see you dance a little."

"Please, Leatherwood," Joe appealed to him, "I'm lame, you know I can't dance."

"Oh, yes, you can."

"No, please, I—"

Nate Sweatt slapped the revolver riding his hip. "The man said dance, Joe. Now dance." And he pulled his gun.

At a table in the far north side of the room, hidden in the shadows of the stairway, sat a solitary figure, quietly observing. His black hat was pulled low over piercing eyes, cigarette smoke curled up around his chiseled features, his black-gloved forefinger tapped rhythmically on the wooden table, and his chest expanded beneath the black gabardine shirt he wore.

He sighed wearily, crushed out his smoked-down cigarette, and took off his hat. Slowly he peeled the tight black leather gloves from his hands and dropped them into the hat. His lean fingers toyed with the shiny panther's claw resting at the base of his brown throat.

Kane rose.

The two large men tormenting Joe South were laughing too hard to notice his approach. Nor did Joe see him. Sweat pouring down his face, Joe stood trembling but rooted to the spot, refusing to dance on his crippled leg. Drawing on the last reserves of pride he was surprised to find he still possessed, Joe prepared himself for the worst. He would not dance; they would have to kill him.

Tears of laughter rolling down his cheeks, eyes locked on the terrified man before him, Damon Leatherwood blindly reached for his whiskey.

And he found firm fingers already wrapped around the glass.

"I believe that's my whiskey, Leatherwood," drawled Kane in his soft Mississippi accent.

Leatherwood stopped laughing. Joe South stopped trembling. Nate Sweatt nervously tightened the grip on his six-shooter.

Kane drank the whiskey.

He placed the empty glass on the polished bar, wiped his mouth with the back of his hand, and said coldly, "And that's my hat you're wearing." Casually he lifted Damon's worn Stetson from his big head and let it fall to the floor. As he ground its creased crown beneath his bootheel, Kane said evenly, "Take off your gun, Leatherwood, and fight this Rebel Indian-lover like a man." His cold-lidded stare never wavered.

"You've had this comin' for a long time, Covington." Leatherwood unbuckled his wide leather gunbelt with its heavy Colt .44 revolver. "I could take you with one hand tied behind my back," he bragged, and motioned Sweatt away from the bar. Leatherwood lifted both beefy fists and winced in shock when Kane tagged him first.

The fight was on.

Leatherwood connected with a harsh blow to Kane's chin. The force turned Kane's dark head to the side and he stumbled backward, almost falling. Leatherwood waded in, eager to cash in on his momentary advantage. His huge right fist shot out but missed its target, connecting with only the air as Kane ducked at the last second, drove a hard fist into the bigger man's stomach, and followed it up with a one-two punch to his head.

Leatherwood bellowed like a bull.

Enraged, he lashed out, pummeling wildly but doing little damage. Agile, surefooted, Kane danced about, striking with the swiftness of summer lightning, delivering a barrage of blows that stunned his opponent.

A crowd rapidly filled the Silverton Saloon as grunts and groans and the unmistakable sound of fists slamming flesh drew a large audience. All were certain it would be a short, swift encounter, the quiet southerner the sure loser.

All but Joe South.

While Kane, his dark face bloodied, his left eye rapidly swelling, traded blow for blow with his formidable foe, Joe South followed the rapid, savage action with pounding heart and utmost confidence. In Kane's lithe, loose body and long muscled arms, he saw unleashed what he had known was there all along: cold deadliness, fierce power, lethal strength.

The fight was brutal. Both men were exhausted, but they kept punching, jabbing, reaching. Kane's right cross caught Leatherwood under the chin, slamming his teeth together, pushing his big head backward. He staggered. Kane struck him in the stomach and felt the raw, bloodied skin slide off his battered knuckles.

Leatherwood spun away, caught his breath, and whirled once more. Kane ducked two wild punches. The third connected with his mouth and bright red blood spurted forth.

His nose was bleeding, his lips were split, his left eye was swollen shut, but still he came, swinging, weaving, evading.

A fierce left hook from Leatherwood tagged Kane's right jaw with a blinding force that knocked Kane across the room and to the sawdust beneath the swinging saloon doors. Leatherwood bore down on the prostrate man, kicking Kane ruthlessly in the ribs.

Kane scrambled to his feet on the far side of the doors; up he came, crouching like a panther. Leatherwood banged out the door after him. On the snowy sidewalk, the violent fight continued, the agonized moans and winces of the combatants drowned out by the loud shouts and applause of the excited crowd.

Leaning back in her judge's chair, Natalie, conducting a bench trial, glanced through the folder before her. Absently running a forefinger under the tight white collar showing above her black robe, she listened to the drawn-out testimony of a witness in a civil case.

The courtroom was overwarm and stuffy, and Natalie battled the sleepiness threatening to overcome her. The droning voice of a circuit attorney further lulled her. She folded her hands before her and focused, with effort, on the young man speaking.

From beyond the courtroom doors, there was noise. At first it was only a low hum. Natalie turned her head, trying to hear what was going on outside. She turned her attention back to the lawyer. But the noise promptly grew louder; the shouts, the whistles, the struggling, sounded as though they were coming from just below the courthouse steps.

Kane was almost out on his feet, but still he lifted his tired arms and swung at Leatherwood, the wet, falling snow washing some of the blood from his dark face. His black shirt hung in shreds, exposing his sweat-slick, muscular arms, scarred back, and heaving chest. His black breeches were soaking wet, and torn at one of his knees. And at his dark, perspiring throat, a sharp panther's claw was crimson with his blood.

Damon Leatherwood was also in bad shape. Two teeth were missing, his left ear was bleeding, his eyes glazed. Blood stained his shirt and trousers and his breath came in labored short spurts. Still he stalked Kane, saying tiredly, "Give it up, Covington." He spat blood into the snow. "You're beat!"

Kane's answer was a well-placed blow to Leatherwood's jaw. The big man went down. Kane staggered to him, bent, and dragged him to his feet. Leatherwood swayed drunkenly. He swung and missed. Kane hit him full in the stomach. Leatherwood groaned and again went down, clutching his belly. Once more Kane pulled him to his feet. Barely able to stand, the two men lifted their aching arms.

With the very last ounce of strength in his lean, powerful body, Kane sent his right fist slamming into Leatherwood's punished face and knew, even as he threw the punch, that the fight was over and he had won.

Leatherwood's companion, Nate Sweatt, knew too. Eyes sliding sneakily about, he eased his gun out of the holster and aimed it at Kane's scarred back.

Joe South urgently called, "Kane! Look out!"

Kane's dark head snapped about just in time to see Judge Natalie Vallance whip a .38-caliber pistol out from under her long black robes, cock the hammer, and fire, knocking the gun from Nate Sweatt's hand. Sweatt's weapon fell into the snow as he yelped in pain. An awed crowd of rowdies stared at the deadly-aiming lady magistrate, her face impassive, the gun still smoking in her steady right hand.

Wiping the blood from his shredded mouth, Kane smiled foolishly, rose, and staggered toward Natalie. Emerald eyes never leaving Kane, Natalie said coldly to the big lawman making his way through the crowd, "Deputy Percell, throw all three of them in jail for disturbing the peace!"

Chapter Twenty-four

Natalie turned and coolly walked away.

Cold winds lifted wisps of flaming red hair about her head and the long black robes billowed out around her tall, slender body. Lowered gun in hand, she calmly climbed the steps of the courthouse while every eye followed her. Including Kane's.

Once inside, she closed the heavy door and leaned back against its carved solidness. And her knees began to tremble. She told herself it was nothing more than a normal attack of jitters. She had, after all, just shot a gun from a man's hand.

This weakness, she silently vowed, had nothing to do with the fact that Kane Covington had come within a hairsbreadth of being killed.

Nothing whatever.

Natalie quickly composed herself. She went to her chambers and shed her judicial robes. But she couldn't resist venturing near the window that afforded a view of Main. She looked out in time to see Kane being escorted into the new jailhouse, his wrists cuffed behind him.

Her eyes clung to the battered, masculine length of him. He was hurting, she could see the pain etched on his harshly handsome features. Natalie winced softly. She could almost feel his suffering. And she had the insane, barely controllable

urge to go to him, to smooth back the dark locks of hair from
his bruised brow, to tenderly wipe his lips, to wash away the
grime and the sweat and the blood.

And the pain.

Kane spent the night in the Castleton County jail and slept
not one wink. His battered right hand throbbed wretchedly
and Kane, teeth gritted, bruised face pale from suffering, quietly paced the small cell while across from him, Damon
Leatherwood and Nate Sweatt snored loudly in the other cell.

The pacing had finally stopped and Kane was lounging on
his bunk when Deputy Percell came to release him the next
afternoon. Joe South, as sober as a judge, waited just outside.

"Sir, you look awful." Joe took the taller man's elbow.

"Thanks." Kane tried to grin, but the effort pulled at his
badly split lip. "Help me to the livery stable?"

"No, Kane." Joe shook his head. "You're going straight to
Marge Baker's; it's been decided. The doc will come by
later."

Kane felt too bad to argue. "You sure Marge has enough
space?"

"She told me your old room is still vacant. You'll sleep
there tonight."

"Let's go," said Kane.

Kane and Joe South made slow progress. They were
stopped repeatedly. Men on the streets rushed forward, eager
to pat Kane on the back, to shake his aching hand. Enthusi-
astic congratulations were offered him. Invitations to buy
him a drink were warmly extended.

The contempt of the past weeks had been replaced with
total awe and respect.

Mildly amused, Kane, with his long arm about Joe's narrow shoulders, smiled and continued on his way.

He halted at the candy store. "Joe, let's go inside. I want to
take Belinda a little gift." Joe nodded and opened the door.

At the boardinghouse, Marge Baker met the struggling
pair at the front door and winced in horror when she saw
Kane's swollen eye, his cut lip, and his bruised face. Hands

flew to her full cheeks and she blurted, "Kane, you look awful!"

The sun was setting when old Dr. Ellroy arrived, black bag in hand. "Well, Mr. Covington," he mused, "looks like Marge and Belinda are excellent nurses." With the assistance of a large, raw beefsteak, the swelling around Kane's left eye had gone down enough so that he could open it. His cuts and bruises as well as his throbbing right hand had been carefully bathed. He wore clean clothes borrowed from a boarding miner, and some of the soreness was leaving his tall, lean body. "That hurt very bad?" The doctor indicated the swollen hand.

"It's killing him, Dr. Ellroy," Marge answered for Kane. Kane nodded affirmation.

"Very well, I'm going to give you a little laudanum, Mr. Covington. It will help you to sleep; you look haggard." The doctor smiled then and said, "You've become a hero, son. Everyone is talking about your pugilistic prowess." He chuckled and added, "And Judge Vallance's quick-draw skills."

After supper, Marge insisted that Kane take more of the laudanum and go immediately to bed. Kane was quick to agree. Saying his good-nights, he headed for the stairs.

"Need any help undressing?" Joe South had stayed for supper.

"I can manage, Joe. Thanks." Kane paused, smiling at Marge and Belinda, whose sweet face made him remember the candy he had brought her. The small paper sack was still on the table in the corridor. "I almost forgot," he drawled sleepily, "I bought you something, Belinda."

"Where, Kane? What?" She was up out of her chair, her dark eyes shining.

"Come with me," said Kane, and left Marge and Joe smiling after him. Belinda beat him into the hall.

She took from the sack the gold-wrapped bonbon and stared at it. Kane stood at her elbow, waiting. At last she looked up at him and in her dark eyes he saw a puzzled expression.

"Kane," she asked, unsmiling, "why did you bring this to me?"

"I thought you'd like it. If you don't, then—"

"No," she said, her eyes holding his. "I do, but . . . why did you bring it to me?"

Kane touched the shiny crown of her dark head. "Because, Belinda, you're my friend."

Belinda's dark eyes flickered. "A very special friend?"

Bewildered, Kane nodded. "Yes, Belinda. We're friends. Special friends."

Belinda's wide lips turned up into a knowing smile. She clutched the shiny gold-wrapped candy to her full breasts and shook her head. "I understand," she told him. "We are very special friends." Her lips fell open in a strangely sensuous, seductive way that baffled Kane.

He shrugged, touched her soft cheek, and said, " 'Night, Belinda. See you in the morning."

Belinda gave no answer. She watched him slowly mount the stairs. She fingered the candy in its gold-wrapper and her mouth began to water.

With his left hand, Kane unbuttoned his pants and eased them down over slim hips. Naked, he slid into bed, blowing out the lamp by his head. The laudanum had not only dulled the throbbing of his right hand, it had left him with a floating, relaxed feeling, a warm sense of well-being that caused him to stretch and sigh contentedly.

Heavy eyelids slipping closed, sounds of the night gently lulling him, Kane didn't fight it when a vision of Natalie appeared. His split lips stretched into a lazy grin as he saw her once more, standing in the snow, her black judicial robes blowing about her small feet, the gun in her hand flashing fire.

Kane licked his split lips.

The image of Natalie Valance whipping a gun out from under those robes was somehow strangely sensual. He drifted closer to the edge of a laudanum-induced sleep and the pleasing illusion grew more pleasing still, as if he were in an erotic dream.

Natalie's glorious cinnamon hair came unloosed from restraints. The thick, glossy tresses fell free about her robed shoulders. She slowly released the gun and it fell, still smoking, to the snow. She lifted a slender arm, waved it in an encompassing gesture, and all the others disappeared and there was only Natalie.

And him.

She smiled seductively and brazenly opened the long judicial robes, looking straight into his dazzled eyes. And she was naked beneath, just as she had been that cold moonlit night in Blackmore's carriage. She wore only the sheer silk stockings with those turquoise satin garters gleaming just above her pretty knees. He stared, hungrily, hopefully, as she let the full sleeves slide slowly down her bare arms and the black robe puddled at her feet in the white snow.

His anxious eyes widened in wonder as she stood before him, serenely nude and gorgeous. Her bare, white body took on a ethereal beauty that entranced him, and he felt he would never get his fill of looking at her. Tall and slender, her soft breasts were high and rounded, stomach flat, hips flaring, legs slim but shapely. She appeared as a perfect alabaster statue; a porcelain goddess of love to be worshiped.

But then she moved.

Her bare arms lifted and beckoned him to come to her. A tremor coursed through his body when she spoke his name huskily and begged him to disrobe. Shaky fingers unclasped his belt buckle and he struggled out of his clothes impatiently, terrified that she would vanish in the gentle winds that were tossing her glorious auburn hair about her bare ivory shoulders.

Naked at last, he looked to her for further guidance while his heart thundered in his chest. She was still smiling even as she looked pointedly at his thrusting masculinity, and her huge emerald eyes held a hot light that pulled him toward her.

He went to her at once and marveled when she swayed slightly to him, offering herself, eager for his touch. His hand went out and reverently roamed over her naked body. The

texture of her skin was baby soft and he watched delightedly
as his dark fingers swept from her delicate shoulder to her
high, full breast. He caressed it for only a moment before
moving on down to the gentle curve of her hip, her thigh,
her . . .

He heard her gentle sighs even as her small hand brazenly
clasped his throbbing male flesh and her honeyed lips opened
beneath his own. And then they were magically stretched out
upon the snow, but they were not cold. Their bodies were
warm . . . so warm.

Kane was sound asleep.

Kane felt the soft, loving hand caressing his groin, his body
responding. Drugged, slumbering, carried away by his
dream, he turned his burning body gratefully toward the
sweet succubus delights of the soft, bare woman next to him
as his erection became total. Eyes closed, he buried his lips in
the curve of her neck and shoulder and murmured sleepily,
hotly, "Yes, baby. Oh, God, hold me."

She wrapped her fingers around the rigid male shaft and
skillfully moved them up and down while her wide, wet
mouth sought his. Just as their hungry lips combined, Kane's
blue eyes slid open to gaze at her.

"Jesus God!" he muttered in shock, tearing his mouth
from hers.

"What's wrong?" Belinda asked innocently, continuing to
slide her fingers up and down his pulsing flesh.

Kane grabbed her hand and jerked it from him. Heart
hammering, breath short, he half sat, half lay upon the bed,
staring, unbelieving, at a highly desirable, very naked Belinda
Baker. Her full breasts were pressed against his bare heaving
chest, and a long, silky leg was thrown over his hip.

"Don't you want to play, Kane?" she asked, leaning forward to nuzzle his hair-matted chest.

Violently Kane shoved her away, bolted from the bed, and
searched frantically in the darkness for his trousers. Completely forgetting his aching right hand, he had the pants up
over his flanks and buttoned in seconds, even as he harshly
issued the command, "Wrap yourself in the sheet, Belinda!"

"Why?" she questioned, and disregarding the request, stretched out on her bare belly, kicking her feet in the air.

Kane ground his teeth and cautioned himself to remain calm. Purposely making his voice low, level, he said, "Belinda, where is your robe? Your nightgown?" She flipped unselfconsciously over onto her back, giving Kane a full view of her naked, voluptuous body. She sat up then, stretching her arms out behind her to prop herself up. "I left it by the door."

Warning himself that he must keep his composure, Kane went for the discarded nightclothes. He came back to the bed and said coaxingly, "Belinda, put on your robe and we'll talk."

She giggled. "Oh, I know. You want to play the game where we leave our clothes on to do it. I like that one." She jumped off the bed while Kane, shocked, mystified, held the robe open for her. Belinda turned her back to him and slid her arms into the soft blue sleeves of the robe. She whirled to face him, smiling, the robe open.

Gesturing nervously, Kane said quickly, "Close it. Tie the sash." After lifting her long, tousled hair out from under the fleecy blue collar, Belinda pulled the robe over her naked curves and Kane felt his lungs filling up with air. "Sit down, please."

Belinda eagerly sat down on the bed's edge, but was no sooner settled than she spread her legs wide apart. "I'm ready, Kane."

Kane almost had a heart attack.

But he didn't let it show. As coolly as possible he said, "No, dear, put your feet together and cover yourself."

Belinda frowned up at him and did not obey. She put her hands behind her on the bed and leaned back, staring at him quizzically. Kane leaned forward, put gentle hands on her bare knees and pushed them together. He hastily spread the folds of the long blue robe over her and sat down beside her.

Keeping a restraining arm lying firmly across her robed knees, he said patiently, "Belinda, this is wrong, very wrong. You should not have come in here."

She looked at him wide-eyed. "But you brought me candy."

"I've brought you presents before, Belinda."

"Yes, but—"

"But what?"

"Well . . . tonight you told me we are very special friends."

"Belinda, we are, but friends don't . . . they don't . . ." He cleared his throat. "Friends do not take off their clothes and get in bed together."

"They don't?"

"No, dear, they don't. You are never, never to do such a thing." His arm tightened protectively across her knees. "Not with anybody, do you understand?"

"But what about—"

"With nobody. Ever. Promise me."

"I . . . I'm sorry, Kane." Tears were filling her huge, dark eyes. "I thought you meant for me to come here. I thought you wanted me to. . . ."

"Why would you think such a thing?" A muscle jumped in his lean jaw. "No . . . never mind, it doesn't matter. It's my fault somehow."

"No, Kane." She was shaking her head. "I thought it was like when I—"

"Belinda, you have got to get out of here at once. Go back to your room before someone sees you." He rose, urging her up with him.

"If this is wrong, Kane, are you going to tell Momma?"

"No. No, I'm not," said Kane, "not if you promise you will never do such a thing again. Now go."

"Good night, Kane," she whispered, and kissed his cheek as though nothing had happened. Kane watched her tiptoe down the darkened hall to the stairs before he quietly closed the door.

He didn't go back to bed. Shakily he rolled and lit a cigarette, fighting desperately to calm his raw nerves. He stood at the window, staring sightlessly out over the darkened valley while he wrestled with his conscience.

The laudanum had worn off. Kane spent the long, pain-filled night worrying about Belinda and wondering if he should go, at once, and waken Marge Baker. It would break the poor woman's heart. He was damned if he did; damned if he didn't.

Kane cringed . . . Belinda had already been with a man. He knew it. He didn't know when or who or how, but he knew that she had. She was far too knowledgeable. She had played sex games with somebody. She had caressed him as if she were an experienced woman, not an innocent child.

Kane was still tormented by the dilemma when the first gray light of dawn crept over the eastern ring of mountains. Exhausted, suffering, he lay down across his rumpled bed. He would act this very morning. His last conscious thought was of the abused Belinda.

Dressed warmly in a heavy woolen coat, Belinda said good-bye to her mother at ten minutes before nine that morning. It was Thursday. Thanksgiving Day. Time to go up the hill to the Blackmore mansion.

"Lord Blackmore said you could cut the cleaning short since it's Thanksgiving, so I'll expect you home before eleven," said Marge Baker as she fondly tied the long maroon muffler about her daughter's neck.

"I'll be here, Momma," promised Belinda, and rushed out-doors. Marge went back to her kitchen as the young girl skipped down the front steps. Hands shoved deep into her coat pockets, Belinda paused on the frozen sidewalk, turned, and looked up at the right front window on the third floor.

Kane's window.

She was still peering up when she sidled absently into the street. Someone shouted, but it was too late. Belinda whirled just in time to see the runaway ice wagon bearing down upon her. She screamed as the snorting, wild-eyed beasts thundered over her.

Her scream jolted Kane wide awake. Heart pounding in his bare chest, he flew down the stairs and out into the cold. Marge had already reached her prostrate daughter. She was on her knees beside the lifeless form, begging Belinda to speak. Kane crouched down, pushed the bloodied maroon muffler away from Belinda's throat, and felt for a pulse.

There was none.

Chapter Twenty-five

Early winter dusk traveled down the snowy slopes of the shimmering San Juan range. A man on horseback, his classic features outlined against the purpling sky, spurred his coal-black mount up into the rugged foothills, disappearing behind an icy ridge of the upland valley.

Over a high-lying plateau he rode, his long black cloak billowing in the rising night winds, horse's sharp hooves drumming a rhythmic cadence on the solidly frozen ground. It was cold night. A snowy Sunday night. A night to be indoors, not galloping across a lake of ice.

Jagged white bluffs loomed in the distance. It was to the base of their shimmering spires that the rider headed. In the deep, black shadows of those needle-like spires, a small, weathered dwelling stood on a small, barren spread of land.

Lights winked from the windows and a curl of black smoke rose from the rock chimney of the dilapidated building. Sounds came from within; deep masculine laughter carrying on the chill night air.

The rider reined in his black mount, his eyes as cold as the ice framing the wooden front porch. He dismounted swiftly and strode purposefully up the sagging front steps of the shack. He did not knock. He burst into the room, surprising the two laughing men seated at a wooden eating table.

"Hello. Come in, come in," said the thin Burl Leatherwood, rising nervously from his chair. "What brings you out tonight?"

The caller ignored Burl Leatherwood. He walked directly to the hulking Damon Leatherwood, where he sat sopping meat juice from his plate with a large hunk of bread. Damon looked up and grinned; the space where his missing teeth had been gave him a comical appearance.

"Hi, boss," said Damon, and pushed the soggy piece of bread into his gap-toothed mouth.

"Stand up," ordered Ashlin Blackmore coldly, his unwavering gaze on the seated man.

Still chewing, and looking puzzled, Damon rose. Towering over the blond, slender man, Damon spoke past the food in his mouth. "What's up?"

Ashlin gave no verbal reply. He lifted his gloved right hand and gave the big man's punished mouth a stinging blow with the back of his hand. Damon's jaw went slack. Half-chewed food dribbled down his chin, mixing with bright red blood.

Burl Leatherwood's light eyes narrowed, but he didn't make a move. Big Damon Leatherwood looked down at Ashlin like a child who was close to tears. Ashlin again slapped him, eliciting a wail of fear and outrage from Leatherwood. Damon's big, bruised hand came up to his face to wipe away the blood as tears stung his shocked eyes.

"You fool." Ashlin finally spoke, softly, stepping back to work his fingers from the soiled black gloves. "I've told you repeatedly to stay away from Kane Covington."

"Yeah, but boss, he picked on me and I was only——"

"Shut your slobbering, ignorant mouth, Damon," said Ashlin Blackmore, shrugging out of his long black cloak and lifting the black fur cap from his shiny blond curls. He strode forward to the fireplace, whirled around dramatically, and said in a low, menacing voice, "I don't give a goddamn if Kane Covington walked up to you on the street and took a piss on your leg. You were not to touch one hair on his head and you knew it."

Damon's chin drooped petulantly on his massive chest and

he made a face. Burl Leatherwood said evenly, "We know, boss."

"Do you?" Ashlin's eyes were fierce. "Do you understand, Damon, why I've ordered you to stay away from Covington?" Damon muttered unintelligibly. "Answer me!"

"Y—yes, boss." Damon reluctantly lifted his head. "But I was—"

Ashlin's gaze swung to Burl. "Burl, I'll say this to you since little brother is too stupid to comprehend. When they find Covington dead, they'll immediately suspect you. It's Damon's fault and I'll not lift a finger to help you. Is that clear?"

"Don't worry, boss," reasoned Burl Leatherwood. "They might suspect us, but they won't be able to prove a thing. Not a thing."

Ashlin's brown eyes were on Damon. "You implicate me in any way and I'll—"

"Never. We'd never do that, boss," Burl was quick to reassure him. "Nobody even knows we're acquainted; I swear it."

"All right, fine," said Ashlin. He stepped away from the fireplace and Damon Leatherwood, eyes darting tensely, stealthily moved closer to his older brother. "Listen to me, both of you," said Ashlin, motioning them to take a seat at the table. Both obeyed and Ashlin purposely came to stand beside Damon, draping his hand on the big man's massive right shoulder.

"Natalie's nosy Texas uncle is finally leaving town tomorrow. Soon as he's gone, I'll take a trip over to Denver. I'll stay gone a full week . . . see old friends, be seen by everyone, establish my alibi. And while I'm away"—his long fingers slid along Damon's massive shoulder to the thick neck, tightening on its bulging muscles—"I want that arrogant southern bastard killed." He squeezed rippling flesh with amazing strength and smiled coldly as he did so. "Do you understand, Damon?"

Damon bobbed his head vigorously. "Yes, sir, boss. I'm gonna kill Covington for you soon as you leave town."

Ashlin relaxed his grip. He smiled disarmingly. "Capital.

You will be well paid when the job is completed." He went for his long black cloak. "Make a mistake . . ." He let the words trail away and his brown eyes once more became hard and cold.

"We won't," assured Burl Leatherwood. "Covington's as good as dead."

"In that case," said Ashlin, "I must be going." He swirled the long cape around his shoulders, smiling. "I'm dining with my fiancée and her uncle and I'd hate to keep them waiting."

He strode to the door, jerked it open, and swept out into the cold night, not bothering to close it. With a flourish, he mounted the big, black steed and galloped away under a canopy of brightly shining stars.

On Monday, daybreak tinted the winter sky outside Kane's mountain cabin. Stretching lazily beneath warm bedcovers of fur, Kane turned his head to peer out the frosty north window. He gingerly lifted his swollen right hand from under the soft furs and flexed it stiffly, then touched his blackened eye to evaluate the damage. Satisfied it was well on its way to healing, he let his hand trail down to his mouth. His top lip was almost mended, but his bottom lip was still raw and tender. Kane ran his tongue over it and winced.

He had been awake for an hour and had little hope of falling back to sleep. He sighed. His thoughts kept returning to the tragedy. To Belinda. His naked chest constricted. The poor child. The poor sweet child.

Kane threw back the covers and sat on the edge of his bed. He rose tiredly and stood scratching his chest, knowing he needed to get away from the cabin—and from his thoughts— for a while. Take a hike in the snow. Walk off some of his stiffness. Clear his head. Watch the sunrise over Lone Cave Peak.

In moments, dressed warmly in fringed buckskins, leather gauntlets, tall brown boots, and black Stetson, Kane stepped outdoors. Colt revolver scabbarded on his hip, sharp hunting knife stuck into the waistband of his buckskin pants, candles and tobacco shoved into his breast pocket, he went forth to meet the rapidly breaking new day.

Blue eyes squinting toward the flaming eastern horizon, Kane began climbing. He went not to the east, nor to the west. He headed straight up the peak, ascending, as though with definite purpose, steadily toward the summit of his frozen, formidable mountain.

He could hear his breath as he scaled frozen rocky shelves of the uplands, zigzagging back and forth along narrow, slippery ledges. Higher and higher he climbed over a steep and rocky path that was extremely hazardous in summer, deathly dangerous on a frozen winter's day.

Perspiration ran down his dark, bruised face and hot pains stabbed at his side, but Kane continued to climb. Winds roared about his ears; thick fog obscured the sun, and his right hand had begun to throb from too much use. An ice ledge gave way beneath his right foot and he groaned aloud as he reached out frantically with his injured hand to grab at a sharp, jutting rock.

Heart thundering, Kane pressed his battered cheek to the cold, slippery wall and fought for breath. Sun suddenly pierced the thick, shrouding fog and Kane, eyes squinting in the blinding glare, looked about.

Dizzy, he closed his eyes, then opened them once more. Not six inches from where his right foot rested—a sheer drop of twelve thousand feet straight down. Kane bit his jaw cruelly. He heard the blood pumping in his ears.

Carefully, he turned his head. And almost reeled with relief. A dim, wide corridor, not three feet away, led behind a towering wall of ragged stone. Kane's left hand reached for, and secured, a firm hold near the entrance to that corridor. Lean fingers curling tightly around a thin upthrust of granite, he slid his booted left foot over and gave a shout of victory when he triumphantly stepped into the spacious passageway.

Patting his breast pocket anxiously for the ever-present tobacco sack, Kane drew a deep breath, rolled himself a cigarette, and felt the calming effects of the tobacco as he pulled the smoke deep down into his lungs.

Looking curiously about, he blinked, not trusting his eyes. He was standing on the threshold of some kind of strange, deserted community. Intricate, masterfully crafted masonry apartments had doubtlessly been built by a people of superior intelligence. Amazed to find such a place directly above his cabin, Kane realized the towering shelf of shielding rock had completely concealed it from his view. And from anyone else's. Shaking his dark head in awe, he stamped out his smoke and went eagerly forth to investigate.

He spent the morning exploring the eerily quiet cave dwellings built into the side of the stone mountain. Reaching three stories high, dozens of rooms appeared as though their occupants had left only yesterday. Quarried stone was as finely spalled as if it had been cut by the most talented of sculptors. High roofs were built of log that had undoubtedly been dragged for miles over the sheer granite side of Promontory Point.

Armed with a flickering candle, lean hand cupped around it, Kane agilely made his way in and out of the dim, deserted living quarters, passing up only the ones whose small, low doorways were sealed with stone and mortar. Room after room was filled with finely molded clay pottery and amazingly beautiful handmade furniture. Kane lifted his candle higher. The walls were covered with paintings and numbers and signs. Entranced, Kane studied the strange artwork, looking for clues to those who had left their messages behind in crimson and umber paint.

In a large room one story underground, Kane discovered the Great Kiva, a ceremonial chamber for religious services. And in that room, artistically carved coffins lined the twelve-foot-high walls, stacked neatly one on the other, reaching to the stone ceiling. The hair on the back of his neck rising, Kane stood in the silent tomb and envisioned the long-dead people who had lived and loved and died in this mountain palace.

Feeling like an intruder into a sacred place, Kane quietly made his way back to the one low doorway, the sound of his bootheels ringing on the smooth granite floor. Outside the kiva, Kane hurried along the winding corridor, and had gone several yards before he realized he was heading in the wrong direction. The opening leading topside was behind him.

He turned, and when he did, he saw it.

Another, narrower corridor led off the one in which he stood. Kane considered it, gave his dark head a dismissive shake, pivoted, and walked away. But he had gone only a few steps when he stopped and turned around.

He felt almost a physical pull toward that small, dark corridor. Smiling at his foolishness, he nonetheless walked back and seconds later was inside the dark passage. Narrow, and so low-ceilinged that he had to stoop to keep from bumping his head, it wound steadily back into the solid rock of the mountain.

All at once Kane stepped out into a light, spacious room. And his mouth fell open.

"Sweet Jesus!" he gasped, and his disbelieving blue eyes took in the dazzling sight before him. Shiny gold bars, stacked like firewood, rose along the rocky walls from the floor to the height of a tall man's head. Heavy chests, filled with gold jewelry—rings and chains and medallions—stood open, their precious contents spilling over the sides.

Gold plates, gold goblets, gold pitchers, and gold candlesticks and bowls rested on huge, smooth tables of stone. The ragged walls and natural ceiling were brightly dotted with glittering, gleaming yellow specks. And Kane knew it, too, was gold.

There was gold everywhere he looked. Shiny, shimmering gold. Soft, pure gold. Yellow, glorious gold. Valuable, spendable gold.

Millions and millions of dollars in gold!

Kane let out a low whistle that echoed through the gold-filled room. Aloud he murmured in stunned awe, "Beyond the dreams of Cortés in Mexico!"

Noon neared and Natalie felt a mounting sadness. She waited beside her Uncle Shelby inside the Wells Fargo office, while he secured his place on the stage to Virginia City, Nevada. She inwardly sighed, wondering if it would be three years before she saw him again. And what would be happening in her life in three years.

Natalie bit her lip. She had told Ashlin that she would see her uncle off on the stagecoach, then come immediately to his mansion for a private, important talk. She knew Ashlin hadn't the faintest clue that she was coming to tell him she could not marry him. How she dreaded it. To hurt a man so kind and good, a man who loved her, who wanted only her happiness.

"There it is, right on time." Her uncle's deep voice shook her from her painful reveries.

"So soon?" she said foolishly, clinging to his arm, reluctant to let him go.

Shelby smiled down at her and guided her outside. "Child, I don't know when I've enjoyed myself so much. It was a wonderful visit. Perfect." They paused on the ice-covered sidewalk, blinking in the bright winter sunlight.

Determined to keep this good-bye cheerful, Natalie smiled back at him. "True, but tell me, Uncle Shelby, was I responsible, or was it Noel?"

Shelby Sutton chuckled good-naturedly. "You both had a hand in my pleasure, darlin'." He winked at her then, and added, "But Noel's departure last week has nothing to do with my leaving, honest."

"Then stay," said Natalie.

"Can't. I'm to meet a man about a claim up in Virginia City before Christmas." His smile flashed bright. "Who knows? Your old uncle might end up a rich man."

"'All aboard," called the lanky stage driver, and Natalie again felt a sinking sensation.

"That's me, hon," said her uncle, touching her cheek.

"Uncle Shelby," Natalie murmured, and impulsively threw her arms around his neck. He swept her close. Into his ear she whispered brokenly, "I'm not going to marry Ashlin. I can't." Her fingers clutched at his neck.

Stunned speechless, Shelby tightened his arms around her narrow waist as he searched for the appropriate thing to say.

Face pressed to her lustrous red hair, his gray eyes strayed to a tall, lean man lounging against a porch across the street. Kane lifted a gloved hand to touch the brim of his black Stetson in silent salute.

And Shelby Sutton began to laugh happily. He kissed his niece's fiery hair and said against her ear, "Why, of course you can't, honey, of course you can't."

Chapter Twenty-six

Natalie stood in the brilliant sun and watched the creaking coach grow smaller. Kane stood on the sidewalk and watched Natalie. Her wistful gaze finally left the departing stage and drifted across the street. She saw him and stiffened visibly. And she promptly turned and hurried away.

Kane could hardly blame her. Not after what he'd discovered this morning. The lovely judge had been an extremely rich young woman until he had shown up in Cloudcastle bearing a deed to Promontory Point. She had every reason to hate him.

And so did Ashlin Blackmore.

Natalie rushed toward the big white mansion at the end of Main Street. Anxious to have the upcoming unpleasantness behind her, she climbed the steps to the imposing dwelling and lifted the heavy brass knocker.

Old William promptly threw open the front door and smiled warmly at Natalie. "Come right in, Mrs. Vallance," said William. "Let me take your wrap."

"Thank you, William." Natalie turned her back to the old servant and released her long pink cape to his wrinkled hands.

"Lord Blackmore offers his apologies. He's—"

Natalie whirled about, interrupting. "He's not gone, is he, William? I specifically asked that he—"

"No, no, ma'am. He's here, but he is tied up right now with a gentleman in the study. Shouldn't take but a few moments." He smiled reassuringly. "You're to go on upstairs and wait for him in the drawing room."

Natalie nodded and patted her upswept hair. "Thank you, William," she said and, lifting her long skirts, ascended the wide staircase. A bright, cheerful fire blazed in the spacious drawing room, but despite its heat, Natalie felt a definite chill. The flames in the marble fireplace licked and leapt erratically around the piñon logs and Natalie looked about, puzzled. She went back out into the hallway, searching for the source of the cold draft.

The door across the wide corridor stood ajar. The door leading into the library. Natalie went inside. She immediately spotted a window across the big room, half open. Frigid air poured into the library, causing the heavy velvet drapes to flutter with its force. A biting chill permeated the room while on top of a tambour desk beside the open window, pages of a small open book were riffling in the cold wind.

Natalie hurried forth and closed the window. Her attention was caught by the open leather book and she laid her hand on it, intending to shut it. But her gaze was drawn to the written word and what she saw there made her green eyes widen. She lifted the book from the desk.

Lips parted, Natalie flipped to the front inside page and read the words *Property of Lord Titus Blackmore.* Titus? Natalie murmured musingly. Ashlin's middle name was Courtney, not Titus. Ashlin Courtney Blackmore. Who was Titus Blackmore?

Intrigued, Natalie flipped to the first page. A bold, scrawling hand had made an entry on May 5, 1859: *Finally got to the United States this date. Will write Ashlin tomorrow to let him know of my safe arrival.*

Natalie turned to a page farther into the yellowing journal. *August 8, 1859. Have reached the wilds of Colorado where I will prospect for gold.* Natalie turned more pages. *February 2,*

1860. My luck is changing. Have met a young Ute squaw. She claims to know of hidden gold.

The blood began to drum loudly in her ears, and Natalie eagerly continued to scan the brittle pages of the leather-covered journal. Titus Blackmore had recorded everything. How the young Indian girl had led him to the gold in the Cliff Palace and how he had meticulously drawn up a map of its exact location. How he had murdered the girl afterward and hidden her body in a fissure of Treasure Mountain. How he was next planning to kill a meddlesome old Ute shaman. How he could hardly wait until the old Indian lay dead so he could take his gold and return to his beloved England.

Natalie heard men's voices in the downstairs corridor. Ashlin was bidding his guest good-day.

Thoughts tumbling over one another, heart hammering beneath the soft pink woolen bodice of her dress, Natalie dropped the leather journal back on the tambour desk, whirled about, and dashed out of the library. Silently crossing the marbled corridor, she slipped back into the drawing room and was standing quietly before the fireplace when Ashlin walked through the double doors.

"Darling," said Ashlin, his hands outstretched, "so sorry I kept you waiting."

Natalie forced herself to smile at the tall, blond man and allowed him to put his arms around her. She stood in his embrace and carefully concealed the dismay threatening to make her ill. Putting the shocking facts together, Natalie wisely kept all burning questions to herself.

Ashlin's lips pressed soft kisses to her temple and he said solicitously, "Tell me, my dear, what was it that was so important?"

Natalie lifted her face to his. "Nothing really, Ashlin. I just wanted to say good-bye in private." Again she smiled and prayed he could not read what lay behind her eyes.

"My love," murmured Ashlin, seeking her lips. Natalie endured his brief caress. Freeing her mouth, Ashlin murmured against her ear, "I've an hour before I leave on the stage for Denver."

Natalie thought fast. "I have a private hearing in my chambers set for twelve-thirty," she quickly lied, and pulled back.

Ashlin sighed, then told her, "I wish I didn't have to leave, but this damned railroad business is—"

"I understand." Natalie was anxious to get out of his arms, out of the room, out of the house. And out of his life.

"I'm glad. You'll keep busy while I'm away?"

"Yes," she quickly assured him, although she had not a single case on the docket for the next ten days.

In the downstairs corridor, Ashlin, standing behind Natalie, draped the pink cape around her slender shoulders. Impulsively, he put his fingers into her hair at the sides of her head and urged her back against his slim body. Huskily, he whispered, "After we're married, darling, will you . . . wear your hair in plaits when we're alone?"

Watching nervously from her private chambers, Natalie felt an overwhelming sense of relief when she saw the Denver stage leave Cloudcastle with Ashlin Blackmore on board.

Troubled thoughts rushed through her mind, one after another. Tahomah asking, more than once, if Ashlin had a brother. Ashlin trying to purchase Promontory Point, telling her it was needed for railroad right-of-way. Kane Covington shooting Damon and Burl Leatherwood while all three were on top of Treasure Mountain. What were the Leatherwoods doing up there? Did they know of the gold? Did Kane? Did Ashlin? Was Ashlin nothing more than a greedy gold-seeker bent on stealing the treasure?

The sun slipped behind thick, dark clouds as Natalie rode home to Cloud West. Natalie began disrobing the minute she walked in the door. Pink cape thrown over the polished banister, she worked at the tiny buttons of her pink wool dress as she climbed the stairs.

The big ranch house was silent; Natalie was alone. Jane had gone to a married daughter's in Arizona. The young woman was due to deliver her first child and Jane planned to stay until her grandchild safely entered the world.

In too great a hurry to light the fires, Natalie shivered as she stepped out of her dress and full petticoats.

Moments later, teeth chattering, she flew down the stairs wearing buckskin trousers and fringed shirt, gunbelt buckled around her flaring hips. From a peg beside the front door, Natalie snatched down the black Stetson her uncle Shelby had left behind. Jamming it down over her upswept flaming hair, she went to the stables for her bay stallion, Blaze.

Natalie headed east as snow began falling from a rapidly changing sky. She looked heavenward and grimaced. A harsh winter's storm was on the way; she could see it gathering in the north. She didn't care. She had to see Tahomah; to question him, to get to the bottom of this nightmare she'd unwittingly uncovered.

"Hell, Burl." Damon Leatherwood scratched his armpit. "It's fixin' to snow again. Can't we wait a couple of days?"

"No, Damon," said his older brother, "get out of that bed and put on a shirt. We're riding over to pay a little visit to Kane Covington." The thin man dropped cartridges into the chamber of his heavy revolver.

Damon Leatherwood made a face, but he rose from his narrow bed. "You know I like a nap after I eat. Don't see what it would hurt to wait till tomorrow."

"We're getting it over with, little brother. Today. This very afternoon."

Damon was still bellyaching when the pair rode away from their little spread in the foothills, heading toward Promontory Point.

Kane returned to his alpine cabin shortly before noon. By the time he had unsaddled Satan and fed him a half bucket of oats, snow had started falling. Kane stepped from the small barn and looked up at an eerily ominous sky.

The storm was blowing in from the north. Likely as not it would be a bad one, maybe bringing a foot or more of new snow. Kane didn't care. He had books to read and liquor to drink and food to eat.

And millions of dollars of bright, shiny gold stashed in the high Cliff Palace directly above him.

Kane went inside his cabin, took off his black Stetson and tossed it onto the coat tree. He would just spend the next two or three snowy days pondering how he could spend all of that money.

Chuckling, he tossed several piñon logs into the fireplace. When the fire was snapping and crackling and shooting tongues of bright orange flame up the chimney, Kane shrugged out of his buckskin shirt, poured himself a tumbler of straight Kentucky bourbon, and dropped into an easy chair.

One long leg hooked over the chair's padded arm, he took a healthy swallow of the dark liquid and smiled over the glass. He was a rich man once more. A very rich man. One of the Territory's richest.

Perhaps he would go again to Europe. Or to New York City. Maybe even down to the Mississippi coast. Buy back his home place and build a new, baronial mansion, grander than the old one. Sit in lazy idleness on the verandah while Gulf breezes and icy mint juleps kept him cool and contented.

Kane sighed and took another drink of bourbon. A twinge of melancholy nudged at him. He yawned with boredom. The newfound money didn't make that much difference. There was nothing he wanted to do. No place he wanted to go.

Kane again lifted the glass, emptied it, and poured another. Hooded blue eyes stared fixedly into the fire and his dark head fell back against the tall, padded back of his chair.

It was quiet and very warm inside the one-room cabin, the only sound that of the hot fire snapping and popping. Kane swirled the whiskey in his glass, drank half the contents, and set it aside.

Yawning drowsily, he scratched absently at his bare stomach, then lifted his fingers to toy with the shiny panther's claw that hung around his neck.

Kane dozed.

Chapter Twenty-seven

The weather had rapidly turned foul.

Natalie felt the cold, driving winds biting through the heavy buckskin shirt and lifting at the too-large Stetson atop her head. One gloved hand clutching the reins, she shoved the hat lower, stood in the stirrups, and wheeled the big bay in a southeasterly direction, putting the winds to her back.

Snow that had been light only moments before was now falling fast and heavily, and the sky was white. A total, complete whiteout. No sign of the horizon in any direction. It would be easy to get lost on such a day.

Natalie was unworried.

She knew the way blindfolded. She and Blaze had climbed these bleak slopes toward the El Diente pass in every kind of weather. She leaned over and patted her mount's wet, sleek neck, trusting the powerful beast to carry her safely around and over the snow-covered spires rising like threatening shadows out of the milky mist.

Blaze, never breaking pace, suddenly tossed his great head and whinnied. Natalie wondered at his action, then saw the coil of black smoke curling up into the snow-white sky. She was not fifty yards from Kane Covington's cabin. Blaze had likely smelled Kane's horse, even through the storm, and was reacting. Distracted, the bay stumbled, quickly recovered his stride, and lunged forward.

"This is dumb, Burl, I can't see a danged thing," complained Damon Leatherwood.

"Will you put a lid on it, Damon, we're almost there," warned his older brother.

"I don't like this, I don't—"

"Wait," said Burl, and pulled up on his horse. "What's that just—" He squinted and raised a bony hand to wipe rivulets of water from his cold face.

"I don't see nothing," whined Damon, turning his dun about.

Burl's pale eyes blinked, then blinked yet again. "It's him," he said quietly. "the fool's out for a ride."

"Where, I don't . . . oh, yeah."

"That him?"

Damon strained to see. "Has to be. Man in buckskins and black Stetson astride a bay stallion. Who else could it be way up here?"

"This makes it easier for you, Damon."

"Easier for me?" Damon grumbled. "I thought you was going—"

Interrupting, Burl said resolutely, "You're going to shoot Kane Covington, little brother." His cold eyes swung to the bigger man. "Were I you, I'd try my best to get him before he spots you. He might be wearing his gun."

Fear registered in Damon's wide eyes. He swallowed hard, dug his big-roweled spurs into his horse's belly, and shot forward, Colt revolver drawn.

A shot rang out.

Kane sprang from his chair. Snatching his Colt. 44 from the holster hanging beside the front door, Kane dashed outside, mindless of his bare torso. Gun raised, he stood poised in the swirling snow, a figure of dormant power, eyes savagely alert, coiled muscles tensed.

And then he was running, his long, powerful legs bounding

over the deepening snows to a horse whickering in panic. Blue gaze cautiously sweeping about as he ran, Kane neared the frightened, riderless animal and felt the heart inside his bare chest constrict with fear.

He recognized the big bay.

The horse's great head was low; held down by a hand clinging tightly to the drooping reins. That hand belonged to a prostrate form upon the snow and Kane knew, even before he reached her, that it was Natalie.

Shoving the revolver into the waistband of his trousers, Kane rushed to her, fell to his knees, not realizing that he had let out a loud wail of despair.

She lay upon her back. Hat gone from her head, her fiery hair was fanned out like strawberry lace upon the snow. Her eyes were closed, long, thick lashes resting on pale cheeks. Her head was half turned to him and her lips were slightly parted.

Kane immediately laid his ear to her chest, heard nothing but the hammering of his own speeding heart. He straightened, put his hand to her throat, and encountered metal. Pushing the shiny gold disc out of the way, he pressed his fingers against her wet flesh and felt a faint, steady beating. He uncurled her slender, gloved fingers from the horse's reins and gently picked her up. And again groaned when he saw the crimson circle of bright red blood staining the crystal snow beneath her.

Tucking her head beneath his chin, Kane ran through the blinding snowstorm, the woman in his arms as lifeless as a rag doll. Inside the cabin, he carried Natalie directly to the eating table in the center of the room. He laid her down upon her back, then carefully turned her over onto her stomach.

From the cupboard he grabbed a sharp knife and quickly sliced away her bloodied buckskin shirt and crimson-stained chemise. The bullet had entered her right shoulder an inch from the armpit and had not exited. It was lodged in the soft tissue and muscle and was bleeding profusely. It would have to come out soon.

Kane's deft fingers unfastened the gold chain from around

her throat. Shiny gold disc resting in the palm of his hand, he carried the dazzling necklace to the night table beside his big bed. Then he turned back to Natalie.

Kane knew what had to be done. Dr. Ellroy was too far away. The snowstorm was growing worse. The wounded judge would never make it down the mountain to Cloud-castle.

Pausing only a second to gently cup a pale white cheek in his hand, Kane went into action.

Within five minutes of entering the cabin, Natalie was stretched out on the table, which was now covered with freshly laundered linen. Unconscious, lying on her stomach, she was naked save for her lacy underdrawers and a covering sheet draped across hips and legs. The wound had been thoroughly bathed and cleansed with warm water and Kane, his hands scrubbed sterile as any surgeon's, stood over her. Nearby were boiling-hot water, several clean white towels, sponges, and a razor-sharp knife that he had held in the blaze of a candle for sterilization.

Kane flexed the stiff fingers of his injured right hand and picked up the gleaming knife. Keeping his eyes off the pale, beautiful face of the helpless woman lest his calm resolve depart, Kane put the point of the sharp knife to soft flesh and felt his insides twist.

With steely determination, he probed the wound, ignoring the instinctive flinching of the bare white back. A soft moan issued from Natalie's parted lips and it, too, was ignored by the dark man who was inflicting the pain. With a single-mindedness born of necessity, Kane went about his work, his blue eyes narrowed in concentration, his stiff hand miraculously steady and strong.

The deadly bullet was extracted and dropped into a dish. For want of a better antiseptic, Kane poured bourbon over the wound and dressed it with white gauze. And it was not until he had put one of his clean white nightshirts on Natalie and had placed her in his bed, that his hands began to shake uncontrollably and he felt so faint, he had to dash out of doors to draw a breath of fresh, cold air.

And then his long vigil began.

Kane drew up a straight-backed chair beside the bed and straddled it. Long, bare arms folded over its back, chin resting on top of them, Kane stared steadily at the pale, pretty face upon the pillow. Long, anxious minutes passed slowly and that face kept growing paler. And paler.

Alarmed, Kane rose and peeled down the bedcovers. Gently, carefully, he slipped his fingers beneath Natalie. They came out wet and bloody. That's why she was getting paler. She was still losing blood. Kane bit the inside of his jaw and crossed the room to the fireplace. He picked up the heavy black poker and looked at it. And he looked back at the deathly-white face upon his pillow.

Kane placed the poker directly into the flames.

He took a deep, slow breath, wondering miserably, Can I do it? Can I actually press that glowing piece of iron against her bare, beautiful back? Can I forever scar such feminine perfection? Even as he pondered, bright red blood oozed out of the bullet wound.

Kane carried Natalie back to the table and stripped away the soiled nightshirt. Again he cleaned the wound. Without further delay he strode to the fireplace, wrapped a heavy cloth around the handle of the fire-red poker and drew it from the flames. Heat from it caused his blue eyes to squint, but he opened them wide when he reached Natalie.

His hand was steady when he pressed the searing iron against her wound. The sizzling sound and immediate stench of burning flesh was almost as big a jolt to Kane as the heart-wrenching cry from an unconscious Natalie.

The poker slipped to the floor from his now sweating hand, and he said raggedly, "Sweetheart, forgive me, forgive me."

Impulsively, he bent his dark head and placed a gentle kiss on Natalie's white face, straightened, and saw that there was blood on her cheek. The taste of blood was strong in his mouth; he had bitten his lip. It was his blood staining her cool face.

Kane gently washed her face and took Natalie back to the bed. He put no clean nightshirt on his patient. He left her naked from the waist up and pulled the warm covers up only to her hips.

He spun around and immediately went about building up the fire. Tossing more piñon logs onto the already blazing inferno, he spoke aloud as he worked. "It's all right, Natalie," he said in low, calm tones, as though she could hear him, "I'll keep the room warm so you'll not get a chill. If I leave the wound uncovered, it will heal much faster. It needs air; that's why I didn't bandage it. That's why I'm leaving the nightshirt in the drawer."

The fire snapped and leapt and burned brightly, hotly. Kane, perspiration gleaming on his bare chest and shoulders, crossed the warm room to Natalie. He stood above her, intense blue eyes upon the small, seared imperfection on Natalie's lovely, slender back. She looked so vulnerable, so tiny, lying there in the middle of his big bed.

So helpless. So dependent. So innocent.

Kane whirled away. He stalked directly to the half-full whiskey bottle and, eschewing a glass, turned it up to his lips and took a long, fiery pull. He wiped his mouth on a gleaming forearm and set the bottle aside.

And he went back to his patient.

She lay unmoving, and time and time again Kane leaned close to place fingers directly in front of her parted lips, assuring himself she still breathed. More than once he found his hand strayed, almost of its own volition, to the strawberry-gold hair fanned out on his pillow. Like a child stroking a newborn kitten, Kane silently marveled at the silky texture of the luxurious tresses spilling through his fingers.

Hours passed.

Night had fallen. The winds had risen. The snows continued, blowing in eddying torrents from the snow-lightened night sky. Kane lit the lamps, stoked the fire, and returned to his vigil at the bed.

It was nearing midnight when, still seated stiffly on a chair beside Natalie, he heard a loud, determined knocking on the front door. Tired muscles tensing, Kane instantly pulled the sheet up to Natalie's shoulders, rose, drew a rifle from the rack, pulled back the bolt to throw a lead bullet into the chamber, and went to the door.

"Who is it?" he called through the closed wooden door, and stood to one side of the portal, rifle raised, alert blue eyes narrowed.

"Open the door, Scarback. Is the shaman, Tahomah," came the Ute's gruff voice from outside.

Kane set the rifle down and swiftly swung open the door. The old Indian came in out of the storm, his ugly face shiny wet and creased with worry, his long gray hair beaded with ice. In his gnarled hand he carried his black medicine bag.

"How is she?" he asked gravely.

Kane stared incredulously at the old man. "How did you know, Chief?"

Tahomah ignored the question. His flat black eyes went immediately to the pale young woman in Kane's bed. He lumbered across the room to stand above her. Kane followed.

"Chief, she was shot," Kane hastily explained. "I took out the bullet. It wouldn't stop bleeding; I had to cauterize the wound."

Tahomah solemnly nodded. He dropped the medicine bag onto the chair and pulled the sheet midway down Natalie's bare back. Kane watched the somber black eyes flicker with . . . hate? Fear? He wasn't sure.

"Leave me, Scarback," Tahomah ordered, turning to Kane.

Kane didn't question the old chief. He backed away, found his discarded shirt, jerked it over his head, and left the cabin. Outside, he reached for the bridle of the Ute's paint pony and, ducking his head against the wet, blowing snow, tramped upward to the small stables, leading the paint. At the wooden corral gate, Natalie's horse, Blaze, stood shivering, still saddled.

"Come on, boy." Kane patted the big mount's cold muzzle and took hold of the trailing reins. "How about a few oats and a warm stall?"

Blaze nickered gratefully and willingly followed the stranger out of the storm and into the shelter. Kane unsaddled both beasts, rubbed them down, and fed them, all the while ignoring the audible protests of his own stallion, Satan. Satan finally calmed; Kane did not. Nervously he paced the drafty barn, and when he thought he had surely killed enough time, he trudged back to the cabin.

Cautiously, he stepped inside. The shaman looked over his shoulder from his cross-armed perch upon the chair, and said in a low, commanding voice, "You may enter. I am finished."

Kane gratefully came forward. "Thanks, Tahomah."

The shaman opened his square hand. In his palm the golden disc of Natalie's necklace lay gleaming in the firelight. "All of this is my fault." He stared down at the shiny metal. "Nothing but death will come from—" He stopped speaking, laid the lavaliere back on the table. "I have placed a poultice made of herbs and alum on the wound. Do not wash away for twelve hours." His obsidian gaze lifted to Kane's. He saw the worry in Kane's brooding blue eyes. The Indian rose and motioned Kane away from the bed.

Kane brought down a new bottle of bourbon and two glasses. He filled both, slid one across the table to the old Ute, and said in a deep, low voice, "I was sleeping in my chair early this afternoon. The sound of a shot awakened me. I ran outside and saw Natalie's stallion, riderless. She lay in the snow, shot in the back." Kane's brown fingers gripped the heavy glass. "I didn't see who did it." His eyes leveled on Tahomah. "The shot was meant for me, Chief."

"I know," said Tahomah. He drank, and held out the empty glass for more. "Have you found it yet?"

Kane knew he meant the gold. "Yes."

The Indian stiffened. "Scarback, no white man will take it out and live."

Kane made no reply. Tahomah said no more on the subject. The two men spent the long, snowy night drinking, talking, caring for Natalie. Daybreak at last tinted the sky and a weary Tahomah rose to leave. He walked to the bed, briefly touched the gold necklace, then leaned down and placed a fatherly kiss upon Natalie's smooth, pale brow.

Tahomah murmured to her in his native tongue, but Kane

understood the language. The chief said, "I will not see you again on this earth, chosen-daughter. Good-bye, Fire-in-the-Snow." His blunt fingers went to the crown of fiery hair. He touched the gleaming red tresses in wonder, just as Kane had done earlier. When his hand dropped away and he straightened, Kane saw the tears glistening in the old man's black eyes and quickly lowered his own.

Kane felt a cold fear possess him. The Indian was telling Natalie good-bye. Did the ancient shaman actually believe she was going to die?

"I'll take care of her, Chief," Kane said, seeking to reassure the sad old man. "Don't worry, she'll make it."

Tahomah lumbered to the door, paused, and turned to face Kane. His black eyes settled on the shiny panther's claw resting at the base of the other man's dark throat. He put a gnarled hand on Kane's shoulder and gripped it affectionately for a moment, though he remained silent.

Kane said, "Thank you for coming, Chief. Your strong medicine will help to heal Natalie."

Tahomah's hand fell away from Kane's shoulder. Suddenly he smiled. And he said, "Love is the best healer of all."

Chapter Twenty-eight

While Natalie Vallance lay unconscious in Kane Covington's remote cabin high on the silvery-white slopes of Promontory Point, an exhausted, travel-weary man checked into a fine hotel on the other side of the Continental Divide.

It was near five in the afternoon when, stiff, tired, chilled to the bone, Ashlin Blackmore, blond curls falling over his high forehead, gray cashmere cloak whipping about his slim form, strode through the heavy glass-and-brass doors of the newly opened opulent Hotel Tremont, his presence causing an immediate stir in the crowded lobby.

All eyes turned to him. Just as he had planned.

Grandly he strode to the marble reception desk, while behind him, two uniformed bellmen struggled with his many leather valises. Speaking in clear Oxford tones, so that all of the curious might hear, Lord Blackmore told the beaming, bowing desk clerk of his horrendous trip over the storm-ravaged Rockies.

"I say, it was truly frightening." Ashlin took the proffered pen and, with a flourish, signed the guest register. "We left Cloudcastle at one o'clock sharp yesterday afternoon." He laid the pen down. "Twenty-eight hours of bumping and hurling along through a blizzard!" He could almost hear the inaudible sighs from the scattered crowd in the tall-ceilinged lobby.

"I'm terribly sorry your journey was so arduous, Lord Blackmore," sympathized the thin, sallow desk clerk. "Your suite is waiting; shall we have your dinner sent right up?" He smiled up at the taller man and his thin, black mustache gave a little twitch.

"No." Ashlin's voice was low, yet it carried throughout the room. "I'll be having dinner with the boys." He smiled then, and whirled about. It was unnecessary to identify "the boys." Everyone who was anyone in the Colorado Territory knew that "the boys" were Denver's elite, the illustrious entrepreneurs of the West, the newsmakers of the day, the possessors of the vast fortunes in Denver's golden noontide of prosperity.

The boys were Haw Tabor and John Evans and Dave Moffatt and a handful of others whose every move was watched and commented upon by the admiring citizens of the booming mountain metropolis. They were men who were envied and gossiped about and kowtowed to. They were smart and rich and handsome. Fun-loving and adventurous and urbane.

And they were impressed by nobility.

Ashlin closed the suite's heavy door behind the departing bellmen. He crossed the large sitting room to the bedchamber, where floor-to-ceiling windows were hung with burgundy cut velvet and ivory Irish lace. A massive carved bedstead stood across the carpeted room. An elaborate chandelier hung suspended from the high frescoed ceiling. A cheerful fire blazed merrily in the marble fireplace.

Ashlin sighed wearily. He had no time to relax. He went at once to the hot bath that had been drawn for him in the giant marble tub. In moments he was leaving his suite once more, slightly light-headed and pleasantly exhilarated, adrenaline pumping from lack of sleep—and from the sure knowledge that Kane Covington was no longer among the living.

Ashlin, the life of the gathering, held court at the head of a long, damask-draped table in the hotel dining room. Before him sat a long-stemmed glass of bubbling Dom Pérignon champagne, a large china plate of oysters on the half shell, a silver basket of crackers, lemon wedges, pats of butter, and a tall pepper cruet.

He ate sparingly, but he drank thirstily and laughed and talked and enthralled the all-male gathering with great ease and charm. His bright, winning smile stayed firmly in place even when Dave Moffatt leaned close and said above the din of loud male voices, "Ashlin, are you aware that a Colonel James Dunn has been making inquiries about you?"

Ashlin, brown eyes shining, absently twirled the delicate stem of his fluted champagne glass in long pale fingers. "Oh?" he said in even tones, "I don't recall meeting a Colonel Dunn." He shook his blond head thoughtfully. "Who is the gentleman, Dave?"

Moffatt lifted his elegantly suited shoulders in a shrug. "I met the man a time or two. He's a territorial official, Ashlin. I'm not certain what his interest is in you. It seems . . ."

Ashlin had a very good idea what Dunn's interest was. He recalled Colonel Dunn's being one of the witnesses to Kane Covington's deed to Promontory Point. The two men were acquainted. Likely as not they had kept in touch. Covington wanted Dunn checking up on him. Ashlin was sure of it. The suspicious, meddling southern bastard's death had come none too soon.

Ashlin took a drink of icy champagne. The relaxed posture of his slim body belied the unease within as he said levelly, "I suppose I shall only begin worrying when I no longer elicit interest, eh, Dave?"

At meal's end a noted Denver photographer appeared as if by accident. It was no accident. Ashlin had planned it down to the moment the talented man was to make his entrance. Despite much good-natured complaining and grumbling about "not wanting to be photographed," Ashlin's coddled cronies were soon posing themselves and smiling brilliantly for posterity. And in the very middle of them all, positioned so that every eye would fall quite naturally upon him, stood Lord Blackmore.

The photographer had hardly packed away his paraphernalia before Ashlin yawned, raised a slender hand to his mouth, and said regretfully, "Chaps, I really must be going to my bed."

"No! The party's just beginning," came the collective protests. But Lord Blackmore turned a deaf ear. He had what he had come here to secure. An ironclad alibi. Recorded on film. He had paid the photographer handsomely to return at once to his studios and do whatever was necessary to prepare the tintype as quickly as possible. And when it was ready, he was not only to have a courier speed a copy up to the Blackmore hotel suite, a copy was also to go to the newspaper offices of the *Denver Post* in time for its next edition.

Head throbbing dully, shoulders and back aching, Ashlin climbed the broad stairs to his suite. Inside he immediately caught the scent of expensive French perfume and felt his exhaustion falling away.

A small, satisfied smile began to play at his lips as he crossed to the bedroom. He paused in the portal, a hip leaning against the carved frame.

A beautiful, bare-bosomed prostitute smiled at him from the depths of the big bed. As requested, her long, dark hair had been carefully plaited, the ends tied with bright gold ribbons. Naked and laughing, she crawled out of the bed, crossed the room, knelt down before him, and said teasingly, "How may I serve you, milord?"

Ashlin pushed away from the door frame. Slim hands going to the fly buttons of his tight trousers, he said huskily, "Stay on your knees."

Natalie struggled to emerge from the depths of darkness. Eyelids fluttering weakly, finally she managed to lift them. Strange shapes and images swam before her clouded vision and she had no idea where she was.

The dim, dark outline of a man appeared. Framed in leaping fiery flames, he sat unmoving, his head bowed, his shoulders slumped, as though unaware he was afire. Natalie screamed as loud as she could, and pushed herself up.

Kane, dozing in a chair before the fire, heard Natalie softly whimper. He was up in an instant and at her side. She continued to softly sob and thrash about restlessly, attempting to turn over onto her back. Kane captured her flailing hands and held them.

"Don't, sweetheart," he said softly. "No."

Natalie's nightmares and terrors continued and she kept struggling. Kane held her down for more than an hour. Still she fought to rise, so finally Kane took two silk neckerchiefs from a bureau drawer and gently, loosely tied her wrists to the shiny cylinders of his bed's brass headboard.

"I had to do it, sweetheart," he soothed, checking to make sure the soft silk restraints were not too tight. Natalie continued her endeavor to free herself, while Kane looked on helplessly, murmuring to her, "Rest now, sweetheart. I'm here. I'm here."

Natalie fought frantically against the curtain of darkness engulfing her. Through slitted eyes she discerned a shape above her. She tried to move and realized to her horror that she was tied down. Outrage penetrated the deep fog she was in, and she lifted her head off the pillow. A man swam almost into focus. He looked for all the world like Kane Covington! But that could not be. It couldn't, because this man kept calling her sweetheart. Kane Covington would never in a million years call her sweetheart.

"There, sweetheart. Yes." Kane gave a great sigh of relief when at last Natalie calmed down and slept peacefully. But that peace was to be short-lived. By dark she was running a fever. Her face was flushed and burning while her small, perfect teeth chattered and her slender body shook with hard chills.

Kane built up the fire and pulled the soft fur counterpane up to her shoulders. Still she shook and jerked piteously at her silk manacles, trying impotently to free her arms so that she might curl up and get warm.

Kane sat beside her and watched helplessly while she suffered. Natalie was freezing to death in the hot, stuffy room. She shook; she pulled; she whimpered; she froze. And Kane could stand it no longer. He took off his boots, stood and stripped off his shirt. His hands went to his belt buckle and he sent the buckskins to the floor. Bending over her, he gently untied both her wrists.

And Kane got into bed with her.

Carefully tucking her slender arms between their bodies, he placed her on her side, facing him. With one long arm beneath her, the other hand holding her naked shoulder so that she would not turn onto her back and bump the healing wound, he kept her warm. Unknowing, Natalie snuggled gratefully to him, seeking his body heat.

Kane felt the heart inside his naked chest beat erratically when Natalie, squirming innocently closer, burrowed her hot face in the curve of his neck and shoulder and slipped a small hand around his back to draw him nearer.

While the sick woman in his arms lay shivering and shaking against him, Kane, perspiring profusely, held her to him throughout the long winter's night and fought the waves of unforgivable desire heating his blood. When he felt her hand rubbing against the hair of his chest, he ground his teeth. And when that hand moved and he could feel her bare, soft breasts pressing against him, he groaned aloud.

Desire rushed unbidden through his long, lean frame and his face flushed hotly beneath the darkness of his complexion. He could not stop the hardening of his body and silently cursed himself for his weakness. Wondering how any man could be low enough to feel such unbridled lust for a sick, helpless female, he lay in agony, suffering far worse than the woman in his arms.

"It's all right, sweetheart," he assured her, "even I'm not that big a bastard. You're safe. You're safe, sweetheart."

Natalie's fever broke at sunup. Peacefully she slept in Kane's arms and Kane, tired, wrung out, flaring passions long since dissipated, dozed too. Unfortunately, it was Natalie who awakened first.

At midmorning she slowly roused. Successfully casting off the imprisoning chains of unconsciousness, she begin to come around. Half awake, half asleep, she lay with her eyes closed, resting, stretching, inhaling. Senses languidly awaking, one by one. Through a rapidly lifting haze she heard the snapping of the fire, the howling of the winds. She vaguely smelled whiskey and piñon wood and a unique, unidentified scent. She tasted a dusty dryness in her mouth. She felt warm, smooth flesh against her own.

Natalie's emerald eyes slowly opened. The first thing she saw was a shiny panther's claw resting on a dark male chest. A little half smile touched her lips as her eyes slid closed once more. Feeling wonderfully safe and secure, she whispered softly, "Tahomah."

A deep, drawling voice said softly, "Natalie, Tahomah was here earlier and he—"

Natalie's eyes flew open in shocked alarm. And she saw a dark, handsome face inches from her own. She was staring into the azure eyes of Kane Covington.

Heart hammering with indignity and frustration, she suddenly became overwhelmingly aware that the two of them were in bed together and that her breasts, totally bare, were pressed to his broad naked chest. Violently she shoved him away.

"You bastard!"

Chapter Twenty-nine

Natalie struck out viciously, hitting Kane, and felt a white-hot pain stab through her right shoulder. She winced and again shouted angrily at him, certain he was responsible for her agony.

Kane swiftly grabbed her flailing fists and held them firmly in one of his hands. He twined lean fingers into her tumbled tresses and held her head immobile.

"Listen to me, Judge." His face was inches from hers, blue eyes calm, voice low and steady. "You are hurt. You must lie still. If you don't settle down, you'll do irrevocable damage."

Natalie tried to turn her face away even as tiny beads of perspiration dotted her upper lip and she felt she might faint from the pain. Kane's restraining fingers slid from her auburn curls around to grip her jaw.

"What have you done to me?" she wailed, near hysteria. "You've beaten me, you . . . you . . ."

Not surprised that she would jump to just such an outlandish conclusion, Kane continued speaking in low, quiet tones. "I'm guilty only of saving your life. You were shot, Justice Vallance, while riding on my property and I . . ." At the word *shot*, Natalie's emerald eyes widened and her thoughts snapped instantly back to the strange journal she had found at Ashlin's mansion. She shuddered. ". . . and brought you to my cabin. I removed the bullet from your back," Kane was saying.

"Who shot me?" she demanded, continuing to squirm against his restraining hands. "Who?"

"I don't know."

"You're lying," she said, her brain spinning with confusion. "You're lying and I want out of here! You let me up, I'm leaving right now." Natalie's bare breasts rose and fell rapidly with her short, nervous breaths, and she glared at Kane.

"You'll leave when you're better."

"I'll go now, damn you." She continued to struggle, her spirit unbroken despite the pain and weakness.

"You wouldn't make it, Judge. There's a raging blizzard and you—"

"What do you care if I make it or not?" she lashed out at him. "Don't pretend concern, Covington. When have you ever cared about anybody but yourself?"

Coolly, he responded, "You are absolutely correct. It's myself I'm thinking of now. I'll be damned if I'm going to let you die and have the whole of Cloudcastle blaming me." A muscle twitched in his hard jaw. His bare chest, so close to hers, was heaving and Natalie, even though she was in pain, hissed at him, "You are touching me and I'll not have it!"

Kane responded by urging her closer, purposely pressing her breasts to the damp, curling hair covering his broad chest. "You'll have anything I hand out. You're not in your courtroom passing down sentences, Judge. You're in my home and I make the law here."

As she trembled with fury, her emerald eyes shot daggers at him. "You're holding me against my will, Covington, and I . . . I . . . demand that . . . you . . . you . . ." Her words trailed weakly away and Kane felt her slender body sag tiredly against his own, her strength completely spent. Tears of frustration were gathering in her angry eyes and her pale bottom lip was trembling.

"Judge, Judge," said Kane, releasing her wrists and gently laying her down upon the bed. He pushed her wild red hair back off her pale, pain-drawn face, and with only a thumb brushed big tears from the corners of her eyes. "Justice, you're sick. You must rest here for a time. Until you are better."

"I want my clothes," Natalie ordered feebly, folding tremulous arms protectively over her bare bosom. "You stripped me!"

Kane rose from the bed and pulled the sheet up to her chin. "I left you undressed to give the wound fresh air." He paused then, his eyes searching hers for understanding, comprehension. There was neither. He continued in a low, steady voice. "I was determined to do anything necessary to safeguard your life. Blood poisoning or gangrene is always a danger, so I cauterized the wound." His deep blue eyes flickered with dread. He fully expected her temper to flare anew at the mention of cauterization, the certainty of a telltale scar marring her smooth, fragile back. He waited for the outburst. She remained mute, staring up at him distastefully, nose wrinkling.

As though she had not heard him, Natalie said scathingly, "Where are your britches?"

Kane retrieved the discarded buckskins, stepped into them, and stood facing her, buttoning the pants up over his flat belly. "Excuse me, Judge."

Eyeing him warily, she questioned, "Why were you in this bed with me?"

"Because," said Kane quietly, raking a lean hand through his disheveled coal-black hair, "you were running a high fever and freezing to death. You've been delirious at times and barely conscious at others. You were restless and thrashing and cold, so cold. I kept you warm. That's all." He presented her with an appealing, little-boy grin.

Unmoved, but wisely surmising that to order him about would be futile, she asked, "May I please have my clothes?" She was, after all, quite helpless; totally dependent upon him. The best strategy would be to pretend acquiescence while she thought things out.

Kane's boyish grin broadened and he gave her bare shoulder a pat. "Tell you what. I'll wash your wound and bandage it; then you can put on a nightshirt. Fair enough?"

Natalie considered the offer for only a moment. "Fair enough."

While he sat on the bed behind her, meticulously bathing and bandaging the heat-blackened bullet wound, Natalie didn't tell Kane that she was experiencing a great deal of discomfort. Her wound was throbbing, and knife-sharp twinges of agony were going down her right arm, up her neck, and beneath her shoulder blade.

Kane sensed it.

"Hurt bad, Judge?"

Natalie, facing away from him, shook her head no. "A little. Not much."

"All done," announced Kane, and obligingly lifted a spanking-clean soft cotton nightshirt down over her red head. "Let me," he commanded gently when Natalie tried to lift her weak arms into the long sleeves.

As one might dress an obedient child, Kane gingerly worked her slim arms through the long white sleeves of the nightshirt. As soon as small, white hands peeked out from the rolled-back cuffs of the big nightshirt, Natalie snatched the garment down over her breasts, her pale face flushing hotly.

Suspicious of the unfamiliar kindness shown by this man whom she knew to be cynical, cruel, and cold, Natalie was totally confused. And frightened. And alone. Whom could she trust? Someone had shot her, Kane said. Someone had tried to kill her. But who? And why? It had something to do with the journal. With the gold. With Ashlin? Or was this dark man lying about the whole thing?

"You said Tahomah was here?"

"Last night." Kane nodded his dark head.

"He knew that I'd been shot?"

"He did."

Natalie frowned and bit her lip. "Why did he leave me here? I must speak with him. I must go to him at—"

"Later, Judge. You can see Tahomah later," said Kane,

confident she was going to get well; certain the old chief had been mistaken about not seeing his chosen-daughter again.

Too tired for further argument, Natalie thought about the old chief's warnings about Kane being in danger and the revelation that after the twelfth moon she would no longer need to guard the Manitou gold. She absently watched Kane from beneath a veil of lowered lashes as he thoughtfully fluffed her pillows, smoothed the sheet up over her night-shirted shoulders, and spread the lush fur coverlet up to her waist.

That done, he rubbed his hands together and walked away from the bed. Over his shoulder he said as he reached for a teakettle, "Food. We need food."

"Fix yourself something, Kane. I'm not hungry." Her eyelids slipped closed as the pain in her right shoulder sharpened.

Kane gave no reply. He went about banging pots and pans, heating water, rattling china. Natalie's eyes opened slowly and she let them slide inquiringly around. There was only one room to Kane's mountain cabin. One large, cozy, comfortable room. The big bed where she lay was placed in the cabin's northwest corner directly below two tall, curtained north windows. A heavy night table sat to the right of the bed.

The kitchen area, where Kane now hummed tunelessly, was in the southwest part of the room. A sturdy eating table occupied the room's center, three straight-backed chairs pulled up to it; the fourth chair was beside the bed. In the very center of the east wall, a tall, rock fireplace blazed brightly. Before the fire, a long horsehair sofa sat at an angle, facing two upholstered easy chairs. Surprisingly, a deep-piled rug of a rich brown hue covered the floor from wall to wall.

There were windows on all sides and between those windows, tall bookcases reached to the ceiling. A small scattering of leather-bound books rested in the smooth-grained shelves. On pegs beside the front door hung a black Stetson, leather gunbelt, and various coats and slickers. There was a heavy front door on the south, a back door to the north at the foot of the bed. The many windows were tightly draped and both doors were bolted.

Kerosene lamps, scattered throughout the room, burned low, casting soft, easy light. The pungent scent of strong, aromatic tea mixed with the faint smells of leather and tobacco and fresh-cut pine. Natalie automatically inhaled deeply . . . then closed her eyes against the sights and scents of her powerfully masculine surroundings. She longed to be home in her safe white bedroom with its white, white bed and white sheets and white rug and white curtains.

Idly she wondered what time it was. It could have been noon; it might have been midnight. Natalie, too weary to think clearly, felt her closed eyelids growing heavier.

A shadow above caused her to lift them. Kane loomed over her, his bare chest now modestly concealed in a clean white shirt. The handsome, hard-planed face was still covered with a dark stubble of beard and his usually clear blue eyes were slightly bloodshot.

But he smiled engagingly and lowered a tray across her lap. Natalie's eyes fell on a large bowl of steaming hot liquid that looked totally unappetizing. Wafer crackers and a cup of tea looked a bit less distasteful, but far from inviting.

"I can't, Kane," she told him.

"You will," said Kane, taking a seat on the bed facing her.

"I won't. It's time I went home. If you'll be good enough to saddle Blaze for me I'll—"

"You're far too weak."

"I'm not weak. I'm fine and I'm leaving."

"I'll make you a bargain. You eat the broth and drink the tea. You can go home."

Natalie eyed him skeptically. But she picked up the silver spoon. Amazed at how outlandishly heavy a simple soup spoon could be, she shakily raised the full ladle toward her mouth and barely made it. Exhausted, she lowered her hand and sighed.

Kane's keen eyes said *I told you so,* though he did not speak. He lifted the linen napkin from the tray, unfurled it, and tucked it in the neckband of Natalie's borrowed nightshirt. He took the spoon from her, dipped it into the hot, nourishing broth, and lifted it to her lips.

She had no choice but to let him feed her. She was well aware she could not manage the task herself and if she was to be released from this mountain prison and her dark jailer, she had to eat to fulfill her part of the bargain. It was an ordeal even with his help. Feeling as though the bottom of the big white bowl would never appear, Natalie took ladle after ladle of the dark, salty liquid, stopping now and then to rest. The tea, piping hot and inky black, scalded down her throat and was delicious.

The ordeal ended at last. Natalie sighed with relief when Kane rose and removed the tray. His back was to her when she put her left hand to the mattress and laboriously levered herself into a sitting position. Breathing raggedly, she pushed at the heavy fur covers and white linen sheet. Managing, after a couple of aborted attempts, to free her bare feet from their folds, she swung her legs over the edge of the bed, biting back a cry of anguish as the movement caused renewed throbbing in her wounded right shoulder.

She sat there, head bowed, long, disheveled hair falling about her pale face, silently commanding herself to step down onto the floor. In answer, she assured herself she would do just that as soon as she took a moment to rest. She was in that position when Kane approached her.

"What in the name of God are you doing?" His fear for her welfare came out in the form of irritation.

With great effort she lifted her sagging head. "I'm going home."

"The hell you are," he said coldly.

"You promised," she reminded him with as much haughtiness as she could muster. "You said if I ate, I could go."

"I lied," he told her coolly as he bent and placed an arm under her knees. He lifted her bare feet from the floor and laid her back on the bed, pulling the covers up once again.

Angry that he had tricked her, too weak to fight him, Natalie sank down into the pillows and attacked him in the only way possible. Verbally.

"How could I have trusted someone as unprincipled as you, Kane Covington? I might have known believing one word you say is a fool's game. Well, you win and shame on me. But know this, you lying southern son of a bitch, I am going home just as soon as you fall asleep or look the other way or go tend the horses. You can't keep me here, you won't keep me here. I am going home and I— Oooohh . . ." her high brow creased with pain and her eyes clouded.

"What is it? Judge, are you—" His eyes clouded too, with fear, and he was beside her, his hands on her shoulders, his heart racing.

The sharp pain passed and Natalie shrugged violently. "Take your hands off me."

Kane's jaw hardened. He moved his hands, but he placed them, palms flat, on either side of her slender body and leaned menacingly close. And his voice became flint-hard and deadly quiet. "Lady, I saved your life. Well, I owed you one for saving mine, so now we're even. Still, while I expect no thanks from you, I'm in no mood to listen to your foolish chastisement. You're a very sick woman and there's a blizzard going on outdoors. I'm as eager for you to get out of here as you are to go. Do us both a favor, behave yourself and gain a little strength, then I guarantee you I'll take you home myself."

His dark, unshaven face, so close to hers, was set and evil-looking, his full lips thinned and stiff. The blue eyes were hard as stone and above them heavy black eyebrows slashed straight, menacing lines above those mean, hooded eyes. Natalie stared up at him. Speechless.

Wisely remaining silent, she drew a shallow breath and lowered her eyes from his ice-blue stare. And she gave an inward sigh of relief when finally he rose and left her. She watched as he moved about the big room, drawing the dark, heavy drapes. He didn't stop until every curtain covering every tall window was open.

Natalie blinked as the pervading, all-encompassing white of the snowstorm poured eye-punishing light into the spacious room. As bright as any summer sun, the swirling, blowing snow was blinding in its intensity. The large cabin and everything in it were suddenly illuminated with dazzling brilliance that caused Natalie's head to ache, her eyes to squint and water.

Kane, moving back to the bed, his brief flare of temper again submerged, said in a low, kind voice, "Judge, there's a terrible storm out there. Won't you stay until it is over?"

Natalie, eyes smarting from the light, looked up at him. And she smiled. "I will. If you'll close the curtains; the light's hurting my eyes."

Kane threw back his dark head and laughed. Blue eyes at once becoming devilish, he came directly to the bed, shoved his hands deep into his pants pockets, and grinned down at her.

"Say please." Chuckling softly, Kane waited for her upbraiding.

"Please, Kane."

Chapter Thirty

Kane's laughter ceased.

His blue eyes narrowed cynically as he gazed down at a strangely sweet-tempered Natalie. She was smiling prettily up at him and it unnerved him far more than her angry chastening had. He didn't trust her. Not for a minute. He could practically hear the wheels of a quick brain grinding inside that lovely red head of hers.

Mentally cautioning himself to watch her every move, he said simply, "Glad to, Judge. We both need more rest." Hands eased out of his pockets and he turned away.

Heart drumming in her chest, Natalie watched him move agilely, silently about the room, darkening one by one the tall rectangles of blinding snow-bright light. A scheme was rapidly taking hold. She knew Kane must be tired. Very tired. Likely as not he had slept only two, maybe three, hours since he'd brought her in out of the snow.

"Kane," she said softly when the last of the heavy drapes had been pulled. "I'm a little sleepy. Would I be imposing if I ask that you lower the lamps as well?"

"As good as done," said Kane congenially, and went about blowing out lamps, saving the one on the night table beside the bed until last. As his lean brown fingers lifted the glass globe, he looked down at Natalie and said in a voice barely above a whisper, "Sweet dreams, Judge," and the room was cast into semidarkness, leaving only the glow from the stone fireplace.

Natalie, head turned on the pillow, watching, held her breath. She saw him move from the night table and become swallowed up in the shadows. Praying he would go to the long, horsehair sofa where he could stretch out and fall quickly asleep, she waited hopefully, listening. She could hear no footfalls but reasoned that he was a lithe, cat-footed man and the carpet was deep and muffling. Tentatively, silently, she lifted her head off the pillow and squinted in the dimness, straining to see the couch . . . and him upon it.

She jumped, startled.

Kane, touching only a forefinger to the back of her hand, said quietly, "I'm right here, Judge. I'll just sit beside the bed and watch you sleep."

Natalie snatched her hand away, mindless of the piercing pain shooting through her shoulder. "Sit. Lie down. Or stand up all day long for all I care," she bit out, and turned her face away.

Kane grinned, drew a cigar from atop the night table, and lit up. Contemplatively, he smoked in the quiet, warm room, his eyes on the mane of tumbled red hair on the pillow, his thoughts on the men who had put it there.

The bullet had been intended for him; of that he had no doubt. She'd been on a bay stallion identical to the one he rode, and she was dressed in men's buckskins. A black Stetson lay beside her upon the snow. They had seen her, mistaken her for him, and shot her.

The Leatherwoods? Sure. But who gave the orders? Ashlin Blackmore?

Natalie, pain quickly overriding her anger, found her thoughts returning to her would-be murderers. She desperately needed to talk to Tahomah. There was no one else she could question; no one else to whom she could relate her dark fears and suspicions. The damning revelations of the worn diary could not be explained away. A sense of terrible foreboding claimed her as she finally allowed the awful truth to surface.

Ashlin Blackmore was mixed up in this attempt on her life. The bullet had not been meant for her. It had been meant for Kane Covington. Someone wanted Kane dead and out of the way. The Leatherwoods, she suspected, fired the shot. But someone else was responsible. Some one else had given the orders. Someone else had reason to want . . .

Natalie dozed.

Kane crushed out his cigar, yawned tiredly, hunched his wide shoulders forward, laced his fingers between his knees, and peered at the sleeping woman. In her slumber her face had turned back toward him. The green eyes were closed, the soft, pink lips were parted. Her abundant cinnamon hair was in wild disarray about her head, a fiery strand falling across her left cheek.

"Judge?" Kane murmured softly. "Judge?"

There was no answer. Kane expelled a sigh of relief, leaned back in his chair, and catnapped.

Natalie came painfully awake. Stifling a groan of agony, she looked at the sleeping man beside her bed. She had waited for this moment. But now that it was here, she couldn't take advantage of it. In fact, instead of being delighted to find Kane asleep so that she might slip away, Natalie heard herself whisper through thinned lips, "Kane."

Instantly he was awake. "Judge," he responded, his alert eyes on her face, "what is it?"

Feeling as though she might scream from the intensifying pain, she managed weakly, "I . . . don't feel too good, Kane."

"Fever again?" His hand shot out to her face.

"No . . . but . . ." Her eyes rolled back in anguish, her face paled, and instinctively she gripped his hand.

"Pain?" he quizzed, leaning close. "The wound hurting?"

Biting her lip, she nodded.

Kane hastily lit the lamp. He threw back the covers and sat down on the bed. Easing Natalie onto her side, he shoved up the nightshirt and undid her bandage. Relieved to see the wound, however painful, was already beginning to heal, he deftly redressed it, pulled the nightshirt back down, and rose.

"I have no laudanum, Judge, but there's no more effective anesthetic in the world than whiskey." He turned questioning eyes on her pale, drawn face.

"Maybe one," she agreed, beads of moisture dotting her stiff white lips.

It was a terrible hour for both of them. In all her life Natalie could not recall the kind of pain she was experiencing. Valiantly fighting to be brave lest her cynical companion think her a foolish, complaining female, Natalie let wave after wave of blinding pain throb joltingly through her without uttering a sound.

Kane, holding the half-full shot glass, watched helplessly as wrenching pain dimmed the beautiful emerald eyes of the suffering woman so foolishly trying to be strong for pride's sake. He knew better than to tell her it was all right for her to cry or moan. She was far too stubborn to listen to any reasoning from him.

"Take another small drink, Judge," he gently urged, and raised the whiskey to her lips. Natalie sipped, made a sour face, and thought the cure must surely be as bad as the cause.

But the horrid throbbing soon abated slightly and Natalie turned to Kane. Almost timidly she said, "Can I have a bit more whiskey?"

Not an hour later, a pain-free, very tipsy Natalie had downed almost three full shots of strong whiskey and was nodding her head yes to more. She drank from the glass Kane held for her, licked her lips, and did not frown at all.

And she fell to talking. She talked and talked and never noticed that the man with whom she was holding a conversation said little more than "Yes, Judge" or "No, Judge" or "Go ahead and say it."

Kane obligingly tipped the whiskey glass up to Natalie's thirsty lips. He knew she was growing drunk, very drunk, and was afraid she would pay for it later by becoming nauseated. But for now her torturous pain was gone and her eyes shone with the radiance of well-being. She was comfortable and relaxed and happy.

And talkative.

". . . first female magistrate of Castleton County . . . did you know that, Kane?"

"Yes, Judge."

". . . and Devlin killed in the war . . . Tahomah's chosen daughter . . . Ashlin Blackmore came to Cloudcastle in . . ." Information spilled from her soft lips like water from a well. Kane, listening keenly, learned more about Natalie Vallance than he'd ever before known.

". . . never truly loved him. . . ." Kane leaned closer. "But he seemed so kind and caring and . . ." Abruptly her eyes clouded and she stared into his. "I found a journal at his mansion, Kane . . . and . . ."

"What kind of journal?"

"A diary . . . a . . . it was . . ." Natalie shook her head. He knew the subject was forgotten when suddenly she smiled and, staring at him like a wide-eyed curious child, reached up and unabashedly touched his right ear. "Did I ever tell you that you've got the nicest ears I've ever seen on a man?" She giggled then, happily, and traced the convolution of his ear with examining fingertips.

"Thanks," murmured Kane, allowing her access to the part of his face that so fascinated her. "About the diary, Judge . . . what did—"

"They lie close to your head and the hair grows just so in wavy swirls above them," Natalie interrupted, concerned only with Kane's ears. He knew it was useless to question her. "Another drink?" she said, abruptly losing interest in his ears and falling back onto the pillow.

"Judge, don't you think you've had enough?"

She laughed. And her voice was girlish and almost musical when she said, "Not really. Don't be mean to me, Kane. Please don't." Before he could answer, Natalie thrust her slim fingers into her hair on both sides of her head. "Oh, Kane, it's dirty. My hair's so dirty!"

"I'll wash it tomorrow."

"Really?" She released the long, tangled tresses and reached for his hand. He took it and held it in both of his.

"Really, Judge."

She found that terribly amusing for some reason. Tinkling, giddy laughter issued from her lips and she tried to speak as she laughed. "You're teasing . . . me . . . you don't . . . you wouldn't . . . you . . ." And new peals of laughter overcame her.

Kane continued to hold her hand. She continued to laugh and talk. She laughingly demanded—and received—one more glass of whiskey. She charmingly suggested that he drink with her. They shared the same glass, she urging it to his lips as soon as she had sipped. And she continued with her incessant talking, the liquor loosening her tongue. But it was all nonsensical.

And flirtatious.

". . . say they think you're good-looking . . ." Her eyes impaled his dark face. Kane gave no reply. "I said I didn't agree, but you know what, Kane? I do. I always have. You're a very handsome man, but you're . . . hmmm . . . scary." She twisted her hand from his grip and lifted it once more to his face. "Your features are so sharp, Kane . . . you look mad and dangerous half the time." Slender fingers outlined his prominent nose, his strong jawline, the soaring cheekbones. "Are you, Kane?" she asked saucily. "Are you angry? Are you dangerous?" And her hand slipped to his mouth. Two inquiring fingers traced the sculpted contours of his sensuous lips and she felt them move beneath her touch.

"The easiest-going man you could ever hope to meet," said Kane Covington.

"I doubt it, but your mouth is . . . your lips are so . . ." Her words trailed away and Natalie yawned sleepily. "I'm tired," she said softly, her fingers continuing their exploration of Kane's mouth.

"Sleep, Judge," urged Kane.

"Hmmm . . . all right . . . if you'll . . ." The sentence was never finished. Natalie lay silent, her eyes still open, fingers still touching Kane's warm, smooth lips. They remained like that for a time. She reclining sleepily, her hand on his face. He, indulgently still, letting her play, watching as her eyelids grew increasingly heavy.

The fragile hand fell away. The big green eyes slipped closed. An appealing little smile curved her soft lips and she turned her face into the pillow. And she slept soundly for the next eight hours.

She awoke with a raging headache and a churning stomach. Cautiously she turned her eyes toward Kane. He was still in his chair, long legs propped up on the foot of the bed, stockinged feet crossed at the ankles.

As if she had spoken, his blue eyes opened. The laughing, likable woman who'd fallen sleep earlier awoke a sick, wretched one. With the speed of a jaguar, Kane was on his feet and fetching a basin. No sooner had he made it back to the bed than Natalie was retching miserably.

Kane held the basin and held her long hair back from her face while she gagged and vomited, her slender body jerking pitifully, tears streaming down her cheeks.

And when it was over, Kane bathed her pale, white face gently, gave her a cool drink of water and a stick of peppermint to cleanse her mouth.

"I'm sorry, Kane," she said, her emerald eyes glistening with embarrassment and shame.

"It's I who am sorry, Natalie," said Kane, and her breath caught in her throat. He'd called her Natalie. Natalie, her name. Never before had he called her Natalie. Never anything but judge or justice or . . . baby, when they had made love. He'd called her baby then.

Natalie felt a shiver of excitement go through her body. When she'd been semiconscious, she had heard a man's deep, kind voice calling her sweetheart. It was Kane. Kane had called her sweetheart. Several times.

"Kane," she ventured softly. "Did . . . did I say anything foolish while I was—"

"Not a thing, Judge." His voice had lost that soft, seductive Mississippi drawl, his eyes, their glowing warmth.

Kane fully realized that his voice and eyes had changed. It

was done purposely. He had caught himself saying her given name, looking at her with affection. He had no intention of letting this pale, lovely woman get under his skin. And he wanted her to know it.

Natalie lowered her gaze from Kane's cold blue one and said no more. The nausea had passed, but she felt drained and strangely melancholy. She closed her eyes and pretended to sleep, though she lay there awake, wondering at Kane's puzzling behavior. He had been so helpful, so caring, so genuinely tender. Then . . .

Kane's eyes never left her face. He sat silently staring at her, convinced she had fallen back to sleep. Elbows on bent knees, Kane leaned closer, fingers steepled beneath his chin.

He watched her. And as he watched her, a long-forgotten emotion stirred in his broad, tight chest. So long forgotten, he failed to fully recognize it for what it was.

But it was akin to love.

Chapter Thirty-one

The winter storm gripping the Shining Mountains continued to heap wet, heavy snow on the steep slopes of the towering San Juans, on the high-soaring Promontory Point, and on the remote alpine cabin clinging to its southern face.

Inside the warm shelter of that well-built cabin, Natalie Vallance spent some of the worst moments of her life. And some of the best.

The throbbing pain in her back returned and Natalie, refusing Kane's offer of whiskey, lay clutching the sheets tightly, her eyes opening and closing in agony.

Kane paced the floor catlike, cursing softly under his breath, and begged her to drink some whiskey. Fearing what she might reveal if she again became drunk, Natalie staunchly refused.

So they both suffered.

At intervals her pain would miraculously pass and there would be a lazy, pleasant interlude of calm relaxation. Both would lightly doze or talk quietly or just rest, not speaking, hardly thinking.

It was on the fourth day that Natalie, almost entirely free of pain, remembered Kane's earlier promise. He had said he would wash her hair. She knew he hadn't meant it, but he was in a good mood and she was too. She felt like teasing him a little.

"Dr. Covington," she called softly to him.

Kane, drinking hot coffee at the table, looked up, his expressive eyes at once troubled. Rising, he said, "You're worse."

"No, no, I'm not, Kane. I'm fine." She gave a negative wave of her left hand. "I didn't mean to alarm you."

Relieved, Kane eased back down in his chair. "Doesn't matter. What can I do for you, Judge?" He drank the last of his coffee.

"Ummm." She stretched, wiggling her toes beneath the soft fur. "Remember when I complained about my hair being dirty?" She smiled but fully expected to see the hardening of his jaw, the dismissive lowering of his lids over bored blue eyes.

"Want to wash it this afternoon?"

Natalie blinked. "Could I, Kane?"

"No," he said, carrying his cup and saucer to the cupboard, "but I can." He turned, leaned a hip against the cabinet, and folded his arms over his chest. "Want me to?"

Natalie's heart gave a funny little skip. "I want you to."

Kane whistled as he went about building up the fire. Satisfied the cabin was warm enough for a sick woman to wet her hair, he went about his preparations, a mild excitement filling him. He so enjoyed touching that glorious, strawberry-gold hair, and she was going to allow him to wash it. He couldn't think of a more pleasant task. Scratching absently at his stubbly chin, Kane, shirtless, heated water, laid out several clean white towels and a bar of soap, and lifted a tin basin from under the sink.

Natalie, amused, watched him go about his preparatory chores and felt as though she could hardly wait to feel hot, cleansing water saturate her hair.

Kane came forward with a pan of water. He placed it on the chair beside the bed. Natalie looked quizzically up at him.

"Why are you bringing the water over here? I thought I'd get up and go to the—"

"Who's washing your hair? You or me?" But a warm, friendly light gleamed in his eyes and his full lips were stretched into a grin.

"Why, you are, Dr. Covington," replied a smiling Natalie.

In seconds the covers were at the foot of the big bed and Natalie, lifted gently by Kane, lay on her back across the mattress, head over its edge, supported in Kane's hands as he sat beside her on the bed.

And then that delicious moment. He lowered her head into the warm water and Natalie felt it lapping up to her ears. It was wonderful, glorious, and she didn't hesitate to let him know.

"Paradise, Kane Covington, absolute paradise."

"I know," said Kane, and she never realized that he meant it was paradise for him.

Strong fingers combed through her long wet tresses, briskly massaging her scalp. And all the while they chattered and laughed and behaved like two foolish children.

Several soapings and numerous rinsings left Natalie's long hair squeaky clean. Head in Kane's encompassing hands, she waited for the towel to go about the sodden locks. With one hand he reached for a dry, clean towel, but paused before draping it around her head.

"I nearly forgot," said Kane, grinning down at her. "Young ladies like to use a rinse on their hair, don't they?"

"Well, yes, but it's all right. . . ."

"Stay where you are," Kane said, and eased her wet head back down into the clean water.

Flat on her back, she could not see him but could hear him as he moved about in the kitchen. When he returned, he was grinning as though he'd performed a great feat. In his long-fingered right hand he held a small object wrapped in yellow tissue paper.

Natalie smelled the fresh lemon even before he unwrapped it and held it out for her to admire. He was gone before she could comment, then right back with the pungent lemon,

sliced in half. He crouched down and squeezed the juice over
her hair, and Natalie didn't have the heart to tell him he
should have diluted it with water. Ignoring the stinging of the
sharp citrus on her pink scalp, she said simply, "Thank you,
Kane."

He dunked her head into the water and told her, "That
will make your hair shine."

"It will. But how did you know?" she questioned as he
lifted her head and squeezed the excess water from her hair.

Tossing a large white towel over her head, he sat her up,
turned her about, and took a seat behind her.

"Sharon," he said, vigorously toweling her hair. "Sharon,
my little sister, used to rinse her hair in lemon juice."

"Tell me about her, Kane"—Natalie's voice was soft, persuasive—"while you dry my hair."

And so the two of them passed that cold, snowy afternoon
propped up in the middle of Kane's big bed; Kane drying,
brushing, combing his fingers through the mane of clean
flaming hair; Natalie allowing him to cradle her head to his
chest whenever he felt she was tiring. And all the while she
coaxed him to talk about his family, his Mississippi home, his
past life.

"Sharon's hair was beautiful, like yours," he told her. "It
was shimmering gold and silky, and when she'd brush out it,
why, it went down past her waist." Kane spoke of Sharon's
death, and of his mother's and father's. He told Natalie of his
big, beloved old plantation on the coast. ". . . and we would
sit on the verandah in the evenings, cooled by the gentle Gulf
breezes, the fragrance of Mother's oleanders and magnolias
perfuming the humid air. I spent some of the happiest days of
my life there."

He talked and talked, telling her things that touched her
heart. Stories of boyhood pranks that made her laugh. Warm,
delightful stories of a family close and loving. Tales of poi-
gnant, personal experiences that caused tears to fill her eyes
and made her want to turn and give him a big, warm hug.

Kane, transfixed by the long, shiny tresses now dry and
spilling through his eager fingers, would have talked forever

to keep her as she was. Hardly realizing what he was saying, his deep voice droned on while his hands and eyes remained on the shining glory that was her hair. It had been ages since he had enjoyed anything quite so completely as sitting behind Natalie and brushing her beautiful hair while he talked quietly of the days long since dead.

It was Natalie who, finally lifting her good left hand to stay the brush, turned her head, smiled, and said, "Kane, that was lovely, truly it was, and I thank you."

Kane, reluctantly rising from the bed, said apologetically, "I've kept you sitting up far too long." He laid the hairbrush aside and helped her sink back among the pillows. "Hungry?" he inquired, grinning down at her.

"I am, but . . ."

"Yes?"

"Well," she began, and reached for his hand. He gladly gave it to her and she toyed with the strong fingers. "Since my hair's all clean and nice . . ."

"Beautiful," he corrected her.

Her eyes went pointedly to his black scratchy beard. "I was thinking that perhaps we might . . . ah . . . try to look our best for supper tonight."

Kane smiled. "If you want me to shave, say so."

"Shave, Kane." Her eyes drifted down to his bare chest. "And put on a shirt."

"I'll bring you a new nightshirt. Then you rest while I clean up. Agreed?"

"Agreed."

She meant only to rest. She was tired and relaxed and hungry. She would laze contentedly while he cleaned up and fixed their meal. Then perhaps he would let her eat sitting up at the table. Natalie smiled a little at the thought. And felt a measure of anticipation.

As dusk descended, Kane lit a kerosene lamp and carried it across the room. Humming, he soaped his whiskered face with thick lather, stropped his straight-edge razor, and began shaving.

Still bare-chested, he lifted both muscular arms. His right

hand held the sharp razor, the left lifted tight, stubbly skin for the stroking. As he did everything else, Kane Covington shaved with easy deftness and grace. Natalie was intrigued. She watched every long, sure stroke of gleaming blade on lathered flesh until the dark, harshly planed face was completely free of black whiskers.

Expecting him to wipe away the excess lather and move from the mirror, Natalie was puzzled when Kane again lathered his face and started over. She'd have to ask him about that.

Her gaze dropped to the wide, tanned shoulders and remained there. Firelight flickered on the satiny-smooth skin and turned the brown flesh a deep brick hue, the white ribbon-like scars a pale pink. His shoulder blades lifted and lowered with the movements of his arms, and Natalie found it fascinating.

All too soon he had, for a second time, shaved all the white foam from his face and was lifting the towel that hung around his neck. Natalie was almost sorry the performance had ended.

Kane looked appraisingly at himself in the tall mirror, turning his face first this way, then that. His fingers skimmed searchingly over the smooth-shaven jaw, and he winked at himself.

Casting a glance over his shoulder, Kane went about his bath, the changing of his clothes, the cooking of their meal, with a boyish expectation. It was almost as if he and Natalie had a dinner engagement and he was looking foolishly forward to the evening.

Snow still fell outside and cold winds howled, but Kane found the wild weather only added to his stimulation. Inside it was warm and safe and intimate. Smiling happily, he unfolded a white cloth and laid the table. From below the cupboard came a bottle of Château Lafite '55. Candles soon flickered on china plates and crystal glasses.

The meal was about ready. Kane, checking to be sure his clean white silk shirt was modestly buttoned to his throat, turned on his bootheel and strode across the room.

"It's ready, Natalie. Dinner's—" He stood beside the bed. His wide shoulders slumped in disappointment. Natalie was sound asleep.

Kane considered waking her, but he knew she needed sleep more than food. She could eat something later, when she awakened. He leaned over her, wistfully touched a long, shiny lock of clean red hair, turned, and walked dejectedly away.

Bending to blow out the candles, Kane ate alone. Appetite gone, he quickly pushed his plate aside, barely touched. Uncorking the bottle of expensive wine, he held it up over his shoulder to the woman peacefully sleeping behind him. "To you, sweetheart," said Kane, lowering the chilled bottle and turning it up to his lips.

It was much later when Natalie woke.

Only the fireplace gave illumination. Natalie sat up in bed, looking about. She saw the untouched dinner on the table. And she saw Kane seated in one of the easy chairs before the fire. Sleeping.

He was trousered in black, his long legs stretched out to the fire. His snowy white shirt hung open to his waist, the sleeves rolled up over the sinewy muscles of his long, powerful arms. Black, thick curls clustered over his high forehead, falling almost to his closed, dark-lashed eyes.

He looked for all the world like a sleek, sleeping tiger and as Natalie leisurely studied him, she decided he was more dangerous, more deadly. Even asleep the man was a threat, because the sight of him reclining there, so masculinely beautiful, so effortlessly potent, made her long to throw back the covers, run to him, and fling herself into his arms.

Natalie felt a tiny moan choking her. Kane had shaved, twice, and bathed and put on clean, expensive clothes. He had cooked a meal and lit candles and uncorked wine. And he had done it all for her. It was flattering. Appealing. Devastating. Dangerous.

There was only one thing to do. Leave. Leave before the sleeping tiger awakened and rendered her totally helpless against such overwhelming, powerful charm. Leave before those all-seeing blue eyes looked straight into her tortured soul. Leave before he sensed that she cared much too much.

Leave before she got down on her knees and begged that sleeping symbol of beauty, power, and mystery never, ever to let her go.

Chapter Thirty-two

As quietly as possible, Natalie eased the sheet and fur counterpane down, her watchful eyes never leaving the man slumbering before the fire. Swinging her long, slender legs over the edge of the bed, she stepped down onto the carpeted floor and, hand clinging to the mattress for support, stood up.

Waves of dizziness engulfed her and she felt the room about her spinning out of control. She managed to sink back onto the bed before falling. Patiently waiting for the world to right itself, Natalie, heart racing, debated abandoning her plan to flee. Surely within two or three days Kane would take her home.

Two or three days . . . Two or three more days of hearing that deep, drawling voice speaking softly, patiently to her, its pleasing timbre spreading warmth and sweet lassitude throughout her being. Two or three more days of watching the play of muscles in his sleek physique as he went about naked to the waist, the pale slashing scars across his long, smooth back beckoning her to touch, to stroke, to caress. Two or three more days of feeling those long, powerful arms go about her as he lifted her, tended her, doctored her. Two or three more days of looking into those hypnotic blue eyes that drew her so effortlessly into their fathomless depths.

Natalie rose once more.

She did not black out this time. She moved cautiously across the dim room, casting quick, nervous glances at Kane's sleeping form. She managed to find the buckskins she had worn the day of the shooting, and her boots. The shirt had been thrown away. No matter; she would leave on Kane's nightshirt.

Struggling, Natalie managed to work the tight leather britches up over her hips. Winded by the chore, she leaned against the cabinet to rest for a minute, eyes on Kane. Stuffing the long tail of the nightshirt down into the buckskins, she got the pants buttoned, with effort, and carried the boots with her to the table.

Gritting her teeth and squinting her eyes as though that would cover the noise she made, Natalie pulled out a straight-backed chair, took a seat, and went about drawing on her leather boots. With no stockings on her bare feet, it was almost impossible to pull on the boots, but she made it.

Again she paused to rest, seated there at the table where the evening meal remained untouched. Rising, she walked on booted tiptoe to the coats hanging beside the front door. Choosing a warm-looking heavy wool jacket, she shrugged hurriedly into it. By now her shoulder was hurting from all the exertion, but she ignored it. Soon she would be home; nothing else mattered.

Natalie struggled with the bolt lock, finally heard it slide clear. Anxiously she turned to look once more at Kane. And her hand trembled on the doorknob. Peacefully, unknowing, he slept there in his chair, the firelight flickering over his face, his raven hair, the wide silk-draped shoulders. In slumbering repose, the harshly handsome face looked almost boyish. But the long, lean body was that of a man: a strong, powerful man.

Natalie eased the door open only enough to slip out. She shut it behind her and drew in a quick, frigid breath. It was cold, freezing cold, and snow swirled down out of the murky night skies. Wrapping Kane's heavy coat more tightly about her slender body, Natalie put her head down and made her way to the stables, knowing, down deep, she was behaving foolishly.

Determined that she would saddle Blaze, ride home to Cloud West, and sleep safely in her own bed, she overlooked the discomfort of her wounded back and the danger of the mountain blizzard.

Through the blowing snow she made her way to the stables, panting and sagging against the plank stalls once she was inside. A coal-oil lamp hung beside the door, sulfur matches on the ledge. With cold, stiff hands Natalie lit it and looked around.

Blaze saw her and neighed a greeting. Natalie smiled but lifted a forefinger, placing it vertically to her lips, murmuring softly, "Shhh, boy. Please don't wake Kane."

He paid no attention. He continued to wicker and snort and to nuzzle her as she summoned all of her strength and lifted the heavy saddle onto his tall back. Kane's stallion, Satan, threw his great head back, and whinnied and pranced, to let her know she was disturbing him.

Natalie used up all her strength lifting the saddle. She leaned against Blaze, breathing heavily, exhausted, trembling. The horse turned his head and nuzzled her cold shoulder, making soft, reassuring noises deep in his throat, as though he fully understood.

Natalie raised her head, fought for breath, and finished the task, tightening the cinch beneath the horse's shiny belly. Blaze obligingly opened his mouth wide when Natalie drew the bridle over his face and in seconds she was leading the helpful mount out of his stall.

"It's you and me, boy," she said softly, patting his withers before climbing onto his back. She urged him to the door, ducking down as he stepped through the low doorway out into the storm. She held the big horse to a walk, afraid to risk the sound of hoofbeats clattering across the frozen ground.

Neck reining the faithful steed down the incline behind the cabin, Natalie saw something move. Jerking up on the reins, heart thundering, eyes wide with fear, she watched a shadowy figure move through the thick snow toward her. He loomed closer and stepped into view. The fine silk shirt was plastered to his chest, raven hair sprinkled with snowflakes. The dark, hard face was wet with snow and rigid with wrath.

Natalie gave a little yelp of despair and dug her heels into Blaze's flanks. The big bay lurched forward, straight toward the approaching man. Kane did not move out of the way. His arm shot out with a speed that frightened the confused horse. He grabbed the bridle, jerked the stallion's head down, and reached for Natalie.

Incensed, frantic, she fought him, hitting at him, kicking, screaming. It did no good; he hauled her down and roughly jerked her along with him toward the stable, ignoring her shouts and struggles. One-handed, Kane unsaddled the nervous beast, his face a mask of dark fury, his fingers biting painfully into the flesh of Natalie's arm.

He said not a word and that alarmed Natalie far more than if he had shouted at her. The horse restabled, Kane turned, swept Natalie up into his arms, and walked out. Panicked by the deadly-mean expression in his hard blue eyes, Natalie continued to struggle against him, afraid of what he intended once he got her back inside his cabin.

Kane was livid.

Holding the battling Natalie in his arms, he stalked down the snowy incline. She was wriggling and hitting and screaming and he had difficulty holding her. Snow was blowing into his face, wetting the silk shirt he wore and plastering his hair to his head. His legs were weak with fright and he could feel the deep snow sucking at his boots, making the steps treacherous.

He was almost to the cabin when he stepped into a hole and lost his footing. He felt himself sinking into the snow and cursed. Down they went, the angry, worried man and the fighting, frightened woman. Forward they fell into a deep, wet snowbank, Natalie screaming, Kane cursing.

He never let go of Natalie. The pair lay immersed in the freezing snow, two bodies melded together, buried in a white, cold grave. He was up in a second, she in his arms, both wet from head to toe.

Back inside, Kane kicked the door shut behind him and roughly set Natalie on her feet. Contrite now, subdued and more than a little afraid, Natalie said, through teeth that were beginning to chatter, "Kane, I—"

"No!" he warned her, his voice as cold and deadly as his eyes. "Don't say a goddamned word! Not one!"

Teeth chattering with cold and with fear, she stood there silent, dripping snow and water on the brown rug. Afraid to speak, afraid to move, she watched him work with swift power and speed as he threw fresh logs into the fire. She winced when he turned and reached for her.

Ignoring the flash of fear in her eyes, Kane jerked her toward the fire and pulled the wet, heavy jacket off her. Violently, he threw the sodden jacket at the front door. Natalie jumped when it smacked loudly against the wood and slid down to a soggy heap on the floor.

Kane's hands went to her damp nightshirt. Natalie silently protested, raising her hand to stop him. He brushed it away wordlessly, and glared menacingly down at her. Knowing she was beaten, she lowered her eyes, and said nothing when he lifted the nightshirt over her head and tossed it aside.

Refusing to allow her to do it herself, or even to help, Kane undressed her. He clamped her down into a chair and struggled with the wet leather boots, letting them fall where they fell. He jerked her up, unbuttoned her pants and peeled the tight buckskin trousers down over her rounded hips. He didn't stop, he didn't speak, until Natalie, furious and freezing, stood naked in the firelight, sopping hair streaming over a bare shoulder, dignity discarded with her pants.

Kane abruptly walked away from her. She took a cautious step. He whirled about. "Stay right where you are!"

She did.

Directly he returned, bringing with him several towels. She reached out for one; he withheld it. He turned her about to face the fire and began drying her wet body, her soaked hair. Hands sure and masterful, he stood behind her and swiped the towel over her shaking shoulders, taking care not to hurt her wound. Natalie fought back tears of humiliation when she felt the towel move down to her rounded buttocks, onto her thighs and the calves of her legs.

She gasped when Kane took hold of her left arm and turned her to face him.

"Please, Kane," she murmured, reaching for the towel, and saw in his icy eyes that it was hopeless. He would not listen to reason.

Kane lifted her long, wet hair up off her shoulder and neck, blotted at the heavy mane, rubbed it between the folds of the towel, and fanned it through his fingers until it was only damp. Then he wound it neatly atop her head and covered it with a clean towel, knotting it over her brow.

Natalie's fear was swiftly turning to anger. She stood, her hands at her sides, no longer trying to cover herself. And she lifted her chin proudly. She would not beg this cruel, domineering man for anything! Naked and helpless she might be for the moment, but she'd be damned if she would weep and plead as though she were the naughty child, he, the tyrannical father.

So she looked straight into those low-lidded blue eyes while Kane, having dried her throat, face, and shoulders, let the towel come to rest on her bare breasts.

His lids slid even lower over the unforgiving eyes and the rapid, almost rough, movements of his hands slowed and became exquisitely gentle. Natalie caught her breath when his towel-draped hands covered her wet breasts. The silence was suddenly deafening. She could hear the thundering of her heart and wondered if his sensitive hand could feel its furious beating.

Gazes locked, they stood staring at each other, Kane's eyes as cold as ever, Natalie's filling with heat. Kane's brown fingers patting, drying, touching; Natalie's white breasts trembling, peaking, filling his hands. She heard his breath, slow and heavy. And he heard hers, soft and labored.

Abruptly his toweled hands moved down to her rib cage and Natalie's eyes slid closed in shame. Her breasts had swelled beneath his touch, the nipples stood out in tell-tale tight buds.

Eyes closed, she felt the abrasive towel moving in circular motions over her quivering belly, her gleaming thighs. Lids opened cautiously to see Kane crouching down before her. Dark head bent, breath warm upon her skin, he dried each long, slender leg, while Natalie's nude body tingled and trembled and silently she prayed for this terrible torture to end.

Slowly he rose before her, looked directly into her eyes, and purposely pressed the towel to the damp auburn triangle between her legs. Dark face remaining ungiving granite, he blotted away the beads of moisture from the tight curls— taking what seemed forever—then slowly released the towel, letting it slip to her feet on the floor.

Gripping her arm, Kane guided her to the bed, turning back the covers when they reached it. Tired and mortified, Natalie crawled between the sheets and sighed her gratitude when Kane spread the warm, soft fur up over her bare shoulders. Toweled head upon the pillow, she burrowed down into the warmth of the mattress, turning onto her side, pulling her knees up.

Kane was back across the room, removing his wet shirt. He undressed there before the fire, just as he had undressed her. Natalie didn't pretend to turn her head away. She watched him strip to the dark, wet skin and stand before the fire, his back to her, feet apart, leisurely drying his long, lean body, his damp raven hair.

The white-ribboned scars on his back pulled and danced, the sinewy muscles in his wide shoulders and his long, powerful legs bunched and slid with his movements. Abruptly, he turned around and Natalie quit breathing. He stood perfectly still. A naked god framed in the glowing firelight.

Natalie stared in wonder and felt an erotic heat spreading throughout her body. Idly she wondered which radiated the most heat; the blazing fire or the naked man. Both were warming her; making her hot. Both held her transfixed. Both could burn her if she got too close.

He moved. She tensed.

Natalie was terrified Kane would walk across the room and get into bed with her. And she was terrified that he would not.

Chapter Thirty-three

Kane lowered his muscular arms, letting the towel slip slowly through his fingers and drop to the floor. He stood unmoving, his steady gaze riveted to the bed. Anger and arousal made his blood surge hot, his bare body harden. In that state it was easy for Kane to tell himself that Natalie deserved any form of punishment he chose to mete out.

She had behaved like an ungrateful, empty-headed fool, causing him no small measure of despair. His heart had sped out of his chest when he awakened to find her missing. The vision of her lying frozen in the snow had caused him more pain than she would ever know. Scared speechless, throat constricting with a panic that choked and strangled him, he had rushed outside, praying to find her alive, feeling he could not bear it should anything happen to her.

And now she calmly lay there, unrepentant and proud. Safe and naked in his bed because he had gone out into the storm and, for the second time in a week, saved her luscious neck. Shouldn't he be rewarded? Didn't he deserve a little thanks?

Kane drew a labored breath. Let her fight him if she chose; he would have no trouble subduing her. He wanted her, had wanted her from the first moment he'd laid eyes on that glorious hair flaming brightly under the blazing New Mexico sun.

Wanted her with a passion that burned as hotly as the roaring fire heating his backside. Wanted her with an animal hunger that tempted him to fall upon her and take her violently, ruthlessly, turning a deaf ear to any pleas for mercy. Wanted her with an overwhelming, disabling tenderness that nudged him to kneel worshipfully at her feet and beg for her sweet kisses, her gentle caresses, her silky body.

Kane shook his dark head vigorously and gave a great groan of despair. Damn her! Damn her to hell! The flame-haired Jezebel would have to torture some other man until eternity! Not him. He didn't need her, didn't want her, would not let her into his heart. He would not hold her again and allow those pale arms and legs to wind around him like silken vines, holding him, imprisoning him, choking him!

My God, he was far from being the only man who had been between her legs. Only one of the many who'd tasted the sweetness of her lips, her breasts, her . . . The thought sickened him. She was exactly like Susannah; the face and body of an angel, the heart and soul of a whore.

Kane whirled about and flung himself facedown on the long horsehair couch, snatching a coverlet over himself. Teeth grinding, total erection throbbing painfully between the cushions and his bare, tight belly, he lay in agony, his blue eyes glazed with unsated desire.

And he never knew, never dreamed, that not twenty-five feet from where he suffered, Natalie suffered as well. She'd not taken her eyes from his fine masculine form; had not once looked away. Snared, she watched unblinkingly while he stood there before the fire facing her. She saw the full arousal of his powerful male body and guiltily admitted to herself that she was glad it had happened.

He wanted her.

Kane wanted her just as she wanted him and he would simply walk across the room and take her. A gentle throbbing began low in her belly and a wet heat between her legs made her instinctively part them: waiting, expectant, eager. She arched her back and felt the pleasing abrasiveness of the sheets upon her tight nipples. Her body was as ready as Kane's.

Natalie's eyes widened in disbelief and she flinched when a great groan issued from Kane's lips and he threw himself facedown on the sofa. She lifted her head from the pillow and stared at his long, reclining body, the back of his dark head. She opened her mouth to call to him. Closed it without uttering a sound.

Tears stung at the backs of her eyes and she slowly sank back to the pillow. It seemed an eternity that she lay there in agony, desiring him, needing him. Then, at long last, finally, mercifully, passion passed and Natalie sighed tiredly as the sounds of Kane's sure, even breathing told her that he slept.

And she was grateful that the naked, sleeping man had not come to her bed. Surprised that he was apparently much stronger than she. And puzzled that, knowing his body, if not his heart, had wanted her—he had not taken her.

Natalie yawned and turned sleepily onto her left side. Never would she understand the strange paradox that was Kane Covington.

Bright light awakened Natalie. Slowly she raised up, hand holding the covers over her bare breasts. All the drapes had been opened to a brilliant Colorado sun, its first showing in five days. The snow had stopped, and through the tall north windows Natalie could see vast stretches of bright blue sky.

At the foot of her bed, on top of the soft fur comforter, a pair of clean tan trousers and a navy flannel shirt were folded neatly. Men's dark stockings and snowy white underwear lay on the shirt.

Natalie's eyes drifted to the horsehair sofa. It was empty. Cautiously, she looked about and saw Kane pouring coffee into one cup. Fully dressed, he came to the bed and handed her the coffee.

"Th-thank you." She struggled to preserve her modesty and at the same time take the cup from him, her eyes regarding him nervously.

"You are welcome." The hard-planed dark face was inscrutable. He stood by the bed, booted feet apart, eyes on the steaming coffee. He slid his right hand under his belt at the small of his back and his steady gaze lifted to her face.

"I've work to do in the barn. If you're still dead set on leaving, I'll not stop you. In a couple of days some of the deepest drifts should be melting; if you can wait, I'll take you then."

"I'll wait, Kane."

He nodded curtly, turned, and walked away. Natalie sipped the hot, black coffee and watched him shove long arms into his coat. He took his black Stetson from its peg and, twisting the brim in long, lean fingers, said, "I've filled the tub with hot water for your bath. You can take your time; I won't come back in before noon. I laid out some clothes; they'll be too big, but I thought you might like to sit up for a while today."

"Yes," she said, "I would like that. I'm feeling much stronger and . . . I . . . Kane, about last night . . . I'm sorry."

"So am I," said Kane, and Natalie knew he was speaking of more than her attempted escape. She blushed in the bright, glaring sunlight, recalling how he had stood before her, naked and aroused. And her reaction to the sight of him.

He turned away, opened the door, and stepped out onto the porch.

Natalie shook off all thoughts of the night before. She had plenty to worry about besides her primal passion for Kane. There was Ashlin and the journal. She had to get to the bottom of it all. Ashlin would return from Denver in three days. She'd be back at Cloud West by then. She would have to confront him, question him, seek the truth.

Natalie finished her coffee, took a warm bath, and stepped into the tan trousers. To her chagrin, she found that although the fine gabardine pants were far too long—she rolled the cuffs up several folds—they were almost too snug about her hips, so lean were their owner's flanks. Natalie settled the pullover navy flannel shirt above her head and had a terrible time trying to maneuver her stiff right arm up through a sleeve.

She sighed with triumph when finally she smoothed the soft navy wool down over her breasts. The shirt, a style meant to hang outside the trousers and strike the body just below the waist, reached to Natalie's thighs. She smiled fleetingly, buttoned the two buttons at the shirt's yoke, and went about searching for Kane's hairbrush.

She found it in a shelf of a bookcase, a comb stuck into its fine bristles. Other personal articles rested there as well. Several coins and some folding bills. A small sack of pungent smoking tobacco, papers, and sulfur matches. Onyx shirt studs, a gold-cased pocket watch, a pearl-backed pocket knife.

Natalie looked with interest at Kane's scattered valuables. As though she could find some insight into the man himself by studying his things, she touched the shiny watch, fingertips gliding over the smooth case, the attached chain, the glass face. She picked up the pearl-cased knife, put it back.

She smoothed the folds of a shiny black silk bandanna, and felt something solid beneath it. Natalie lifted the shimmering scarf and stared down at a small, shiny object. Eyes narrowed, she let the black silk flutter to the shelf and reached for the gold-tipped arrowhead. It lay heavy in her palm and Natalie felt the fine hair of her nape rise.

Kane knew of the gold! He had found the Cliff Palace, she knew it. Her fingers closed around the shiny metal arrowhead. She couldn't let him attempt to take the treasure. It was dangerous; Tahomah had told her no white man would take the gold and live. She would tell Kane. As soon as he came inside, she would warn him. And pray he would listen.

Sighing, Natalie placed the gold-tipped arrow back on the shelf, laid the black bandanna on top of it, and removed Kane's comb from the brush. Her mind on the arrow, she lifted the brush to her tangled hair. Stroking absently, she moved to the books in the next shelf. Scanning the titles for something that might hold her interest, she saw leatherbound volumes of Dickens's *Tale of Two Cities* and *Great*

Expectations. Fitzgerald's *Rubáiyát of Omar Khayyám.* Hugo's *Les Misérables.* There were Shakespeare and Keats and Shelley. Tolstoy and Mark Twain and Dostoevsky.

And there was a worn, well-thumbed, black leather Bible. Natalie laid aside the hairbrush and took it down. Feeling the need for guidance and comfort in this time of uncertainty, she turned swiftly to some of her favorites passages; Scriptures that offered solace and strength.

Choosing one of the favorite chapters she had memorized as a child, Natalie flipped the fine parchment pages to the Twenty-third Psalm. But she didn't read a word.

A faded, much-fingered daguerreotype caused her to blink and raise the Bible closer. An angelically beautiful young girl was smiling up at her. Long dark curls cascaded around a flawless, heart-shaped face. Huge dark eyes looked straight into the camera and into the eyes of anyone holding the Bible. Perfect, turned-up nose, rounded, healthy cheeks, small, full-lipped mouth. Lovely throat and shoulders revealed in a gown of some soft pastel.

And across a full left breast, the inscription read, *My darling Kane, I shall love you until eternity. Your adoring Susannah.*

Natalie read and reread the words. And she looked once more into the dark, sparkling eyes of the breathtaking young beauty. Speaking aloud, she addressed the absent woman.

"Susannah," she said scornfully, "you are a fool and you have from now to eternity to realize it." She shook her head sadly. "And I am too."

Suddenly unreasonably angry with the smiling Susannah, Natalie slammed the Bible shut and put it back on the shelf. But another secret treasure had been hidden inside and it fell from the pages and fluttered to the floor.

Natalie leaned over and picked up the curiosity from the carpet. A lock of hair. Holding the shimmering strand between thumb and forefinger, Natalie went to a window. Strong winter sunlight turned the soft lock of hair a fiery reddish-gold.

Natalie tossed her head, swinging her loose, long hair

about to fall over her shoulder. She bunched the reddish-gold tresses up in her hand and, with shaking fingers, laid the fiery lock amid her own red curls.

A little gasp of wonder escaped her open lips. It was her hair! Her own hair; the exact same shade and texture as the unruly mass now spilling down over her breast. Natalie again lifted the lock before her face.

Instantly the hot day at Spanish Widow came rushing back. With vivid clarity she could see the lock of hair she now held lying on the wooden floor of the adobe weigh station. Snipped off clean by the speeding bullet of a bloodthirsty Apache warrior. *If you wish to keep it, you'd best keep your head down* had been the words uttered coolly by a stonefaced Kane when the incident occurred.

That was the last she had thought about the clipped hair. She didn't recall seeing the auburn lock again. Had no idea when or why Kane had picked it up. Staring at it now, her pulse quickened. She felt a wave of hope and happiness surge through her.

That dark, hot night they had spent together at Spanish Widow had meant something to him, just as it had to her. He had taken the lock of her hair and put it in his shirt pocket. He had brought it to Colorado with him. He had saved it all this time. He had cared a little.

Natalie found herself eagerly looking forward to Kane's return from the stables. She tried to read, but her eyes kept lifting from the printed page, going to the door, expectantly, impatiently. She put the book aside and again brushed her long, red hair until it snapped and crackled and shone with fiery highlights.

At long last she heard him coming toward the house, booted feet crunching across the frozen ground. He stopped on the porch and stamped the clinging snow from his boots, and Natalie, seated on the horsehair sofa, hurriedly bit her lips to give them color, fanned her long, flowing hair out over her shoulders, and waited, smiling.

Kane walked in and looked directly at Natalie. Her red hair lay in shimmering waves about her face and shoulders, the strong sunlight coming from behind setting it afire. Her emerald eyes were upon him and behind them lay a glow, as though some inner happiness illuminated them. Her full lips were red and moist and parted. She was smiling warmly at him. She wore his clothes, the navy flannel of his shirt concealing the curves he knew lay beneath, his tan trousers tight about her feminine hips. Bare feet peeked out from beneath the folded pants legs.

Never had she looked more adorable.

And that rankled Kane. Made him mad as hell.

He had purposely spent the morning away from her. Had stayed alone in the cold stables, telling himself that his pretty patient was a brittle, experienced woman; a woman as hard and jaded as he.

And now there she sat, looking for all the world like an innocent sixteen-year-old who had just laid aside her dolls to smile sweetly up at her very first beau.

"You might have cooked something for our lunch," he said harshly, jerking his Stetson off, releasing a shock of raven hair.

"I'll do it now." She rose, at a loss, her smile slipping a bit.

"Forget it." He hunched out of his jacket. "I'll do it myself." He waved her back to the sofa.

They ate in strained silence after she made several attempts at conversation and he answered coldly with clipped one-word replies. And then they were like two polite strangers, avoiding each other's eyes, saying little, watching each other cautiously.

Kane's dark and sullen good looks unnerved Natalie. His quiet, moody presence made her long to slap him smartly . . . or to pull his dark head down and kiss the hardness from his lips. Natalie's soft beauty, the expression of puzzlement in her huge green eyes, made Kane want to jerk her up and shake her by the shoulders . . . or to lift her in his arms and kiss her half senseless.

The strain was taking its toll on them both, so two days later when Kane woke Natalie and said quietly, "I'll take you home now," she replied honestly, "Thank God."

Chapter Thirty-four

"Sure you'll be okay?" Kane stood framed in the doorway of Natalie's white bedroom at Cloud West.

"I'll be fine," she assured him from the depths of the big four-poster with its white silk bed-hangings and white lace-trimmed sheets and pillowcases. She smiled at him, plucked nervously at a lacy white cuff of her nightgown, and added, "You've taken care of everything." She indicated the blazing fire in the white marble fireplace, the silver tray with hot tea and toasted bread on the marble-topped table at her elbow.

As soon as the pair had reached Cloud West, Kane had built a fire in Natalie's big upstairs bedroom, put water on to heat, and gently ordered her to take a hot bath and get into bed while he tended the horses.

When he returned from the stables, he put on the kettle for tea, sliced the bread, and searched until he found a small pot of blackberry preserves. He entered her bedroom to find her primly in bed, her long cinnamon tresses gleaming on the snowy pillow.

"I don't like leaving you alone." Kane's jaw tightened.

"My housekeeper will be back in a few days, Kane."

"I'll be on my way, then," Kane said. And did not move.

"Thank you for everything. And Kane . . ."

"Yes?"

Natalie drew a deep breath. Then hastily, "You've found the Manitou gold, I know you have." Kane looked at her, said nothing. "Don't take it, Kane. It's not safe, you'll be . . . it's dangerous, truly it is, you—"

"Good-bye, Judge," drawled Kane, and his hands went to his slim hips. He stood there unmoving, his hooded eyes accusing, cynical. Slowly he pivoted and walked out into the corridor.

The sound of his footfalls going down the stairs mixed with the deep, deriding chuckling coming from his broad chest. Natalie sighed, shaking her head despairingly. He didn't believe she was worried for his safety. He thought she was only concerned with keeping the gold for herself.

Impetuously, she threw back the white silk covers and leapt from her bed. She flew across the floor shouting, "Kane, Kane!"

Kane halted midway down the steps, turned, and looked quizzically up. One hand gripping the polished banister, the other holding up the flowing white nightgown, Natalie rushed down the steps, her bare feet skipping hurriedly, flaming hair in wild disarray about her shoulders. She stopped on the step where he stood in a wary stance.

For one brief instant her fingertips and forehead pressed the hard male chest before her as she leaned to him and said into his shirtfront, "I'm not going to marry Ashlin."

She was gone then, flying back up the stairs while Kane's astonished blue gaze followed the shapely bare calves and small feet rapidly retreating. He said nothing. He stood motionless there on the stair, long after her slender form had disappeared inside the bedroom and the heavy white door had slammed shut with a resounding bang behind her.

Kane was halfway up the stairs. And halfway down.

Half ready to rush back up and take her in his aching arms. Half afraid to trust her with his heart. Half elated to know she would not be another man's wife. Half disappointed that she would not be another man's responsibility.

Kane lifted wide shoulders in a shrug of frustration and walked down the stairs.

Natalie, her back against the closed bedroom door, her heart hammering in her chest, closed her eyes and listened, hoping against hope that he'd turn and climb the stairs. For what seemed an eternity, she heard nothing. Nothing but the snapping of the fire, the pumping of the blood in her ears.

Silently she prayed, Please, God, please. Tell him to come back . . . make him . . . Her eyes flew open. She turned her head to listen, lips parted, throat tight. And she heard Kane's distinctive step on the stair.

Going away. Leaving her.

Natalie slumped against the door, head sagging on her chest. Her eyes swam with tears that did not fall. Then she straightened, walked slowly to the tall bed, and climbed between the sheets. She felt suddenly weary, more tired than she could ever remember being.

The toast and tea cooled, untouched, on the tray. The fire burned low in the grate. And Natalie lay listless in her big white bed, her green eyes clouded. Unhappy and alone.

At dusk Kane finally lowered the heavy ax. He stood for a while with the solid oaken handle gripped tightly in his hands. He looked at the huge log below him, grumbled a loud curse, and lifted the ax high over his head. With all the strength left in his lean, powerful body, Kane brought it down, burying the gleaming iron blade in the wood.

He released the ax handle and looked at his blister-riddled bare hands. Shrugging, he lifted a forearm to wipe the sweat from his face. And he laughed at himself. Since returning from Cloud West at midmorning, he had been chopping firewood, and he had chopped with unremitting vengeance. Now, everywhere he looked, piñon-pine logs were stacked neatly, row upon row, some as high as his waist. Enough firewood to last all winter.

Grinning, feeling more than a little foolish, Kane looked about, surveying the fruits of his anguished labor, shaking his dark head. Tiredly, he headed for the cabin, his long arms weak, the broad muscles of his back aching.

Inside he ate a cold supper, bathed away the sweat and

grime, and dropped into his easy chair to sip a brandy and smoke a cigar, certain that by the time he finished, he could fall into an exhausted sleep.

He sat quietly staring into the fire, lean, muscular body unwinding, relaxing. Tiredly, he sighed. His thoughts, as they had been all day, were on Natalie. Again he was looking down upon a fiery head pressed to his chest and hearing the words *I'm not going to marry Ashlin.*

Kane drained his brandy glass. Cigar stuck between his strong, white teeth, he rose and crossed the room to his bed. Deftly unbuttoning his buckskin trousers, Kane stepped out of them and crawled naked between the sheets, leaning up on an elbow to blow out the kerosene lamp.

He lay back then, lazily puffing on the hot-tipped cigar. Eyes on the ceiling, he smoked the cigar completely down to the tip, snuffed it out, and turned his face into the pillow, closing his eyes. His eyes opened. Kane groaned aloud. The faint scent of lemon clung to the pillowcase where, until tonight, a fiery head of hair, rinsed in lemon juice, had lain.

He missed her. Missed her much more than he would have imagined. For the past week his cabin—and his life—had been full. Now both were unbearably empty.

A weary but confident Ashlin Blackmore stepped down from the Overland stage at noon the next day. Brown eyes bloodshot, golden hair disheveled, he put a hand to his aching neck and looked about, expecting Natalie to step forward, happy to see him.

She was nowhere about and Ashlin felt a surge of irritation that his fiancée had not seen fit to welcome him home. His gaze drifted up and down the street, warily searching for another face. A face he knew was not there. Could not be there.

Kane Covington's bones were already turning to dust beneath a snowy grave in the Cloudcastle cemetery, Ashlin joyfully reminded himself. The thought cheered him no end, and he felt his weariness magically lifting. A quick bath at the mansion would revive him. Refreshed, he would ride to Cloud West to see his beautiful fiancée.

Ashlin smiled in the bright midday sunlight. Perhaps he could persuade Natalie to become his bride this very day. Or tomorrow. Tomorrow would be better. Meantime, he could transport a load of gold out of the cave.

Ashlin began to chuckle evilly as, without bothering to greet his faithful servant, William, he climbed into his gleaming, crest-emblazoned coach. Settling himself back against the tall leather cushion, he let his thoughts paint sensual pictures. He envisioned a naked Natalie, her flaming hair in plaits, lying open-thighed upon a bed strewn with glittering gold coins.

Yes, tomorrow he would marry her.

Natalie heard the resounding clatter of hoofbeats on the frozen ground, and stiffened. She knew at once that the lone rider was Ashlin. She rose, went to the tall bureau, drew a small pearl-handled pistol from the top drawer, and calmly loaded it.

A robe of soft blue flannel tied tightly about her narrow waist, the revolver concealed in a deep pocket, Natalie descended the stairs, apprehensive but resolute.

She opened the front door. Backlit by the blinding sun, Ashlin stood framed in the portal, smiling happily. He reached out for her, but Natalie took a step backward.

"Ashlin," she said, holding the door wide. "Please, come in."

"Darling, what kind of greeting is this?" his voice was gently scolding. The smile immediately left his handsome face. "You're not dressed. Natalie, are you ill?"

"No, Ashlin, I'm not," said Natalie. "Take off your cloak and come into the drawing room."

A strange unease tightening his chest, Ashlin Blackmore shrugged out of his fine cashmere cloak, unwrapped the white silk muffler from his throat, and followed Natalie into the warm, sunny room.

She strode to the fireplace, inhaled deeply, turned, and announced, "I was shot, Ashlin."

"My God! No!" he exclaimed. "When? Where?" He rushed forward.

Natalie put up her hands. "Don't, Ashlin. I want to talk."

"Certainly, darling, but you must tell me what happened. Where were you? Whom were you with? Who on earth would want to shoot you?" His face was flushed with shock and outrage.

"No one, Ashlin."

"No one? You just said. . . . Darling, you're speaking in riddles. What are you saying? Tell me. . . ."

"I'm saying that someone mistook me for Kane Covington and shot me in the back."

"No, that couldn't . . . Who found you? Took you to the doctor? Are you all right? Dear God, this is ghastly, unbelievable . . ." His words trailed away.

"Someone in Cloudcastle wants Kane Covington dead. They rode onto his property to shoot him. They hit me by mistake and Kane saved my life."

Ashlin again started toward her. "Darling, this is horrible. Did the doctor get—"

"There was no doctor, Ashlin. The blizzard made it impossible for Kane to get me to Cloudcastle. He removed the bullet; he saved my life."

"I shall be eternally grateful to him, Natalie. Did . . . did Jane help him and—"

"Jane was not here. I've been at Kane's cabin for the past week. He tended me there."

"I see. . . ." His eyes flickered. "You and Kane alone all this time? Surely you could have—"

Natalie cut him off. "Your brother, Ashlin? Your brother, Titus?"

She watched a tiny muscle jump beside his bottom lip. "My God, what's gotten into you?" He shook his golden head. "You've been listening to that ignorant old Indian telling tales!"

"I haven't seen Tahomah, Ashlin. A diary in your house."

The blood drained from his face and his brown eyes narrowed dangerously. "You were snooping through my things?"

"Yes, Ashlin." She looked him straight in the eye. "Titus was your brother, wasn't he? He found the Manitou gold. That's why you came to Cloudcastle. Why you wanted to marry me."

"Natalie, Natalie." Ashlin felt everything slipping out of his control. Fighting the panic gripping him, he said forcefully, "You have everything confused! You don't know what you're talking about, darling. I know nothing of any gold and I—" Swiftly he stepped closer and took hold of her shoulders. "I want to marry you because I love you. You're going to be my wife and we'll—"

Natalie plucked at the restraining hands holding her. "No, Ashlin, I'm not going to be your wife. I'm not going to marry you."

"You can't mean that! You're upset, that's all. You're ill and not yourself, not thinking clearly." He smiled then, a strained, tight smile that did not reach his worried eyes. "You foolishly meddled about and you think you found something. You'll see it was all a mistake." He urged her to him.

She managed to pull away and her right hand went into the robe's pocket to rest on the revolver. "Ashlin, I will not marry you. I intend to find out just how deeply you are involved in the attempted murder of Kane Covington."

Livid, Ashlin nonetheless managed to hide his anger from Natalie. "I? Involved? Darling, that's the most absurd thing I've ever heard." He nervously drew a gold cigarette case from inside the pocket of his fine silk shirt. "I've been in Denver for a week, remember? I couldn't possibly have—"

"A man needn't pull the trigger to commit a murder," Natalie said evenly.

Ashlin knew if he did not leave at once he was going to give himself away, so upset was he. He put the cigarette case away. Nothing had worked as he had planned. The stupid Leatherwoods shot the woman he was to marry! And Kane Covington, whom he thought dead, was not only alive, he had spent the week alone with Natalie in his remote mountain cabin, poisoning her mind. And making love to her?

"Darling," Ashlin said softly, "you're overwrought and confused. I understand, truly I do. I want you to go straight to bed and rest. When you're feeling better, we'll talk."

"When I'm feeling better, I'm talking to the sheriff." She fought the weakness claiming her slender body. "Don't leave town, Ashlin. You've some explaining to do."

Ashlin stared incredulously at the woman who had once agreed to be his wife. She was looking up at him as though he had committed some terrible act, as though he were a criminal. His reserve wavered; his calm voice rose in frustrated anger.

"Natalie, I'll hear no more of your foolish insinuations. It's obvious that Kane Covington has been putting ideas in your head. You'll forget all about this in a few days." He moved toward the corridor. "I've business I must handle. I'll be back when I can."

Natalie followed. "No, Ashlin. Don't come here. Not ever again. I'll see you in court."

Ashlin whirled the long cloak about his shoulders. Eyes wild, face demonic, he spun on Natalie, grabbed her before she could react, and jerked her up against him. Through thinned lips he said, "You'll see me tomorrow! We're getting married in the morning; I'm out of patience with you!"

His lips came down on hers in a punishing, ruthless kiss that left her staggering and fighting for breath. Abruptly he released her. She sagged against the banister of the stairs as Ashlin slammed out of the house, ran down the walk, and mounted his horse.

Trembling with rage and weakness, Natalie battled the waves of blackness threatening to engulf her. Gasping for air, fighting the dizziness, she made her way up the stairs.

She collapsed across her bed, closing her eyes against the reeling room. And her eyes remained closed even as the rotation slowed and stopped. Wrung out from the confrontation, exhausted from an almost sleepless night, Natalie fell asleep.

It was late afternoon when she awakened. Rested, stronger, Natalie rose and began dressing.

Kane stood in the setting sun. He heard the muffled hoof-beats and his heartbeat quickened. Foolishly expecting to see Natalie's bright coppery hair silhouetted against the lilac sky, he turned hopefully. And the smile left his face.

The riders were upon him; he had no chance. His holstered gun was in the cabin, a hundred yards from where he worked. He dropped the heavy load of piñon and started walking fast, strides long and purposeful, eyes riveted to the approaching pair. One rider, a big, beefy man, was grinning broadly; the other, pale and thin, smiled not at all. One led an unsaddled gray gelding behind him. Both carried unholstered rifles.

The mounted men swiftly blocked Kane's path, their horses dancing on the snow. Kane halted.

"Get off my property," he said levelly.

Damon Leatherwood snorted loudly. "Shut your dammed mouth! You've caused us enough trouble, Covington. Lord Blackmore's mad at me and my brother. And that makes us mad at you." Burl Leatherwood remained mute. Aiming his rifle straight at Kane's head, Burl nodded.

In moments Kane found himself astride a barebacked gelding, wrists tied behind his back, gag between his teeth, noose around his neck, its end tied securely to the branch of a gnarled pine. And flanked by the armed, mounted Leatherwoods.

Damon talked nonstop. His beefy face freshly battered by an enraged Ashlin Blackmore, the big man taunted and tormented and nudged Kane in the ribs with his rifle. "Ever seen a man hanged, Covington? Terrible sight, terrible sight. He flops around like a fish out of water, gagging and eyes popping and kicking up an awful fuss." Kane's blue eyes stared straight ahead. "You're gonna swing 'cause that's the way Blackmore wants you to die. He made us promise not to shoot you. Said that would be too quick."

Burl Leatherwood leaned close. His long, skinny fingers

sank into Kane's dark hair and jerked his head backward.
The sallow man put his lips near Kane's ear and spoke for the
first time.

"Know why you're dying, Covington? Because you've been
sticking your greedy southern hands in the gold . . . and
your stiff southern cock in the judge."

Chapter Thirty-five

Natalie topped a snowy ridge below Kane's cabin and her eyes widened in horror. "No!" she tried to scream, but no sound came forth.

Damon Leatherwood gave the gray gelding's rump a loud whack. The frightened beast lurched wildly forward and galloped away. The two mounted men, one silent, the other shouting triumphantly, thundered after the gelding and out of sight.

Staring horrified at the dark-haired man dangling helplessly from the end of a rope, Natalie dug her heels into Blaze's belly as she drew her revolver.

The big stallion lunged over the snow-covered ground. Natalie fired at the rope; it snapped in two, and Kane fell into the snow. She was off her horse and beside him in an instant.

"Kane, Kane, speak to me!" She threw herself down beside him, gloved hands immediately tearing at the choking rope encircling his dark throat. Tears of panic streaming down her cheeks, she jerked the gagging bandanna from his mouth and entreated, "Kane, oh, Kane! Don't leave me, Dear God no!"

His deep blue eyes were open, looking at her, and as soon as she loosened the noose he croaked, "Calm down, honey. I'm alive."

"Oh, Kane," she screamed exultantly, and fell upon him,

framing his flushed face in her gloved hands, kissing his eyes, his brow, his cheeks. "Yes," she murmured, breathless, heart racing. "You're alive, you're alive. My dear, you're alive!" She lifted her face from his and saw pain in his eyes. "You're hurt bad, Kane! Your neck is—"

"It's not my neck, honey," he rasped. "I'm lying on my hands and—"

"Kane! I'm sorry." She immediately eased him onto his side and with trembling, clumsy fingers, untied his wrists, grimacing at the telling red, raw flesh burned by the rope.

"Thanks," Kane managed, and levered himself into a sitting position. He sat in the snow, rubbing at a chapped wrist but smiling reassuringly at Natalie.

On her knees beside him, worriedly studying his face, Natalie rashly pulled his dark head against her breasts and murmured "You're safe now, Kane. I'll take care of you; don't you worry, I'm here."

"Let's get inside," said Kane into the wet lapel of her coat.

"Of course!" She was up at once, tugging on him. "I must get you indoors and get a doctor."

"No doctor, Judge." Kane stood on shaky legs. "A shot of whiskey; that's all I need."

"Anything you want, Kane," assured Natalie, stepping to his side, "anything at all."

With her arm wrapped around his trim waist and her slender shoulders supporting his long right arm, Natalie helped Kane to his cabin while Blaze eyed the pair and shook his mane and fell into step beside them.

Natalie paid the stallion no attention. Her total concentration on the tall, dark man beside her, she thought of nothing and no one save Kane. It was he who said, when they neared the cabin door, "Natalie, I can manage now." His blue gaze went over her head to the neighing horse. "Blaze wants to be off."

Her reply brought a smile to Kane's tight lips. "Let him be off, then; I'm staying with you."

Inside, she guided him to the bed, issuing orders as if she were a commanding general. "You are to get in bed at once.

I'll heat water while you undress. I'll bathe your neck and wrists and determine whether or not a physician is needed. If so, I'll ride Blaze into Cloudcastle and . . ." She looked at him. "What are you waiting for? Undress!"

"Yes, ma'am," drawled Kane hoarsely, waiting for her to turn away. She didn't. She reached for the fringed hem of his buckskin shirt, shoving it up over his ribs. Together they got his shirt off and Natalie, eyes on his rope-burned throat, said shrilly, "The panther's claw! Where is it? Why aren't you wearing it?"

"On the night table," Kane told her, and seeing the censure in her flashing green eyes, added, "I always wear it. I forgot this morning." He lifted bare, wide shoulders apologetically.

She sighed, stepped closer, and put her hands to Kane's belt buckle. She felt his fingers close over hers. "I'll get the pants, you get the whiskey."

Her eyes lifted to his. She blushed and turned away. In moments she was back with the whiskey bottle and one glass. Kane was in bed; his clothes discarded on the floor. Natalie poured, handed him the whiskey, and watched him grimace as the fiery liquid burned his raw throat. He lowered the half-full glass and Natalie took it from him.

"I need this worse than you," said she, and tossed it down. Kane chuckled while she coughed and blew and waved a slim hand before her face.

And then Natalie tended her patient. With gentle hands, and gentler eyes, she hovered over him, pressing clean, wet cloths to his chafed throat, his red, roughened wrists. And as she bathed the raw, punished flesh, they spoke at last of the men who had done this to him.

"Kane," murmured Natalie softly, painstakingly surveying the damage to his brown throat, "was it the Leatherwoods?"

"Yes."

Her eyes met his and her tenderly probing fingertips came to rest at side of his neck. "Did they tell you anything?" Kane nodded his dark head. "Ashlin?"

"Yes. It was Ashlin."

"You found the Manitou gold, didn't you, Kane?"

"I did."

"Ashlin knows of the gold. That's why he tried to murder you." Her eyes lowered. "That's why he wanted to marry me."

"I'm sure the gold was only part of it."

They talked and talked. Natalie told him of Tahomah and the Anasazi legend. Of her promise to guard the gold. Of finding the diary at Ashlin's mansion. Kane told her of stumbling onto the Cliff Palace. Of Tahomah warning him of danger and giving him the panther's claw. Of suspecting Ashlin Blackmore from the beginning.

"Talk no more, Kane," Natalie finally warned, "you'll hurt your throat."

"All right," he answered. "Again I thank you for saving my life. It's getting to be a habit." Natalie rose from the bed. Kane grinned boyishly, and added, "You'd better leave for home now while there's still a little twilight."

"Leave?" Her hands went to her trousered hips and she stared down at him. "Who's leaving? I'm not leaving. I've not fed you your dinner yet." She turned and crossed the room, took her coat down from the peg. "I'm only going to stable Blaze, then I'll be right back." She walked to the door, saying over her shoulder, "I'm spending the night."

The sun had slipped below the western ridge of the Rockies and a near-full moon was rising. Ashlin Blackmore, feet propped on top of a cluttered eating table at the Leatherwood shack, hands laced behind his blond head, leaned back in the wooden chair and said, "Are you certain he's dead? I won't tolerate any more mistakes. You damned near killed my fiancée!"

Burl Leatherwood poured himself a straight whiskey. "We've explained a half dozen times, boss. The judge was dressed like a man and riding near Covington's cabin. It was a natural—"

Ashlin waved a silencing hand. "Answer my question. Is Covington finally out of my hair?"

Burl, tight-lipped, nodded yes.

"He's dead, boss," affirmed Damon Leatherwood. "That gray gelding is still running somewhere!" He laughed loudly and sank heavily down into a chair. "The shots came from far away. Whoever fired couldn't have possibly reached Covington in time."

Ashlin's arched blond eyebrows lifted questioningly in Burl's direction.

Burl backed up his brother. "Damon's right, boss. I guarantee you that by the time the intruder reached him, Covington was nothing more than a slab of dead southern white trash swinging in the breeze."

All three men laughed.

"Who do you suppose was shooting?" Ashlin's laugh quickly gave way to frowning inquiry. He directed the question to Burl. "Think it was that old Indian?"

"Who else? That nosy old bastard shows up like he's been sent a message."

"He has to be killed. Right away."

Burl Leatherwood looked straight into Ashlin's brown eyes. "I told you before, you want him dead, you kill him."

Damon nodded vigorously in agreement. "We ain't gonna do it. That old Ute has powers; he spooks the daylights out of us."

"That's nonsense," Ashlin Blackmore scoffed, and sipped his whiskey. "Let me repeat, I will pay you double what I gave you to kill Covington. Hunt him out tomorrow and get rid of him. I want to go up to the cave while this thaw's on; take out some of my gold. You can have your earnings in gold coin."

"We're not killing that shaman," said Burl Leatherood firmly, "for any amount of money. Or gold."

"Very well." Ashlin Blackmore sighed wearily and yawned. "I'll take care of it myself." He rose on tired legs. "Now I must have some rest. I've not slept in forty-eight hours."

* * *

Natalie flung open the door and marched outside, calling to her horse, "Okay, Blaze, it's suppertime. Follow me to the barn." Kane heard the whickering of the beast as the door slammed shut. When she returned, she said breezily, "The temperature is rising."

"You're teasing me," said a skeptical Kane.

"I'm not. Looks like a chinook is blowing in from the west."

"Chinook?"

"Yes. A strangely warm, dry wind that occasionally blows across the Rockies in the winter. It's very odd. By midnight the mercury will have climbed dramatically. For the next day or so it will be almost as balmy as spring."

Kane watched through amused blue eyes as Natalie, a dish towel tied around her waist, went about preparing their meal. It was a simple, priceless pleasure to watch her move around his tiny kitchen, her flaming hair now wound up into a tight knot atop her head, her hands covered with white flour, her small rear end moving rhythmically as she held a big pottery bowl in the crook of her arm and vigorously beat thick biscuit dough.

Proudly, she came to the bed bearing his tray and looking to him for approval. "Mmm." Kane winked at her, inhaling deeply. "Smells good, looks good."

Natalie smiled and admitted, "Kane, I've never made biscuits before." She looked at the large, misshapen rounds of too brown bread, then at him. "I don't know why I did tonight."

She placed the tray across his lap, feeling suddenly foolish. "Whatever your reason, I'm grateful," said Kane. "I haven't had beaten biscuits since the last time my mother made them for me. How did you know they were my favorites?"

They ate a leisurely meal, Kane assuring her that her biscuits were as good as his mother's. They sipped hot coffee and Kane told his rapt audience of one more about his life in Mississippi.

"They were remarkably golden days, Natalie, those years

before the war; years when I was a young man." He smiled, remembering. "I roamed up and down the old Gulf Coast—New Orleans, Pass Christian and Biloxi, Gulfport, Port Gibson . . ."

"It must be beautiful down there. I've never been past Texas but I . . ."

"You would love the Gulf, Natalie." Kane's blue eyes gleamed. "So warm in the winter, you need only a light wrap to go about; so sultry hot in the summer, you cast aside your clothes for a swim in the surf. . . ." Kane's voice was growing hoarser as he spoke and Natalie, though longing to know more, put silencing fingertips to his full lips.

"Kane, you sound worse. Don't talk anymore. You need rest. Think you can sleep?"

"No," answered Kane truthfully.

"Well, try," ordered Natalie. She rose and leaned over to blow out the lamp.

"The fire is getting low." Kane's rough voice followed her across the room. "Think I should build it up before we sleep?"

"Don't you dare get out of that bed," scolded Natalie. "We won't need more fire. I told you, a chinook is coming through. You'll think you're back on your warm Gulf Coast come sunrise."

With the soft glow of the dying fire supplying the only light, Natalie stood at the long horsehair sofa. Her back to Kane, she undressed. Wearing only her lace-trimmed chemise, she stretched out on the couch, pulling up a coverlet from its foot.

She lay on her side with a bent arm tucked under her cheek, looking toward the bed. Moonlight streamed in through the north windows, illuminating a dark, handsome head, broad, bare shoulders, and brown, muscular arms.

Long, sleepless hours later, Natalie's eyes were still fixed on the bed. But she could not see the man. The moon had set. The fire had burned itself out. It was dark in the room, very dark. And warm, so warm. Dark and hot. Like the night they met.

The sudden flare of a match made Natalie's eyes widen. Kane had awakened. Or was still awake. Perhaps he had not slept either. Maybe the same thing keeping her awake was plaguing him.

Entranced, Natalie watched the red tip of a cigar moving back and forth to Kane's mouth. The cigar would glow hotly as he drew on it, then dim slightly as it moved away from his lips. Back it would go to his mouth, to burn brightly, to cast a tiny disc of orange light over his full lips, to ignite a smoldering fire deep within the watching woman.

Natalie lay in the hot, heavy darkness allowing her simmering passions to surface and conquer. She was alone in this remote place with her dark southern lover, just as she had been that night at Spanish Widow. All she need do to know the ecstasy of his arms was to cross the darkened room to him.

With cool determination, Natalie threw off the covers and sat up. Silently she lifted the chemise over her head and let it flutter to the floor. Naked, she sat for a second on the sofa, back rigid, slender legs tense, her gaze on the pinpoint of orange light once again brightening as Kane drew on the cigar.

She rose.

Wearing nothing but the shiny gold disc at her throat, Natalie went to Kane. She said nothing as she crossed the room. Like a moth to the flame, she followed the beacon of Kane's hot-tipped cigar, not stopping until she stood with her bare knees touching the edge of the mattress.

She sat down on the bed facing him, and heard Kane's sharp intake of air. She reached for the nearly finished cigar. Taking it from his lean fingers, she snuffed it out in a glass ashtray; tiny orange sparks showering outward. Unhurriedly, Natalie lifted and lowered the thin cigar, methodically tapping; extinguishing each and every minuscule bit of burning ash.

The room was cast into total blackness.

Natalie laid a warm hand upon the dark, handsome face

she could not see. "I want you," she whispered in a low, throaty voice.

Kane, heart drumming in his naked chest, smiled in the darkness. He had said those very words to her that hot, dark night at Spanish Widow. Just that. Nothing more. He recalled what her answer had been on that fateful evening. In hoarse, teasing tones he repeated it now.

"Don't hurt me."

Chapter Thirty-six

Kane's strong, warm hands lifted to Natalie's bare shoulders. Gently he pulled her down to him. Shuddering at the touch of naked flesh, Natalie waited breathlessly. For a time he held her quietly, strong arms around her, a firm hand cradling the crown of her head.

Open lips pressed to his warm, muscular chest, eyes closed in the darkness, Natalie heard him murmur against her temple, "Natalie, I'd like to be tender . . . I'm not sure I can; I want you too much."

Natalie smiled and lifted her head. She brought a hand up to his tense mouth, touched the full, warm lips with her fingertips, and told him honestly, "Tenderness can come later, Kane. I'm as impatient as you." She laughed then, a soft, sensual sound in the darkness, and added playfully a line her Uncle Shelby often used: "Let the joy be unrestrained."

"Ah, baby," rasped a delighted Kane, and his mouth came down on hers.

They did, indeed, let the joy be unrestrained. The very first kiss was deep and passionate and flaming. Little tenderness; much ferocity. Wildly they kissed, mouths open wide, seeking, exploring, devouring. While their heated lips were locked in that raw, ravaging caress, their bare bodies touched, pressed, strained, and burst into scorching flame. And their hands, brazen and eager, shamelessly searched planes and curves and hollows of blistering bodies.

When their bruised lips finally parted, Natalie found she was on her back lying across the bed, Kane's lean body beside her. They were tangled up in the sheet, both fighting to be free of it, far too aroused to halt the lovemaking.

Long arms wrapped around her, Kane kissed all the warm, naked flesh he could find, his questing lips feasting on delicate shoulders, swelling breasts, and narrow rib cage, leaving a moist trail of fire in his path. His knee was between Natalie's parted legs, pressing, rubbing, igniting, through the barrier of rumpled sheet trapped between them.

Panting, breathless, Natalie sought closer contact with that obliging knee, pushing up against it, her entire body arching and lifting and giving itself over to her dark lover's fiery lips, masterful hands, hard, muscled body.

A soft cry of joy came from her open mouth when she felt the obstructing sheet jerked away and in its place Kane's skilled fingers caressing her, readying her. Tensed, on fire, aching, she felt his long, lean body shifting over hers and then . . .

"Ahhh," moaned Kane as he slid easily into her.

"Ohhh," she breathed as his powerful, throbbing masculinity sank into her, stretching her, filling her, enthralling her.

As with the first kiss, there was no tenderness. Violently, vigorously, they mated, abandoned, unrestrained. He thrust rapidly, rhythmically, shoving forcefully into her, burying himself as deeply as possible in the hot female sweetness. She clutched at his scarred back, lifting rounded hips, bucking wildly against him, gripping him tightly, begging for all he had.

The carnal coupling was bawdy but brief.

Hot and hungry for each other for far too long, they quickly exploded into earth-shattering orgasmic ecstasy. Natalie's startled sobs mingled with Kane's loud groans of gratification, the odd chorus ringing in the darkness of the room. And when the sobs and groans died away, two spent, sweat-drenched lovers lay in the thick, hot darkness.

And laughed.

They laughed with the sheer joy of being alive. Of being in each other's arms. Of being young and lusty and rapturously sated.

Legs and arms entwined, slick bodies shaking with their glee, they tumbled about on the rumpled bed and giggled uncontrollably, tears streaming down their happy faces, stomachs aching from the continuous jerking, breaths short and labored.

They laughed and laughed. One of them would calm a bit, the other would still be caught up in fierce fits of laughter. Then the calmed one would burst out once more even as the other quieted.

At last two exhausted, peaceful people lay on their backs, their knees pulled up and bent, soles of their feet flat on the bed, hands held between their limp bodies, fingers loosely entwined.

It was Natalie who finally broke the close, comfortable silence. "Kane," she said, turning her head to press a kiss to his damp, hot shoulder, "I think it's time we talked."

She felt his long, lean body tense against her.

"All right," answered Kane. He rolled up onto an elbow and leaned over her flushed face. "I'll light the lamps." He gave her lips a quick kiss and was up in one fast, fluid movement. Natalie sat up, scooted across the bed, shoved fat pillows against the brass-cylindered headboard, and curled her long, slender legs beneath her.

A lamp flickered to life, illuminating Kane's darkly handsome face and tall, muscular body. He looked at Natalie and smiled nervously. A fleeting, little-boy smile that reached her very soul. He looked for all the world like a shy tiger. Never had he been more appealing, more lovable. More unsure.

"My darling," she said, beckoning him, "come here." He came to her almost reluctantly, as though fearful of what she was going to say. She read the unease in his beautiful blue eyes. Touched, heart filled with love, she drew him down beside her, put a hand up into his thick black hair, and questioned, "What is it?"

He captured her hand, brought it to his lips and kissed it, then placed it on the thick, dampened hair of his chest. The little-boy smile had fled; his face was set. The blue, blue eyes narrowed. He was Kane once more, the hard, skeptical man who had seen most everything in life and disliked much of it.

The woman who loved him understood. Understood both his shyness and his cynicism. This big, fearless man was afraid of her. Afraid to care. To love.

She looked straight into those hard blue eyes and said, "Kane, my foolish darling, don't you know how much I love you?" His eyes flickered, full black lashes lifting restlessly. "I do, you know," she crooned softly. "I love you very, very much, and you love me as well. Don't you?"

Kane gave no reply, but the heart beneath Natalie's splayed fingers thumped rapidly, giving him away.

"Don't be afraid to love me, Kane. Please don't." She smiled at him and added, "I'm not the loose woman you think. You are the second man in my life. The other was my husband." She waited for him to react.

"It doesn't matter to me if you—"

"Yes, it does, and I'm glad. I've never made love to Ashlin. I swear it."

"Why would you—"

"Make love to you as soon as we met?" she finished for him. Smiling, she said, "I thought it would be my first and last chance what with those deadly Apaches breathing down our necks." She sobered then and told him, "I'm not sure, Kane. I wanted you, I needed you. Who knows, perhaps I loved you even then."

"I'm not much of a prize," said Kane in the soft Mississippi drawl she had grown to adore. "You really love me?"

"With all of my heart, Kane." Her hands went up to frame his dark, chiseled face. "And I fully intend to make you love me." She leaned toward him, kissed his smooth jaw, and said, "But for now, may I please have a bath?"

They bathed, they ate, they drank hot black coffee and sipped warm amber brandy. And they talked. Natalie gently convinced Kane, through her seemingly spontaneous conversations regarding her background, her family, her dreams and hopes, that she was far from a deceitful, unprincipled wanton. She was instead a warm-blooded, trustworthy woman capable of abiding, long-lasting faithfulness as well as deep, glowing passion.

She spoke openly of the relationship she had shared with Ashlin. She had been fooled by Ashlin's intentions and had agreed to become his wife even though she had never been in love with him. She admitted to believing that she would never again fall in love as she had with her husband, and told Kane she longed for children as any woman might.

As she spoke she looked unwaveringly into his eyes, letting Kane read the sincerity and truthfulness of her words. Open and honest, she said if there was anything he wanted to know about her, he need only ask.

She could tell that the man of stone was quickly softening, though not yet had he said he loved her, despite her telling him repeatedly that she was in love with him, loved him more than ever she'd loved a man. She was unworried that Kane had not spoken of love. The words would come in time.

They sat at the table, remnants of a half-eaten supper before them. They had talked for so long, the coffee was cold in their cups, snifters of brandy emptied. And Natalie, her eyes on the raw bruise circling Kane's brown throat, said softly, "Kane, it's time you went to bed. You need some sleep."

Kane's dark hand reached across the table and closed over hers. He smiled and said, "It isn't sleep I need."

"What are we waiting for?" said Natalie, and started to rise.

"Stay where you are," ordered Kane gently.

She didn't question him. She remained seated while Kane, wearing only a pair of tight trousers, got up and moved about the room lighting every lamp and candle he could find. He left none darkened. All were illuminated and soon the spacious room was filled with far-reaching yellow-white light. No corner remained in shadow. Everywhere was light; bright, radiant light.

Kane returned to the table and offered Natalie his hand.

She took it and stood, looking questioningly up at him. He smiled down at her. "We made hurried love in the darkness. Let's make unhurried love in the light."

"Kane," she murmured happily, and threw her arms around his neck.

"I like the way you say my name," he told her as he picked her up and held her high in his arms, against his bare chest. He kissed her, and said against her mouth, "I'll be tender, sweetheart. I'll make it up to you."

Natalie couldn't answer. She buried her face in the warm curve of his neck and shoulder and felt him moving gracefully across the floor. At the bed he stood with her in his arms for a moment, and against her hair he told her his intention. "I'm going to undress you now. I want to take down your beautiful hair. Allow me these pleasures, sweetheart. Will you do that?"

Her breath already coming quickly, she managed, "Yes, Kane, yes."

Slowly he released her, lowering her bare feet to the floor. He took a step backward and let his blue, appreciative gaze slide slowly over her. Over her doeskin trousers she wore a dark shirt of shimmering silk that he had loaned her. His lean hands went to the pearl buttons going down the shirt's front. Languidly he released buttons from buttonholes, his gaze holding hers.

Natalie's breath caught when finally all of the buttons were undone. She expected Kane to swiftly push the silk shirt from her shoulders. He did not; his hands lifted up to her hair. Gently he removed the pins holding the hastily wound knot of red curls atop her head. Natalie watched his eyes. An expression of awe filled them when the tangled mass came spilling down about her shoulders.

Transfixed, he put his hands into the flowing hair and combed his long fingers reverently through it, murmuring hoarsely, "Such hair. I see this flaming hair in my dreams."

Natalie swallowed and her hands lifted to Kane's trim waist. "You'll help me wash it again sometime?"

"Always," he breathed, and Natalie's heart rejoiced.

Hands still entwined in her hair, Kane leaned down to her. Their mouths came together in a slow, tender kiss and he gently drew her against him. His lips were soft and warm and undemanding. And when they left hers, he smiled down at her, his eyes as tender as his lips.

He pressed her close to his tall frame and said, just above her ear, "I've a fantasy, sweetheart. Shall I tell you?"

Lips resting on his warm, rope-punished throat, she said, "I insist."

"You are naked to the waist. Your beautiful red hair is long and loose, as it is now. I part it in the back, draw it over your shoulders and breasts." Kane paused, slid his hands out of the hair and locked them behind her back. "Then I search through all that silky red hair for rosy nipples." He grinned and added, "With my mouth."

Natalie shivered. "Let's live your fantasy," she murmured in a soft, seductive voice.

Then her breath grew heavy when Kane, releasing her, put his hands to the front of her shirt. Slowly, sensuously he parted it, exposing her flesh to his eyes. Her full, trembling breasts blossomed beneath his gaze and ached for his touch.

The soft silk shirt slid down her arms and off. Kane drew in a breath and touched her cheek. "You're beautiful." He kissed the corner of her mouth. "I'm glad. And I'm glad you're here with me."

"I am too," she breathed. "I love you, Kane."

Kane took her arm and gently turned her around. He stood behind her, and Natalie, heartbeat erratic, fingers curling into fists, felt the light touch of his hands once more on her hair. Expertly he parted the tousled mane down the middle at the back of her head. Then carefully placed equal portions over each bare shoulder.

The silky hair tickled and teased Natalie's bare, sensitive breasts. Her eyes lowered, and to her surprise the tingling nipples were completely hidden beneath thick, heavy locks of hair. She felt Kane's warm hands cup her shoulders.

He pulled her back against his tall, lean frame and wrapped long arms around her, crossing them over her chest, above the hair-covered breasts. Her nervous hands moved backward to clutch at his hard, trousered thighs.

"Kane," she whispered breathlessly, "I so want to please you."

His lips pressed the side of her temple. "No one has ever pleased me more." His arms fell away. "Turn around, sweetheart."

Natalie exhaled and slowly pivoted. His erotic eyes were on the two thick portions of long red-gold hair draped over her shoulders. His hands enclosed her narrow waist and Kane bent his dark head. He lowered his face even as Natalie came up onto her tiptoes. And she found Kane's fantasy as provocative as he did.

Nose and mouth nuzzling amid the auburn tresses, Kane made a delightfully arousing game of locating Natalie's tensely waiting nipples. When he uncovered the left one, she sighed with pleasure. He pressed a warm, moist kiss to the pink satin bud and went in search of the other. When both were unveiled and worshipfully caressed, their crests peeking proudly out of the cascading hair, Kane raised his dark head and enfolded Natalie gently in his arms.

"My God, you're sweet, so sweet," he said, holding her close, feeling the hard nipples brushing his naked chest. "Can I hold you on my knee for a minute?"

Natalie inhaled deeply, loving the masculine scent of him. "Forever."

Kane dropped down onto the bed's edge and pulled Natalie forward to stand between his bent knees. Teasingly blowing his warm breath on the pale breasts before his face, he went about the task of unbuttoning Natalie's tight trousers. It took a while. With each button he released, with each inch of flesh he bared, he paused to place a kiss on the area he had exposed.

By the time the soft doeskin pants were sliding down her quivering thighs, Natalie's slender, naked body was afire from the top of her flaming head to the tips of her toes.

Dizzy with desire, Natalie clung to Kane's wide, bare shoulders and swayed helplessly to him. She closed her eyes

as Kane seated her on his left knee, an arm around her. His
fingers brushed her chin, trailed over the curve of her throat
to her shoulder.

Natalie opened her eyes.

"There are so many things I want to do with you; so many
ways I want to love you," Kane told her. As he spoke his
hand moved over the contours of her throat and down to a
shimmering white breast. He covered it with his brown hand,
squeezed it gently, then began to rub the taut nipple with a
feather-light touch of his thumb.

That arousing hand moved down to her stomach. The lean
fingers spread there and stroked her tight, flat belly, brushed
the smooth skin of her thighs, and came to rest on the flaming red triangle. "Sweetheart, sweetheart," he murmured
softly.

Natalie felt herself being borne backward onto the big bed.
Kane's mouth was on hers, kissing her tenderly, warmly,
over and over again. Weight supported on an elbow, he lay
stretched out beside her, his lips toying with hers, tongue
doing sweet, lovely things to her tingling mouth.

Natalie lay on her back, glorying in the unhurried way he
was loving her. She was glad he'd insisted on the lights. She
liked lying stretched out before him, totally naked and open,
offering herself for his intense scrutiny. She experienced a
delicious sense of vain power over this man so eagerly paying
homage to her. His eyes told her he thought her beautiful; his
hands and his lips told her more.

Serenely nude, Natalie stretched and sighed and clasped
her arms around Kane's neck while he continued to kiss her
with restrained passion and devastating tenderness. Natalie
gave a soft little whimper of pleasure when that warm, wonderful mouth finally left her swelling lips and went to her
throat.

Nudging aside the shiny golden disc gleaming at her
throat, Kane unhurriedly, tenderly, kissed her throat, her
ears, her shoulders. He kissed the undercurve of her breasts,
he pressed the gentlest of kisses to the aching crests. He

kissed her stomach. Soft, butterfly kisses that made her lift and sigh and want more, much more.

"Remember how I loved you at Spanish Widow?" Kane's voice was low, raspy. He lifted his dark head and looked at her.

Her eyes met his. "I remember." She felt the hot blood race through her veins. "Love me that way again, Kane."

"My sweet baby," said Kane, and changed positions. Still wearing his tight pants, Kane lay between her parted legs, his lips brushing kisses to her navel, her hipbones, the pale insides of her thighs.

Natalie waited, her eyes opening and closing, her curled fingers gripping the mattress beneath her. Kane made her wait; prolonging her pleasure, loving her tenderly, sweetly, until she was breathlessly calling his name.

When Kane leaned down and nuzzled his nose in the tight triangle of auburn curls, Natalie's back arched. "You tasted so good that night. I've been starved for you ever since," said Kane, and then he lowered his face and he kissed her.

"Kane . . . please . . ."

"Yes, my love, yes," Kane soothed, and Natalie squirmed and moaned as he sank his dark head, as eagerly as a thirsty man bending to drink, and pressed his burning lips to her. He buried his face in her and she put her fingers into his thick, black hair and pulled him to her. He kissed her, stroked her with his tongue, while his hands grasped her bare bottom and held her up to him.

Natalie had no idea that loud gasps and moans were tearing from her tight throat. She knew only that the dark, handsome head between her burning thighs was giving her the most frightening, exquisite pleasure she had ever known and that she wanted to keep him there . . . kissing her . . . caressing her . . . loving her forever.

She would never release him, never let him up. Would not allow him to take his lips from her flesh. Would command him to remain where he was until she . . . she . . .

"Ka—Kane . . ." she sobbed as the contractions in her belly became violent and her deep, shuddering climax began.

Kane's loving mouth stayed fused to her until total, draining ecstasy was attained and Natalie lay back, tears of joy filling her huge eyes, slender body limp.

Only then did Kane lift his head. Lithely, he slid up beside her, gathered her into his arms, and whispered, "There, honey. You're okay, I've got you."

She lay silent for a long time, clinging to her lover, pressing her bare, warm body to his. At last she softly said, "Kane."

"Yes, baby?"

"Don't ever do that to me again." But she was smiling; a catlike, satisfied smile.

"I won't," he promised, kissing her damp forehead. "At least not before tomorrow."

Chapter Thirty-seven

Kane held her until she was totally calm. Then he eased her down onto the pillows, gave her eyelids a kiss, and spread the fur covers up over her damp, naked curves.

"Where are you going?" she questioned drowsily when he rose from the bed. "Don't leave me."

"Never, sweet," assured Kane, "I'm only going to douse some of these lights so we can sleep."

"Mmm," she mumbled contentedly, and watched from beneath droopy lids her tall, dark, godlike lover move about the room like a mountain cat, easy and smooth and remarkably graceful. Muscles flowing beneath swarthy, satin skin.

Natalie felt a delicious surge of possessive pride. This magnificent man whose rock-hard muscles rippled with each lift of his long arm was hers. All hers. This man of mystery whose tight trousers revealed the powerful sinew of his thighs and lean buttocks had just made intimate, exquisite love to her.

Natalie sighed happily and her sleepy but fond gaze slipped downward from Kane's furred chest to his groin. She bit her lip. She was so tired, so sleepy, so fulfilled, she felt as though she couldn't possibly make love again. Not even with Kane. Yet she knew it was unfair and selfish to leave him in this unsated state.

Eyes still following his every move, she watched Kane extinguish the last of the brightly burning lamps. He returned to the bed carrying a tall new white candle, freshly lit. He set it on the night table and, looking directly at Natalie, unbuttoned his tight trousers and sent them to the carpeted floor.

He stood there proudly naked, the shadowy candlelight softly licking at his tall, bare body and his fully aroused, thrusting masculinity. He didn't make a move until Natalie's gaze finally lifted from his groin and came up to meet his burning blue eyes.

Kane got into bed with her, gathered her into his arms, and whispered, "Good night, Natalie. Sleep well." But before she could answer him, his lips, soft and moist, covered hers and his fingers had encircled her fragile wrist and carried her hand down to his throbbing erection. He gently guided her, letting his fingers cover hers, sliding hers, with his on them, up and down slowly, provocatively, over his engorged flesh while his mouth remained melded with hers.

To Natalie's surprised delight, she felt her sleepy lassitude slipping rapidly away. She never knew when Kane's instructive hand left hers. She knew only that her caressing fingers, gliding easily, rhythmically on his rigid shaft, were eliciting moans of pleasure from deep inside his naked chest. And enkindling a slow-burning fire within her.

Kane's lips left hers and he laid his dark head back on the pillow. And Natalie did just what he'd hoped she might do. She slipped up onto an elbow—embracing hand never leaving him—and leaned over his face, her long russet hair falling into his eyes, across his throat.

He felt the fluttering tip of her moist tongue against his open lips and sighed while shivers of expectant ecstasy coursed throughout his hot, tensed body. With a nimble toe, Kane kicked at the fur counterpane. Natalie sensed his wish to be uncovered, and lent a hand. Or a toe. Lips and tongue still playing with his heated mouth, hand still full of pulsing maleness, she kicked vigorously at the covers and felt them sliding away.

Kane sighed anew when sheet and heavy fur coverlet

rested at the foot of the bed. And he sighed yet again when Natalie, finally taking her sweet, teasing lips from his burning mouth, tossed her heavy hair out of her eyes and let her curious gaze slide downward.

"Kane," she whispered breathlessly, her heavily lashed emerald eyes shamelessly observing what she was doing to him, "does that feel good?"

"Oh, Jesus, honey," groaned Kane expressively. "Too good, I can't take it anymore."

With that he snatched her hand from him, kissed it gratefully, and eased her onto her back. And when he moved anxiously over her and thrust into her waiting warmth, he asked, "Natalie, does that feel good?"

"Oh, Jesus, honey."

They slept like two innocent children. Come morning, Natalie was awakened by bright Colorado sunshine streaming in the tall, uncurtained windows. She lay quietly, unmoving, while Kane continued to slumber peacefully. Backed up spoon-fashion against him, his long arms wrapped tightly around her, Natalie listened to his deep, even breathing and smiled contentedly. If she had her way, this is how she would greet each new morning for the rest of her days.

Natalie inhaled and let her lazy gaze follow a drop of water making its slow, steady descent down the crystal pane of the tall north window. Her eyes lifted. From eaves of the cabin's roof, long, spiky icicles were dripping. Melting.

Natalie cautiously lifted her head from the pillow and looked across the room. The fire in the grate was nothing but blackened ash and yet, naked though she and Kane were, covers at the bed's foot, she was not cold. Kane's long, protective body pressed to hers gave warmth, but it was more than that.

Natalie lowered her head back to the pillow. The weather had taken a great turn, no doubt about it. The chinook winds had obviously come through in the night, blowing their hot breath across the snow-gripped San Juans.

Natalie felt a sudden surge of panic.

It was December 12. The day of the twelfth full moon. Tohamah had said that with the passing of noon on this date, she would no longer need to guard the Manitou gold.

Natalie felt her heart begin to pound. What had he meant? What was to happen before noon?

An icy fear began to spread through her bare body as she recalled Kane's low, determined words spoken sometime in the long, love-filled night. "Tomorrow I'm going to the Cliff Palace, Natalie. I'll kill two birds with one stone."

"I don't understand," she had whispered fearfully.

"Ashlin will come, I'm sure of it. And when he does, I'll—"

"No, Kane, please!"

"When I've dealt with him, I'll take the gold."

"You've heard nothing I've said, Kane. I told you that Tahomah has warned against it!" Natalie sought to make him understand, to believe. "The shaman can determine the origin of ill fortune and can safeguard a man's future if he will only—"

"Ah, Natalie, you're so sweet, and you're far too intelligent to believe in Indian superstitions."

Natalie, sick with worry, lay now in the arms of her sleeping lover and believed with all her heart that to keep this dear man safe, she had to keep him away from the Cliff Palace. At least until noon passed.

Kane was right; Ashlin would show up there, eager and greedy for the gold. And if the pair met . . . Why did it have to warm up? Why couldn't another blinding blizzard have roared over the mountains making travel impossible and keeping her precious love safe here in this mountain hideaway with her. If only they were cut off from town, as they had been the week before, and Ashlin couldn't come here. If only she could persuade Kane to see the sheriff and let him take care of the murderers. If only . . .

Kane stirred behind her. His arms tightened around her, a dark hand straying up to fondle a bare breast gently. In a sleep-hoarse voice he murmured close to her ear, "I feel sorry for them."

"Who, Kane?"

"For all the people who are not in love."

"Darling," she exclaimed happily, at once forgetting her worry. She turned in his arms and looked into his sleepy blue eyes. "You . . . You . . . ?"

His lips closed over hers in a slow, lazy good-morning kiss. She pulled away, heart racing, eyes questioning. "I love you, Natalie Vallance," drawled Kane. "There! I've said it. Satisfied, sweetheart?"

She fell upon him, scattering happy kisses over his dark unshaven face, "Yes. Yes, yes, yes," she exclaimed in a high-pitched, excited voice. "No!" She lifted her face. "Say it again. I want to hear it over and over."

"I love you. I love you. I love you."

"Oh, Kane," she breathed, "I love you too. So much."

Kane grinned and turned her to face away again, pulling her once more into the curve of his frame. They lay cuddled together, his body around hers, her slender, silky-skinned back and naked bottom pressing his hair-covered chest and belly, both reluctant to let this lovely moment go.

Longing to please this complex man who lay whispering that he loved her, Natalie at last interrupted teasingly, "I must rise and make coffee for my dark master." Radiantly happy, she plucked away Kane's restraining arms and got to her knees.

Kane's quick blue gaze took in a temptingly beautiful sight. She twisted her torso to smile at him over her shoulder and he was rewarded with a fleeting glimpse of a bare, bouncing breast, tipped with dusky rose. Wild, sleep-tumbled red hair spilled down her ivory back. Her waist was astoundingly small, her shapely thighs pale, and her firm bottom as white as the snows covering the mountains.

"No," Kane commanded, and his hand went to the back of her knee.

Kneeling on the mattress, Natalie trembled. Kane's warm fingers moved up the length of her inner thigh, to gently stroke and caress that most feminine part of her. Her breathing quickened, her eyelids slid low, and a moist heat soon revealed her arousal to Kane.

A whoosh of air exploded from her lungs when Kane gripped her hips and pulled her onto her side, returning her once more to her former position against him. His dark, strong hands reached in front of her, moved over her flat, quivering belly and the red-gold triangle of hair to touch and tease the tiny bud of her passion.

Natalie squirmed and moaned and felt Kane's powerful erection throb against her bottom. "Kane . . ." she breathed raggedly, opening her legs and arching her back that he might enter. Then again, "Oh, Kane . . ." as she felt the hard, heavy flesh move between her legs and push into her.

"Am I hurting you, sweet?" Kane's breath was hot on the back of her neck.

"No," she told him, "but I'm not . . . I don't think I know how to . . ."

Open lips pressing a heated kiss to her ivory, bullet-pierced right shoulder, Kane's voice was little more than a husky whisper. "You're doing fine, just fine." He thrust farther into her. "I'll help you, baby, I'll show you."

Kane's masterful hands guided her movements. He pressed her hips back to him, even as he thrust forward into her, pushing warily, slowly, until his full, throbbing length was deep inside her.

"Okay, angel?" he softly inquired.

Natalie could only gasp and nod violently, her disheveled hair tossing in his passion-hardened face.

One of Kane's dark hands stayed between her legs, the other moved up to fondle and caress her swelling, aching breasts. Those talented hands increased Natalie's ecstasy, and his own. The fused pair moved together in erotic splendor there on the sunlit bed, and when the first blinding waves of release began, both knew it was going to be an almost painful climax, so deep and grinding were the beginning tremors.

But neither was quiet prepared for the intense pleasure that gripped and buffeted them. The spasms were acute, prolonged, extreme. And wonderful. Not of this earth, never to be forgotten, wonderful.

And when they passed, two limp, awed lovers lay still joined, silent in their bliss, more deeply in love than ever.

When Kane finally slid out of Natalie and gently turned her to face him, he kissed her brow and said teasingly, "Judge, may I say I find being 'in your chamber' more than pleasurable."

Natalie gave him a playful punch in the stomach and lifted her head. "Counselor, having, as you so crudely put it, been 'in my chamber,' are you fully aware that you must now pay your debt to society and to me?"

"Oh?" His blue eyes narrowed in mock fear. "Am I not allowed a trial?"

Natalie, green eyes twinkling, put on her grave, judicial face. "Covington, you shall be awarded a bench trial, as this case could best be described as civil." Her somber face screwed itself into lines of laughter and she added naughtily, "Although I'm not sure I would call what you just did to me 'civil' or 'civilized.' "

Kane smiled and pulled a shapely ivory leg up over his hip. Hand slipping around to cup her firm buttocks, he kidded, "May it please the court, I must point out that my esteemed colleague, Her Honor, Judge Vallance, did in fact and in kind behave in a manner at once as primitive as the accused."

"Counselor is out of order! The court is not on trial here. Any further outbursts and you will be asked to leave my bed!"

"Beg pardon, Your Honor." Kane leaned forward and kissed her nose. "If defendant is found guilty, will bench please pass down the sentence and bring these proceedings to a close."

Natalie raised herself onto an elbow. "Kane W. Covington, you have been found guilty of the heinous crime of making a helpless, unsuspecting female fall victim to your dangerous charms and animal lusts and did cause said victim to submit to wild passions of the flesh and in so doing fall everlastingly in love with you! Forthwith you—"

"Come on, Judge," Kane disrespectfully cut in, "tell the poor trapped guy what you're going to do with him."

Natalie placed her hand in Kane's thick, dark curls and spoke in a firm voice. "Under the authority vested in me by the sovereign Territory of Colorado, I sentence the defendant, Kane W. Covington, to take the oath of matrimony. And to remain loyal and true to your oath until—"

"You sure you want to marry me, honey?" Kane's dark face turned somber and he abruptly ended their game.

"More than I've ever wanted anything in my life," Natalie said, and kissed him. "Marry me, Kane," she murmured softly. "Marry me." She snuggled down onto his chest.

He held her close. "Sweetheart, sweetheart," he said hoarsely. Then abruptly he loosened his long arms and said, "Get up, baby. I have to take care of—"

"No!" Natalie's arm tightened over his chest. "You can't go to the Cliff Palace, I won't let you! I've told you, it isn't safe. I'll lose you if you—"

"I'll tell you what isn't safe. The two of us lying here."

Natalie tensed. "You're right, Kane. Let's ride up to Tahomah's lodge. I know the way, I'll take you." She raised up and looked at him hopefully.

He touched her cheek. "Good idea. We'll bathe, have coffee, then I want you to go to Tahomah."

"But . . . you're coming with me?"

"No, sweetheart, I'm not." Kane gently eased her arms from around him and swung his long legs over the edge of the bed and sat up.

Natalie was up at once, on her knees behind him, arms wrapped around his wide shoulders. "Please, Kane, don't try to . . . darling, I'm afraid. Ashlin is a dangerous and terrible man."

"I can handle Blackmore."

Her arms tightened and she leaned around to lay her cheek against his. "Kane, don't do it. Don't go after them; they'll kill you. Let's ride into Cloudcastle and alert the sheriff. He and his deputies can pick them all up and . . ."

Kane gently tore her arms away and rose. He turned and,

looking down at her, took the panther's claw from the night table and lifted the leather necklace over his dark head. He put out a hand and pulled her to her feet. Naked, they stood in the morning sunshine looking at each other. Kane's dark, lean fingers toyed with the shiny gold disc resting in the valley of Natalie's cleavage.

"Sweetheart, it's thawing outside. Blackmore will be coming; we both know it. Unless I intercept him, he'll show up at Cloud West for you. After all, the man still thinks you're engaged."

"But, Kane, I—"

"No, Natalie." Kane's dark face had taken on that set, chiseled look. "I'm going after him. Now make some coffee while I heat water for our baths. I'll take you to Tahomah, or down to your girlfriend Carol Thompson's, but I'm going after Blackmore."

"Is there nothing I can do to change your mind?" Natalie said sadly.

"No, my love. Nothing."

Chapter Thirty-eight

A woman deeply in love, Natalie sat in Kane's deep tub and racked her brain, trying to come up with a scheme to keep him occupied until noontime. Idly she passed a soapy sponge over her slick throat and watched Kane shave.

Towel wrapped around his slim hips, he stood before the mirror shaving his face covered with creamy white lather.

The ribbon-white scars on his deeply cleft back pulled and lifted with his movements. Natalie felt a quiver deep in her bare, wet belly as she remembered the first time she'd seen them. She had watched him wash up that hot evening at Spanish Widow, eyes drawn in fearful fascination to the pull and play of the satin scars. And she had assumed he was a desperate outlaw, that he had gotten them in some life-threatening, violent struggle.

Natalie bit her bottom lip. Those terrible scars had been delivered by a Federal's deadly, slashing sword. This man deftly shaving his handsome face was a Rebel, the brand of southerner she had hated with a fierceness bordering on obsession. Not a day had passed when she had not vowed never to forgive or forget what had happened in the war.

Now it seemed so long ago. So unreal. So far unremoved from all that was most important in her life. She no longer cared which side Kane had fought on, or even how many

Federals he might have killed. She only cared that this tall, scarred man who had taken her in his powerful arms and awakened her from a ten-year sleep, was in danger. Dear God, she might lose the treasured love of her life just when she'd found him.

Natalie rose from the tub. She patted at her body with a white towel. "Kane, do you suppose we could go by Cloud West so I can pick up a few things?"

Razor poised over a high, dark cheekbone, Kane looked at her in the mirror. "There's no time."

Unruffled, Natalie pulled the bathtowel about her slender body, tucked in the edge over her breasts, and crossed the room. "Kane," she said, stepping up behind him, "it wouldn't take long."

Kane lowered the razor. "Sweetheart, you'll only be at Tahomah's for a day or so. I'll come for you soon."

Natalie slipped her arms around his trim middle. Leaning close, she pressed a kiss to his scarred flesh. "Darling, I'm afraid men don't always understand." She laughed softly, and added mysteriously, "There are things a woman needs that are found only in her own home."

It worked.

"Uh . . . I . . . well, no longer than fifteen minutes. You hear me?"

Hiding her triumphant smile against his warm back, Natalie kissed his shoulderblade and murmured, "I hear."

Outdoors, Kane shook his dark head and remarked on the puzzling warmth of the sun-brightened morning. Hand in hand the pair climbed the gentle incline toward the stables, Kane's blue eyes squinting disbelievingly. Instead of the familiar crunchy hard-frozen icepack beneath their boots, there was wet and watery snow with patches of dark green showing through some of the sunnier spots.

"This is the damnedest thing I've ever seen," Kane said in amazement.

"I know," Natalie agreed. "I told you; it's the chinook winds. Almost like the spring melt-off."

Kane flashed Natalie a bright grin. "Well, ma'am, I can't

say how you Yankees feel about this weather, but this Gulf Coast southerner finds it to his liking." He released her and shrugged out of his coat.

"Rebel," teased Natalie, "you're soft."

Matched bays carrying them over the slippery mountain slope to Cloud West, the two lovers rode knee to knee, the bright sunlight beating down on them, their horses' sharp hooves leaving deep prints in the slick, melting snows.

They crossed a narrow brook. A deep, clear stream—almost always frozen solid from early autumn until late spring —was flowing, rushing loudly; its frigid water, filled with broken, jagged ice blocks, hurtled over boulders, loosening great ridges of ice from its banks.

Again Kane smiled at her as Satan pranced proudly through the noisy spring. "Want to go wading?" His eyes twinkled devilishly and he gave a great shout of laughter.

Natalie smiled, shook her head, and carefully kept a new fear to herself. Waiting until Kane had again turned to the path before them, Natalie lifted worried eyes to the high peaks towering above. Turning her head a little to the side, she listened for any strange or unusual sounds thrumming through the soaring San Juans.

She heard only the deep, rumbling laughter of her lover, and with one last, hasty glance about, she turned her attention fully back to him.

At Cloud West, Kane kneed Satan into the big, roomy barn after Natalie, then swung down out of the saddle and reached for her. On another day she might have reminded him she was perfectly capable of dismounting without his help. It so happened that, with little time to set her well-laid plans in motion, this solicitous offer of assistance played right into her hands. And she was quick to take advantage of the opportunity.

Smiling winningly down at him, Natalie agilely brought her long, trousered leg over the horse's back, put her hands on Kane's wide shoulders, and slid from the saddle, making certain her body brushed his on her descent. When her toes touched wood, she did not release his shoulders. She stepped closer, blatantly pressed her pelvis to his, and said softly, "Kiss me, Kane."

A flicker of interest mixing with irritation in his expressive eyes, Kane grabbed her by the belt, bent his head, and gave her a quick peck. Then he turned her about, released his hold, and gave her shapely bottom a little spank.

"Ouch," she protested, rubbing the seat of her trousers. "You'll pay for that."

"Fine," said Kane, "but not today." He took her arm, guided her out into the glaring sunshine and toward the big ranch house. Inside all was silent, only the slow, rhythmic clanking of Kane's spurs on the hardwood floor of the corridor.

"Want to lay a fire, Kane?" Natalie looked up over her shoulder at him while he freed her arms from the heavy coat and tossed it across the polished stairway banister.

"Do you need it for . . . ah . . . whatever you might want?"

Natalie turned to face him. "I've a feeling I won't be needing a fire." She gave him an enigmatic smile and lifted her hand to his chest. With a dexterity that startled him, she opened the top two buttons of his shirt before he realized what was happening. She slipped a warm hand inside and spread her fingers in the thick, crisp hair.

"Damn it, Natalie, this is no time for games." Kane captured her brazen hand and withdrew it. "I've told you, we have to hurry."

"Mmm," she murmured apologetically, but grinned slyly and nuzzled her nose in the open V of the shirt before whirling about and stepping onto the stair. "I'll be good," she promised, walking away from him, hips swaying beguilingly.

Natalie timed him. She would give him five minutes. No more. If he had not followed her up the stairs in five minutes, she would bring out the big guns. She was going to keep him with her until the stroke of noon, no matter how she had to go about it.

In the bedroom, Natalie opened the shimmering white silk drapes. Blinding bright sunshine flooded the big white room.

Her huge, silk-hung bed with its snowy counterpane shimmered in the fierce light. The deep-pile white carpet, the white brocade couch and wing chairs, the white marble fireplace, shone a dazzling silver-white in the winter sun.

Kane's five minutes passed.

Natalie frowned. She undressed with the speed of one possessed, discarding her boots, pants, shirt, belt, and underwear in her dressing room. From the top drawer of the tall armoire, she drew a shimmering white satin nightgown. Pulling it over her head, she felt the fabric slink down her belly and thighs as though it were warm honey being poured from a pitcher.

It fell to the white carpet over her bare feet and Natalie, snatching at the pins restraining her long hair, looked down at herself and smiled wickedly. A daring, enticing bit of fluff she had never before worn, the white satin gown covered little and tended to accentuate the female curves beneath its clinging softness.

If this didn't entice the preoccupied man downstairs, nothing would. Natalie hurried to the bed, drew back the ivory silk spread, the downy comforter, and the silky top sheet. She punched up the many fat, white lace-trimmed pillows and stepped back, pleased.

Natalie crossed the big room, enjoying the feel of sun-warmed satin sensuously hugging her naked curves and the deep pile carpet beneath her bare feet. Easing open the bedroom door, she ventured out into the hall, paused at the top of the stairs, and anxiously looked down.

Kane was where she had left him.

He lounged there at ease against the wall, unaware of her presence. His black Stetson was pushed back, the two top buttons of his shirt were still open. A cigarette protruded from his sculpted lips and a thumb was hooked in the gunbelt that slanted across his slim hips.

Natalie's heart began to pound beneath the straining satin as her eyes fondly beheld this extraordinary man. She said nothing, but Kane's head slowly turned and he looked up.

"Kane," she said softly, and descended a couple of steps.

Kane's blue eyes narrowed with surprised interest and he felt a sharp lurch in his chest. She stood above him wearing nothing but a daringly provocative nightgown of some shiny white material. Her flaming hair was brushed out, a thick, loose lock curling appealingly about her ivory throat. The bodice of the gown slashed low, exposing the milky skin of bare shoulders and slim arms. The shimmery fabric clung to her full, jutting breasts, flat belly, and flaring hips. Though it was not transparent in the true sense of the word, Kane could see through the gleaming white satin the distinct outline of large, rose-hued nipples as well as the shadowed loveliness between her thighs.

"Kane," she repeated, and ventured another two steps.

"Yes?" he finally managed, removing the long-ashed cigarette from between tight lips, his hot gaze locked on her seductively clad body.

"You recall how you told me of your fantasy?"

"Yes. Your hair brushed over your—"

"And I indulged that fantasy, didn't I, darling?"

"You did."

Natalie smiled and floated down to him. She stopped when she reached the second step from the bottom. She stood just above him, her scantily draped torso on the level of his upturned face. Smiling, she lifted a hand and removed the black Stetson from his head. Dropping it on top of the newel post of the banister, she said, "I have a fantasy, Kane."

Kane swallowed hard. "Tell me."

Natalie inhaled deeply, toyed with his stiff shirt collar, and said, "My fantasy is to see your very dark, very bare body on my very white bed in my very white room." She shuddered a little, as if envisioning it. "You lie there on your back, perfectly still and relaxed, and allow me to make love to you."

She turned then and slowly ascended the stairs.

"Damnation!" cursed Kane as the smoked-down, forgotten cigarette suddenly burned his fingers. Frantically looking around for an ashtray, Kane saw none, crossed anxiously to the front door, and sailed the smoke out into the snow.

Slamming the door with a resounding bang, he threw the

heavy bolt lock and climbed the stairs so swiftly, he intercepted a softly laughing Natalie. Sweeping her up into his long arms, he pressed his hot face into her free-flowing red hair and growled, "Woman, you are the devil's own daughter."

She kicked her bare feet and giggled. "It's heaven I'll take you to when you're naked in my bed."

Natalie hurried into her dressing room while Kane disrobed. She gave her hair a few more strokes of the brush, then unstoppered her most expensive perfume and nervously dabbed the fragrance over her pulse points and between her breasts. Pinching her cheeks for color, she let her eyes drift appraisingly over her body.

Determined to be as seductive as possible for Kane, Natalie rushed into the bathroom, took a spanking-clean washcloth from a neat stack and dipped its corner into a basin of icy cold water. Lowering the bodice of her satin gown, Natalie bathed her soft nipples with the cold cloth until they stood out in chilled, rigid points. Gown pulled back up, Natalie nodded approvingly at the sight of hardened nipples standing out beneath the white satin. She turned and went out to Kane.

The effect she hoped to have on him was at once eclipsed by his effect on her.

His clothes lay in a pile on the deep white carpet. One black leather boot sat upright; the other lay on its side. Over the foot of her intricately carved bedstead hung his buckled cartridge belt, smooth black leather swinging gently. Sunlight glinted on the brass bullets it held, but the heavy black Colt was missing. It rested on the white marble-topped night table near Kane's dark head.

Kane lay on his back in the very middle of the white bed. As naked as Adam. Long legs crossed at the ankles, one arm folded beneath his head, the other resting on his furred chest, he was all any warm-blooded woman, who ever dared to daydream of a handsome brown Adonis, could ask of the gods of love. He was as perfect a specimen of manhood as ever lay naked before an awed, aroused female.

And Natalie, looking upon him lying there, all dark and gleaming on her sun-brightened white bed, brought a hand up to clutch at her throbbing throat. Her eyes shamelessly went to his groin; to that maleness nestled amidst a thick brush of tight, black curls.

She drew a shallow breath and went to the bed.

"Kane," she said softly, and sat down facing him, a hand stopping him when he started to lower his arm from beneath his head. "No, darling. This is my fantasy. You must do as I say."

All his love in his eyes, Kane spoke softly, "I will. Just tell me."

Natalie slowly leaned toward him and kissed the corner of his mouth. Lips resting there, she murmured, "I want you to lie quietly and let me love you, Kane. Don't reach for me, don't pull me down, don't stop me when I touch you." Before he could reply, she again kissed him, licking at his mouth, nibbling gently on the fleshy inside of his full bottom lip, toying with him while her long, free hair covered his face in a cloak of red silk.

Kane closed his eyes and enjoyed it.

Natalie, making certain her gossamer-draped breasts rested enticingly on his naked chest, continued to press whisper-soft kisses to his lips while her hands framed his face, stroked his ears, his temples, his firm chin. And Kane lay dutifully still, arm folded beneath his head, wondering how long he could endure her sweet torment.

Natalie abruptly lifted her head, tossed her hair back off her face, and sat up. "Kane, you're beautiful," she whispered, her hands raking through the thick, black mat covering his broad chest. "So beautiful"—she leaned down and pressed warm lips to the hollow of his throat—"that I love to look at you. To touch you. All over. May I do that, Kane?"

"God, yes." Kane's drawling voice was low and strained. "But I'm not pretty, Natalie. Men aren't—"

"You are, Kane." She raised her eyes to his. "No . . ." she warned when he brought his arm from under his head, "don't reach for me, Kane. Not yet." Kane's hands flattened on the white sheets and he gritted his teeth.

But he sighed when soft, gentle fingers played along the muscular ridges of his chest, moved back up to skim the tops of his shoulders, then traveled down his arms. And he winced when those hands stroked his tight belly and brazenly slipped lower, to touch, to caress, to arouse. To send the hot blood rushing into his already rigid masculinity.

Bold emerald eyes locking with shocked blue ones, Natalie stroked, gently squeezed, and felt her own blood scald through her veins at the touch of his flesh, which radiated fierce, animal heat. Her brazen hand continuing to pleasure him, Natalie leaned over Kane's heaving chest and began pressing warm, moist kisses to the flat muscles, the heated flesh, the curly hair.

Kane, eyes still wide open, watched in nervous ecstasy while this goddess of desire led him skillfully toward the heights of passion. Natalie put out her tongue and licked a sweet, wet path along the heavy black line of hair going down his flat abdomen.

Kane held his breath.

Natalie laid her cheek on his flat stomach. "Kane," she whispered, "you're holding your breath."

"Yes," he gasped, "I'm terrified you'll stop."

Natalie brushed a kiss over his hipbone. "Breathe, my love, I won't stop. I'll never stop loving you."

Kane released a tentative breath and let his eyes come to rest on the fiery head bent to him. Her hand had released him and now played in the damp hair of his groin while her lips continued to move ever closer to that stiffened shaft of desire pulsing on his brown belly not an inch from her nuzzling mouth.

And then Kane's heart stopped beating, because Natalie lifted her lovely, glowing face and, looking directly into his passion-darkened blue eyes, told him, "I want to love you the way you loved me. Tell me that I may."

Kane choked. Couldn't speak. Couldn't say a word.

Could only watch in fearful, expectant awe as the woman

he loved lowered her open lips to him. His eyes slid closed. His agonized breath came bursting from his chest and his hands left the bed to tangle in Natalie's long, red-gold hair.

Kane allowed himself this forbidden ecstasy only a short time. For only a brief, blessedly sweet moment he lay there beneath her, his toes curling, his fingers gripping her head, his belly contracting. Fleetingly wishing he could lie there stark naked on her soft white bed, with Natalie's warm mouth enclosing him, for all the rest of his life, Kane abruptly pulled her up lest he explode in a gushing climax.

With swift agility he sat up, lifted the white satin gown over Natalie's head, and, still holding it in his right hand, lay back and hoarsely entreated, "Climb astride me, baby."

Natalie murmured softly, "Yes, Kane, yes, darling," and swiftly straddled him, guiding him into her. Kane groaned with pleasure, feeling the moist tightness swallow him up. Satin nightgown slipping through his fingers, Kane's brown hands came to Natalie's hips while his eyes went to where the two of them were joined.

His dark body was melded with her ivory skin. Hard male flesh with soft female flesh. Raven curls with red. God's two gloriously different creatures, now one. Joined in the age-old act of physical loving.

Kane sighed and lifted his gaze to Natalie's flushed face. There was a wicked wildness in her huge emerald eyes and her soft, wet mouth was sensuously open. Her tousled red tresses spilled about her bare shoulders, and her breasts, their pink centers diamond-hard, bounced seductively with the movements of her rotating hips. Her hands gripped his ribs as she rode him expertly, rhythmically, hotly.

As it had been when her lips were upon him, Kane felt that this surely must be the ultimate in bliss. And he wanted it to last. To endure. He would hold back for a long, long time. He would lie here and let this brazen beauty ride naked astride him forever. He would withhold his—

"Ba—baby . . ." he groaned helplessly as all his dreamy intentions were lost in the surging climax pumping hotly into her.

Natalie, near the edge, let herself go with him. Her joy matched his. Together they reached the apex of ecstasy, rocketing high up into a sexual nirvana of their own making, reveling briefly in a hot heaven of love before exploding completely to float weightlessly back to earth.

Natalie collapsed atop Kane and they lay there in the bright Colorado sunshine, panting, resting, silently thanking each other.

Natalie, still astride him, knees hugging his ribs, hands gripping his shoulders, cheek pressed to his damp, heaving chest, said lazily at last, "Kane."

"Yes, baby?"

"How did you like my fantasy?"

Kane chuckled and his lean fingers slipped from her narrow waist to move up over the rise of her bare bottom.

"Beats the hell out of mine."

Chapter Thirty-nine

Ashlin Blackmore calmly buckled his gunbelt. He placed not one but two fully loaded heavy Colt .44-caliber revolvers down into the leather holsters on his black-trousered thighs. He stood before the tall beveled mirror in his sun-splashed bedroom, pale, slim fingers resting lightly on the silver-plated gun handles.

Like a gunfighter soon to be pressed into action, Ashlin Blackmore practiced his draw. Dexterously, he drew, reholstered, and drew once more, gleaming steel clearing black leather with respectable swiftness.

He had never in his forty-one years fired a gun for any purpose but sport. And that had been target practice or fox hunting in his native England. He had purchased the six-shooters when he had first arrived in the Colorado Territory but had worn them for a brief time only, feeling foolish and vulgar as he strolled down the wooden sidewalks, the heavy revolvers impeding his step.

Quickly he had made friends with the townsfolk, and, convinced Cloudcastle was not a dangerous place for a respected English nobleman, Ashlin had hung up his guns . . . and also had quickly formed a secret liaison with the feared Leatherwood brothers.

The Leatherwood clan's reputation for meanness had intrigued and impressed Ashlin. He had wasted little time in recruiting them, certain he would find a need for them in the future.

Ashlin again reholstered his gleaming Colts and his lip thinned angrily. The Leatherwoods were not mean and fearless after all. And now he, Lord Blackmore, a titled, aristocratic blueblood, was forced to go out and dirty his own fine hands. He would have to kill the old Ute shaman himself.

Ashlin eyed himself speculatively in the tall, clear mirror. And he began to smile.

He was not afraid of some superstitious old savage. He would ride quietly, secretly up into the mountains, hunt down the meddlesome old chief, and shoot him dead. That done, he would head for the Cliff Palace, fill his black saddlebags with gold coin, and go for Natalie. He had been patient with Natalie much too long. It was time she learned who was master, who was servant. Today was as good a time as any.

Ashlin's lips slowly curved wider into a sly grin and he nodded, pleased, at the reflection in the mirror. He saw a handsome blond man attired in black, a brace of pistols on his hips. A man sure of himself and of his future.

By sundown he would be at Cloud West making lewd love to Judge Natalie Vallance on a bed scattered with shiny gold coins. He would take her by force if necessary, show her he could be quite different from the acquiescent gentleman of the past. He'd seen the way she unwittingly responded to the lusty male presence of the crude, insolent Kane Covington. Maybe that was what she preferred. Perhaps, despite her intelligence and gentility, she longed to be enslaved by a strong, ruthless male.

Ashlin's evil smile broadened and his right hand slid from gunbutt down to the erection straining against his tight black trousers.

He would be delighted to see that Natalie got her secret wish. He would have her at his feet by midnight, whimpering and subservient. He would conquer her with old tricks that would be entirely new to her. By the time they took their wedding vows, the very prim and proper judge would be reduced to an obedient, wide-eyed plaything, catering to his every whim, gladly indulging his every hunger, eagerly learning and being rewarded by her master.

Just like Belinda Baker.

Shortly after eleven in the morning, Natalie and Kane rode away from Cloud West. Despite her efforts to hold him there past noon, Kane, with only a small, silencing kiss, had risen from the white bed, stepped into his buckskins, and said, "Put on your pants, sweetheart. We're leaving."

Now she rode ahead of him, defeated. It was still an hour until noon. There was nothing more she could do to detain him. She was sure that he loved her, but Kane could still be a hard, uncompromising man. Repeatedly she had warned him of the danger of disturbing the Manitou gold, yet he remained unmoved.

"I love you, Red," he had murmured, nibbling on her ear while she held him fiercely, tightly to her naked breasts, "but I don't share your superstitions. The gold is there for the taking and I intend to help myself." His mouth had moved down to the gold chain around her neck. His tongue followed the delicate chain to the shimmering yellow medallion resting in the hollow of her throat. "Didn't this little trinket come from the Cliff Palace?"

"Yes, but—"

"You're white, honey. You took some of the gold and nothing bad has happened to you."

"No," corrected Natalie, "I did not. I have never taken anything from the Cliff Palace. Tahomah gave me the medallion, but he told me that—"

"Sweetheart, I lived with the Comanches for more than a year. They were forever predicting my demise because I refused to believe in their myths and fables. I'm still here." He raised his dark head and smiled down at her.

"Kane." She lifted loving fingers to the bruise beneath his left eye. "Don't you love me?"

"I do. You know I do." He grinned and added, "So much

that I want to give you everything a woman could ever desire."

"You're all that I desire, Kane."

But Kane did not fully believe her; she could see it in his brooding blue eyes. The memory of another life, another love, had not been completely vanquished. Kane was not entirely certain that she would not behave like the avaricious, fickle Susannah. He was not yet secure in the knowledge that she loved him—would always love him—whether he be rich or poor.

Natalie, silently riding ahead of the dear, foolish man for whom she feared, unconsciously rotated her aching right shoulder. Thoughts on Kane, she was unaware she was doing it, hardly realized that the small gunshot wound was bothering her.

Kane saw the reflex action and immediately spurred Satan up beside her. "That shoulder hurting bad, sweetheart?"

She smiled at him. "Not really, Kane. A little sore, but . . ."

Kane frowned. "We're near the hot springs. A good soaking would ease it."

Natalie's emerald eyes lit up immediately. "Yes! That's exactly what I need." Surprised that Kane had suggested it, she thought not of her wound, nor of the healing powers of the springs, but of the time it would kill. One last delay. One more chance to save Kane from impending danger. One final opportunity to keep him safely with her as high noon approached.

Elated that she'd been handed another reprieve, Natalie gave Blaze a slap of the long reins and altered her course toward Escalante Canyon. Kane followed. In moments the pair rode around the ragged upthrust of jutting rock and into the steep-walled canyon.

Inside it was dim and chilly. But high, high above, the Colorado sun beat down through a cloudless blue sky. And beneath that glaring sunshine, heavy banks of snow, thawed by the warm chinook winds, began to shift and move. Deep melting had begun, slicking the jutting, dangerous slopes.

Setting the stage for disaster.

Kane and Natalie hurriedly dismounted and, hand in hand, walked toward the small man-made stone enclosure hugging the flat floor of the dim canyon. Natalie commented on the workmanship of the spring house. Kane proudly pointed out that just inside the opening was a small room for dressing and undressing.

They ducked in out of chill air and onto the flat, rocky apron of the gurgling springs.

"Oh, Kane, let's hurry." Natalie's fingers flew to her belt buckle. "I can't wait to feel that heat."

Kane grinned, but shook his dark head. "You hurry, honey. I'm not getting in."

"You must." She turned to him. "It would be good for you too. Tell me you're not still a little stiff from all you've been through."

Kane's lean fingers went to the buttons of her tight pants. "You worked all that stiffness out of me, Natalie." He shoved the trousers down over her flaring hips. "I'll sit here and watch you."

"Suit yourself," Natalie said, disappointed, twisting her long red tresses atop her head. But she didn't stay disappointed for long.

Splashing naked down into the thigh-high bubbling, vaporous water, she sighed with delight. Kane, crouching down beside the steamy pool, sat on his heels and watched, squinting to see through the thick clouds of rising white vapor.

"Warm enough?" he inquired, grinning at her obvious pleasure.

"Hot!" she assured, backing away from him, dipping down to sit on the smooth stone bottom. "Perfect! Wonderful!"

Kane chuckled and drew a cigarette from his breast pocket. He leisurely smoked and enjoyed the sight of this beautiful flame-haired woman playing before him in the high-wilderness hot spring. Natalie knew he was enjoying it; and she knew that the longer he enjoyed it, the more time would pass.

Each ticking moment counted.

She rose from the steam. Rivulets of water ran down her shoulders and over her full breasts and belly. She pirouetted, fingers trailing, skimming the warm surface of the springs. She lifted her hands behind her head and drew deep, moist breaths. She lowered her arms and backed away from Kane. Clouds of thick white steam obscured him from sight. And her from his.

"Natalie." Kane's soft drawling voice caressed her through the thick curtain of mist. "Honey, I can't see you."

Natalie smiled. "Do you want to see me, Kane?"

"What do you think?"

Quietly, rapidly, Natalie moved through the dense wall of fog, not stopping until she reached the rocky edge of the pool where Kane crouched. She stood directly below him, glowing face tilted up to his. Her bare, gleaming breasts were visible for only a moment before she spun about and backed up between his bent knees.

"Kane, how does the wound look?"

Cigarette jammed between his even white teeth, Kane gently touched the wet flesh of her right shoulder. "Healing quickly, honey."

"Hmm," she sighed. "Rub it? Scratch it a little?"

Kane obliged. Natalie moaned and rolled her shoulders and leaned her head against his left knee. Slowly but surely, Natalie began to turn toward him while his massaging hand remained on her wet flesh. And Kane found himself grinding out his cigarette beneath his bootheel and bending to taste her wet, parted lips with his own.

While he kissed her, Natalie turned to face him. And Kane's hand no longer stroked her wet, silky back but was filled with her full, slippery breast. Their lips separated and he raised his dark head. Fingers gently toying with a slick, firm nipple, he looked into her emerald eyes.

Natalie raised a slim hand to his knee. Holding his heated gaze, she let inquiring fingers travel up the inside of his muscled thigh to his groin. Playfully, she touched the restrained fullness there and said, "Have you ever made love in a hot spring, Kane?" Kane felt his groin rapidly expand.

"Have you?" he said huskily.

"Not till today." With her forefinger she drew a line down the straining fly of his tight pants, smiled naughtily, and splashed away.

Ashlin Blackmore curtly told his puzzled manservant, William, that should anyone—anyone at all—come to pay a call, the visitor was to be informed that he, Ashlin, was upstairs in his bedroom, ill, and could not be disturbed. Brushing past the old man, he jerked open the heavy back door and rushed down the steps.

Supple jacket of ebony leather concealing the heavy pistols, Ashlin mounted his coal-black horse, dug evil-looking silver spurs into the beast's shiny flanks, and whirled him about, heading into the foothills behind his mansion.

It was the long route up to Promontory Point, but Ashlin could not afford to be seen. He would ride over the icy ridge of the upland valley, then circle back, skirting Cloudcastle as he headed northeast. He would not travel Paradise Road. He would cut through the forest, climb up out of the trees on the far side of Covington's cabin, and make straight for El Diente pass and Tahomah.

The reflection of the bright sun against the snow caused Ashlin's squinted brown eyes to tear. Wet, slippery snow slushed beneath the pounding hooves of his galloping black steed. Gazing up at the sun-warmed slopes above him, Ashlin felt a twinge of unease.

He dug the spurs deeper into the horse's belly. Big eyes wild, the beast thundered faster, great breaths labored as its long, fragile legs ate up the slippery white terrain.

It was after eleven, the sun almost hot, when Ashlin, circles of perspiration staining his fine silk shirt, neck-reined his lathered mount around the high peaks of Promontory Point toward El Diente pass.

It was eerily quiet. No sound at all, save the rhythmic

clomp of his mount's sharp hooves on the sun-drenched snow. Ashlin pulled up on the big black. Suddenly the wet circles of perspiration beneath his arms grew icy cold. He shivered. He felt the fine, silky hairs on the back of his neck lifting.

Ashlin nervously dismounted.

Holding the reins loosely, he let his searching gaze make a wide, slow sweep of the countryside before him. He lifted wary eyes to the tall, sheer peaks above. He saw nothing. His heart abruptly began an erratic beat. He could feel eyes upon his back. Quickly he whirled about, panic rising.

"You came." The bass voice reverberated in the silence. "I have been expecting you."

Chapter Forty

Paroxysms of fear rendering him temporarily helpless, Ashlin stood speechless, fixed in place by a pair of black, deadly eyes in a broad, granite face.

Ashlin's tight, burning chest told him he had ceased breathing. He gasped frantically and sucked in a gulp of thin, dry air. The new supply of oxygen snapped his brain back into action and he ripped the heavy Colt revolvers from their black leather scabbards.

"Yes." His voice sounded less than steady. "I have come to kill you." He aimed his right pistol straight at the broad chest of the Ute shaman, nervously noting the colorful black and white paint across the Indian's flat coppery cheekbones, the fancy shell- and hair-decorated turquoise velvet tunic atop the worn buckskins. The absence of weapons.

Tahomah's mouth turned up into a scornful grin. "You could not persuade your lackeys to do me in," he correctly accused the slender blond man who was pointing the brace of pistols at him, silver-plated barrels gleaming in the Colorado sunshine.

Ashlin's slim right finger tightened on the trigger. "I asked no one to kill you, old man; it's a pleasure I saved for myself."

"You are not only a coward and thief, Yellow Hair, you are a liar."

Ashlin felt the need to defend himself. "No Blackmore has ever been a coward! From the thirteenth century every blue-blooded Blackmore male has—" He suddenly shook his blond head. "My God, I am wasting words on a stupid savage!" His eyes narrowed and, with the fully loaded revolvers aimed at the heart of the unarmed Indian, he admitted calmly, "If I am a coward, you are a fool." He smirked and indicated Tahomah's lack of weaponry.

Tahomah's words unnerved him. "There is no need for weapons against a coward."

Composure shaken, Ashlin snapped angrily, "You old fool! You put on that hideous shirt and expect it to deflect bullets."

"You know little of the Ute," said Tahomah in a low, quiet voice. "This is not my ghost shirt." He lifted a gnarled, age-splotched hand to his massive chest. "My chosen-daughter, Fire-in-the-Snow, made this. It is my burial blouse. I wear it to honor the great spirit, Manitou."

The image of Natalie painstakingly stitching the turquoise velvet shirt flashed through Ashlin's mind, and his jaw tightened. "Well, old man, I'm delighted my lovely fiancée made you a colorful shroud. I'll see to it you meet the spirit people, but first . . . did you kill my brother, Titus Blackmore, a dozen years ago?"

Tahomah lifted enormous shoulders in a noncommittal shrug. "Perhaps. I kill many white-eyes." He grinned then. "All look alike to me. White-eyes like ants; no matter how many I stamp out, they keep coming."

"You killed nobility!" Ashlin told him angrily. "My younger brother was the second son of the—!"

"He was a noble thief and murderer. Just as you are, Yellow Hair."

Ashlin bristled. "Enough! I should have killed you long ago. You've been a thorn in my side from the . . ." He began to smile an evil, pleased smile. "Take this thought with you, old man. By sundown, when the crows come to pick out your ugly black eyes, I will have taken the Manitou gold—and your precious Fire-in-the-Snow!" Eagerly anticipating a look of horror on the old man's face, he was disappointed, and strangely fearful, when the Indian authoritatively replied,

"You will have neither the gold nor my chosen-daughter."

"Ah, but I shall." Ashlin's voice cracked. "You can't stop me, you'll be dead."

"I will be with the Manitou," Tahomah calmly agreed. "But hear me, Yellow Hair, the hour of your decay is near at hand. It has been foretold that at noon of the twelfth full moon, a terrible creature that flies without wings, strikes without hands, and sees without eyes will—"

"Shut up!" Ashlin shouted, firing wildly. "Shut up!" A bullet pierced the old Indian's fleshy left earlobe. Bright red blood squirted onto his weathered cheek, his powerful neck, his brand-new turquoise spirit shirt. The black, obsidian eyes remained unblinking.

Ashlin stared, hypnotized, at the drooping bloody mass of flesh that had been Tahomah's earlobe. And he whimpered like a frightened child when old Tahomah, smiling slightly, took a step forward, reaching an arthritic hand up to tear the bloody, loosened flesh away, dropping it to the wet, snowy ground.

Horrified, Ashlin shouted, "Stay where you are!"

Blood dripping, Tahomah advanced, black eyes gleaming, mouth smiling.

"God damn you!" Ashlin again fired. His hand shook; the bullet hit the approaching Indian just above the left knee. Tahomah never faltered.

Terrified, unbelieving, Ashlin swallowed and tried to take aim. He fired two rapid volleys. The first bullet slammed into Tahomah's massive chest. The second shattered a collarbone.

The Indian, his beautiful turquoise velvet shirt saturating rapidly with blood, continued the march toward his executioner. The smile remained on his broad face.

Incredulous, Ashlin emptied one Colt into the stalking savage, tossed it away, and began firing the other. Sheer will keeping the walking dead man on his feet, Tahomah neared

Ashlin. He stood not five feet away, his big, squat body a mass of bloody bullet wounds.

"Die, you red bastard!" shouted Ashlin hysterically, squeezing off the final bullet straight into the proud redman's face. He heard a sickening, crunching sound as Tahomah's right eyeball exploded in its socket.

Silently, regally, Tahomah went down. But with his good left eye, he saw the cowardly tears in the other's frightened eyes. And the telltale stain wetting the tall blond man's dark britches. Tahomah smiled contentedly and closed his eye.

The old Ute warrior died there in his beloved Shining Mountains below the gold-filled tomb of the Anasazi, while high above on the majestic, cloud-high peaks, a great mass of wet, heavy snow, loosened by the echoing reports of gunfire, shifted ever so slightly.

Eyes smoldering, Kane lithely rose and stripped. Natalie giggled happily when he stepped naked into the steamy pool. The laughter choked off in her throat when he reached out and grabbed her wrist.

Sexually intoxicated by Kane, Natalie felt a delicious tremor of fear when she looked into his passion-darkened blue eyes, which impaled her through the thick, rising white mists. Kane's dark, moisture-beaded face looked fierce, and when he swiftly pulled her up against his hard, bare body, Natalie was sure he would take her immediately, roughly, eschewing any preliminaries.

In trembling awe she looked up at him while his powerful tumescence pulsed against her wet belly. A lean, dark hand captured her uptilted chin and his harshly handsome face started its descent.

Natalie anticipated a ravaging kiss of uncontrolled passion.

Ever an enigma, Kane suddenly softened his cruel-looking mouth and, lips hovering just above hers, said, "You've got the sweetest kisses. I can't get enough. Never enough."

His lean fingers released her fragile wrist and tenderly he enfolded her in his long arms. And he kissed her. Languid kisses. Delicate kisses. Brief, soft kisses of infinite tenderness. Long, deep kisses of simmering passion.

And while he kissed her, Kane's right hand moved from Natalie's narrow waist to her hip. Mouth hotly melded with hers, his hand slipped easily down her thigh to encircle her knee.

The first thing she knew, her leg was hooked up over his bent arm, and he was showing her just how uninhibited lovers went about making love standing belly-deep in a pool of gurgling mineral waters.

It was difficult. It was strange. It was awkward.

Natalie stood there in the vaporous heat on one tiptoed foot, clinging to Kane's wet, wide shoulders while he urged her right leg around him and plunged into her, his hands guiding the movements of her slippery hips.

Brown feet planted firmly apart in the swirling, hissing spring, balance sure and perfect, Kane looked down into her half-frightened green eyes while he loved her. The intense heat of that blue gaze coupled with the firm, deep sliding of his hard, wet flesh inside hers, rapidly turned the unusual mating into a gloriously hot dance of ecstasy.

Natalie quickly found his rhythm and moved with him, eyes locked with his, lips parted. The perspiration of sex and the hot springs dampening their thrusting bodies, they slipped and slid, flesh on flesh, flesh in flesh, flesh afire.

Natalie could feel Kane's climax, and her own, beginning and building. And when it happened, it came with the thunder and power of a great mountain avalanche.

Gasping and shuddering, Natalie clung to Kane and shook with explosions so powerful, she could hear as well as feel them. They sounded like Fourth of July firecrackers.

"Ka—Kane, listen . . ."

Kane's mouth closed over hers and stayed there until the last tiny tremors had ceased jerking her bare, slender body. Only then did he raise his dark head. "Gunshots."

Chapter Forty-one

Tears of despair slipping down her hot cheeks, Natalie knelt on the rocky floor of the candlelit burial chamber deep inside the Cliff Palace. Above her stood Kane, head respectfully bowed, mutely watching the sad young woman saying good-bye to the dead shaman, Tahomah.

"He truly was a father to me, Kane."

"I know, sweetheart."

"This is where he wanted to be buried. Here with his ancestors. Here with the Anasazi." A sob escaped from her tight throat. "Th-thank you for cleaning him up, Kane, he was . . . there was so much blood, so—"

"Don't, honey. Don't."

She was silent for a time, her cold fingers absently patting the chief's broad, wrinkled hand, which rested on his unmoving chest. "Who will look after me now?" she wondered aloud, feeling like a lost, confused child.

Kane crouched down beside her. A long, protective arm encircled her slender, shaking shoulders. "I will, darling. I will look after you." Gently, he pulled her to him. Natalie rested her weary head on his solid chest. Vision distorted with tears, she saw the blurred outline of a polished panther's claw resting in the hollow of Kane's dark throat.

"Yes," she said, sniffing and hugging him tightly. "Tahomah knew you would, didn't he?"

Kane kissed the silky crown of her head. "He must have, sweetheart." Slowly, Kane rose to his feet, drawing her up with him. "We have to go now, Natalie."

Natalie nodded, looked one last time at the dead Ute chief, and turned away, murmuring, "I'll send a wire to Metaka, his granddaughter."

The pair wound their way back through the stone corridor toward the cave's wide mouth. It was silent in the Cliff Palace, no sound but the hollow echo of their bootheels on the flat stone floor. Only the flickering, wavery light of the candle Kane carried gave illumination.

Kane and Natalie blindly blinked when, finding their way back into the huge anteroom at the cave's opening, their dilated pupils were assaulted with bright, pervasive sunshine.

It was nearly noon.

The sun was directly overhead, its powerful ultraviolet rays pouring down on the sky-high snowy tops of the towering San Juans, the southern slope receiving the full impact of its burning brilliance.

While Kane and Natalie mounted their waiting horses below the sun-drenched opening of the Cliff Palace, high over their heads a huge mass of heavy snow, loosened by the earlier echoes of gunshots, groaned and hissed and shifted.

And gave way.

Natalie had heard the distinctive sound once before in her life and would never forget it. A cold dread immediately claiming her, she lifted horrified eyes upward and saw the faint white mist beginning to rise high into the clear blue sky.

"Follow me!" she commanded, kicking Blaze into a rapid trot.

Unquestioning, Kane galloped after her as the strange hissing grew louder and the giant white cloud advanced rapidly. In seconds they reached a jutting granite overhang, both bending low to duck as they guided their nervous mounts under the snow-covered, protective ledge.

They stood clinging together beneath the ledge as the entire mountain seemed to start falling. High above, a vast wet snowbank had broken away from the lofty peak and was pouring down the southern slope.

From their vantage point beneath the protective shelf, Kane and Natalie witnessed the deceptively beautiful movement of tons and tons of snow on the rampage. Like a huge tidal wave it plunged downward, the terrific thunder of the falling mass booming and rumbling and shaking the very earth around them.

The giant, deadly cloud advanced with ever-increasing speed, threatening to swallow up everything in its path. Unleashed fury with the power of infinite destruction swept down the sunny slope, scraping away layer after layer of deep snow as it tumbled.

Through the great white cloud, Natalie's unbelieving eyes spotted a man emerging from the Cliff Palace. Golden hair gleaming in the sunlight, a colorful carpetbag in his right hand dripping gold coins, he dashed madly out of the cave and ran frantically down the steep slope, mouth open in a scream of terror that was drowned out by the deafening roar of the rapidly descending avalanche.

Millions of tons of heavy snow cascaded after him, the horrid hissing becoming a deep, swelling bass hum with high whistling overtones.

Kane saw the doomed man and tightened his arm around Natalie. Both watched in helpless horror. Ashlin Blackmore released his hold on the heavy gold-filled bag and it fell to the snow, spilling out its treasure. Uncaring, Ashlin fled blindly down the vibrating mountain in a hopeless race for his life.

The deadly white cloud, rising higher in the air, careened down the slope in pursuit. Gathering up snow, scouring every gorge, tearing loose immense boulders of solid granite, the powerful avalanche overtook the running man and buried him in a icy tomb.

The thundering White Death swept on past the timberline, ripping trees up by their roots. In seconds it took Kane's alpine cabin, shoving the structure down the mountain, ripping it apart, splintering piñon logs and glass and furniture.

Gaining momentum, the avalanche plunged to the high mountain valley, ran completely across it, and rammed into the mountain on the opposite side, the grinding crash echoing throughout the soaring San Juans.

It was over almost as suddenly as it had begun. Silence followed the fading echoes, and all was eerily quiet.

It was five minutes past noon.

Chapter Forty-two

Gold glittered and gleamed and glistened.

The gold-leaf bell tower of the First Presbyterian Church on Cloudcastle's Main Street caught the strong afternoon rays of the warm June sunshine.

Inside the gold-domed structure, a wedding was taking place. Friends and neighbors packed the high-benched pews and spilled out onto steep marble steps.

Blond and pretty, Carol Thompson, seated near the front, held hands with her faro-dealing beau, silently vowing to herself that she would be the next to the altar. Esther Jones with her adoring husband, Ben, and their two boys were seated across the aisle, dressed in their finest.

The bride, lovely in a gown of pale peach, wore a look of serene happiness. Calmly composed, she held a bouquet of vivid blue columbines resting on a white Bible that shook not at all in her small hands.

Beside her, the beaming bridegroom shifted his weight, his hair slicked back off his forehead, his eyes dancing, face as pink as the rose in his lapel.

At his elbow the tall, self-assured best man stood erect, hands at his sides, eyes resting on the magistrate conducting the services.

The official spoke in a soft, clear voice: ". . . and do you take this man to be your lawful wedded husband, to cherish and honor, through sickness and in health, until death do you part?"

Marge Baker, her plump face dimpling with happiness, said breathlessly, "I do."

The judge smiled at the bridegroom and told him he could kiss the bride. Joe South, sober now for the past six months, awkwardly embraced the new Mrs. South and bussed her briefly, his pink face turning scarlet.

The organist pounded out the wedding recessional. The newlyweds exited the church, Joe limping hurriedly, Marge, clinging to his arm, accommodating her steps to his, her sparkling eyes filling with tears of emotion. Everyone followed the glowing pair into the street, throwing rice, shouting, and whistling.

Only the best man and the magistrate remained behind inside the flower-scented chapel. Without a word the tall, dark man stepped up onto the platform, plucked the rose from his buttonhole, tucked it into the shimmering red hair falling over her small left ear, took the robed justice in his arms, and kissed her.

Kane lifted his head and looked down into Natalie's beautiful face. "Let's don't go to the reception, sweetheart. Let's get a room at the Eureka and—"

"And what?" Natalie teased softly. She pulled back a little, placed her hand on her huge, robed belly, and laughed. "You know what Dr. Ellroy said. No more 'unrestrained joy' until after your son has entered the world."

Kane's lean protective hands joined his wife's on her swollen stomach. "Hear me through, will you?" Kane had solicitously accepted the fact that the days of their wild and wonderful lovemaking were over until after the arrival of the baby in July. "You'll tire yourself," he told her, "that's all I meant. We could take a hotel room and you could lie down—"

"Kane." She abruptly pivoted, showing him her back so that he might help her shed the long, hot robe. "I have never felt better in my life." She turned again to him. Face suddenly screwing up in a worried frown, she said wretchedly, hands once again on her stomach, "But I've sure looked better, haven't I?" She suddenly flushed as red as the shy bride-groom had earlier. Kane was ashamed of her! He didn't want her going to the party. Didn't want their friends to see her fat and ugly body when it wasn't discreetly covered by the bil-lowing judicial robes.

Doubts seized her as they had repeatedly in the last un-comfortable few weeks of her pregnancy. Kane was so strik-ingly handsome, so tall and lean. And successful as well. In a matter of months her husband had become a prominent and very busy attorney in Cloudcastle, drawing clients from all over the Colorado Territory. Some of those clients were women. Rich, beautiful women. Slender, attractive women.

Natalie was overcome with jealousy.

As though he had read her thoughts, Kane gently pulled his wife into his comforting embrace and said against her cheek, "Listen to me, Mrs. Covington. Never in your life have you been more beautiful than you are today. No other woman is as lovely; no other exists. I love you, sweetheart. Worship you and always will." He felt her go limp against him and he smiled. "Now kiss me and let's go wish the new-lyweds well."

The June sun had changed from a white, blinding disc high in the clear blue sky to a sinking orange ball resting on the western horizon, tinting the low, puffy clouds a pale lavender.

The green valley where the spacious white Cloud West ranch house sat was fully in the shade, had been in the shade for the past two hours.

Kane Covington, naked to the waist, sat alone on the rail-ing of the wide front gallery, facing the lush valley spread out before him. Natalie, wearing a white, loose-fitting robe, no shoes on her feet, silently joined him, stepping out onto the wide verandah. Standing behind him, she studied her hus-band's smooth, dark back with its slashing ribbon-white scars and felt a shiver of excitement. She wanted to touch him . . . had to touch him.

She crossed to him, skimmed a forefinger along the smooth leather thong around his neck, then placed her hands on his bare shoulders and leaned her chin on his dark head. Kane smiled lazily and drew her hands across his bare chest. She felt his steady heartbeat beneath her flattened palm at the same time that his unborn child gave her a forceful kick. She was not certain which made her happier.

Natalie sighed contentedly. Her dreamy eyes slowly lifted to the towering southern peak of Promontory Point. Flowers now blazed color down the rocky slopes; the delicate pink of the wild rose, the blue of the columbine, the vivid yellow of the snow buttercups.

Squinting in the fading light, Natalie searched for the location where the Cliff Palace's wide opening once had been. It was there no more. The avalanche had sealed the cave forever. The vast cavern with its Manitou gold lay buried beneath tons of solid, savagely beautiful rock formations.

"Kane."

"Hmm?"

"You're not sorry, are you?"

"About what?"

Dreamy green gaze still fixed on the sealed sanctuary, Natalie said softly, "You didn't get the treasure."

Kane lifted one of her hands to his lips and kissed the soft palm. "I have the treasure, sweetheart."

Natalie smiled. The Anasazi could rest in peace. And so could she.

MONTANA

Angel

THERESA SCOTT

Amberson Hawley can't bring herself to tell the man she loves that she is carrying his child. She has heard stories of women abandoned by men who never really loved them. But one day Justin Harbinger rides into the Triple R Ranch, and Amberson has to pretend that their one night together never happened. Soon, the two find themselves fighting an all-too-familiar attraction. And she wonders if she has been given a second chance at love.

___4392-0 $5.99 US/$6.99 CAN

Dorchester Publishing Co., Inc.
P.O. Box 6640
Wayne, PA 19087-8640

Alluring Adversary — Marti Jones

Bestselling Author Of *Blind Fortune*

Wealthy and handsome, Reese Ashburn is the most eligible bachelor in Mobile, Alabama. And although every young debutante dreams of becoming the lady of Bonne Chance—Reese's elegant bayside plantation—none believes that its master will ever finish sowing his wild oats. Then one night Reese's carousing ends in tragedy and shame: His gambling partner, James Bentley, is brutally murdered while Reese is too drunk to save him.

Entrusted with the care of James's daughter, Reese knows that he is hardly the model guardian. And fiery Patience Bentley's stubborn pride and irresistible beauty are sure to make her a difficult ward. Still, driven by guilt, Reese is bound and determined to honor Bentley's dying wish—as well as exact revenge on his friend's killers. But can he resist Patience's enticing advances long enough to win back his pride and his reputation?

_3943-5 $4.99 US/$6.99 CAN

Dorchester Publishing Co., Inc.
P.O. Box 6640
Wayne, PA 19087-8640

Robin Lee Hatcher
Midnight Rose

Adored and protected by her father and nine older brothers, the high-spirited beauty Leona has always chafed beneath their loving domination. An arranged marriage with a total stranger is the last thing she will tolerate now, even if that stranger is the most handsome man she's ever seen. Diego has come to California to honor his father's pledge to an old friend, but he doesn't plan to make good on a marriage contract written before he was born. But then, he never expects to find violet-eyed Leona awaiting him at Rancho del Sol.

___4504-4 $5.99 US/$6.99 CAN

Dorchester Publishing Co., Inc.
P.O. Box 6640
Wayne, PA 19087-8640

Please add $1.75 for shipping and handling for the first book and $.50 for each book thereafter. NY, NYC, and PA residents, please add appropriate sales tax. No cash, stamps, or C.O.D.s. All orders shipped within 6 weeks via postal service book rate. Canadian orders require $2.00 extra postage and must be paid in U.S. dollars through a U.S. banking facility.

Name_____
Address_____
City_____ State_____ Zip_____
I have enclosed $_____ in payment for the checked book(s).
Payment <u>must</u> accompany all orders. ❏ Please send a free catalog.
        CHECK OUT OUR WEBSITE! www.dorchesterpub.com

MIDNIGHT SUN

AMANDA HARTE

Amelia Sheldon has traveled from Philadelphia to Gold Landing, Alaska, to practice medicine, not defend herself and her gender to an arrogant man like William Gunning. While her position as doctor's assistant provides her ample opportunity to prove the stubborn mine owner wrong, the sparks between them aren't due to anger. William Gunning knows that women are too weak to stand up to the turmoil of disease. But when he meets the beautiful, willful Amelia Sheldon, she proves anything but weak; in fact, she gives him the tongue lashing of his life. When the barbs escalate to kisses, William knows he has found his true love in the land of the midnight sun.

___4503-6 $5.50 US/$6.50 CAN

Dorchester Publishing Co., Inc.
P.O. Box 6640
Wayne, PA 19087-8640